THE BOOK OF CHOCOLATE SAINTS

by the same author

fiction
NARCOPOLIS

poetry
COLLECTED POEMS
THESE ERRORS ARE CORRECT
ENGLISH
APOCALYPSO
GEMINI (two-poet volume)

as editor
THE BLOODAXE BOOK OF
CONTEMPORARY INDIAN POETS
DIVIDED TIME:
INDIA AND THE END OF DIASPORA

libretto
BABUR IN LONDON

The Book of Chocolate Saints

JEET THAYIL

FABER & FABER

First published in 2018
by Faber & Faber Ltd
Bloomsbury House
74–77 Great Russell Street
London WC1B 3DA

Typeset by Faber & Faber Ltd
Printed by CPI Group (UK) Ltd, Croydon, CR0 4YY

A CIP record for this book
is available from the British Library

ISBN 978–0–571–34149–8

2 4 6 8 10 9 7 5 3 1

In memory of
Dom Moraes
(1938–2004)

Contents

What is the mark that dist[illegible]
good from the bad, in wh[illegible]
Holiness is precisely [illegible]

Eric Gill

What is the mark that distinguishes the
good from the bad, in works as in men?
Holiness is the only word for it.

Eric Gill

Prologue

Praise the broken world for it will vanish in a day and in a day be replaced by nothing. That was the city's message for the rainy season. A fire truck raced somewhere, followed by police jeeps, their beacons flashing on the store windows of Electric House. In the hush that followed, a horse carriage clattered to the seafront and a bus went past and the conductor blew his whistle. Under the covered arcades of Colaba Causeway the pavement shops pulled their shutters for the night and the street sleepers prepared their bedding. The lamps glowed dull and gold among the skinny trees in their dented metal skirts. Then the rain came again, dropping like pebbles against the tin roof of the verandah. Inside the apartment a woman's unceasing tirade rose to its usual pitch of anguish. It was his wife shouting at the neighbours as she did most evenings; but tonight Newton Francis Xavier heard his mother's voice not his wife's and he felt his skin prickle with fear.

He stood at the bookcase and found his notebook and made a quick pencil sketch of a young woman in an untidy hotel room. He worked roughly, from memory, using a Japanese marker with a fine 0.1 tip, listening all the while to the sound of his wife's voice, Lula's famous Swiss-schooled voice coarsened now by smoke and drink and Hindi curses. He was ready to hide the sketch if he heard her footsteps approach from the next room, but she did not come. The tirade continued. When he was finished he put the notebook away at the back of a shelf stocked with history and biography, books he knew his wife would not disturb. In the notebook were fifty pages of drawings of the young woman in different rooms and moods, in poses both explicit and demure.

Later that night after his wife had gone to sleep he would transfer the notebook to the drawer of her bedside table where household bills lay among manuals and warranties. The sketches were preliminary efforts at a painting he was working on; they were expendable. In a day or two, after he had gone, she would open the drawer to look for the month's electricity and water bills. She would find the notebook and the sketches and understand: after eighteen years of marriage, after threatening to do so a hundred times, he had finally left her.

Early the next morning he will shower and dress and Kuthalingam will take his suitcase and typewriter to the waiting taxi. He will leave the books collected over decades and he will leave the paintings his friends the artists have presented to him. He will leave on the shelf in the bedroom the copies of his own books and the magazines, anthologies, and art journals that have featured his work. He will leave most of his clothes and his shoes, his shelf of bronze sculpture and his collection of Russian icons painted on wood. Before his wife is fully awake he will leave the house. He will not kiss her or take her leave. He does not trust himself to do this without mishap. He will shut the door and take the lift two floors down to the street and there he will tip Kuthalingam for the last time and step into the taxi that will take him on the first leg of his journey out of Bombay. His flight will land in Delhi in the afternoon and the young woman in the drawings will be waiting at the airport. They will drive into the city and check into an overpriced hotel with an unashamedly colonial past and name. Over the next few days they will discuss the immediate future as they have done off and on for a year. Again he will ask her to accompany him to New York where he owns an apartment and a reputation. She will agree.

But all of that is yet to happen. For now, Sunday night lies before him. As the voice falls silent in the next room he returns to the window and the blank rain that breaks on the dead street; and because the young woman's name is a talisman that will get him through the night he says it to himself, very softly, and then he says it once more.

Goody Lol.

BOOK ONE

From Those to Whom Much Is Given

Saint Mummy

the Lonely; flew things from buildings,
her flightless birds; could not abide
people, for sin she smelled inside;
knew knives & loud forebodings;

her bird bones bundled in aspic;
dragged by doctors; immune to harms;
held at distance her husband's charms;
holy woman preached Joan of Arc;

soul in extremis; hunter of devils
or flatly insane; maker of insane
son, whose company of brown saints
she rebuked; starved herself for thrills;

physician who could not heal herself;
poor memsahib who died in debt
one summer when the power died;
girl who wished she was someone else.

from *The Book of Chocolate Saints: Poems* (Unpublished)

Paulita Ribeiro, neighbour, interviewed by Dismas Bambai in Forgottem, Goa, February 2005

Until the day she went after him with a bread knife we thought his mother was the most ordinary woman in the world.

We called her Burial because she was always so cold and formal. My husband's joke, her real name was Beryl. She thought she was better than the rest of us poor camponês because she was descended from a long line of doctors. She said her mother or maybe her grandmother was the first female doctor in the country. We didn't know she was mad until much later. The first time I thought about it, about her sanity I mean, was when she force-fed the poor old cook, shoved a tube into her mouth and poured in a mixture of honey and mustard. She did it quietly so the neighbours, meaning me, wouldn't hear. But Cook told the whole countryside. She said Burial would go from room to room, anything breakable she smashed to the ground or threw out the window. Cook said the servants locked themselves in the kitchen. After that bit of news nobody wanted to work at crazy Burial's house, believe you me.

Karma bites you in the backside, doesn't it? These Hindu chaps get it right sometimes.

We weren't friends to begin with. I suppose we became friends without meaning to, accidentally, you might say. She called me when she needed help with the house, or the servants, or finding the right butcher or liquor supplier. Once she had rats in the eaves. I told my youngest and he went up with a stick. Goa's old houses are like old people, there's always something that needs taking care of. Sometimes she came over just to look at my floor, just sit with that long ago and faraway look on her face, counting her rosary. Or cry for no reason, endless tears, a reservoir of tears, and not a word of why.

She took lemonade with salt, not sugar. She'd sit on the bench at the kitchen table and sip her salt. Her eyes were the colour of very dark chocolate, and she had a birthmark on her neck that always reminded me of Australia or the United States or maybe the Black Sea.

I asked her once, "Ber, do you think we Indians are qualified to run the country? At least the British knew what they were doing. They were qualified to administer. Look at what-all they gave us."

She was Portuguese so I knew it was safe to say such things. If she was some true blue Indian I would have kept my trap shut.

"What did they give us, Paulita?" she said. "My husband says they robbed us for two hundred years."

"That's when he's in editor mode. He also has good things to say about them, no?"

"I'm not sure. Around guests he is so charming, so brilliant is the conversation. Otherwise it's silence as unto the grave, just like his son."

She was quiet for a time and then she tells me, "What did they give us, Paulita? The British?"

"So many things," I tell her. "Tarred roads, the law, Victorian architecture, the steam engine, the watch, the language we speak."

"Frank says these are double-edged swords. He says the question we should be asking is, what did they take from us?"

"But what do you say, Ber?"

"They took everything from us and Frank took everything from me."

"Ber, we are in the midst of a war for independence. This is your war also. You are allowed to have an opinion."

If she had one she kept it quiet. Some people are born secretive. Even when she went crazy she went crazy quietly. For example, when she punished the cook there was no shouting. She admonished the woman softly and held her down with those medical practitioner's hands. The shouting was a later development in her life and once it started it didn't stop. She would shout for hours, always at the same pitch, controlled but crazy. She'd shout at her son, at the cleaning woman, and also when she was alone at home. She'd stand at the window and shout. One day it came to me, who she was shouting at from the window. Me! The only one she didn't shout at was her husband, Frank the Great. Some days she'd shout and some days she smashed things. Once I saw her in action at the top-floor window, throwing clothes, shoes, a cut-glass vase, framed photos, beautiful porcelain. I stood at my window and watched everything smash on the lawn. She didn't shout then. She did the smashing silent.

What she did to the cook was terrible but what she did to her son was much worse, believe you me. Probably I should have done something or said something, but what?

What happens when a mother goes mad? I've thought about it a lot because of Burial and poor Newton. An only child grows up thinking his parents are the world. This is what it means to be an adult, he thinks. What he knows of reality he learns from them. But what if one of his parents is insane? And not his father who is mostly absent but the mother who gave birth to him, who fed him, who never smiled or laughed whole-heartedly, who never relaxed because she didn't trust anyone, not even her own son. What does that do to a boy?

Fr Joseph Pereira, former principal of Saint Britto High School, interviewed by Dismas Bambai in Mapusa, Goa, February 2005

In my experience it's always the brightest that you have to watch. They cause the most trouble. As you must know, my experience is vast. Incredibly vast. I retired as principal after fifty years. I served through Partition and Independence and the terrible years that followed, and through the time of Indira Gandhi's Emergency, which in my opinion was a brave and necessary measure, and through the years of regulated liberalisation introduced by her son. Half a century of experience! So I think I can safely say that when it comes to young students my judgement is simply impeccable.

He was a scholarship boy who arrived directly from the village of Forgottem. We published a few of his poems in the school magazine. He called them sixteen-line sonnets, strange formal inventions that featured wizards and damsels and swords. In other words they were the kind of English poems that the English no longer wrote. I tried to tell him that India also was a fit subject for poetry, that Indian birds, the crow, for instance, or the kite, or the saddest bird in the world, the grief-stricken monsoon koel, these birds were as worthy of poems as robins and doves. But it was no use. His imagination was soaked in English literature. He couldn't hear me, not then. Years later, he heard loud and clear. I found him a far more interesting poet after he dropped the Englishness and turned to India as the source of his torment and material. It gave him a second wind. I'd say it brought him back to life.

When he came to us he was about ten or nine, already such a serious boy. I don't think I ever heard him laugh or smile in a natural way. His presence was ghostly but also photogenic, as if he was smiling for a camera hidden behind the bushes, as if he was already in apprenticeship to the future. The only inkling of his later career was the poem about his mother, 'Saint Mummy', which, as it turned out, was the last of his poems to be published in *The Brittoan*. I was gratified to see that there were no elves or kestrels or gratuitous Merlin references. Do you know that a koel makes an appearance in one of the later poems? For this important development I must take a modicum of credit.

Beryl Xavier, mother, interviewed by Dismas Bambai at the Bangalore Institute of Mental Health, Bangalore, June 1998

I remember everything. Believe me it's a catastrophic condition. You develop the long view whether you like it or not. You see the future as one side of a coin and the past as the other, a coin in which both sides are heads, or tails if you prefer – the past and the future, the same! In between, separating them and holding them together, is the narrow edge of the present. For example, you see me here and now, a woman well past her prime in a questionable institution in the shallow south of India, but I am at the same time a young doctor and mother and wife in Bombay and Delhi, and my knowledge and experience are all of a piece. Do you see? Good, it's such a relief to speak to one's equals. Some of the people here, goodness me, I have no idea what kind of accreditation process they underwent. Were they vetted at all? It's a mystery willed by the Good Lord in his inscrutable wisdom. The Virgin Mother herself would be hard put to keep her patience! In my hospital they would have been dismissed for incompetence, if not prosecuted for malpractice. Things here are a little different, as you will see. Look at the personnel. The boys are like inadequately tamed animals, and the girls, goodness, just look at the girls! Let me tell you something about this so-called Institute of Mental Health. Every girl here says she likes Audrey. They say: I'm so Audrey! Let them say what they want about Audrey, it doesn't matter. But the minute someone says, I'm so Holly! I say, oh no you're not. They love Holly because they love Audrey. Do they even know that Holly was a prostitute?

When I first got here they called it a lunatic asylum. I thought it was a good enough name for a place where lunatics are given asylum from the world. I didn't see anything wrong with it. Neither did any of the other lunatics. But they changed lunatic asylum to mental hospital. In those days there were no bars on the windows and the doors were always left open. The driveway was a dirt path. You could leave the building and walk through the dirt and slip right out of the gates if you felt like it. I didn't feel like it then. I liked Dr Feroze who used to see me on Tuesdays and Fridays. He lent me detective stories. That's what I like to read, thrillers, the bloodier the better. Dr Feroze liked them too. Sometimes he'd lend me a book I had already read and I'd remember some of it, but the whodunit I would forget. I think that's one of my gifts. I am able to remember everything and forget some things but only if I put some work into it. Especially the forgetting part! For example, I borrowed *Gaudy Night* from Dr Feroze, which was one of the first Dorothy Sayers books I'd ever read. That was the book that made me want to read everything she'd written, including the poetry. And I am no fan of poetry, I can tell you. I saw how miserable it made my son. In any case I read it again, *Gaudy Night*, and I made myself not remember the mechanics of the plot. Not remembering is an art and I'm a master of it. Sometimes Dr Feroze and I discussed the books he lent me. What do you think, Beryl, he said. What do you think of *Gaudy Night*, is it any good? It's better than good, Dr Feroze, I replied. In fact I do believe it may be the first feminist detective story ever written. And then Dr Feroze looked at me as if I had said something terrible and the Fear came to me. I thought I had exposed myself to a mortal enemy who would use the information to kill me. Instead of murdering me, he said, I see why you would come to that conclusion, Beryl, and I think you're absolutely right.

When he told me he was leaving I wrote my address on a piece of notepaper. Of course he knew the address. That isn't why I did it. It was a way of asking him to write to me if he felt like it. He never did. Psychiatrists are not allowed to write to their patients, did you know that? It's unfortunate, yes?

Paulita Ribeiro, neighbour, interviewed by Dismas Bambai in Forgottem, Goa, February 2005

She was outnumbered. Her husband was a writer and so was her son. Two writers versus a doctor, do you see what I mean? They excluded her. If you keep treating a woman like an alien, soon she'll begin to act like one. They'd talk about some writer or painter, some Delhi artist whose lovers numbered in the hundreds, whose affairs were common knowledge but only to people like them. And they would leave her out of it. She read a lot of crime novels, which was the only thing she and her son had in common other than God. But they would discuss things she knew nothing about. As a woman I understood. Women know what it means to be silent. We know what it means to be cancelled, to not exist.

Not long before she was sent to the asylum she asked me to accompany her to Fontainhas in the old part of Panjim. There was some sort of gallery in a church there that she liked to visit but she didn't want to go alone. It was a good day for a drive, hazy, one of those rare days when the sun wasn't blazing in your eyes. Still, I put on sunglasses and a scarf on my head. I like to wear sunglasses and a scarf when I'm going for a drive. We got into her Premier Padmini, sky blue it was, with tan leather seats that stuck to your skin. As soon as we set off I knew I had made a mistake. She drove so fast. There wasn't much traffic but there are always animals wandering around the roads of Goa. You don't see them until it's too late and then you're upside down.

We sped off on that road crowded with buses and trucks and bikes and bullock carts and every once in a while she would turn to say something to me and I would see her black eyes focused on a spot above my shoulder. Those were the worst moments. Eyes on the road, Ber, I'd say, not that it made a difference. At first she wanted to talk about prayer. She said it helped her cope with almost every kind of situation in life. She said it calmed her down to talk to God when she was confused. I told her she was lucky. Nothing calmed me down when I was in a tizzy, not even God. Then we talked about the rainy season in Goa, which is not easy to adjust to even for people who have lived here their whole lives. She asked how I got bed sheets dry in the rain. Nobody can dry bed sheets in the Goa rains, I told her, give them to the dry cleaners. But keep your eyes on the road, Ber, I said. Then I told her the story of my nephew, Mario, a wonderful singer who had formed his own a cappella band. He was riding home one night and a cow crossed the road and he didn't see the tether. The motorbike landed on his head. He was in hospital for a year. He forgot how to sing.

I said all this but she didn't slow down and after a while I decided to trust her and let the day unfold as it would. Then something came to me, an insight, you might call it. I saw a system in the way she accelerated into clusters of traffic. I decided her style of driving was similar to the technique of Zen meditation, which I once tried. She drives in a state of no mind, I thought, which she achieves by minimum use of the brake and horn. Instead of slowing down, she speeds into turns even with traffic approaching and then somehow she finds an opening and pushes the small car into it and out the other side.

The usual scenery flew past, the dusty brown trees and people of Goa. We kept overtaking State Transport buses, which you should never do if you are a woman driver. But there was no point telling Burial these things. She was silent, lost in her Zen meditation. And then she said, I think it's important that family members have fun with each other. Don't you think so, Paulita? No, I really don't, Ber, I replied. Families are there to help each other. Burial shook her head. You don't understand anything, Paulita. Your husband will support you whether you are wrong or right. There's someone on your side no matter what.

Do you see, Paulita? This is why you don't understand a thing, said Burial. I was about to say, look, Beryl, you may be right or I may be right but whatever is the truth of it, do you mind keeping your eyes on the godforsaken road? But then another thought occurred to me. What if saying this made things worse? I held my peace.

She slowed down when we neared the old city. She had no choice, no? The streets are too narrow for fancy driving. We took the old Patto Bridge over the Querem creek and she parked in a shaded spot near a church and then we stepped out of the car and stretched our legs. Burial led the way to a room above the main building and when my eyes adjusted to the darkness I picked out life-size figures of wooden saints with smudged pieces of paper stuck to their arms and legs. A female saint stood guard near the door. She wore a cape and she was bleeding from terrible wounds in her neck. A note was pinned to her sleeve, "Saint Catherine TORTURED on the wheel & DECAPITATED." A thin-faced man was slumped against the wall with his torn head in his hands. Two children knelt on the floor and reached for their missing eyes. Francis Xavier was in the back of the room where he regarded the wreck of his body that was missing toes and fingers and whatnot. In his one remaining hand he held the earth. As we watched, people came up to the wooden saint and touched him and kissed their fingers to their lips. They left small pieces of lined notepaper on a makeshift shrine. Burial unfolded one and passed it to me:

> Tell me, O Lord, how does the penitent child pass?
> Only on his knees.
> Why, dear O Lord? Why must he pass on his knees?
> For if he pass on his feet he surely must be decapitated.

I could make no sense of it but Burial gazed at the note for a long time. By now I was ready to leave and I wondered how long this mad adventure would take. I had to get home and attend to life. Come on, Ber, I said, some of us have work to do. She didn't say a thing. She didn't even smile, just kept staring at a painting of Saint Xavier on his back with a bottle of whisky between his feet. The painter had made his skin bright yellow and the eyes were lit red. There was not an ounce of extra flesh to be seen. The face was like a mask of one who had suffered the terrors of hell. Beside it was a painting titled *The Last Journey*, in which a sickly Saint Xavier clutched at a cross that was beyond his grasp. A small boy massaged his feet and a Chinese monk held a candle and cried a single tear. A sticker on the painting said, "I am watching night and day for the return of the merchant who has agreed for 20 pices to convey me to Canton."

Poor Burial looked as if she too had become a statue, except for her hands, which were always moving. What was she looking at? I was about to rouse her when she said, what do you think pices are, Paulita? Do you think it is a misspelling of pesos or a misspelling of pieces? I don't know, I replied, and I had never said a truer thing. I had no clue. How could I? Those paintings were like nothing I had ever seen. I wondered who had painted them and how had he got away with depicting the patron saint of Goa as a homeless fellow and alcoholic? Burial examined the canvases from every angle, lost in her own thoughts. In the car, we sat in our seats and neither of us said a thing. When she turned the key in the ignition I steeled myself.

But the return trip was better. She wasn't driving so fast. We stopped at a courtyard restaurant in Candolim where we ordered tea and sugar biscuits. I balanced my sunglasses on top of my head. The air had turned balmy and it was almost enjoyable to be sitting there sipping tea like two leisurely ladies. We talked about the Congress Party, about Jinnah, about what India would be like after Independence. My husband and I were thinking of moving to Portugal, I said, though most likely we would stay right there in Goa. And what about you, Beryl, I asked. She sipped her tea and nodded. She didn't know what she would do, she said, or where she would go. She said she liked Berlin because the weather was so terrible that you could stay home and never feel like you were missing out on life. And then she talked about the cemeteries of Montparnasse and Père Lachaise and Montmartre, and how they were like miniature cities. She mentioned the trees of New York and in passing she described the dirt and noise of Rome, which she found more welcoming than the clean streets of Geneva. These were cities she had visited with her husband when they were young and childless, when they were newly and happily married. She knew the names of the streets and the names of the rivers and central stations and she even listed some of the restaurants and hotels they had visited. She was an encyclopaedia. Beryl, I said, you're better than a travel book. I was going to tell her how lucky she was to have travelled the world but I noticed that her black eyes were wet. Never mind, I said, everything will be fine. She shook her head. Nothing would be fine again, she said, the tears streaming down her face. She pulled the note out of her pocket then and smoothed it on the table, the wretched note about the penitent child and decapitation. This is for Newton, she said through her sobs. He used to love visiting churches with me. We had a game. Whenever we saw a brown saint, not a white saint but a brown one, and there are several if you know where to look, then the one who saw it first would give the other a pinch. He's forgotten the game now that he's growing up and away from his mother. She smoothed the horrid typewritten note. I'll give it to him for his ninth birthday, she said. I saw her wet black eyes and I saw the black birthmark on her neck and right there and then I knew something terrible would happen, and the hair on my arms, I'm not joking, my hair stood on end.

Fr Joseph Pereira, former principal of Saint Britto High School, interviewed by Dismas Bambai in Mapusa, Goa, February 2005

Frank Xavier was well known for his peppery editorials during the Independence movement. We used to quote them verbatim! The boy would have been about ten at the time, or less, nine maybe. Ten years later after the Annexation of Goa he too would make peppery statements in the press that made him unwelcome in his own country. His grandmother was famous, the first female surgeon of the state. His mother too was a well-known doctor. To me she did not seem disturbed but withdrawn. We had no inkling. Not then. The boy was bright, as I say, among the best I've taught but also the worst, a natural ringleader. Even at the age of nine he married his talent to negativity. In my mind he was a boy nihilist. I had no choice but to do what I did.

We started as the Sacred Heart School for boys and girls. When the school was handed over to the Jesuits Goa was still under Portuguese rule. The Jesuits renamed it Saint Britto High School and made it exclusively for boys. Good thing it wasn't co-ed when Xavier got here, if you follow me. He would have imploded in a worse fashion than he did. Of course I did not know then that his mother was going through her troubles. I thought he was a natural born ruffian and nuisance.

In his first week, during the morning recess, Vic Menezes was laughing about something, excited to be talking to a group of the older boys. Menezes was telling a story or a joke and nodding at Xavier. At lunch Xavier cornered Trev Coutinho in the hall and asked what Menezes had been saying.

"I don't know," Coutinho said.

"You were laughing and you don't know why?"

Poor Coutinho had already begun to sweat.

"Tell or I shall kick you."

Coutinho was a crier, a delicate child. When anxious he'd hold his breath until he turned blue. Xavier grabbed him by the collar and out it all came, that Menezes had said Xavier's mother was as funny as a three-cornered jam tin. She acted like a great aristo but actually she was an upstart bag lady. Xavier went directly to Menezes and called him a filthy bugger and banged the older boy's head against the wall. They were on him in a minute, Menezes and his friends. They roughed him up and I think they would have caused some damage if I hadn't put a stop to it. The strangest thing was that Xavier was having the best time. He was egging them on. He wanted them to hit him. Go on, is that the best you can do, a big fellow like you? Are you a sissy boy? I should mention that Menezes was a senior at the time. He was two years and a few months older than the Xavier boy and bigger in every way.

The drawing appeared a month or so later, a line drawing on the wall of the boys' toilet, the outer wall, mind you. So perfectly detailed, such an accurate anatomical study I knew immediately who had done it. He was the best draughtsman in the school. The drawing was art, of course, but explicit in a way that was decidedly vulgar, if not pornographic: a red-haired giantess with red nipples and red eyes and a black phallus-shape in her belly.

He didn't deny it. If anything he took some pride in the work.

"Where did you get the paint?" I asked him.

"From the workroom. I had to make do with black and red because there were no other colours."

"Are you quite pleased with yourself?"

"No, Father," he said. "I think there is far too much red. I should have been more sparing with the colour."

I would have let it go. We whitewashed the wall and forgot about the incident and one morning there was a new drawing, a woman in a hat and a sundress through which you could see her naked figure. I took Xavier to the scene and asked him if he had done it. He said someone else had done it and he had tried to correct it. He pointed out which lines were his. He said he hated bad drawing.

How could I have allowed it? I had to do something. It was a calculated slap in the face of our authority and it didn't end there. Certain members of the faculty had no hesitation in expressing their grievances in writing. In short I had no alternative but to expel him. I wrote a discreet recommendation and I made a call to a former student of mine at Saint Mary's in Bombay. I suppose I should mention that the caption to the pornographic drawing was something I taught him, a saying of Saint Francis's that the body is a cell and the soul a hermit who lives therein. The rascal had the nerve to sign it with the school motto, *Facta non Verba*, followed by a single letter that announced the culprit's name. X.

I don't mean to brag but I think I may be able to take some credit for the religious nature of his art. I may deserve a footnote in the story of his life. Do you remember the epigram that accompanied his Chocolate Jesus exhibition? Thirty boys in the class were told the quote and it registered only with one. I remember it well. I've always had a photographic memory for those moments in which I have felt myself inspired or moved by the highest calling, if you will. The summer months in Goa are the schoolmaster's nightmare. The fans are clicking overhead and not a thing moves in the room, certainly not their brains. I told them the quote and I watched the twitch of thirty hands. I heard thirty pens scratching on paper and I knew exactly what the writing was worth. I looked at their hands and for a moment I thought of the tiny fishes that swim together in the wake of bigger fish. I looked at their eyes and I saw ghastly fish eyes, glassy undersea minnow eyes, spherical eyes without feeling or intelligence.

What was the quote? Good, that is the correct question. Revelation, Chapter Ten, Verse Ten, such a lovely symmetry, ten colon ten: "And I took the little book out of the Angel's hand, and ate it up; and it was in my mouth sweet as honey; and as soon as I had eaten it, my belly was bitter." It was a game I played against myself. Throw a thought among them and see what happens. Would one of the minnows bite? Or would they toddle on without a thought in their heads? I hoped for the former and expected the latter. I recited the quote and told them it was not the only instance in the Book in which a prophet ate the words of the Lord and reported a taste in his mouth *as of honey for sweetness*, a sweetness that cannot last. What I hoped to communicate to the boys was that success in this world is a passing thing. Only Newton heard.

Beryl Xavier, mother, interviewed by Dismas Bambai at the Bangalore Institute of Mental Health, Bangalore, June 1998

He didn't listen. The taller he got the less he heard. I had information that might have lifted his life into the blessed radiance if only he had listened. I was forced to resort to drastic measures. What else could I do? I am a mother and I did what mothers must, I entreated the Virgin. I spent the days in my room and on my knees I prayed to the Virgin Mother. I asked for guidance and I begged and after many hours of pain and entreaty I found my answer. Raise your voice, she told me, raise your voice without anger and then he will hear you. One morning when I went to wake him for school I stood at the doorway and addressed him in a loud even tone. I said, wake up, Newton, I wish to tell you about your ancestors. I thought I'd got the tone exactly right but he continued to lie there with his eyes closed, pretending to be asleep. If only he had listened. I told him about Joan of Arc, our direct ancestor, about the links between the Goddess Kali and the Black Madonna of Byzantium. I told him to pay no mind to the pale scientists who speculate that the Black Madonna and Black Child had turned that colour from the accumulated grime of votive candles. If that were the case why were the vestments not black as well? My Black Madonna is the true Madonna, I told him. Was she not a woman from the east? I told him and he did not listen and then I did not speak any more. But I am a mother and I cannot give up. I gave him other opportunities to correct himself. For example, the following Sunday after church we had lunch at a restaurant in Panjim, just he and I. His father was travelling. I told him about a recurring dream in which God came in disguise to give me secret information about the origins of man and his likely demise. When I told him this he looked at me the way he looked at his father when they discussed poetry, that is to say he looked at me with great interest. But then he went back to his chorise and pau. He didn't say a word. I remember I had dressed him in a white shirt and bow tie, with pressed long shorts and shined black shoes. I like to dress up for church and I like my son to dress up too. He was drawing in the margins of a book, faces, always faces and busts, knights and maidens, dragons and wizards. He drew our cook and a schoolmate of his from Saint Britto's and his Sunday school teacher (a horrible woman I had never liked) and a portrait of his father in a suit and a portrait of Nehru; in other words, anybody and everybody, except for me. He had never painted a portrait of his mother. I was cutting my roast beef and suddenly it came to me that he had never tried to be a proper son. At least I had tried to be a mother. I looked at the meat leaking on my plate and I put down my knife and fork. I thought of Nehru and his daughter, his clever daughter who had always resented me. She had a soft spot for Frank and she was exceedingly kind to my son. I was nothing more than the fly in her ointment. When we got home I told Newton to draw a picture of me, his one mother. What kind of a picture, he asked. Draw me the way you see me, darling, I said.

Paulita Ribeiro, neighbour, interviewed by Dismas Bambai in Forgottem, Goa, February 2005

We all know the story of his expulsion. How did he know to draw a picture like that at such a young age? He was eight years old when his mother came after him with the knife, and she's a doctor, you getting me? She knows how to use a knife. Then he watched her being dragged off to the asylum. It was the best asylum in India of course, goes without saying. My kids say I should call it a mental institution. I say, call it what you want and it's still a loony bin. Personally? I think his mother traumatised him into art. I'm not saying artists need trauma but it helps, believe you me.

Even after they put her in the bin, sorry, mental institution, she was swanning around saying she was a doctor and her fellow inmates were her patients. Imagine! I felt sorry for her, no? By then I thought of her as my friend. But one thing, it's true what they say about doctors. They have no feelings. When they look at us they don't see a friend or husband or son. They see case histories, contagions, ailments. His mother was that kind of doctor.

He drew a picture on the wall of his room. I saw it after she was taken away and I helped Frank wrap up the house. What a sight the boy's room was. It seemed to me that nobody was living there because there were no toys or books or clutter. Just a desk against the wall and a narrow bed with a single pillow and above the bed a wooden cross. Like a monk's cell it was. And there was the picture near the window of his mother naked in a tub, beehive hair and strawberry breasts and skinny arms, oh it was her all right, believe you me. I could see it right away and I knew he had the gift. No wonder she hated it. I heard her shouting. This is the picture the devil loves! Even in her madness she was fully Catholic. She cursed him with hellfire. Stinking brimstone upon your head! We heard nothing more for a long time and then I heard her screaming and the boy ran to my house. She has a knife, he said. What knife, I said. I felt stupid to ask but it came out of my mouth. He said it was the bread knife from the kitchen, of all things. I saw a cigarette burn on his wrist and I asked if she had done it and his reply made me sad. Yes, he said, but it was his own fault. Afterwards he had locked himself in his room as his father had taught him and when he saw his chance he left the house. I called Frank and told him what had happened. In the meanwhile, Burial had stopped shrieking. There was a moment of respite and we all took a breath thinking the worst was over, but it was not. There was a crash and a marble side table came sailing through the window to the lawn. Even then the boy was calm. He had a cup of tea and waited for his father.

After the men in white coats took her away father and son went to Bombay and then out to the wide world. Goa was too small for them. Snobs they were, snobs to the end. Be that as it may the point is the boy is eight when his mother tries to kill him with a knife. And the next year three things happen. His mother is committed to a loony bin, his father takes him to Bombay, and India becomes Independent. How can you not see the significance of these dates? Why do you think he had such a love for English history and literature? He knew more about London than most Londoners. It was his way of belonging to something. More important, it was his way of escaping his mad mother. I think he hated India because of her and once he left he wished never to return.

Fr Fo Hernandez, former teacher at Saint Mary's School, interviewed by Dismas Bambai in Byculla, Bombay, July 1998

It was old Father Joseph who asked me to take in that Xavier fellow. Father Joseph, what can you do when he booms at you? What a voice! What a stentorian instrument! Booming, booming, for no reason at all and one thing you don't do when that voice booms in your ear and your spine straightens of its own accord and you know you're done for, the one thing you don't do is say no. He'd be after you like a trio of blasted Furies. So of course I accepted the Xavier fellow although he'd missed a term and I knew from the outset he would be trouble. But let me be clear. I had no blasted choice in the matter!

And by the way, I knew this would happen. I'm only surprised it took so long. I knew someone would come nosing around wanting to know about his school days. There's no getting away from the fact that we schooled him and we must be responsible in some way for the cock-up that followed. I'd say some self-examination is in order, some extended soul searching. Fact: he attended three Jesuit schools before leaving India for the United Kingdom. I myself am a Jesuit born and bred, so I think I may be allowed some leeway here. We teach by example. And what is that example? One, personal freedom, tempered by, two, an awareness of one's social responsibility, and, three, an understanding of what it means to be fully human. With some of our students this teaching may have unforeseeable consequences. In effect they turn to the opposite end of the spectrum. Sensation, nihilism, excess. They turn against their training.

The day I got the call from old Father Joseph I felt a kind of stench blowing down the line from Goa to my office in Byculla, a wind-borne stench I could not identify. I will describe it as a combination of rotting fish and fresh flowers. And at that moment I knew the voice would bring only bad tidings.

"I've written him a recommendation," said Father Joseph. "His father is a friend. See what you can do, will you?"

So loud I had to hold the phone away from my ear. And I knew the old man well enough to know that in Father Joseph's world "see what you can do" means "you better get to it right away, boyo". I held the phone away and still the voice boomed and the ill wind blew and I caught a whiff of fish and desperation. I told myself, you do what you must do.

I took him, missed term and all I took him. And the minute he arrived in my office and took a seat, his chin sunk into his neck, silent as the grave of the martyrs, the minute I saw him I knew. Something about the exceedingly slouchy posture and the shifty gaze that would not hold one's own and his way of speaking as if each word issued from a mouth full of marbles, I knew only bad luck would follow. You see how right I was!

The first time I called him in was about a week after he got here. He refused to speak in class. When it came to written assignments he was good enough, perhaps even exemplary, but he refused to speak and so I called him into my office. At the time we still used corporal punishment. I believe it can be useful when used judiciously and I knew that one of my colleagues had marked his palm with a ruler. Not that it did any good.

I asked him to sit and when I saw the expression on his face, those resentful eyes, dear lord, I knew I was in for it. I thought of Father Joseph's overbearing voice and I wished I had had the gumption to tell him no. No, I should have said, this Xavier fellow sounds like a bad customer to me. I don't want him. You keep him. But it was too late to wallow in regret. Here we were, the miscreant and I, and we had to play our respective roles. So I asked him what he hoped to achieve with silence. Tell me, I said, I have an abiding interest in the circus of personality. He had no reply, of course. Whereupon I had an idea born from bitter experience. I've dealt with my share of bad apples and I've learned a thing or two. I called for tea for the both of us and placed sugar and milk near his cup. Then, as if I didn't have a worry in the world, I went to work on drafting the speech I was going to make at a schools meeting the following week. In other words I left him alone and minded my own business in a companionable way. He added sugar but no milk and drank his tea and sat quiet for a time. Just as I was getting used to the silence and hoping it would continue blessedly all day, he said something in that infuriatingly soft voice I had learned to distrust, a voice that was the opposite of Father Joseph's ear-splitting boom. I didn't catch it because I wasn't expecting it. I'm sorry, I said, what did you say? As if it was the most natural thing, as if we were two old friends having a bit of a natter. I had to pull my chair closer to the table. I had to lean forward to hear him.

"Father, why are there no museums in Goa?"

I may have spluttered a little. The fellow was asking a serious question. Well. All my training collected in my spine and I sat up straight. This was a real question even if it had been asked so softly it would take a bleeding superhuman to hear it.

"Of course there are museums in Goa," I responded. "What makes you think there are not?"

But he had again lapsed into that impermeable, that irredeemable silence and soon I went back to my draft. I was using a red pen to correct and highlight before I made a fair copy. About ten minutes later he spoke again.

"Father, why are there no non-Christian museums in Goa?"

"Because Goa is predominantly Christian," I replied.

For one thing I wasn't sure about museums in Goa. I would have to investigate but of course I wasn't going to tell him that. The more I looked at him sitting on the office chair where a hundred boys had sat, still and silent in his white shirt and blue tie, the more certain I was. I knew he was bad medicine. I could smell it just as I had smelled the stench of rotten fish and wildflowers the day this merry imbroglio had begun. I realised he had more to say and this time I knew how to get it out of him. I went back to my speech. I pretended that ghastly boy wasn't staring at me. When he started to talk I didn't look up and I didn't lean over. I let him speak.

"There is no sense of history in Goa," he said, "that goes back further than five hundred years. For Goans the idea of time begins with the Portuguese and the advent of Christianity: there is no notion of a pre-Christian civilisation though there must have been one, wouldn't you say? Is the idea of living history tied to the idea of religion and picked from the air as casually as we take our sense of sunshine or moisture?"

I was astonished. It was the longest speech I had ever heard him make and as it turned out I would never hear another that was comparable, at least in length. I should have ignored it. I should have made him sit outside. I should never have offered him tea. And once he made the speech I should never have asked him to write it up. And after he'd written it up I should never have sent it to a newspaper I knew.

If I had ignored it I might have saved us a lot of trouble.

Subir Sonalkar, journalist, interviewed by Dismas Bambai at Gokul Permit Room, Colaba, Bombay, July 1998

Poets, man! They're the same all over. Mendicants, martyrs, lapsed monks convinced the world owes them an explanation or an apology or a meal, wine included. But fuck the dumb shit. I tell you this, if you're planning a revolution or founding a new religion go to the poets. Don't waste your time with fucking scriveners. Go to the source, the bards. At least you can count on them to be true to their essential nature. And what is this nature? Ruthlessness, I say! Enlist the poets and expect blood. There will be a lot of it. Enlist the poets and stay away from the novelists because novelists are feckless. They have no feck at all. They are yes-men hungry for approval and patronage, always looking out for their own best interests. As for playwrights, all they do is talk, talk, talk about the revolution and social justice, women's empowerment, humanism, anarchism, but it never goes anywhere because that's all it is, big talk, back talk, chitchat, gossip. They're good at it because this is how they gather material. When it comes to putting words into action? They'll be the first to disappear. You will also come across scriptwriters and screenplay doctors. Be warned. They live in their own reality and it rarely coincides with anyone else's. I advise you to tread carefully with those bastards. Walk among them as if you're in a den of goddamn vipers. Count on nothing and you'll be okay. The only ones you can trust are the short-story writers because they're like poets in at least one respect. They shoot their shot in one go and this leads to an understanding of luck and discipline. They learn early that discipline lies in waiting and allowing the circumstances for luck to arise. The point I am trying to make is that poets are born with certain unenviable traits. For example, paranoia. For example, they believe in persecution by persons of lesser sensibility. For example, they admire self-sabotage and the perverse. And for a last example, they are born with a capacity for cruelty, followed by an infinite capacity for remorse.

How do I know this in such intimate detail? Because for a time in the seventies I was a poet too, though I was never a good one. No good. I knew that and it might have been the thing that fucking saved me. Or it might be the thing that brought me to this table, sitting with you, lifting my endless glass of Old Monk to the murky afternoon light of Gokul.

I know it's hard to imagine but once when I was young I wrote poems. I fancied myself a Maoist. I joined the CPI-M-fucking-L. I read Proudhon and as if I had come up with the idea all by myself I announced that property is theft is property is goddamn fucking theft. I read the usual poets. Baudelaire of course, or should I say Rimbaudelaire? Because Baudelaire led me to Rimbaud who led me to Mallarmé and inevitably I found Verlaine and Villon, to continue with the theme of theft, and Michel Butor, although I only read *L'emploi du temps*, I couldn't find anything else, and Blaise Cendrars, Tristan Tzara, Robert Desnos, Jean Follain, Francis Ponge, and finally, unavoidably, Alfred Jarry, because *Ubu Roi* from its first word, "Shit", is poetry, also Isidore Ducasse, obviously, which young poet does not read Monsieur Ducasse? Also, René Char, André Salmon, Max Jacob, and so on, the usual lot, as I said, and I read them exclusively for two years and more. It was my French phase. All poets have one but that's hardly new and it's not the point of this speech. What I'm trying to say is that once upon a time the weight of the world rested on my slender underfed shoulders. You see, I wrote poems.

Let's say I gave the poetry life a go. Or the poetry life gave me a go and found me wanting. Ezekiel published me in the *Illustrated Weekly of India* though not in *Quest* and I did some reviews and opinion pieces for the newspapers. I was living in a one-room chawl at Crawford Market, a proper Bombay tenement with shared bathrooms and balconies where you saw entire families live their lives in a single room. I lived in a chawl named poverty. For me that is the essence of the goddamn poetry life. There's a reason those words are so similar in sound and spelling and separated only by a V pronounced the Indian way, we.

POETRY = POVERTY.

I was half a name in the cultural life of the city and Frank Xavier was the editor of the best newspaper, the *Back-Bay Dispatch*. I wrote a weekly column for his paper and we became friends. This was after his wife had been committed to an asylum somewhere in the south. For a while he took as mistress an American photographer who tried to be a mother to the boy, except Newton was not interested in acquiring a new mother.

When the father showed me the son's poems the first question I asked was about his age. Fifteen, he said, and I said, come on, Frank, pull the other one. Frank said he was not joking: Newton had just turned fifteen. I asked if he had helped edit the poems. Everybody asks that, said Frank, a handsome man who was always in a suit and tie, always elegantly provided with a glass of good whisky at his elbow. Come to dinner, he said, and judge for yourself.

They lived in one of those new apartments near Navy Nagar, wall-to-wall windows and a view of the sea. We had a drink and then Frank sent for his son, who arrived wearing a summery short-sleeved white shirt. I remember it was beautifully pressed. I noticed that kind of thing because I didn't press my clothes. I was a communist. I also remember that he was smoking an unfiltered local brand called Cavenders. Frank smoked imported cigarettes and used a holder. They were quite a sight, father and son, perfectly poised and smoking in harmony.

How do you do? Newton said, like the perfect English gentleman he wasn't. He was a skinny Indian kid who'd never been out of the country. It was unnerving to say the least, as unnerving as the heavy fucking silence he brought with him. Nobody said anything for a while and then, just to lighten the air a bit, I told him I liked his poems. He nodded and stared at the floor as if I had asked him to promise me, on pain of death, that he would never again write another word. He hung his head and smoked and stayed completely silent. I feel I should say a word about the quality of that silence. It was not the kind of silence that allows sweet meditation to flower and neither was it companionable. He was only a boy but his silence felt like oppression, a sense of the slave ship, the sharp stink of the lash below decks, also a sense of aphasic fucking bewilderment. He smoked and looked into the distance of the floor. Perhaps he was shy but I don't think so. For me there was a kind of violence in that silence, a torturer's sly pleasure. I felt it was up to me to say something because clearly the kid was beyond speech. So I asked how many poems he'd written. He looked stricken, as if I had said something unforgivable, as if I had asked a question about his mad mother or enquired as to whether or not he was a virgin (there was no doubt that he was, you could tell from the way the poems idealised women). He said nothing for a long time. How long I don't know but it was an interminable stretch of murderous goddamn silence. Then he lit yet another unfiltered fucking Cavender. He said, about a dozen, maybe ten that I'm sure of. That's not bad for someone your age, I said, relieved now that there was some semblance of a conversation. He nodded in a solemn way and said with an old man's gravity that he would have had more but he'd just completed a book on cricket. A small press was bringing it out. I forget the title, something like *The Green Grass of Home* or *How Green the Grass*. Frank said the boy was thirteen when he started writing the cricket book and that was when it struck me. I said, are you the Xavier who writes the cricket commentary with the line drawings and Yeats epigraphs? Yes, said Frank, that's him. First I was surprised and then it made sense to me and all of a sudden I knew he had written the poems himself with no assistance from his father or anyone else. I was a fan of his cricket pieces but I didn't know how to say so without embarrassing us both. We talked about poetry. He said he was reading the Symbolists and we had a long conversation about the French poets and after that he said nothing more for the rest of the night. When we moved to the dining table his father allowed him a glass of beer. The food was Goan, pork and rice, cutlets and a salad and a heavy bebinca to finish. He smoked during the meal and sipped silently at his beer. I'll tell you what else I remember. He had the most delicate hands and he knew it. And he had a way of holding a cigarette as if to show off his hands. It was the only sign of vanity I noticed.

Glory Pande, former live model, interviewed by Dismas Bambai at Bangalore Club, Bangalore, March 2005

I was one of the first women in India to model nude. I come from a family of writers and artists on both sides. My aunt streaked on Juhu Beach in 1974. She caused a scandal and she was invited to the best parties in Bombay. My uncle was a novelist and poet, three novels, four books of poetry, and a collection of essays. In his sixties he was accused of sedition for a novel he had written thirty years earlier, a novel that had known only moderate success until some right-wing busybodies discovered literature. My uncle said the charge of sedition was the best thing that ever happened to him. It restarted his career, made him a legend. My mother wore bell-bottom jeans in 1972 when nobody else had them. It was the first time anyone had seen an Indian woman in groovy pants. My father says she stopped the traffic on Flora Fountain, including the double-decker buses. So when I began modelling nude it really was not a big thing. The work was "artistic" as we used to call it. In other words, it was tame and tasteful. Until Newton came along, that is. I was live modelling once a week in the evenings and he was the youngest student in the class. He painted a series of pictures that were similar in a way, fully dressed women around a naked man. Eerie. I was nude, he painted me fully dressed, and it was the first time I felt as if someone had seen me naked. He was a boy and already there was something in the way he depicted the female form. Oh, I know what some people will say. I was treated like a sex object. I was a repository for male leering. The truth is simpler and more complex. I was in my twenties, yes, but he was in his teens and if I was objectified then so was the man in the paintings and the man was always Newton and he always painted himself with so much self-loathing, such violence directed against his own person, the blemishes placed under a magnifying glass as if he saw himself in the future when his youth and talent had faded. In one picture he made himself an old man with a broken nose and white beard. Uncanny when you think about it. I saw a photo a few weeks ago of Newton with a broken nose and shaggy beard, as if the early work was some kind of prophecy. And another thing about the "Portraits of a Ladie" series, he made himself ugly and he made me beautiful. If that's objectification I have no objection.

Subir Sonalkar, journalist, interviewed by Dismas Bambai at Gokul Permit Room, Colaba, Bombay, July 1998

He was a master of manipulation. He understood the necessity of style. Nothing else matters in our line of work. Style is all there is, the image, you get me? He worked at being obscure the way other people work at being rich or disciplined. He fucking worked it, mainly because he was a manipulator but also because he did not want to be found. No, wait. First he wanted to be found. When he was doing those jagged geometric hallucinations that were like no landscapes anyone had seen? At that time he wanted to be known. He wanted to be a name and a face. Then he tried something ambitious, what they came to call his Chocolate Jesus Period, and the moment he became a face and a name he didn't want it any more. He was like that. If he knew you admired him and liked his work he treated you badly. If you cared nothing for him he would turn on the charm. The show that followed the Chocolate Jesus pictures was the biggest thing he had ever attempted. The Forest of Knowledge, do you remember? No, nobody does, except those of us who were there. A forest of trees infested with termites or poison and primed to disintegrate over a period of one or two years. It was his comment on the annihilation of the planet and it was long before everybody began to talk of climate change. The critics crushed it, all of them panned it, they didn't get it and they flattened him and in my opinion that was when he decided he would give them substandard work, give them shit and see what happens. We know what happened. They liked it. They fucking loved it. That was the impetus behind the Any Colour You Like show, the work painted in whichever colour his buyers wanted, whichever disgusting colour matched their disgusting living rooms. They loved it and he hasn't looked back since. That, in my opinion, is the single event that determined all that was to follow, the nihilism, the world-weary world wandering, the reclusiveness and contempt for critics and the general public. This is my take on the matter, of course. You don't have to agree.

The day Frank invited me over to meet his son I walked in the room and found a copy of *Les Chants de Maldoror* on the bar. I held up the book and I asked Frank what was going on. I was going to offer my condolences, right? Oh poetry is quite beyond me, said Frank. That's Newton. He's a bit of a genius. When the genius arrived in his pressed white shirt, I said something flippant. I said a boy of fourteen should not be allowed to read the good goddamn Count of Lautréamont-Ducasse. He smiled at this sad witticism, smiled sadly as if he were humouring me. Much later in the evening he told me he had translated some of the French poets as a way of learning French. I asked if I could hear one of his translations. At this point, Frank, discreetly I thought, vanished into the kitchen to confer with the cook. The boy said nothing for a long time. Oh the quality of that oppression, the steamy depths of that silence. How it weighed upon one's head and how it leaked malaise into the room. A long silence and then he recited from memory a poem that sounded familiar to me. I pretended to know who it was because I did not want to expose my ignorance to the kid, but in my head I made some educated guesses. I knew it was a sonnet so I thought there was a good chance it might be Baudelaire. But it didn't sound like him. I thought of Verlaine or even Apollinaire, though I should have known that it could not be goddamn Apollinaire. Not Apollinaire and certainly not Victor fucking Hugo! I gave up trying to guess who it was but I liked the translation and I asked for a copy. At home I looked up my French poets. It was Rimbaud of course. I noticed that he had mistaken right for left in the last line and I called and pointed it out with some pleasure. The following week I sent the poem to Nissim Ezekiel who published it in *Quest* and became a friend and role model to Newton. (Isn't it strangely fucking interesting that both of Newton's early mentors were poets who edited magazines funded by the CIA? I mean, his first publishers were Stephen Spender's *Encounter* and Nissim Ezekiel's *Quest*, serious literary journals, and also, as we now know, secret 'cultural freedom' weapons of the cold war.) Ezekiel's mentoring technique in those days was to take you out for a cup of coffee where he looked at your poems and then he would take you for a walk on Apollo Bunder or Marine Drive or some other sea-struck cityscape and he would be extremely critical about said poems. Then, seeing the look of defeat on your face, he would drop two or three well-chosen words of hope into your misery. "Work harder." Or, "We must labour to be beautiful." In any case it was young Xavier's first poetry publication in a national magazine. I have a copy if you're interested:

Lush green hollow and crackling river
Where the mountain sun, brighter than our sun,
Throws to the grass crazy rags of silver:
The little valley brims with light and sound.

A young soldier, head bare and mouth open,
Neck bathed in watercress of latest blue,
Lies asleep, stretched out under the heavens,
Pale in his bed of green; the light eddies true.

His feet in swordgrass, he sleeps. The smile
Of a sick child on his lips, he rests a while.
Mother, lull him warm – he is very cold.

No plant makes his nostrils quiver, no scent.
He sleeps in the sun, hand upon his silent
Chest. In his right side are two red holes.

Glory Pande, former live model, interviewed by Dismas Bambai at Bangalore Club, Bangalore, March 2005

I try to remember those days and it isn't easy, let me tell you. It's like the seventies. If you remember, you were not there, or you were in the wrong place. I mean, it's true too that my memory falls short in general. What happened yesterday? For the life of me I cannot remember. I want to say nothing happened but this can't be true. Then let it be said like this, yesterday nothing happened that was worth recording. I remember the old days better, when we were young and the world was beautiful.

This is before he became a citizen of everywhere, before London and New York and Paris, before alcohol claimed him like an only child. He was fifteen or so, awkward around people. The only time he seemed confident was when he was working. Getting a word out of him was like squeezing blood from a stone. Impossible. He would just look at you with those big eyes and if he was moved for some reason or trying to communicate without words, which I often felt he was trying to do, then he'd vibrate. I'd feel him vibrating.

He was called the Genius of Saint Mary's. That was the first thing I heard about him. He wrote poems, I wrote poems. He painted, I modelled nude. It was only natural we would be drawn to one another. I was older and wiser in the way girls are wiser and he liked to follow me around. I suspect he was a bit star-struck. I think he liked it that my family was famous for its poets and writers.

One day he asked me out. He said, would you care to join me for luncheon tomorrow at the Taj? And I realised two things. One, it was the first complete sentence I had heard him utter. Two, he had an English accent though he had not been to England. But how could I have refused, a boy with perfect manners asking me out? I said yes, yes, of course. By luncheon he meant dinner. He arrived on the dot of six in a taxi and held the door for me. We drove from Walkeshwar all the way down Marine Drive to the Gateway of India. He didn't say a thing. At the restaurant we ate and drank in complete silence. But I felt it throughout, the vibrations that came off him like waves of static. He spoke with his hands and he smoked continually.

He wanted to marry me. Perhaps if he'd stayed I would have said yes. It couldn't have been more of a disaster than his other marriages, though it surely would have been more of a disaster than my one and only marriage. The following year he was gone to Jesus College and then came fame. I didn't see him again until twenty years later, after his first and second marriages had ended and he returned briefly to India. And then I met him again last year in Bangalore at a wedding reception for the son of a dear friend. He was with his lovely partner, I forget her name, and he was wearing a black straw hat. It was the first time I had seen him in a hat and all of a sudden I realised he was old. And then something far worse occurred to me. I was old too. I mean, it stands to reason. I met him when he was a boy and now here he was in his sixties. It was a shock, I'll tell you that. We didn't have much to say to each other. When I looked at him it was like looking into a mirror that had cracked. I'm sure he felt the same way.

Miss Henry, author, actress, and artist's model, telephone interview by Dismas Bambai, January 2005

I saw the whole bloody thing, didn't I? The first thing I noticed? I'll tell you, darling. It was his way of smoking. So thoroughly affected, do you know what I mean? So affected, but affecting as well. Look at the photos from that period. Look at the cigarette held at the very tip of index and middle fingers, hand up near his face as if he was trying to decipher something written on his palm, some lost or forgotten language, Classical Aramaic or Phrygian or Sumerian or Linear A. That was the first thing I observed, the beautiful hands and doe eyes and total silence at all times.

Most people dream visually, in a stream of pictures. I don't. I dream in text. Print scrolls in my nightmares and sometimes in my dreams. Words seduce me first, not looks or money, though those qualities certainly help. Oh, my dear! Words are my erogenous trigger, in which case how did this silent boy manage to win me over? Easily explained. I'd seen some of his poems, hadn't I? Poor Ralph showed me some crumpled pages while I was holding the fort at the bookshop one day. The first thing I noticed was how beautifully the text was shaped, perfect rectangles. The language too was beautiful. I told him so, which pleased him because he wanted to publish a selection in his Archer Press Poets series. That was the point about Ralph. He had no patience for the second bloody rate. I asked him once how he chose the poets he published. I realised I had never seen him reading anything other than newspapers and magazines. Do you know what he told me? He tapped his nose. I can smell them, he said. Not that they smell bad, which some of them do of course, dear me, they haven't the most scrupulous hygiene. It's the nose, Miss Henry, never lets me down.

Well, then. I read the poems aloud and to my ears they sounded like the Old Testament, the Song of bloody Solomon transplanted to England's green and pleasant land. And when Newton came in one day his silence did not unnerve me as it did most people. I heard him in my inner ear and what I heard most clearly was a sort of mute entreaty and immediately I understood. He didn't so much as say hello. He might have swayed in my general direction and I was ready to go home with him. I was. Of course he was too shy to suggest any such thing. His way was to simply position himself in my general orbit. That was the entirety of his seduction technique in those days. I noticed that he began to spend a lot of time at the bookshop. He would come in early and help me set up for the day and then we'd have lunch and sometimes dinner as well. It was extraordinary. A courtship conducted entirely in silence.

One night I asked him to take me to the cinema. We went to a Peter Sellers film. *The Naked Truth* or *Naked Is the Night*, something that had the word 'naked' in the title. I was hoping for a racy comedy but it wasn't a comedy and it wasn't racy and throughout Newton kept his hands to himself, so proper I realised I should have to make the first move. Afterwards we walked on the streets of the West End, past the tube station and the girls in the doorways, and we might have kept walking all bloody night if I hadn't taken matters by the lapel, by the scruff of the bloody neck. I told him I'd the key to a friend's flat. Would he like to go there with me? I thought his reply remarkable but only because it was a complete sentence and most of the time he was given to monosyllables. I couldn't possibly, he said. And I thought, oh well, it's only a matter of time.

His father had put him up in an Asiatic boarding house somewhere in Shoreditch, of all places, or it might have been Hackney. Somewhere dire at any rate. Frank knew the owner of the boarding house. It was a way of keeping Newton safe before he went up to Oxford. But daddy couldn't keep him safe enough, could he, from the likes of me?

When I couldn't bear it any longer I told him one night that I was going home with him, whatever his thoughts on the matter. We took a taxi to Shoreditch or Hackney or Hoxton, somewhere, and we stumbled up the stairs and he unlocked the door to a room lit by a naked hanging bulb. The bed and dresser were covered in drifts of debris. You see, he couldn't pack, it was a sort of disability. He could not pack and it goes without saying that he could not unpack. Clothes and books and bottles everywhere and an ashtray on the floor and damp towels on the bed and a smell of old socks and damp. The toilet was not en suite, you'll be surprised to hear: it was at the end of the filthy corridor. It struck me as appropriate lodgings for a foreign poet and I felt very much at home. My only complaint was that he was much too tender. I had to teach him how to be rough with a woman, how to use his open hand. Once he got over the shock he was a fast learner. I stayed a week and then came an unforeseen piece of luck. It turned out my former husband had left me a house. Newton and I moved in of course.

Call me Miss Henry. I don't have a second name. I might have had one once but it was so long ago I don't recall it, really I don't. For a time I called myself Henry Xavier. But I dropped that soon enough. Didn't like the ring of it, did I? I mean, there's nothing sadder than a divorcee using her married name, don't you think? Although to tell you the truth, to drop a little truth bomb, we never did divorce. We split up, we separated, we became ghosts to each other but we never made it official. It was the sixties, darling, when Newton and I tied the knot, 1962, to be precise, and we didn't believe in marriage. Nobody did. If you don't believe in marriage how can you believe in divorce? The point is, his later marriages, the two I know of, they were illegal, weren't they? Stands to reason. Not to put too fine a point on it, he was a bigamist, a trigamist, a serial bloody matrimonialist.

I saw the whole thing, I did. The transformation of the silent young poet to drunken raconteur, all in the space of a year or two. It began around the time he won the prize, in 1958, at the jaded age of twenty. When he first got to London before going up to Oxford he didn't say a word. He was so bloody shy. But that lasted for as long as it takes to down a breakfast Bloody. He took to the life as if he'd been rehearsing for it from the age of ten. He was a natural. And do remember, darling, they used to call me the Queen of Soho. I should know.

We needed so little then. Half a crown for a pack of Player's and a drink and then the day would settle into itself. The days, the days, how I loved them because they were always the same. First thing in the morning, meaning second or third thing, we'd go to the Café Torino on Dean Street for a vol au vent and coffee, if we had the change to spare. Otherwise just the caffeine. It was across the street from the French, Gaston's pub, which had another name of course, a name nobody bloody used. We called it the French because Gaston was French, just the loveliest man with the most elegant way of lending you money. You'd say, I'll take a Pernod, please, Gaston, and do you think you might be able to lend me a fiver? And he'd bring you the drink and change from a fiver and you were set for the afternoon. We'd sit at the Torino and watch until the French had filled up and then we'd tumble across the street and fall in, always from the side entrance on the left and always we'd exit from the right. One must have one's little rituals, must one not? At the French, then, the parade would begin, the endless talk and gossip and innuendo. In the afternoon we'd go to a drinking club and to another in the evening. How rude we all were! Hello cuntie, Muriel said to everyone at the Colony Room, man, woman, and child, meaning Newton, who was always the youngest person in the room, eighteen when we met. The first time someone was rude to him it was as if a cloud had descended. He was mortified. It didn't last, needless to say. Soon he was ruder than any of us. He could aim an insult from ten paces that would leave you breathless.

Bacon and he had a rivalry, didn't they? Who could be more of a bastard? It was a rivalry based on the usual thing. First Newton painted me and then Bacon wanted to paint me. Newton didn't like it but he couldn't quite bring himself to forbid it, either. Besides, I wouldn't have bloody obeyed. I was born in Simla but I wasn't a quiet Indian housewife beholden to her husband. And how on earth could one refuse Bacon when he was always so generous with the champagne? He drank nothing else as we all know. The second time he painted me, and he always painted me nude and spread-eagled on an unmade bed, well, that afternoon we went back to the Colony Room and there was Newton. Bacon asked if he would like a glass of bubbles and Newton said, certainly fucking not! Do I look like a champagne drinker? I told him, darling, don't be jealous. Bacon doesn't like girls except as models, don't you know?

He didn't know.

Ralph's Archer Press published *Songs for the Tin-Eared* when he was nineteen. The next year the book won the biggest poetry prize in

England, a prize they hadn't awarded in fourteen years and certainly not to a non-Englishman, and some time after that we were married. By then I was an old woman of thirty-something, or let's say twenty-nine, yes, twenty-nine's better, and he was famous, details of his life, of our life, splashed across the newspapers, and always the same word in the headline, *Poet*, and none of them knew poor Newton's secret. The poems were few and far between. I hardly ever saw him working. He tried to write but it was a hard slog and very little came of it and he blamed me. Who knows, maybe it was my fault. I'm the first to admit it. I'm a handful, I am.

One morning I went out to buy some Player's and a pimply-faced git waylaid me, my first paparazzo, clicking away, and there I am unwashed in me pyjamas and he says, Miss Henry, Miss Henry, what's it like, life with the poet? Is it all it's cracked up to be, then? I drew myself up to my full height. It might have been my finest moment.

I said: Piss off, darling!

Reggie Ashton, former English tutor, Jesus College, Oxford, telephone interview by Dismas Bambai, February 2005

It was one of those moments, extreme flux in the air, the sixties not quite upon us. One had to keep a wary eye out for the rabid socialist, as you know, who was absolutely everywhere one looked. And the socialists hadn't yet become Utopians. This may be the main reason one looked the other way at the outré behaviour, because of his background, as it were. The exotic Oriental! The beautiful brown boy fresh off a boat from the tropics! The baby poet! One saw a letter of introduction from Stephen Spender, no less, and Auden had read him and liked him, and Barker and Bacon were his friends, and the Archer Press was about to publish him. It did strike one that he seemed to have no interest whatsoever in the study of English Literature. I've seen a number of essays in my years at this hallowed institution, as you may well imagine, and still I recall the first he submitted. Even now, after all these years, when one cannot remember if one has taken one's morning medication.

The wild horses of the mind, what? We are but riders holding on for our lives, if you see what I mean. Let me try to explain about the essays. They were full of the most marvellous and convoluted images, upside-down girl-trees, cadaverous monster-writers feasting on bowls of blood, and so on, but there was no content whatsoever. It was plain to see that he had dashed them off in ten minutes. The first essay he gave me began with this statement, and I am not paraphrasing, "Byron was born with a silver spoon in his mouth. Pope was born with a wooden spoon. And Keats was born with no spoon at all." The essay then went on to discuss in extraordinary detail the comparable tactile qualities of silver versus wood, and it ended with an anthropological interpretation of the use of cutlery and the societal meaning of eating together in a group. There was no further mention of Byron, Pope, or even poor Keats. Still and all, it was apparent to most of us that his only interest was poetry. Fun for him, what? One realised eventually that one had to surrender to the inevitable. From the day that realisation dawned things improved considerably. When Mr Xavier arrived at my rooms I would make myself comfortable in my armchair. I would put my feet up and light a cigarette and rest my eyes upon the green field of the quadrangle. The poet would read aloud from his essays, or he would read his poems, of which one remembers certain phrases even now, much as one recalls a melody one has heard in one's youth. After some weeks of this I must say I began to enjoy the sessions in the way one enjoys certain types of fiction, or the sound of birdsong in the streets of London. One enjoyed listening to the words as a purely experiential sensation in which one is liberated from the tyranny of meaning. Once I reached this somewhat mystic, not to say profound appreciation of Mr Xavier's talents, I was able to relax. Thereafter we got along rather famously. I understood him and he understood that I understood. Aut insanit homo, aut versus facit.

He and his friends, the poet Peter and the filmmaker Julian, threw rather interesting luncheon parties. More often than not they were liquid luncheons. But Newton would always cook some one thing, a one-pot meal, coq au vin or pork stew or goulash. His idea of a meal was rather avant-garde to say the least. Bacon and wine in everything.

Bacon-wrapped chicken, bacon-wrapped fish, bacon-wrapped bacon. Rashers in the pudding! I jest, but the fact is he could not get enough of the pig. And his future wife was there of course, whose main interest was the rolling and smoking of cannabis cigarettes, who was rather visibly pregnant, who announced one day that she had stopped drinking whisky and switched to vodka and orange juice, for the vitamin C, don't you know? She was quite the hit. One noticed she was most comfortable when she was the centre of attention and surrounded by a crowd of admiring male faces. That was when she came, so to speak, into her own. She was a one, really. Poor Newton suffered terribly.

Miss Henry, author, actress, and artist's model, telephone interview by Dismas Bambai, January 2005

A detail. I was pregnant when I first met Newton, and I disappeared for a time. I went to the baby's father and tried to make a go of it, as one does. Not that it worked. Or it worked for some time and then it did not. I was lucky in that I had an easy time of the delivery, possibly because I was in the Colony Room when my waters broke and Muriel took me upstairs. There was no time to drive to a hospital and she said she had some midwifing experience. Come along, cuntie, she said. Exactly the kind of invitation I could not resist in those days. She put me in the bathtub and she perched on the toilet. And the baby's father, a man whose name no longer passes my lips, he was on the floor. When it was time I told Muriel, it's coming, I do believe it's coming, and she said, well, I better get my suitcase. Back in a moment, cunties, she said, and went downstairs. The baby's father was of no help whatever. I realised it was all up to me. Isn't it bloody always, though? I told myself a few things.

- The same energy that puts the baby in will bring the baby out. Harness the womanly energy.
- Breathe: one breath, two breaths, three, four. Relax and count.
- It is like dying, trust and let go.

- It is not enough to experience the door. You must open.
- Travel down into consciousness. All is written inside. The knowing. The future.

I would have liked to stay in the water but the bathtub was too small. At which Muriel said one can rent a birthing pool and put it in the living room. It's a bit late, isn't it, darling? I said. My daughter was born at that very spot, in the bathroom where I knelt. Muriel told me to reach down and pull her out with my hands and I did just that. I reached down and pulled. It was so easy. I knew as I pulled out my baby that Newton would find me and we would live together in a house, though I never would have guessed Islington, and I knew too he would leave me, as he did, twice.

The first time he disappeared Nannie and I went to find him. But where do you find someone in London if he does not wish to be found? We tried the obvious places, the Colony Room, the French, the Coach and Horses, Bacon's studio, a barge on the Thames on which an acquaintance used to live. I thought he might be holed up in somebody's rooms in Oxford and I resolved to go there. And then we had a bit of luck. I ran into a friend, a cat burglar if you must know, someone who had helped me out on occasion, and she gave me an address in Pimlico. Nannie and I went there and we found a flat without heat or running water. But my cat burglar had come through, for there was Newton in an armchair, nervously smoking a cigarette. He was Nannie's favourite. She used to call him Newski because he'd read all the Russians. He was pale and unwashed and trembling in a fisherman's sweater. Newski, said Nannie, what have you done? And we carried him home and fed him and put him to bed and I saw something on the pillow. It looked like a moving spot of blood. Lice. His head was full of lice. Nannie had to get a special shampoo and wash his hair, at which point he mumbled something about how Verlaine's wife had found lice on a pillow used by Rimbaud. And off he went, a story about Rimbaud and Verlaine in Brussels. How had he landed in that hovel in bloody Pimlico? He never said. Or he had a different story each time I asked. I think that was the thing that drove us finally, finally apart. Newton had a shifting relationship with the truth. He liked to keep a respectful distance. When hemmed in he told the most fantastic lies.

A week later, after he'd recovered, after he'd been fully deloused, he said he was off to the shops to buy cigarettes. Back in ten minutes, darling, is what he said. For a month, for two months, I heard his footsteps on the stairs. I imagined he was lying beside me. I saw him at the newsagents or on the tube. I imagined the worst. Dear, dear dotty me, I thought, I must be losing my tiny mind. Of course I never saw him again.

Gill Temple, sound engineer, telephone interview by Dismas Bambai, January 2005

I know that story. "See you in ten minutes." It became a kind of catchphrase in their circle. My mother had heard all the stories, true and false, and she had no illusions. She married him and had a baby with him and tried to make a go of it. I take some comfort in the fact that my mother is the only one he did not leave. He didn't have the chance, really. She left him first.

This was in 1975 when I was about five. Newton had been commissioned to paint the Prime Minister of India and we three went to Delhi. The portrait was never completed. It was the time of the Emergency and Mrs Gandhi was sensitive about her image and I think she had reason to be. Also, the government had just blacklisted Newton's father, my grandfather, the journalist Frank Xavier, and I think Mrs Gandhi must have been asking herself why she had commissioned the portrait in the first place.

My mother was present at their first meeting. Her job was to take notes while Newton interviewed the prime minister and made preliminary sketches in his notebook. She said it was a complete disaster. Newton would ask a long leading question and Mrs Gandhi would reply in monosyllables. Newton pointed out that India had arrested its intellectuals and politicians for speaking out against the government. Was this not an extreme response to a fairly common democratic tradition?

No, said Mrs Gandhi. Newton asked if the Emergency would continue indefinitely despite the fierce criticism it had drawn in India and the world. Yes, said Mrs Gandhi. Did it not bother her that history might judge her as one of the most autocratic of Indian rulers, asked Newton. Mrs Gandhi paused for a moment and regarded the floor with disapproving eyes. She took her time to reply. No, she said. There was only one question to which she did not reply with a monosyllable. Newton asked if her father Jawaharlal had had a great influence on her policies. She looked at him for the first and only time in the interview, frightening him with her eyes, and said, why does everybody who interviews me have to ask the same questions? And that was how the meeting went, according to my mother. Mrs Gandhi never came around.

My mother said the preliminary interview was Newton's technique. He asked questions, made sketches, and took detailed notes, meaning my mother took notes. Then he examined and dissected each reply and created a composite psychological portrait of the subject before going to the canvas. There were no sittings. He preferred not to have the living subject before him while making a picture. He preferred to let his imagination have the final say. I think it's true to say that this remained the case throughout his life. For him nature was a springboard. He had no interest in mimesis. He was interested only in transcendence.

By then he was no longer writing. He announced that he had given up the word and taken up the line. According to my mother he was doing neither. She said his self-appointed role was to drink and because he was working for the prime minister everything was on the house, cases of liquor delivered to the door whenever required. There was an endless stream of visitors as well, journalists and poets, artists of all kinds, and the only thing they had in common, according to my mother, was the whisky and the rum. They drank like it was going out of style. She said he was drinking so much that he came to see the work as an interruption. He switched from oil to acrylics because acrylics dried faster. He was in a hurry to be done. No wonder Mrs Gandhi had her doubts about the portrait.

Unannounced she came to inspect the studio one morning. My

mother and I were in the sitting room when the bodyguards arrived. Then she came in, so swiftly and noiselessly that I was scarcely aware a tall lady had sat down beside me on the couch. I was crying for some reason I don't remember, and she took my hand and spoke in a very soft voice. I don't remember what she said. You are a strong girl and you must always be strong, she might have said. Or she might have said, be brave and everything else will follow. Whatever it was it made me stop crying immediately. She was wearing a white sari and no jewellery and she had short hair and sat very straight. When she smiled I was surprised at how girlish she seemed, not at all like the Indian ladies who came to visit my parents. She was simple in her dress but still there was something queenly about her. I thought she was wonderful! I admired her as only a five-year-old can admire someone. She knew she had made a fan of me.

Newton was asleep or he was sleeping it off and my mother didn't know what to say. How do you tell the prime minister to come back later? Besides, the portrait was highly visible, placed by the window in a corner of the room. Mrs G stood in front of it for no more than two or three minutes. The smile left her face and her whole manner changed. She became positively glacial. I don't blame her, do you? He had made her a blob of black against a background of newspaper headlines about the Emergency. It was a special kind of black. Really, it was the absence of all colour. And all you saw in the elongated humanoid blackness were a pair of eyes and the famous streak of white in the hair. It was the first of the paintings he came to call 'Alterations', where he would use a magazine cover or a newspaper photo and paint over it. Mrs Gandhi gathered her white sari around her and turned her terrible gaze to my mother. She said, tell him I will not be demonised. Then she left and never returned. In the afternoon there was a phone call from her office informing Newton that the portrait had been decommissioned. It was as if he had been waiting for just such a setback. He started to drink in earnest. My mother decided she'd had enough. Early one morning we got into a taxi and went to the airport while Newton was still asleep. I remember it, empty bottles everywhere and full ashtrays and rubbish and my father passed out on the couch near his frightening portrait of

Mrs Gandhi. My mother and I tiptoed around him so he wouldn't wake up. It was the last time I saw him.

Years after my mother had left him a journalist asked her about their life together. Oh, Newton, she said, he was poet for a day. Of course they took the quote and made a news report out of it.

He was on one of his trips to London when she fell ill and he was here when she died. Everybody called to say a few words, complete strangers called. He did not. That's the kind of thing you remember all your life. She was so young, I was so young, but not a word from him. Then, weeks after Edna's death, I saw an interview and I will always remember the headline. *Nothing sadder in the world than the death of a young woman, says Newton Xavier.* The interview was mostly black comedy. He was blackout drunk. He kept asking for an ashtray and when they got him one he kept missing it, he ashed the floor. He misheard questions. He insisted there was a third person in the room and when the interviewer said, no, it was just the two of them, Newton took a swing at him. Then he took a drink. He was of the opinion that there was no situation in the world, however unpleasant, that could not be improved with alcohol. Whisky was his stock response to life. Except not everything in the world can be solved by drink. "Nothing sadder in the world than the death of a young woman." Words are cheap when you're talking to the press.

Two years after she died the phone rang and it was a voice I did not know, a man who claimed to be my father. He wanted to meet me. I'd like to drop in, if I may, he said. But why now, I asked. He said, you were a child when I last saw you and I have no idea what kind of young woman you've become. I told him he needn't trouble himself to be a father for a day. He asked if he could see me even if it was only for a moment. I disconnected the phone. When it rang again I did not pick up.

I changed my surname and took my mother's maiden name. I'm happy to say that I have taken after my mother in every possible way, from my colouring to my eyes to my general outlook, which is sunny. Of course I take after my mother. I work with music and everybody knows Newton is tone-deaf. The title of his first book is autobiographically accurate. I'm telling you this for the record. I have nothing more to add.

Reggie Ashton, former English tutor, Jesus College, Oxford, telephone interview by Dismas Bambai, February 2005

It occurred to me that one should bring together birds of an exotic feather. Newton was in the dailies. It was the first time the Hawthorn had been won by a Wog, by which I mean Westernised Oriental Gentleman. Mind you, one uses the word in its best sense, as a term of affection if not quite endearment. Also in the news for other reasons was young Vidia Naipaul, who too had been a student of mine. One hesitates to say one taught him everything he knows, but one must say so as he is not the sort to credit his masters. Vidia had published a brace of amusing novels set in the islands. The comic mode, as it were. And just that year he'd come out with a collection of short stories, also set in the islands, also amusing. In other words he received some attention in the better newspapers. I don't know why, or perhaps I do, perhaps I was being devilish, and I set up a meeting between Newton and Vidia. Newton had gone down from Oxford and was living somewhere in London with the soon-to-be-infamous Miss Henry. He suggested the French Pub as a meeting place, which wasn't its name, incidentally. One doesn't wish to be thought of as a pedant, or perhaps one does. The point is the establishment's name was the York Minster. Only its shaggier denizens called it the French. Newton was a regular for the simple reason that it was Miss Henry's favourite pub in all of London and possibly the world. Vidia had never been there in his life. He was no bohemian and in any case he wasn't one to go out to lunch unless someone was picking up the william. So there we are, Newton penniless, Vidia parsimonious, and luncheon at the York Minster. How one would have liked to be a fly on the wall during that meeting, you know, between the lauded young poet and the future Nobelist. One has no doubt it was a liquid affair on the Newtonian side of the table. Carpe Cerevisi! And it serves one well to remember that the two were of the same generation, separated by six years, Newton being the younger. I spoke to Vidia soon afterwards and asked him how things had gone. "He wasn't interested in me," said Vidia. "He was interested only in English writers." One detected a curious note of hurt. And believe me, Vidia is not given to sentiment of any kind. Purely in the interests of research I asked Newton the same question. How had the meeting gone? He said, "Much as I thought it would. We had nothing to talk about and nothing in common, except that he is very shy and so am I." Then, some years ago when Newton was on one of his forays to London, I persuaded him to stop by the college for a glass of sherry. I was nearing the end of my innings and had already begun to take my leave, intellectually, from my immediate surroundings. In the course of things he mentioned that he had met Naipaul at the Neemrana festival in India. This is decades after their first, rather disastrous meeting at the York Minster. How did Newton find the new laureate, I asked. "He can be witty and wise, when he allows himself the liberty," he told me. "Alas, he prefers to be the great man of letters. There has been a change in the shy young writer I met in 1959 and change isn't always for the better."

One never quite believed they had nothing in common, you know. They were born in the thirties and started to publish at around the same time. Both converted to Englishness as if to a new faith and both felt they were outsiders in a house of privilege. Both arrived in Oxford in their late teens. They thought and spoke and wrote in English and did so better than some Englishmen but they were treated like immigrants. Perhaps most tellingly both were cruel to the women in their lives. It makes one wonder if spousal abuse is an Oriental attribute.

The greatest point of convergence is one that is rarely mentioned in literary society, which is nothing if not polite, alas! Newton and Vidia were superb incarnations of the true Wog, a tribe that is vanishing from the multicultural world we have created. They arrived in London from the former Empire at around the same age, seventeen or eighteen, young writers who wished to locate themselves at the centre of English life, and they acquired, almost before they arrived, the properly fruity accent of their new environs. Remarkably, we tend to forget that neither had set foot upon these isles until their late teens. Audio, Video, Disco. Or rather, Audio, Vidia, Disco, and the learning, the soaking up is extant. All quite laughable, what? Except one must not laugh, not if one cares about one's career and reputation. As you can see, I do not. Indeed, I am become exempt, am soon to become extinct. I have had my career. I may speak freely.

Rama Raoer, former professor of English Literature, Bombay University, interviewed by Dismas Bambai at Dolly Mansions, near Dadar Station, May 2005

If this is a story about art then it is a story about God and the gifts he gives us. Also the gifts he takes away. God has it in for poets, that's obvious, but the Bombaywallahs hold a special place in his dispensation. Or so I believe, with good reason. Much has been taken from the poets of Bombay. Bhagwan kuch deyta hai toh wapas bhi leyta hai.

What a time it was for poetry and poets, Xavier and Doss and so many others. In my mind those two are inextricably twinned, Doss and Xavier, Xavier and Doss, and your call brought it all back. But first let me apologise for my rudeness on the phone. I wasn't raised to be a barbarian. When you said you were a journalist I went into automatic attack mode. I don't trust journalists as a rule. I learned the hard way. They ask you an innocuous question, you make an innocuous reply, and the next thing you know there's a screaming headline. *GAY PROFESSOR DEFENDS UNDERAGE SEX*. Or something of that nature, something vile, something so embarrassing you will wish you had never opened your mouth.

Let me ask you a question. Why has no one written about the Bombay poets of the seventies and eighties, poets who sprouted from the soil like weeds or mushrooms or carnivorous new flowers, who arrived like meteors, burned bright for a season or two and vanished without a trace? It had never happened before, poets writing Marathi, Hindi, English, and combinations thereof, writing to and against each other, such ferment and not a word of documentation. Why not?

The fiction has been done to death, features and interviews and critical studies and textbooks, and not one of the novelists is worth a little finger of the poets. They were the great ones and they died. All of them died. If you want a moral, here it is: what God giveth, he taketh away. In this story art is god. And if god is art, then what is the devil? Bad art of course. But we'll talk about that in a minute or we won't. Kuch bhi ho, yaar.

I'll tell you something no one knows. It was Narayan Doss who came up with the infamous name, the Hung Realists, as opposed to the famous name, the Hungryalists. It was Doss. Not the Bengali poets but a Marathi poet, a lower-caste or casteless Marathi poet. Of course the Bengalis took credit for it, as they do, but the truth is more and less clear-cut. The name did not come from Chaucer as some have claimed. It arose out of a misunderstanding. Someone misheard a joke made by that infernal joker Allen Ginsberg and a historical witticism was born.

When Doss arrived in Bombay in 1977 he knew nobody. He was nobody. But in a month or two he was at the heart of the scene, if scene is what it was. This was why he left his small town and came here, or one of the reasons he came, to be part of the milieu of Bombay in the seventies, which, as you know, was nothing if not glamorous, a saturnalia, a phantasmic playground for the rich and famished. Doss knew it would be closed to him because of who he was, his brilliant and terrible personal history. So he came up with an audacious scheme. He told everyone he was engaged in a revolutionary remapping of the continent of poetry to be published by the much-imitated never-equalled poetry collective Clearing House, a definitive anthology, inclusive rather than exclusive, with a hundred and fifty poets in all and a wide representative sample of each one's work, a door-stopper of a book weighing in at about a thousand pages. This got him invited to the homes of the poets and they hosted him and paid his bills and no one ever thought of checking with Clearing House whether the anthology had been commissioned. Doss was a poetry hustler. We knew it and still we fell for it. We fell for him.

You must understand that he was a beautiful young man. Not handsome or good-looking. Beautiful! Dark skin, swollen lips, Neanderthal eyebrows, wild black hair, a bit like a promiscuous Russian ballet star, Nureyev rather than Baryshnikov. In short he looked the part of the poet. And the Untouchability? In the mid-seventies it was a badge of honour. It only added to his allure. We thought it was simply a part of his rebel genius and Luciferian ambition to appear out of thin air and make those authoritative pronouncements about the strongest among us, the blanket condemnation and praise and weird insights into our work and into our heads. It was as if a fully formed baby poet had appeared in our midst to hold us to the light and destroy us – or make us better.

We were entranced and we let him get the better of us. That's the truth of it and by now it's well known. People talk, word gets around. Everybody knows what became of that anthology, kuch nahin, one big anda, zero se zero tak. The true anthology was something nobody expected. It burned the old maps and all those who expected to be in it were excluded. It was something he and Xavier dreamed up. All of that is known. But here's something else nobody knows. He brought a book of poems with him when he arrived in Bombay. Did you know that? A genuine book, poems he'd been working on since he was a teenager growing up on the wrong side of the river in that heartless Indian village he was in such a hurry to escape. Not a slim book – God save us from slim books of verse – no, no, it was a hundred and thirty pages, a substantial selection, and the poems were like nothing we had seen, loose-limbed, improvised, shaggy laughing monsters of violence and pity, also sweetness, also rage.

The question I will leave you with is this, what happened to the book? Why did it appear in Marathi and disappear immediately thereafter? Why was it never translated into Hindi or English when lesser poets were being translated left, right and centre? And what was the nature of the encounter between Doss and Xavier? Enough, I've talked enough for today. I'm an old man and I need my rest. We'll pick it up again tomorrow.

I'll leave you with a last thought. What I'm telling you is a story with no end and no beginning. From those to whom much is given, much will be taken away.

Peter Priestley, former Oxford Professor of Poetry, email interview by Dismas Bambai, Cornwall, October 2005

It's rather heartening that you should contact me now. There was a time journalists wrote to me every other day, around the time he became the first non-white winner of the most prestigious poetry prize in the land. They said it was because he was the youngest recipient but what they really meant was something quite different. He was the first winner of the prize who was not to the manor born. You must keep in mind how racist England was in those days, not that it isn't so now. It's just that we do a better job of hiding it.

One afternoon, it was one of those afternoons of our lives when all was ahead of us still, summer, the brilliant water, the lovely weeping trees, a hump-backed bridge and a trio of friends, and I said, New, in twenty years we're going to want to remember this. He was silent for a long time. His eyes were closed in the sun and I thought he had not heard me or he had heard me as one hears the sound of water, and just as I was beginning to sink into my own silence, he said, in twenty years, Peter, we shall still be friends. He was right. I look upon that unlikely testament as one of the achievements of my youth.

Last year a small poetry press in London acquired the rights to Ralph Godwin's Archer Press publications. The idea was to bring out a collected edition of the various volumes in a single box. On the spine would be the logo, the yellow archer and his arrow poised for flight, with the titles and authors' names, lovely idea, really, and they wanted a quote from me for Newton's poems. Do you want to know what I said? "Learn these poems by heart. Newton Xavier was a guardian spirit of a shamanic age." I meant every word. In a time of performance poets and spoken word poets and jazz poets and poz poets and beat poets and street poets and stand-up poets and sit-down poets, and the poet-next-door and the poet-as-professor, the conversational poets and confessional poets, the poets of the quotidian and the poets of crisis, and the poet as activist and poet as arriviste, and Martian poets and Movement Poets and identity poets and queer poets, it helps to remember that once poetry was prophecy. Ted Hughes's first volume, *The Hawk in the Rain*, appeared the same year as Newton's *Songs for the Tin-Eared*, in 1957. And Geoffrey Hill's first, *For the Unfallen*, appeared soon after. Hughes, Hill, Xavier, a trinity of shamans. Not Larkin, for God's sake, none of those well-crafted limericks. Not Heaney by any yardstick. Hughes was Heaney's daddy and daddy did it first and best. And not Peter Porter or Kingsley Amis or Newton's mentor Stephen Spender. God no. In that context one must mention that the songs in *Songs for the Tin-Eared* traded in certain secrets: the meaning of rivers (they are never silent), of trees (upside-down sense spirits), of predatory creatures from the animal kingdom (blood spirits of violence and life-in-death). And then came the second volume, *Saint Me*, published in 1967, which I can tell you was originally and provisionally titled *Kingdom of the Leashed, Republic of the Lash*, a related suite of poems that presents the intellect as an adequate reflection of the finite and points in the last section to the future, poems that seem uncanny when you look at them today because they predict a world in which suicidal rage and the climate would combine to create the end of days. One marvels at the fact that New's entire reputation rests on two slim books of verse. But what books they were! You will not see the like again. I believe this was the true reason for his inability to continue after the second volume. He wrote as if each poem was his last. I believe he used it all up and he had to switch tracks to his other, lesser gift, the gift that added fortune to his fame.

He told me once that thoughts of the future made him envy the birds because they had no such worries. Well, we can't be sure of that, can we, New? I said. You have a home to go to, he said. Where will I go? And then his English life fell to pieces and his marriages broke up and his father died. The poetry stopped. Eventually he returned to India. Return was not inevitable, not by any means. But he made it so.

BOOK TWO

Adventures in Alleged Bias

Saint Nicholas

or Sinte Klaas in the Dutch vernacular;
Americanised to Santa Claus by settlers;

born in Turkey, not the North Pole;
patron of brides & unmarried girls,

of travellers, sailors, children, & Russians;
washed white in representations;

life story lost, found as Christmas father;
of reindeer, the tetherer.

from *The Book of Chocolate Saints: Poems* (Unpublished)

1.

It was the second Christmas of the new century, a dazed and joyless time in the life of the city. Everywhere we looked the storefronts were lit but the lighting was lurid and wrong. Late in the evening the odd lost Santa walked to the park, his bell silent. On the high branches of the trees plastic bags bloomed like flowers. Residual Fifth Avenue traffic sent up a tidal hiss. Above it all the small sky sat like a lid, a sky of ash and tower dust and who knew what powdered human remains. In the old apartment the old body sounds deepened. The conjectural wheeze of hot water pipes, the bone creak of floorboard, all those unknowable scrapes and knocks. And gust after gust against the window where Goody Lol watched the wintry shades darken from purple to slate and then to black.

Undisturbed on the workspace were the twenty-three pictures she had placed there that morning. Newton's only task for the day had been to make a final selection for the Chelsea gallery where he would be exhibiting for the first time in many years. He wasn't sure exactly how many years because he lost track of decades (and: wives, a war, three cities, one subcontinent). He lost track of simple tasks. It was all extremely annoying until you reminded yourself that he could not help it. He had lost track of himself.

The grandfather clock chimed the half-hour and at the same moment she heard the rotary phone with the big handset and overloud trilling. A moment later she heard him shout.

"Goody, the phone! The phone, Goody."

But New yelled her name so often she'd stopped responding. In public he was unfailingly soft-spoken. Supplicants, civilians and patrons had to lean forward to hear him. His softness of speech had been remarked upon. An interviewer had even speculated that it was "a deliberate ploy to get one's attention".

Goody knew why he called for her. It gave him a sense of purchase in an otherwise unmanageable apartment. There was *stuff* everywhere. Even the master bedroom had been co-opted and the walls barricaded with wobbly stacks of books that had not been touched in a decade. The guest bath had been turned into a darkroom festooned with shiny blackout curtains and clotheslines strung with clips. The bathtub was booby-trapped with stop baths that were not for bathing and encircled by trays of malodorous fixative or curative. *Stuff*. There were LPs and stretched canvases stacked twenty deep in the hallways. Take-out cartons stood on the bookcase. The kitchen was the bivouac of an insurgent army. Every surface had been colonised by objects that had nothing to do with cooking: a rotating globe, illustrations ripped from anatomy textbooks, toy Ambassador taxis from India, an obsolete desktop computer, a shelf of floppy disks, miscellaneous handwritten missives stuffed into folders. Making a cup of coffee was a philosophical manoeuvre. You had to take a position. You had to ask yourself, what is coffee? Why is it consumed? How far would I go for a cup?

The apartment was chaos made visible.

In the early days when she brought it up Newton would air his Theory of Creative Disorder with particular reference to the state of one's living space. He said the attempt to impose order on chaos was the mark of a minor artist, particularly if said artist failed to recognise the world and its manifestations as meaningful; and the impulse to create tenderness or bliss in the midst of chaos was the project of the superior artist. Then he would bring out the Big Guns. Freud, Einstein, Rothko, de Kooning, Pollock. He would reluctantly mention Bacon against whom he had a long-standing grouse. Not a woman on the list anywhere, surprise, surprise. The Big Guns believed in product over process, in the end not the means, in tardiness not tidiness.

"Isolation, ecstasy, and vigil," he said, "these are the things that count, not an orderly desk. Write that down."

She had taken to renting a small apartment downtown that she kept obsessively tidy. But she spent several nights a week at Chaos Central. Tonight in a converted study off the living room where she had commandeered a small desk for herself, Goody was putting the first strokes to a photo of her own face, lining closed eyes with kajal, outlining cheekbones and smudging lips. She was obscuring, obscuring. She was working long hours on her own image but it was the opposite of vanity. It was selflessness. She was making in the name of, for the glory of the master.

"Goody, the phone, dear god!" he shouted, and just then the ringing stopped and she heard him say in a lower, much lower register, "Yes?"

It was probably Amrik hoping to talk him into agreeing to a show in India, something that would make them real money for a change. She put the pen down and touched her shoes, black pumps with a medium heel. She slid a finger into the right one: it was too tight. She needed new shoes and winter boots and a digital camera. Really, she needed more money. For a man who had earned a fair amount of cash in his life, New lived from hand to mouth. There was never enough money to not think about money.

Again on the phone New said, "Yes?"

She would have to move out of the Union Square apartment and into Chaos Central because the upkeep on the two places was too much. Rent, power, maintenance, not to mention his insurance premiums. She had no health insurance because she was self-employed. She had no steady income and was therefore not eligible. Was this the life artistic? If so she'd be better off working in a bank or a nail salon. There was no point telling New she needed to make her own money and work on her own show. He would tell her not to mess with a good thing and to think of their arrangement as an apprenticeship or master class.

"Yes," said Newton for the third and final time.

Later, after they'd been to the gallery where Goody hung the new pictures it had taken her all of ten minutes to choose; after she'd made sure the gallery assistant – whose name was Clare, who had stayed late and was not happy about it – was using latex gloves so she wouldn't nick the polished steel of the frames; after late supper at a newly trendy Francophile bistro in Chelsea where Goody had ordered onion soup, oysters on the half shell and wine, and New a croque madame that he barely touched, but drank a pot of black coffee all by himself; after they'd taken a cab home, though Goody had mooted the idea that it was a lovely evening, cold and full of stars, and it would be nice to walk a little, and they'd stepped out of the restaurant to the sudden sound of air brakes from a bus on the corner and New had cried out, shielding his face with his hands, and that was the end of the walk; after they'd got home and Goody had had a shower and wrapped herself in a bathrobe and gone to her desk where she'd angled a magnifying glass over the face of the rope-bound sari-clad figure lying prone on a sidewalk, her own face; after she closed her eyes and imagined a woman she'd known at Goldsmiths', a maddening gender-conflicted English chick named Megan – these were the women Goody fantasised about, while her nesting fantasies were always with men – whom Goody saw in parts or a single part thereof, in the men's Y-fronts she favoured, Megan, a music major and femme dyke; after Goody imagined pulling the briefs aside at the crotch, not taking them off because she wanted the act to be uncomfortable and intense, she settled back in the chair and used both hands and didn't care if Newton saw.

Pulling the curtains for the night she remembered that she had first come to the apartment at the same time of year with the same wintry view from the window. Though the scene had not been so blank. Blankness was a thing come new into the world.

She had left the bright winter sun of Delhi for the frigid wastes of Manhattan. Her first sight of the city had been late at night through the window of an airport taxi. Much of it seemed as poor and shabby as a city in India. The cab driver played soft music on a tape deck, choosing from a box of cassettes on the passenger seat. The music was full of bounce and yearning and the driver sang softly along, the word 'safiatou' – or was it 'safi a tout'? – repeated in alternating tones of demand and release.

When they got to the apartment New had opened the door with a key he wore around his neck. He made a little speech. They would sleep together and work separately. He would teach her how to put together a show, how to use the press to advantage, how to frame a picture, and so on. Meanwhile, she was free to do as she wished. Her private life was her own business.

He said, "You are too young to be faithful. I'm too old to be monotonous, I mean monogamous."

She had not even put her bags down and he was talking about monogamy or its opposite. For a moment she considered finding a cab, the airport, a ticket home, but his voice pulled her back. He said he was addicted to solitude. He craved it and repudiated it in equal measure. He had grown up with a mad mother and it had marked him. He had started to think about death in his teens and now in advanced middle age or early old age he thought about it in a different way, like a daydream or a treat for the future, and he thought about it more and more as the years went by. Why was he telling her this? Not because he wanted her sympathy or because he was prone to making dramatic statements, which of course he was. He was telling her because she had a right to know that he'd been asking himself the important questions. What makes life worth living? What do you do when the best is behind you and whatever comes next will be a disappointment?

"Look at me," she had said. "I'm next. Are you disappointed?"

She could hear him now moving something in the bedroom and her spirits sank. If he was moving stuff around it meant he was going to be up all night. Which meant he would be wired and unpredictable in the morning.

He stood by the closet in the guest bedroom. On the floor were two open suitcases. In one he'd dumped a pair of shoes and a pile of black T-shirts and one of the ancient Olivettis he liked to use. The other suitcase was empty but for a carton of Pall Malls.

"New? It's late, what are you doing?"

He turned, his eyes demonic or haunted or on the verge of panic.

"I'm packing, Goody, packing if it's okay with you. I'm not leaving things for the last minute, if you see what I mean. I am planning ahead."

"Planning what?"

"I told you, my retrospective and party, the last and final blowout. In India."

"The India trip isn't for a few years."

For a minute it was as if he had not heard her. Then he shook his head. He said, "Next year is a month away."

She led him by the hand into the bedroom. The night had turned cold and outside she heard the high whine of the wind.

2.

The subway car rocked its way due north and the lights failed for four or three seconds. Fear was never far when you were trapped in a moving cylinder deep in the innards of a city under attack. In a subway tunnel you were unseen under the weight of the earth, immured, losing all sense of definition. You were no different from worm, clod, or bony root. A tunnel approximates the experience of burial.

The complexion of the car had changed as the train creaked past midtown and coloured faces gave way to pale, but the expressions were the same. The same look of grievance, of having been wronged, the same averting of the eyes from the dark-skinned man with the parcel wrapped in foreign-language newspaper.

At Fifty-Ninth and Lexington he came out of the subway and continued north. Old snow had frozen hard to the gutters. The air was crisp and he could smell some kind of rot or fermentation. A sanitation truck moved on the street, a single word spray-painted in red on the front bumper. REVENGE. Of the driver all he could see was a reflective orange vest and visored sunglasses. The truck sparked a memory of a front-page item by his friend and colleague Shyam Pereira, a story about sanitation workers who had chased a young Sikh man on the morning of September Eleven as the towers came down. There had been a picture of the truck the men drove. He was certain it was the same one. How many city sanitation vehicles would be emblazoned with such a slogan? Dismas walked a block and stopped when he saw the steam from a hot-dog vendor's cart. He asked for a dog with everything.

"Dirty water dog with onion, sauerkraut and mustard?" said the vendor, who was Hispanic.

Dismas told him no, hold the mustard, and waited while the man made his dog. He paid and took a bite as he walked up the block. He ate some more but something in the meat or the onions tasted off and he put the rest of it into a bin. At the end of the block a man was pushing a cart and Dismas ran to catch up with him. He asked for bottled water. The man said he sold honey-roasted nuts not water.

"Honey-roasted nuts, okay. What do you have to drink?" said Dismas.

The man gave him a Pepsi. He drank most of it standing on the sidewalk with his parcel between his knees. The parcel's Hindi newspaper wrapping had come undone in layers and you could see the frames on the paintings inside. He was tucking the shreds of newspaper into place when a woman in a short fur coat swerved around him. Her yellow T-shirt said I HATE NEW YORK and her hair had a green sheen that was the exact colour of something. What? She glanced at the paintings and smiled. There was something about her that was familiar or familial and he would know what it was in a minute, except the wondrous stranger was going, going, gone, disappearing out of his life for ever. Her hair was disappearing too, hair the exact shade of coolant. And then he noticed the vengeful sanitation truck idling nearby. It had matched his progress up the block. Was he being followed? It was not too far-fetched an idea. The driver was white and Dismas was not and there lay the basis of their antagonism. It was December of the year 2001, three months after September Eleven and a bad time to be 'South Asian' in New York City. Better black, better yellow, better blue than brown. To the sanitation man the street was divided between his people and other (lesser, hued) people. Dismas understood the man's narrow rural *white* point of view, he really did. He too wanted a world cleansed of the foreign and peopled only by Dismas, the comely coolant-haired New York-hater, and a wide flotilla of retail technicians. But there was no time to pursue this line of thought. Wednesday was the day the paper went to press and he had an interview to turn in to his slave-driving editor.

At the end of the block he consulted a Post-it he had stuck in his back pocket. The directions he'd copied were meticulous, which subway, where to exit and to cross, the turns, the street number – all of it unnecessary as it turned out. The Fifth Avenue building was prime Manhattan property and impossible to miss. Park-facing and rent-controlled, the redbrick was so red it might have been fired only minutes earlier.

Against the westside façade was old signage – HARRY'S DEPT. STORE, FOR THE GREATEST VALUE – faded but visible. The building had four floors and no elevator. Wrought iron scrollwork and small recesses set off the redbrick. The bay windows curved and projected just so. The steep mansard roof had ornate touches on the, what were they called, the dormers? The wood-panelled entrance door was a proper step or two above the sidewalk. Three floors of limestone façade and the top floor some kind of light-coloured brick. A florist and newspaper kiosk on the far corner and from the park the sound of birds.

He stood across the street and looked at the building's pre-war stolidity and modest height, so modest nobody would crash a plane into it. Then he saw the Revenge idling on the corner and the insane sanitation driver. It was hard to believe but he was being followed by a garbage truck! Of the many ways to die, the thousands of available permutations, he could think of nothing more shameful than to be run over by garbage.

With an eye on the truck Dismas hurried across the street and into the building. He was not too agitated to notice the exceedingly red Moroccan walls and yellow Siena marble floors. The doorman took him up two floors to a door with no nameplate. A hunched man in a loose pink T-shirt and overcoat opened, a younger thinner version of the face in the photographs. The man's glasses were smudged and he needed a haircut and he had that look, fame turned against itself, a famous philosopher gone intentionally to seed, or a late night television host put out to pasture, trying on his fuck-you beard and yearning for action. More to the point he had no idea who Dismas was or why he had come.

"I called yesterday," he said, holding up the paintings. "Dismas Bambai?"

Some weeks earlier on the wall of a Chelsea gallery he'd seen a black and white flier in the style of a vintage news photo. It announced the showing of new work by Newton Francis Xavier. A blurb from *Art News* said, "These portraits announce the return of the mercurial talent whose pitiless evocations of sex and god remind us of what we've been missing in the modern art scene. His first show in eleven years is nothing less than a cause for celebration – and cerebration." To his editor, Mrs Merchant, he had pitched a story idea. He would interview the artist for a one-pager around the show, with reference to the controversy following his statements about September Eleven. On the Internet he found a Hotmail address for Xavier and wrote an email citing his admiration. He mentioned that he'd bought two Xavier oils in Bombay in 1990 from a dealer who had subsequently been accused of selling fakes. Dismas had brought the pictures with him when he moved to New York. He hoped to meet Xavier and authenticate them. There was no reply. Then the editor approved the interview idea and Dismas looked up the phone book and found, to his surprise, that Xavier was listed. He waited a day before he called. The number rang and rang and then the connection was cut and when he called back the line was busy. That evening he tried again. The British voice that answered was rusty and full of weird pauses.

"Yes?" said the voice, doddering or distracted, in any case distrustful.

Dismas introduced himself and mentioned the email he had sent.

"Yes?" the voice said again.

Dismas repeated the contents of the email in case Xavier had forgotten. Could they meet the following day?

"Yes," the voice had said for the third time, sounding merely aggrieved.

Now the owner of the voice, who was not doddering by any means, led the way through riverine interiors to an oddly shaped central room. There was only one chair and Xavier took it. Work he seemed to have lost interest in was stacked against the bed's headboard. Paint spatters decorated the hardwood floor and the ceiling. An antique Olivetti sat on a bare mattress that was used as a surface for newspapers and loose typescript and books of all kinds. There were no pillows or sheets. Where did he sleep? Facing the park was a rolltop desk, the only uncluttered surface in the room.

Beyond the smeared window was sunlight filtered by the chemical residue that drifted across the city at all times. The window was conceptual, a window in name only, sealed shut with adhesive sealant or some kind of industrial grade resin. It shed no light and allowed no air and had not been opened in a decade or more. The objects on the sill – a silver horse with one hoof in the air, red clay replicas of funerary urns, a voluptuous Venus figurine with its extremities painted wine red, a pair of dice, Ken and Barbie dolls tied up and suspended from the window latch – and the dust around the objects suggested years of untouched repose. Sketched in crayon on the window's bottom panes were twin towers, in the foreground the peaked roof of a church, a rough cross floated above.

Xavier said, "I hate being interviewed but you brought paintings all the way from India and I suppose I feel obliged. Let's establish the house rules. No questions about whether or not I'm married and how many children. No questions about alcohol, do I write with pen or computer, first thing in the morning or at the stroke of midnight. No questions about the difference or similarity between poetry and painting. No comments, positive or negative, about my work. No suggestions for future work. No comments at all regarding the future. Otherwise you're free to ask anything you want."

Dismas didn't know if it was meant to be funny.

To the left of the window was a picture partially hidden by a hanging drape, heavy oils squeezed straight from the tube, a woman in a burkha smoking an opium pipe, her round face lit by lamplight. When he leaned in for a closer look he saw that the pipe was a penis and the penis was attached to the woman, who was smoking herself, her eyes looking directly at the viewer, Chinese eyes, wet and opaque, as if she had died and the information had not yet reached her brain.

"Who is she?" said Dismas.

"She's nobody, or no body, a Bombay ghost."

Then he muttered something about genital amputation and the ghost penis, or he might have said guest pianist. The plummy British monotone was difficult to follow.

An ancient to-do list taped to the window obscured Dismas's view of the street and the possible presence of a sanitation truck.

Xavier gestured at the crayon sketch on the glass, "Based on an old photo taken from Union Square."

"One minute," said Dismas, taking out a pocket tape recorder. "Do you mind?"

He switched on the recorder and took a seat on the bed.

*

In his celebrated chapter-long second account of the meeting, Dismas wrote that the interview began with the appearance of the tape recorder. Xavier's voice and posture were transformed. His mumble disappeared. Now he was *engaged*.

"The photo was taken from the Union Square town house in which the photographer rented modest rooms. He was a recent immigrant, the kind of European whose use of the word 'exile' was never self-conscious, unlike Asiatic immigrants who cannot say it without an inward smirk or shudder. Our Czech was gloomy, as people from those parts often are. His taste in music tended toward the melancholic and melodramatic, gypsy violins, crashing pianos, the operatic expression of grief or jealousy. He did not learn to speak English until he was in his mid-thirties and settled in New York, around the time he found an old Rolleiflex in a pawnshop. Because he came to the language late he used it in ways that struck native speakers as unusual. For instance, he favoured unexpected combinations of words that produced rather odd results. He would say, the hair of my dog is biting me today and I am opting to stay bitten. Or, tonight I am numberlessly sad. Look, Mr X, before you stands a man downcast beyond measure. Whatever his linguistic peculiarities his work habits were singular and remarkable. You see, he took pictures of the towers at different stages of construction from the window of his apartment and from the roof of his building. The pictures were all framed the same way, that is, twin towers in the middle distance and a structure of some sort in the foreground. They spanned many years. As the towers grew taller the Czech's photographs grew dimmer. If you look at the pictures chronologically there is a consecutive darkening as in Rothko. In the final images you can just make out the shape of the towers glowering under layers of cloud. In the last image, by luck, he found a sliver of light and a bird in full flight up where the structures disappear into mist. What kind of bird? What was it looking for among the buildings of lower Manhattan? Had it been blown off course or was it a city bird experimenting with the thermals created by high towers? These were questions the Czech photographer asked himself to no avail. For if he had been able to answer the question about the bird's true purpose and destination perhaps he would have chosen a different course in his own life. As you have no doubt apprehended, soon after the towers were completed he killed himself for no apparent reason, or none that could be discerned since he left no note. All this is exceedingly clear to someone who looks carefully at a photograph. I am wondering if you are able to do that?"

"It was my job at one time," said Dismas, trying to sound humble. "I was an art critic with the *Times of Bharat*."

"Impressive!" Xavier said, in a tone that may have been admiring or ironic or both at the same time. "Then perhaps you can answer the first question his biography brings to mind. Why did he kill himself?"

"Honestly, I wasn't expecting this kind of, this level of interaction."

"An interview is a two-way process. The interviewer must open up too. Do you not think so? Answer the question."

He thought it would have something to do with linguistic isolation or the way the towers filled the viewfinder of the Czech's camera and shut out the light. It would have to do with photographer's light and the lack of it: the slow dying of light across many days and months.

"Wrong!" said Xavier, though Dismas had not uttered a word. "Asking why someone killed himself is like asking why the demon chasing you has a pimple on its nose. The second question, how did he do it?"

"He threw himself from the towers."

"Pish and codswallop. Suicide may be the obvious response to the intolerable but it doesn't, you know, have to be unimaginative. Do you want to check that the tape recorder is working?"

Dismas checked; it was. The palm-sized machine's tiny cogs were in constant satisfying movement, the micro-cassette snug in its groove and the glass dot on the casing a deep electronic red.

"Last question, did the meaning of the bird elude him or did it not?"

But Xavier expected no answer.

"We survived the Age of Woe thanks to efficient pharmaceuticals and the Age of Rage by the skin of our gnashed teeth," he said. "But now we enter the Age of Indecency. This is the common resource of the two thousands, the fountain that will never run dry. After this Age there will be no other. Are you a native of Bombay?"

"Yes," said Dismas.

"The lovely ruins of."

"Ruined, surely. I don't know about lovely."

"Only Bombaymen feel obliged to run the city down. I feel obliged to disparage Goa and lately New York. It strikes me that other cities of the world are more *New York* than New York. London, say, or Hongkong or Melbourne or Berlin. Something has left this town."

Dismas had done his homework. He knew that Xavier had been born in the small village of Forgottem and he was its only famous son. He shared a birthday with Goa's patron saint, Francis Xavier, and had taken the saint's name: Newton *Francis* Xavier. He was expelled from school for drawing on the wall of the boys' toilet a precisely enhanced female figure with a soul- or penis-shaped cavity in the inexact region of the belly. The drawing had been captioned with a quotation from Francis of Assisi, "Wherever we go we bring our cell with us. Our body is the cell and our soul the hermit living in it." He signed it *X*. And even then the boy Xavier had thought of documentation. He had persuaded a friend to photograph the picture.

"Why," said Dismas, "did you name yourself after Saint Xavier?"

Xavier examined his nails, which were chipped though not dirty.

"I rather would like to offer coffee but the truth of the matter is there's no one here to make it."

"I'm good."

"Quite. Do you want the long version or the short?"

"The long."

"Francis Xavier achieved sainthood by unstinting aimless motion. His great wish was to be never at home. *Never at Home* – good title, do you think, for a memoir about professional exiles such as us? I can see by your terrifying stare that you do not think so. The point about saints is they understand the futility and beauty of movement for its own sake. The self-denying artist is a kind of saint and I allied myself to one I felt some affinity with."

Dismas pointed at the window. "May I take this off for a minute, the list?"

Xavier did it himself and pulled the paper from the glass to reveal layered smears, a surface that had never come in contact with soap or water. Dismas could see nothing of the outside but rough fields of green and grey. He would have to stick his head out of the window to see if the street was safe. Where was the sanitation truck and its crazed driver?

Somebody was at the door. A dapper turbanned man, moustache combed out into a walrus, a face Dismas took a minute to recognise.

"You're the guy who was attacked during Nine Eleven," he said. "Amrik Singh Dhillon. My paper interviewed you. Front-page story, above the fold and boxed, written by my friend Shyam Pereira."

"*Indian Angle*," Amrik said. "Interesting guy, Shyam. I don't know how he heard about it but he was on the phone within hours and the article was out almost immediately."

"Right. And then the *New York Times* picked it up."

"My manager," said Xavier, by way of introduction, "and friend, Amrik."

"Just a quick question," said Amrik. "The ICCR festival in Delhi? They want you on a poetry panel. They'll fly you and put you up and pay you an honorarium and a per diem."

"My last book of poems was more than thirty years ago. Nobody remembers."

"Not true. You won the Hawthornend Prize and you're still the only non-white person who's ever won."

"That would be the Hawthorn."

"Right, right."

"Tell him no. I have nothing to say, truly."

"I said you'd go. They'll send an advance against expenses."

"To sweeten the sour."

"You were taking the show to India, I thought, anyway."

"Shall we discuss this outside?" he said, pointing at Dismas.

The two men left the room.

He went to the window, which opened with a moderate struggle. The air was cold and almost fresh. When was the last time fresh air had entered this room? He considered telling Amrik about the Revenge, still out there on the streets of Manhattan, hunting for darkies. But on the street no sanitation truck was to be seen, only taxis, a mob of jaywalkers, and a lone jogger. He pulled the window shut and saw some lines near the sill written in pencil. *The old soothsayer, however, danced with delight, & though he was then, as some narrators suppose, full of sweet wine, he was certainly still fuller of sweet life, and had renounced all weariness.* He took a closer look at the painting of the burkha-clad opium smoker and her penis pipe. It was dated 1982.

When Xavier returned and claimed his chair Dismas pointed at the scribbles.

"Oh, that would be Goody quoting the syphilitic German horse lover." At Dismas's look of incomprehension Xavier said, "Posthumously co-opted by the Nazis? The man with the magnificent flying moustaches? For god's good sake what do they teach you in school these days? It appears to be a message courtesy of Goody and I am somewhat pleased to say that I have no idea what it signifies. You might ask her."

"Let's talk about the Hawthorn," said Dismas. "They call it the most English of prizes. You won for your first book. After the second you abandoned poetry altogether. I know you've been asked this before but could you talk about what happened?"

"I don't know, don't know . . . unpredictable master or mistress." He lit a cigarette and took a deep first drag. "I didn't abandon it. If anything it was the other way around. I think it visited me as a young man and left me when I got older. It happens to poets and musicians. You're on fire for a minute and then nothing but embers. If I had known then that the future was a bereft old age without poems."

"Right," said Dismas, "I think you said that once, pretty much in those words."

"If you ask the same question you get the same answer. Everybody wants to know about writer's block and how terrible it is. They love the idea of the tortured artist. Nobody talks about how super it is. How much like a paid vacation. You are giving yourself permission to not work."

"No poems, but the paintings are plentiful," said Dismas.

"One can only imagine how much worse it could be."

"Sorry?"

"Imagine when both stop and you are left with nothing but your own used-up self."

"Is that going to happen?"

"I started to paint because the poems would not come. I thought of it as left-handed work. Automatic. I didn't put much into it and they loved it. They missed the point. The poetry is the point."

"The buyers and critics missed the point?"

"When you are *on* nothing exists but your working hand. When you are done doubt returns rather quickly. The death of God is unbearable when he is all you've got. What can fill that hole? No amount of fame or love."

"Money? An apartment on Central Park West?"

Dismas wrote in his notebook: "A hint of a smile appears on X's handsomely lined face."

"Art makes nothing happen but it survives. We've known that since 1939 at the very—" Xavier didn't finish. "It survives in the valley of its making. It finds a way of happening and a mouth."

He reached for a glass placed by the leg of his armchair and stubbed out the cigarette. It continued to smoulder.

"Once I thought you could change the world or some small part of the world with a book, a painting, a poem – I was younger and given to arrogance. The suicide knows better, and the terrorist. The only poem that matters is the poem that picks up a gun."

He tugged at his laces and kicked off his shoes, hand-made red leather Oxfords. The beautiful shoes had been treated badly, the leather scuffed, drops of wax melted on the wingtips. Dismas made a note, "Red leather wingtips."

"And knows how to use it."

Dismas said, "In retrospect, did the Hung Realist anthology and your association with Narayan Doss change the world of Indian poetry in any way?"

"I prefer not to live in the past. How long have you been in the United States of Émigrekah?"

"The United States of Amnesia," said Dismas.

"The United States of Amurka."

"I got here in 1998. My first address was Queens."

Xavier said, "Of course. One must be true to one's cliché."

"I don't know. It could have been Delhi or Dacca. I was in a city inside a city."

"The moveable ghetto."

Dismas remembered the frigid Sunday in January when he first caught a glimmer of the immigrant life. Walking home from the subway he'd stopped by Patel Brothers, a fragrant grocery operation on Roosevelt Avenue. Inside the store a Sardar with a flowing white beard and faded turban held a sun-ripened Alphonso to his nose, his pleasure plain to see. When the old man caught Dismas looking he sheepishly put the mango away. Just then a family of five appeared on the sidewalk carrying plastic bags full of provisions, even the small children loaded with vegetables and spices and rice. Mom and Dad were hard to tell apart, their identical hooded parkas tied so tight all you could see were slits for eyes and pursed mouths. One of the children dropped a bag and three red onions rolled to the sidewalk and Dismas picked them up. The child just stood there bundled in too many layers, too cold to accept the onions or say anything. And that was when it hit him, the pitiful half-life of 'South Asians' in New York City.

"Bad timing," Xavier said, crossing his legs, "you are in Amurka at the end of the Amurkan Empire. You left one kind of poverty for another. A dozen apostles of the new apocalypse take down the tallest buildings in the world and the predicament presents itself in the form of a chant or a jingle" – and then he said a mocking phrase that Dismas would hear again – "The beast of the east eats the best of the west."

Dismas consulted his notebook for a bit of breathing space. The conversation was hard and distinctly personal labour. Xavier demanded your complete attention. If he looked away the man would stop talking until Dismas's eyes returned to him, motionless in his ancient armchair, a wax figure animated only by intelligence. He spoke softly but in violent non-sequiturs. It struck Dismas that he slept in the chair, which explained the number of sketches in the vicinity.

"Mr T on the phone," Amrik said as he ducked into the room. He pulled up the antennae on one of the hinged cell phones that people were wearing in holsters clipped to their belts. Dismas hoped to get one too. Unlike Amrik, who didn't have a holster, Dismas would wear his at the small of the back. It would be discreet and noticeable at the same time. "They'll pay a one-time appearance fee of two and a half thousand plus two business class tickets and five-star accommodation. Is it a yes?"

"Perhaps a maybe," said Xavier. "Perhaps he might make it a round five thousand dollars?"

"You heard the man," Amrik said into the phone as he left the room. "Oh, you didn't?"

Dismas was taking the paintings out of their newspaper packing when his pager beeped. Mrs Merchant. He would have to keep her waiting and this was never a good idea. He placed the pictures against the foot of the bed. The glass in one of the frames had cracked but the nudes were as lurid as ever, shaky lines in black marker on the glossy covers of a British men's magazine. In both paintings swim-suited feathery blondes were partially visible under the blurry blue wash of chemical solvents. You could make out some of the headlines, *Melinda Returns* and (*Something*) *Dogs the Cockney Mafia* and *Giant Poster Inside*. Against the washed blue the fleshy Marys were crudely drawn. Something in the lines suggested the Willendorf Venus.

He may not have been expecting a fanfare when he unveiled the paintings but he had hoped for some kind of reaction. Xavier lit a cigarette and examined the coal. When he had determined that it was burning to his satisfaction he brushed at an ashy stain on his trousered knee. He fidgeted. He snuffled. Then he turned to the canvases and appraised them with the eye of a pathologist gathering data for a medical journal. He may have been about to rouse himself to say a word, or even two, when the doorbell rang.

"Goody," Xavier said, and left the room.

Dismas wandered into a hallway packed with video equipment and televisions, heavy box sets that resembled pieces of furniture, clunky and panelled and studded with looped aerials and oversized dials. On a tidy rolltop in a room at the end of the hall he saw a work-in-progress, a Polaroid that Xavier was working on with pen and ink. A rope-bound woman in a chiffon sari lay on a sidewalk as if felled, her face tiny and detailed like a miniature and made up in the style of a fifties Bollywood star. A magnifying glass lay beside the photo and Dismas picked it up to take a closer look. Then he thought better of it and put the glass down.

He was looking at the Two Marys when she came in, the fur coat and yellow T-shirt mostly hidden by paper bags of dry cleaning. The coolant-coloured hair had lost its sheen in indoor lighting. If she recognised him she gave no indication.

Xavier made a gesture. "Goody, meet the Bombayman."

"Dismas, I'm interviewing."

"I know," said Goody. "I know, I know."

She spoke with an accent from the north of England, some place made knowable by twentieth-century British pop. The tone was intimate and oddly reassuring, markedly different from Xavier's Oxbridge accent redolent of high tea and sherry and buggery in the staff quarters.

"We need to be at the gallery immediately if not sooner," she told Xavier, "some vital decisions about seating must be made."

"Must I come?" he asked, in his almost-but-not-quite-inaudible voice as Goody left the room.

They were like actors in a sitcom. British Indians in New York who looked and sounded alike. Her fur and Xavier's overcoat made him conscious of his own clothes. The shapeless Indian jacket struck him as an embarrassment: not warm enough for winter or light enough for spring: unstylish, incorrect, inappropriate for a New Yorker.

He nodded at the paintings. "I've been calling them the Two Marys. I hope you don't mind."

"Yeah, no," Xavier mumbled. "I mean they are mine but I wouldn't swear to it in a court of law, if you see what I mean?"

Was this meant as a cryptic sideways clue? Dismas didn't get a chance to ask. A phone was ringing in the hall and it was a commotion in the quiet, not to say spookily silent apartment. Xavier made no move to get up. Instead he said, "Goody?"

She came in with an open bottle of wine and two glasses on a breakfast tray she placed on the floor.

She said, "New doesn't drink but he won't mind if we do."

Then she unhurriedly left the room in the direction of the ringing phone. Xavier looked at the wine and Dismas looked at his watch. It was not yet noon. At least in this house the cliché about artists was true: red wine in the morning and disorder everywhere. He decided to chance his hand and reached into his breast pocket for a small sheaf of typewritten pages.

"Whenever you have the time," he said. "I'd be grateful for an opinion, even a hurried one."

The poems had been folded lengthways. Xavier took the sheaf reluctantly and began to read. He flipped back and forth across the pages. It took him all of three or four minutes.

"Even if I have but scanned a few pages I can give you a considered opinion, if that's what you want."

"That's what I want."

"Use your ears and your eyes to make the craft shipshape. Indian poets think all you need to write poetry is feelings, and forget that everybody in the world has feelings, and the purpose of poetry is to get away from your fucking feelings. If you do not mind my saying so, you can write but you are crippled by your image of yourself as a poet with a capital P."

He was saying something about youth or truth when Goody returned.

"It's for you," she said to Dismas. Her eyes were wide. "A woman, says she's your boss and she doesn't sound happy about it."

"Sorry, sorry," said Dismas, his voice squeaky. It was his bipolar control-freak editor. How had she found the number? The fact that he was about to speak to Mrs Merchant made the nerves tighten behind his eyeballs and he noted also a contraction in the general region of his sphincter. When he picked up the receiver she was already speaking, yelling before he'd said a word.

"On production day of all days. Haven't I told you not to go off without permission? Have I or have I not? Tell me because I really want to know. Maybe it's not your fault? Maybe I forgot to mention it."

"I left a message with—"

"I want you in the office now, you get me? You have two pages to finish and that includes the letters page, one of the most important pages in the paper. I'm looking at it now and it is, let me see, how should I put it? Shit. Complete fucking shit."

"Sorry, Mrs Merchant," Dismas murmured, hoping Goody couldn't hear him.

"I can't hear you."

"I said, I'm sorry."

"Tell me something."

"Yes, ma'am?"

"Who gave you permission to disappear?"

"Mrs Merchant, I'm interviewing Newton Xavier the artist. I budgeted the story for this issue and I left a message with Pereira for you."

"Pereira? What makes you think I'd listen to a word he says? I don't care where you are or what you're doing. You come here and sign off on the page or I'm sending it just the way it is. You know what that means."

Dismas knew: abject humiliation at the Thursday morning meeting.

"I'm on my way," he managed to say before she hung up.

"Already?" said Goody, when he went in to say he was leaving. "Newton, did you scare him off?"

"We were in the middle of an interview, I thought," said Xavier. His head was in his hands.

"The editor wants me to sign off on a page. I'd really like to talk to you again whenever it's convenient."

"It may never again be as convenient as it is now," Xavier raised his voice. It was the first sign of animation he'd shown all morning.

"It's a question of my job," said Dismas. "Sorry, sorry. I'd much rather stay here."

The front door opened as soon as he shut it behind him, Goody with a Mary in each arm, bracketed by versions of herself, and she also had his tape recorder, which was still running, and his sheaf of poems.

"You're forgetting stuff all over the place today, aren't you?" She pronounced it stoof.

He felt the touch of her hands when she gave him the paintings.

Stepping out of the building he checked for sanitation trucks, speeding or stationary, and on the long walk to the subway he kept open a wary peripheral eye. A fine snow had begun to fall and many of the stores were closed. There was a small crowd outside a basement establishment that advertised yoga classes for dogs. DOGA: FOR YOUR PET'S DAY-LONG MENTAL AGILITY. He passed a phone store and reflexively looked for and found the model Amrik had been using. Motorola StarTAC. He dug out his notebook and made a note of the phone's clamshell shape and 1.3 ounces of weight.

On the facing page he had written a riposte to the hit single off the new Kelis album. He read it again and thought it serviceable enough for *Indian Angle*. "The nature of the beat is moderate, 113 bpm, but why so infectious? Because instead of a drum machine we hear the manjira, trad. Indian hand cymbals, the sound of bhajans imported into American pop." He would always remember the scene in the video when Kelis went into the kitchen of a diner to entertain a mere cook, a short order fry-up man, not even a chef. The democratic impulse was nothing short of revolutionary. She was a titan of modern aspiration, a benchmark figure with only one rival in the field.

On the subway he calculated that if the ride to Twenty-Third Street took ten minutes and the walk to the office five, he'd be at his desk in a little over half an hour from when he had spoken to Mrs Merchant. It wasn't much but it was something.

Near him were two men in hip-hop uniform, spotless footwear and new baggy jeans and tilted Yankees caps. Shopping for blue jeans at Macy's, Dismas had discovered that hip-hop labels were as expensive as, if not more expensive than some of the high-end names he coveted. Functional clothing designed to absorb sweat and repel mud cost as much as designer eveningwear. Phat Farm, Armani, same difference. It was a revelation that made him see the B-boys and Thug Lifers in an empathetic new light. The men beside him were mirror images of each other's clothing styles and the guy on the far side wore Timberlands so new they seemed box-fresh.

"Seen Tupac's new joint?" he said.

"I seen it."

"You fillin it?"

"I fill it."

"Straight-up XL fuck-off black, like Tupac. Classic, see what I'm saying?"

Dismas shut his eyes to hear. It wasn't easy. Subway noise lapped at his ears with a watery roar and in the thick yellow air sound was drained of all clarity. Mixed into ambient wind-borne knocking and the squeal of metal on metal, the voice retained none of its individual timbre, the tone control was off. Dismas leaned in and held his breath.

What was the guy talking about?

"Got to be black and no leather on it. Got to be nothing on it."

Some item of clothing, but what could it be?

"I'm saying it got rules, fool, like everything. Like, if it's cognac it best be Henny."

"Why?" said his friend.

"Open it. That smell?"

It came to him that the man was talking about hoodies, but this was nothing more than a peg for his ideas. In actuality the guy was engaged in an examination of shopping in all its infinite variety. He was a guru, a realised master of the targeted purchase. Here was the act elevated to art. Here was a pure product of America. Dismas had many questions for such a man – for example, which venue offered better value, Banana Republic or Club Monaco? – but Twenty-Third Street was nigh.

Dismas's true reason for coming to America had been to get away from the caste-endowed divisions of his homeland and to avail of consumerism as an opportunity for social improvement. He graduated from Bombay University with a degree in economics and sociology. He'd scraped through with a pass and had no illusions about his academic prowess or lack thereof. He realised early that his talent was a modern one. He was a discerning and intelligent consumer of products, substances, and services. America was a Mecca for a man of his abilities and when the opportunity presented itself he applied for a ruinously expensive Master's at the not-so-prestigious Central University of New York. There he managed to bag a partial scholarship available to needy foreign students. Expenses were another matter. As a student he'd managed to keep them down. He had shopped only when necessary and stayed within the spectrum of toiletries and clothes and music.

Until he started to look for work Dismas had assumed that an MFA in comparative literature would get him a good American job with good American pay in a good-to-middling American university and then would begin his conquest of American retail and American leisure. But before he could find a university placement he ran out of funds and he was forced to take the first job that came his way.

At Apna Bazar Cash & Carry in Jackson Heights he found a tabloid with the unpromising name of *Indian Angle*. It was so shabby and so badly in need of a makeover that he knew he would get a job without too much effort. He cold-called on a Monday and was asked to come in early Tuesday for an interview. The office was on Twenty-Sixth and Sixth and the editor-in-chief was a skeletal woman named Mrs Merchant whose decades in New York hadn't changed her Delhi accent or Delhi-centric view of the world. There was a sloped wooden stand under her desk for her feet and a dog dozed in a wicker basket by her chair. Dismas handed her a CV that said he had worked for the *Times of Bharat* during the years 1990–1995. The claim was true only from a distance. He had never been on staff or accredited in any way. The woman asked what kind of work he'd done. Art critic and cultural theorist, he replied, at which she had narrowed her eyes as if someone had released sewer gas into the room. A moment later he did smell sewer gas. Perhaps it was the dog. She asked if he had brought clippings and he took out a little plastic holder and handed her one yellowing bit of newsprint after another. She pressed a switch on her phone and summoned the assistant editor and the features editor/obituarist. Then she read from the clippings in a tone that sounded earnest at first, even admiring, until Dismas understood from the discomfort on the faces of the two editors that it was meant to convey contempt.

"'Papyrus palimpsests of a disappeared race, hard-won artefacts that embody a Rimbaldian punctum ("Il faut être absolument moderne") transported at great peril across space and time. They tell us that modernity is an age-old idea. Each element in these crowded frames has the function of a prayer and each is a variant exegesis on an ancient prophecy, that the promise of beauty is inseparable from the promise of happiness.'"

She put the cutting aside and took off her glasses to examine Dismas. Then she read from the next one.

"'In this artist's fierce palette of ochres and reds we are witness to a world of ritual slaughter and fertility, menstrual ministrations and hymen hymns, the mystic grammar of a matriarch who embodies the tribe's yearning for transcendence.'"

She repeated the phrase 'menstrual ministrations and hymen hymns' with a little shake of her head, then put the clipping aside and picked up another.

"'What mysteries? What edicts? What frenzied hieroglyphs? These truncated tales in a tortured tongue are the dialect of a people whose entire alphabet consists of two or three consonants and a single fugitive vowel.'"

She coughed and put the cuttings down.

"Bravo, the *Times of Bharat*," she said. "But what do we do with this kind of writing at *Indian Angle*?"

Expectantly, the two editors looked at her.

She said, "What do we do, people? I can't hear you."

Pereira, features editor and obituarist, was the first to speak. "We spike it, ma'am?"

"That's right," said Mrs Merchant, slapping the air with her free hand, "we spike it. And why do we spike it? I know you know so let me hear you say the words."

She cupped her ear. "I can't hear you."

"Because it has no traction, ma'am," Pereira said. "Because our goal is not to create deathless prose but to communicate essential information."

"Close but no biscuit. We spike it because it's shit. I can't hear you."

"We spike it because it's shit," Pereira and the other editor said in unison.

"If you want to work here you'll have to learn how to spike shit," she told Dismas and nodded at the pile of cuttings by her elbow. "You can start with that."

Dismas looked at the cuttings and thought about freedom. There was no question that he needed a steady influx of dollars to be a part of the city's rich inner life of consumerist discernment. Otherwise he would return to India with nothing to show for his time in the United States, time served in the penal sense, in confinement, because he was unable to participate in the glittering life around him that he could see but not touch; and it was an added injury that in America even a janitor, sorry, even an office custodian shopped at the best stores. For example, *Indian Angle*'s custodian Jose wore top-of-the-line Tims while Dismas had come to the interview in Converses.

The next day was his official first day of work and he filed a story about a twelve-year-old Indian-American from Wichita, Kansas, who won a national spelling bee. The finals were broadcast live and it seemed to Dismas that the girl was affected or afflicted by the words she was made to spell. When it came to *elegiacal* she seemed to wilt, as if touched by a sudden melancholy, and when she spelt *narcolepsy* her eyes drooped of their own accord and didn't open for eight seconds, and when in the final round her opponent, also Indian, misspelled *guetapens* she smiled guardedly, and when it was her turn with *stichomancy* her eyes darted from side to side as if she were reading lines on a page or lines from many pages, reading fast and at random. Her technique drew some attention because she traced the words on her hand before saying them aloud. Some commentators said the method was unconventional, if not suspect. They described her win as controversial, which struck Dismas as mildly controversial in its own right, or at least mildly comical, considering the commentators were white men whose subtext was that the girl had used some kind of mystic Hindu divining power that gave her an unfair advantage over her homegrown American competitor. Of course none of this appeared in print. In the *Indian Angle* tradition the story he wrote was anodyne and heartwarming. He put a headline on top and typed in his byline. It was only then that his self-bestowed name seemed real, only when he saw it in print. He was Dismas Bambai, intrepid reporter and investigator of spelling controversies; also, he was Mrs Chatterjee, the Auntie of Agon.

In his first week as an employee of *Indian Angle* he also wrote the following articles for the issue dated 1-05-2001:

- Two thousand words on Bombshell Baby Productions, promoters of a weekly Bollywood Cruise with the memorable name of 'Bhangra on the Hudson'. There was music by DJs Louder and Lasoon and Bombay street eats by Chef Sam Biryani (a minor figure from the Dongri mafia who had switched career tracks and expanded operations to New York). The story had started out in the classifieds and made it to the paper's front page because Bombshell Baby's proprietors were old friends of Mrs Merchant.

- A page three item about a small town that had been given a Gandhi statue by an Indian-American real estate company named American Desi Inc. Mrs Merchant spiked a paragraph concerning council members and residents who were unhappy that a statue to a foreigner was going up on public land; but the story ran to more than fifteen hundred words.

- Fifty words for the ALSO NOTED section in the back of the paper about the vandalising of Georgetown University's Muslim prayer room in an 'alleged' hate crime. There was a mention of President Clinton's Eid message to Muslims on behalf of the American people.

- Thirty-nine words on Pakistan's involvement in the continued destabilising of India and the world. The piece was too short for a byline. He gave it a headline pulled from a quote by the spokesman of an Indian think tank: *The True Locus of Terrorism Is Pakistan*. On Saturday when the paper appeared he discovered that the copy editor had changed 'locus' to 'locust'. The error struck him as correct in its own way.

Two weeks later, with his first paycheque in hand, Dismas went to the Macy's flagship at Herald Square and bought a pair of premium wheat nubuck Tims for $189.99 and a Kangol Two-Tone 504 for $39.99. He wore the cap back to front so the logo would face the world. He packed his Converses in a Macy's bag and wore the Tims out of the store. He picked up the new Alicia Keys and a portable CD player shaped like a frisbee. All the way home he noticed others like himself, recognisably set apart by the bags they carried from various retail giants. The young father in baggy jeans and white T-shirt who proudly carried purchases from The Gap, Urban Outfitters, and Calvin Klein; the elegant older lady with the distinctive Barney's bag; the couple with matching sets of Bed, Bath & Beyond. He was one among them, an extended family on a weekend outing, people from all kinds of ethnic and economic backgrounds bound together by the same great yearning. With his first substantial act of shopping since arriving in New York he felt American at last. Nothing else mattered, not his past, not his caste, not the weight of his degraded history. In this great country the only caste marks were the brand names you accessorised.

Now, waiting for the elevator in the lobby of his office building, he wished for only one thing from the rest of the day: to make it to his desk without running into Mrs Merchant. The small lobby was crowded with office workers returning to their cubicles after lunch, receptionists and information technologists, custodians and CEOs, real estate specialists and day traders, all of them white except for the two custodians – one of whom was Latino, the other African-American – and the half-dozen 'South Asians' headed to the eighth-floor office of *Indian Angle*.

"Are physicians to blame, though?" asked a man wearing pointy new lace-up boots.

"Yups, exactly," said the woman to whom he was speaking. "Pick on the softest target. What's that supposed to mean?"

"We were told to provide relief for pain no matter what the cost. The pressure on us to perform miracles," said the man. "What did they think was going to happen?"

"True fact," said the woman in an undertone heard only by the man with the beautiful boots and Dismas. "But hold that thought, prospective clients in the vicinity."

"Three overtimes. End of the second Phoenix led by one, four seconds left," said Jose, the Latino custodian.

Dismas couldn't see him but he recognised the voice.

"Most a the times tied two-two," said his friend.

When the elevator doors opened the *Indian Angle* employees rushed in first, followed by the doctors and custodians. The small elevator was already crowded and Dismas thought of waiting for the next car but Mrs Merchant's aged cadaverous face flashed in his head and he squeezed in at the last possible moment.

"We were told to make them grade pain from one to ten. Relief was the point. Quality, satisfaction, everything depended on it," whispered the man with the boots.

"Whenever a doctor cannot do good he must be kept from doing harm," said the woman.

"Hippocrates?" asked the man.

"Nobody mentions him no more, it's all Larry Bird this and Magic Johnson that and Michael Jordan the other, you know it?" said Jose.

"Muscles are the real bad guys when it comes to pain in the long term. That's the thing that causes harm, not us."

"That's the game, here today, gone today."

"Users are losers. Opioid heads are born every minute, addicts just waiting to happen. Only explanation. Why shoot the messenger?"

"She brings the same thing every day, black daal, rice, and raita," said a woman, in Hindi.

"Must be going through financial difficulty," said a wide Bengali in a starched black sari. She too spoke in Hindi but for the words 'financial difficulty' enunciated clearly in English.

"Nahi, yaar," said a third *Indian Angle* employee. "Diet it is. Die-yet."

Dismas took an exploratory breath of the close fragrant air and smelled Indian spices and fresh dry cleaning and lavender disinfectant or perfume. The Bengali stood immediately behind him. He could feel her sari rustling against his shoulder blades. Why was she so close? Indians have no sense of personal space, he thought, as his penis came to life against his trousers. He clasped his hands in front of him and glanced up at the numbers flashing much too slowly past three, past four.

"How you can eat same-same every day I don't know," said the woman behind him.

"The pain lobby is as powerful as the gun lobby."

"Dead if you do, dead if you don't. What's that supposed to mean?"

"Greatest game ever? Uh-uh. All I know's from Havlicek's bank shot, fifteen feet, dude, fifteen! And the set-up? It was sick!"

"Are you the only black Celtics fan on the planet?"

It occurred to Dismas as the Bengali's ample bosom brushed his kidneys once and then again that he had noticed her around the office and had never thought of her in any terms other than the maternal and the collegial. She had two children and a husband half her size. The children were as loud and badly behaved as Indian kids everywhere and the husband was a quiet dandy who wore pinstriped suits and polka dot ties. The woman always had house keys hooked to the waistband of her sari and the keys jangled in his earshot several times a day. They had exchanged few words, once when she wanted to borrow a stapler from the news desk and another time when she brought around Diwali sweets. He didn't know her name or her designation. Still, a casual brush in the elevator and here he was with an unruly lump in his trousers. Not that he wanted to follow where the penis led. He had no doubt that the moist folds of her belly and ass crack were coated with talcum powder, that her fingers smelled of methi and masala, and that her idea of sex was hurried missionary coupling in which she lay as still as possible. What would be the point? You may as well come in your hands. She was the exact opposite of Goody, who, he had no doubt, was loud, inventive, and demanding, but there appeared to be some kind of communication mismatch between his brain and his penis. He considered pinching the tip to bludgeon it into submission but the opioid-enabling physicians were much too close.

He was first out the door on eighth.

There were other establishments on the floor but the *Indian Angle* office dominated by size and the number of employees it managed to squeeze into limited floor space. The receptionist's desk was pushed up against the reporters' desk and the one-man advertising department shared a corner with the tea boy. Everywhere was clutter and noise. Natural light was not allowed to penetrate into the warren of rooms. Even before the elevator doors opened Dismas heard the mix of voices speaking simultaneously in Bengali, Gujarati, and Hindi, a mainstream cacophony in which other languages also made a fleeting appearance, less assertive tongues such as Oriya, Malayalam, and Khasi. The only language notably absent from *Indian Angle*'s rank-and-file chatter was English.

"Mrs Merchant asking for you again," said Sheri-from-the-Islands at the front desk. "She upset. I mean, she allus upset but today she more upset than usual, man."

"Did she say what it was about?" Dismas asked.

"Never did but she been calling, calling, asking where you gone missing."

"She knew where I was."

"Man, maybe she did and maybe she did not, but she keep calling. Told me one, two, three time, I *gotta* call her the minute you walk in that door," she said, picking up the intercom.

Stepping into the main room he heard laughter that sounded forced or false and then he heard a male intern's dry sobs and from the compositor's room the sound of traffic or bhangra. He smelled chicken masala and fried fish and the indelible smell of methi and asafoetida, smells that had seeped into the walls from years of lunch and dinner heated in microwaves and eaten off newspapers on the desks. It was no microcosm of America. There were only Indians here. Many employees went from Friday to Monday without speaking English or seeing a white person. They lived in the middle-class 'South Asian' ghettos of Edison and Jackson Heights and came into contact with America only on weekdays while taking public transport to and from Manhattan; and even then America existed dimly, deniably.

Having made it unmolested to his corner Dismas booted up his computer. As with most of Mrs Merchant's rants the severity of the tantrum had little to do with the nature of the crime. He had no idea what he had done wrong. The Xavier interview had been approved. He would have come to the office and made his pages in good time. What had been the reason for her meltdown? He opened a page and started work but such was his agitation that the screen resembled an arrangement of pygmy squiggles and markings. What did it all mean?

Shyam Pereira, the paper's obituarist, immigration expert, and features editor, placed his hairy forearms on Dismas's desk. Behind thick glasses his eyes were mild.

"Listen, agony auntieji," said Pereira, tucking his flower-printed shirt into the high waistband of his trousers. "Joshi and me have a little bet going. He says you don't have the immigrant mark. I say you do. Joshi thinks you're not brown enough. I think you are. He says this is the true reason why Big Bitch is always picking on you. There's only one way we can settle this. Do you have the mark or not?"

He nodded and smiled and waited for a reply. His question was genuine as far as Dismas could tell. He was asking about the vaccination scar that Indians of a certain age carried on the upper bicep like a bar code. Pereira had befriended Dismas in his first week at the office. He had seen Dismas's distress and understood and with jokes and asides he had tried to make things better. A seasoned New York hand above reproach in his work whose byline appeared more often in the newspaper than anyone else's, even Mrs Merchant left him alone. In Dismas's eyes Pereira was the cleverest man he knew. Just then the editor stepped out of her cabin.

"Here comes Big B," whispered Pereira, his eyes wide as he backed away.

Pereira called the editor Big Bitch to differentiate her from Sam, her pet Pomeranian. The animal had a cabin to itself and was not to be disturbed at any time. If you woke it up by accident and it bit you, you had to apologise to the dog in the presence of its mistress.

As she walked past, Mrs Merchant motioned to Dismas to follow. It was a long-established Mercantile tactic. She disliked talking to employees in private: she preferred to have an audience when she was humiliating someone. She stopped at the news desk, near Pereira, the paan-chewing Joshi, a computer guy no one knew the name of, and Sheri-from-the-Islands.

"It's past two. You should have put up the new page," she said to Dismas.

For some reason she had decided not to chew him out about the Xavier interview. That would come later; it would not be forgotten; it would be filed away for the future.

"It's just that I needed to discuss one of the letters with you," said Dismas.

Sheri-from-the-Islands vanished and the computer guy busied himself with his screen. But Joshi and Pereira paid rapt attention.

"Well, what the fuck are you waiting for?" said Mrs Merchant. "I'm here, in case you haven't noticed. I've been here all day. Does everything have to be spoon-fed to you people?"

It wasn't true that she'd been there all day. Mrs Merchant never arrived at a fixed time and never before eleven. Most likely she slept late, had a lazy breakfast, and spent the morning shampooing her Pomeranian or giving it a pedicure or taking it to DOGA classes.

"Tell me," she said.

Dismas explained that a letter had arrived for Mrs Chatterjee, Agony Auntie, from a woman who had lost her husband at the World Trade Center. In the woman's dream her husband would call her on the phone and say in a surprised voice that he was at the door of the family home but he had no key. He was waiting for her to let him in. The woman had been having the dream or variations of the dream for so long that it had almost become a comfort. She wanted to know if she needed therapy or not.

Mrs Merchant folded her arms.

"The husband," she said, "is he Indian?"

"No," said Dismas.

"Listen." Mrs Merchant shook her head and a bit of skin flapped on her throat. "Listen, you're Mrs Chatterjee, *Indian Angle*'s agony auntie. Your job is to make up funny or heartwarming stories for our readers who are Indians, in case you didn't know."

"This is a compelling story, Mrs Merchant. It brings up some important current questions."

"What does it bring?"

"What the city is going through and what the loss of the towers means to the American idea of freedom and the pursuit of happiness. How lasting will be the impact on the city. I think the letter even suggests a view of the future as an unrelieved landscape of economic malady."

"Malady? Did you say malady?"

"Mrs Merchant," said Dismas.

"Malady is a twenty-dollar word for a two-dollar item. What's the rule about using twenty-dollar words around here?"

"Don't."

"Exactly, well done. Don't."

The editor-in-chief sighed and looked at the faces around the news desk.

"Let me ask you again. This woman, is she Indian?"

"No," said Dismas.

"Is the husband Indian?"

"No," said Dismas.

"No Indian angle, no story. For fuck's sake," said Mrs Merchant. "How many times do I have to tell you people, find the Indian angle?"

Joshi and Pereira found their voices after she left.

"Agony auntie, find the Indian angle, no?" whispered Pereira. "I think BB is in heat today. Go to her office, yaar, put her out of her misery. Even old ladies need servicing once in a while. Just don't service the wrong bitch!"

Joshi laughed and his shoulders shook convulsively, while Pereira looked silently at Dismas. Then he laughed too, quietly, into his fist.

Dismas went to his desk and opened up the Agony Auntie page and started filling in column inches. He found the letter from the haunted woman, signed 'I-too-died-that-day'. There was no question that it was real. He put it aside for the moment and got to work making up a letter. His only instruction from the editor had been to make sure that he used Indian English as much as possible. In this way readers would identify with the column and think Mrs Chatterjee was a real person. He put his fingers to the keyboard. On the screen text appeared.

Dear Mrs Chatterjee,

I got married six years ago and moved to America where my husband has been living since college. My parents-in-law live next door to us. They are nice but not as nice as my own parents, who still live in Haryana in our village. Sorry. I should not say that my parents are nicer but I can't help it. It is the truth. Anyway I'm writing to tell you that lately I've been hearing Indian birds here in America. Last night I thought I heard a bulbul outside my door.

When I went to check, my husband said I was mad. He said, "There are no bulbuls in New Jersey, you crazy lady!" Is it true? Are there no bulbuls in America? What about mynahs?

Yours sincerely,

Birdbrain

Dear Birdbrain,

There is no chance that some poor bulbul or mynah will be wandering so far from her domestic route – just imagine – that she'll land up in the frozen tundra of New Jersey. I'm thinking you're suffering from severe case of homesickness. Either you buy ticket back home for a month holiday or rent DVD of *Kuch Kuch Hota Hai*. It is very wonderful way to forget homesickness. I do it all the time, especially when Mr Chatterjee and his parents are in the house.

Yours,

Mrs Chatterjee

He measured off inches and typed in the letter from the woman whose husband had died in the towers. It was something of an occasion, the first real letter Mrs Chatterjee had received. He started to write a reply and managed to bring in an Indian angle; and although it seemed to him the angle was flimsy, nothing more than a trifle, he hoped it would get past Mrs Merchant's beady eye.

Dear Mrs Chatterjee,

My husband died in the staircase of Tower One, as I told you in my last letter. Why didn't you reply? I talked to a counsellor appointed by the state. She told me to try analysis. Well, I did. I tried it. I'm writing to say it was a failure. The analyst said he would never have guessed I had just lost my husband because I seemed so composed. I wanted to say, listen, bozo, how would you know? You've never even seen me before. Obviously I didn't go back. Instead I thought I would write to you. My question is, will it get better? Or will I always think of him with a sinking in my chest? Will time heal me? Okay, sorry, that makes three questions.

Yours sincerely,

I-too-died-that-day

Dear I-too-died-that-day,

Woman to woman, I must quote to you what our wise Indian men of the mountains say. Now it is true they have many unfortunate habits of personal hygiene and some terrible so-to-say substance abuse issues but you can always count on them for perspective. One such holy fellow said, "Time heals not a damn thing." This maybe seems like a cruel thing to tell someone who is grieving but it is not so. It is liberating. Once you're not expecting time to make things better you begin healing. Automatic. The same fellow also said, "At the moment it may seem that the future does not exist, but I assure you, madam, it does."

Yours feelingly,

Mrs Chatterjee

When he looked up Sheri-from-the-Islands was at his desk.

"You better be running up there quick, mister man," she said. "It Wednesday today. It making her mad."

He minimised the page he was working on and hurried across the office to the editor's cabin. She was standing in the middle of the room with her arms in the air while a young Chinese tailor measured her waist. Her face was folded at a frightening angle, as if the muscles had atrophied. She was attempting to smile.

"I hope you got something explosive from the painter? About his comments after September Eleven?"

"I didn't get a chance, Mrs Merchant."

"But why not?"

It was hopeless. She had pulled the plug on his interview before he got started and now she wanted an explanation.

"Meet him again," she said, pirouetting slowly, a cadaverous flatfoot ballerina. "If you get him to talk it's a page one byline. You know that, don't you?"

Her tone was polite, almost tender, and when he brought her the completed letters page she passed it without comment. Even the letter from I-too-died-that-day was passed. She ran her eye over it, then she nodded, ticked the page with a pencil, and it was done. The editor's extreme change of mood was business as usual at New York's Indian newspaper of record. Dismas suspected it was strategy, a way to keep the employees unsettled and always on their toes. The obituarist Pereira had another explanation. He said the tailor was a known gossip popular in her set and Mrs Merchant didn't want to be maligned as a slave driver among her socialite friends.

That night he dreamt heavily and when he tried to transcribe his dream in the morning he came up with two lines about a man in a watchtower. He wrote some more and in a day or two he printed out a long poem in rhyming couplets. The model for the woman in the poem was Goody. He put the printouts in a shoebox and forgot all about them. More than a year later the poem would have disastrous consequences. Here is the unpromising opening couplet:

All day I drink with my eyes on the river,
At night I drink and fear for my liver.

The Loathed, Dismas Bambai's fictionalised memoir of the Bombay poets, part crime thriller and part gossip sheet, begins with an account of meeting the celebrated painter and poet Xavier in New York City in the early two thousands. The future author becomes an irregular visitor to the artist's cluttered apartment on Central Park West. The week after their first meeting Dismas is arrested and Xavier bails him out. As they walk along the streets of lower Manhattan, Dismas worries that the arrest will adversely affect his immigration status. The older man suggests the visa he has secured, the Alien of Extraordinary Ability category reserved for writers, artists, and academics. Then Dismas asks Xavier about his comment to the *New York Post* that September Eleven was a case of "the chickens coming home to roost". Xavier replies that he had only articulated what people all over the world and in America were thinking. And in any case he was quoting Malcolm X. But because he had said it in the vicinity of the World Trade Center's ruins he had been singled out for contempt and controversy. Since then he hadn't spoken to the press. Not until Dismas turned up at his door.

Xavier didn't attack *The Loathed* until after its success when he and Dismas had separately returned to India and when the book's visibility in airport bookshops and lifestyle chain stores made it clear that it had met with a considerable success. He told a reporter the book was "a malevolent fiction with an eye to commerce and a nose for stink". He said Dismas was "a loathsome type of insect who invented everything, everything. Why would I say I liked his poems? I never even saw them." The piece ran in the national newsmagazine *Indus* under the headline *The Poet and the Pest*. Xavier's accusations served to help the book's renown and it was serialised in the same magazine and soon went into reprints. A reclusive theatre director in Poona produced a one-act play based on some of the events described in the book. Experimental and low budget, the play ran to unexpectedly full houses at Juhu's Prithvi Theatre. It won a cult following that made the director briefly notorious, his long grey hair and Arun Kolatkar moustache recognisable in caricature on Amul Butter billboards all over the country. The director then disappeared into a life of womanising and alcoholism. A production house in Andheri made a film version of the book that won an award at a festival in Goa, which nobody noticed. When the film won a second award at the Sundance Festival it came to the attention of a mostly independent New York-based production house that made a new version in which they changed the setting (to Paris) and the characters (to a group of Brooklyn expats) and the story (to a romantic comedy). Dismas Bambai made a little money and a lot of enemies. The book was written partly in the first person and billed as "the autobiography of an era". Its most scandalous passages discussed the sex and artistic lives of Dom Moraes, Arun Kolatkar, Nissim Ezekiel, and Newton Xavier, all of whom were identified by name; also identified were the men and women who orbited around these figures. Its most controversial passage suggested that someone had murdered Moraes, Ezekiel, and Kolatkar. "Who was he, this diabolical murderer of poets," wrote Dismas, in the melodramatic style he favoured, "this dastardly assassin who has never been imagined, much less hunted or apprehended? Was he a failed poet whom the three men had spurned? Had he extracted his revenge in a bloody spree over a few months in 2004? Was it the Pathar Maar, the Stone Killer, returned from Delhi or wherever he'd been hiding for two decades? Or was it a kind of extreme literary criticism that hinted, nay, proclaimed that the best work of the three poets was long past and it was time they were put out to pasture, by force if necessary?" After the film appeared, some journalists woke up to the book's news potential. Editorials and reviews condemned the fact that the nation's most prominent poets had been "vilified and besmirched", according to the *Hindoo*, and "taken down a peg or two", according to the *Times of Bharat*. Only the crime reporter of a soon-to-be-defunct tabloid with a tiny circulation and a tinier readership, the *Tea-Time Herald & Dispatch*, hinted at a false controversy aimed purely at increasing sales. Inevitably, the week the reviews appeared the book hit bestseller lists around the country. But all that was much later. Before Dismas and Xavier became antagonists they were friends and the friendship began with an arrest.

As the snow came down on the anxious city he typed up his last piece for the day, ninety words for the books section cribbed from the back cover and flap of a bestseller about India's Partition. *Indian Angle* reporters were forbidden to read the books set aside for review. It was a reckless waste of time for an item that would run to no more than a couple of paragraphs in the back of the paper. Furthermore, only those books available in the bestseller section of an airport bookstore were to be considered for review.

"Books with traction!" had been the editor-in-chief's exact words. "Traction is action!"

When he was done it was almost seven o'clock. He paged Tony and waited fifteen long minutes for a call back. The address was in the East Village, a good half-hour away. He packed his messenger bag and locked the Two Marys in the bottom drawer of his desk. He found a pear on the compositor's table and stuffed it into his jacket, the office empty except for Jose who was on the phone at the receptionist's desk.

"Nada," he was saying. "Nada lo es todo."

Dismas shrugged at him and gestured to the clock on the wall. Late o'clock.

Jose waved back and told the phone, "Existe el hombre del mal en los suenos del hombre bueno."

Outside the snow had stopped and the air was frigid. He was wearing a beanie and fingerless gloves and under his heavy coat were a twill cardigan and flannel shirt, but the wind sliced through everything. On Twenty-Third Street he stopped at an ATM to check his current account. The Bank of New York held eighty dollars for him, the sum total of his hard labour in the Empire State. After several moments of reflection he withdrew fifty.

He ate the pear on the subway. The woman seated directly opposite was bundled up and layered but her breasts were terrifically vertiginous. Nowhere near Goody's level of gravitas but then what was? A version of Xavier's jingle floated into his head. The breast of the east beats the best of the west. If Goody was the prototype for the Two Marys, Xavier had an in-house model and muse with classic Tang Dynasty, seventies Bollywood, plus size curves. What more could a man want? He licked pear juice off his fingers. The woman got up and took a seat at the far end of the car.

At Bleeker he went up into the end-of-the-year end-of-the-world streets of the East Village. He turned east on Houston and walked three blocks up the Bowery and east again to a building on Second Street and was buzzed up to a one bedroom-hall-kitchen where a small group of unopiated punters waited for the man they called Tony.

"Wake up and hustle on over to the village for what? He's always fucking late," said a guy in western garb.

"He's a busy man, got people to do, things to meet," said a tall man dressed in several shades of blue. He held a cigarette and moved his hand in the Queen Elizabeth wave.

"Easy for you to say, Rico, you're always holding," said Western.

"I plan ahead, darling," said Rico, sitting up straight and batting his eyelashes. "So go ahead, shoot me. Shoot me first."

"Fuck, that line's so old it should be put to sleep."

"Whose line is it? Let's snort it up real quick," said Rico, cackling throatily around his cigarette.

"Yeaha," said a woman lying completely still on a couch in the corner. "Doctor Ricard, famous poet, hung out with Warhol, brown-nosed Schnabel, discovered Basquiat, yadda dada, except it was twenty years ago. Now you can't see talent when it's under your deviant septum."

"Twenty-two years ago, my dear, and I'm not a famous poet. I'm a famous critic and obscure poet. What talent?"

The woman nodded at Western.

"Clayton here," she said. "Three shows already, one solo. That's his stuff on the wall. You see but you don't see."

Only then did Dismas notice the pictures, gleaming acrylics of cowboys in squalor. A blond boy passed out in a tenement hallway with his jeans around his ankles; a boy smoking crack in an abandoned lot; a boy having sex in a public toilet with two obese men. The boys all wore white Stetsons.

"It takes talent to know talent, darling," said Rico. "Maybe I've misplaced mine or sold it or traded it in. Now stop being disagreeable. Our guest must be wondering what fresh hell he's stumbled into."

They all turned to Dismas.

"Well-appointed hell, if you ask me," he said.

Rico cackled again and Dismas noticed a filigree of nicotine stains around his otherwise white goatee. He adjusted the mustard cravat around his throat and pointed his cigarette at the woman on the couch.

"May I introduce you to your host, Lysistrata?"

She said, "Warhol superstar, painter of poems, art arbiter. You were a beautiful boy. What happened?"

"I like that, arbiter, like Petronius."

"Petronius."

"Nero's personal fashion consultant, a man of taste and decency."

"What's taking him so long?" said a woman who was stretched out on the floor. "Fucking Tony, keeps you waiting every time."

She was in the punk uniform of ripped blue jeans and black leather motorcycle jacket but she was well past her teens, too old to carry off the role with any clear authority.

"Part of the life, dear, don't underestimate the lure of being kept waiting for your reward," said Rico, pulling his hoodie over his head.

But in an instant the blue eyes had turned watery and the charm disappeared. “I fronted you a bag and I want it back. If you can take a moment out of your busy life.”

Then the doorbell rang and Tony came in and showed them pictures of his bulldog, Clinton. He stood in the middle of the room, puffy-jacketed, handing out glossy prints of Clinton posed under studio lighting. When it was Dismas’s turn he gave the man forty dollars and received four bags in return. He spilled half of one on his wallet and snorted it with a rolled-up dollar. Then: the slowing of time, the cooling of time, the annihilation of time. Much later he left the building with Rico and the punk woman. On the sidewalk Rico told her she owed him a bag or ten dollars. It was now or never. The woman reached into her purse to rummage. And a stocky man in jeans and a stained Dolphins sweatshirt materialised in front of them.

He said, “All right, open your hand.”

He made them hold hands and walk to a car parked at an angle against the sidewalk. He assured them that he would shoot if they tried to run. They got into the car as he bid, Rico and Dismas in the back and the woman in front. Rico told the cop he’d been through all this six months earlier and could they please come to some kind of arrangement, please? The woman said her name was Rita and could they come to an arrangement too? Only Dismas had no arrangement to offer. At the East Fifth Street station house they were booked for possession and only Dismas had no identification to show. A detective accompanied him to *Indian Angle*. Other than Sheri-from-the-Islands and one of the compositors the office was empty. It was the first bit of luck he’d had all day.

Sheri cracked her knuckles when she saw Dismas and the policeman.

“Oh ho,” she said. “Who this strapping young ’un you bring with you, Dismas?”

Then she squinted and scratched her chin to indicate confusion.

“Man, you in some trouble?”

“It’s a long story,” said Dismas. “I need to pick up a small thing.”

“What small thing now?”

“Passport.”

Inside, the compositor was singing the hit tune from *Kabhi Khushi Kabhie Gham*. Most of the lights had been turned off and there was a terrific smell of methi in the air. The detective examined the open editorial section, the cabins, the stained walls, Dismas's own small desk and battered computer, and though there was nothing grand about any of it the man seemed impressed; perhaps he was comparing it to his own grubby policeman's cubicle with the overflowing trash cans and faulty ventilation.

On the way out Dismas asked Sheri-from-the-Islands for a favour.

"If I'm not in tomorrow tell Mrs Merchant I had urgent immigration work. Can you do that?"

"How you mean? Tell her you go do immigration on office time?"

"Listen, just tell her."

"Sure, man, I tell her and I tell you right now what she say. You want hear?"

And Sheri-from-the-Islands laughed at her own joke.

The detective laughed too.

They drove back to the station house where Dismas was charged. At eleven fifteen he and Rico were in a detention cell for the night.

There was one other occupant. A shirtless man whose rich stink filled the room. He was barefoot; his khaki cargoes bulged at the pockets; he sucked his teeth and said nothing all night. Because they were hungry Dismas and Rico talked about food. Rico said his name was Rene and nobody called him Rico but the crazy lady at whose house they had met. He said some people were of the opinion that the Poles had no cuisine to speak of. They say the Poles are cuisineless but this is untrue and it can be proven, said Rene. Whenever he had twenty dollars to spare, which was not often – and how heartbreaking it would have been if he'd known as a young man in New York City, living that young man's charmed life, that one day dinner would be moot – when he had the money he went to Veselka and ate Polish because it was solace food, nutrition for the disaffected. He had to admit that he wasn't a huge fan of Indian. The restaurants on Sixth seemed to specialise in three dishes, green, red, and brown. Those are not Indian restaurants, said Dismas, they're Bangladeshi and the joke about them is true. All the food comes from the same kitchen. I knew it, said Rene. A nose is a nose is a nose. You recognise quality in one thing you recognise it in another. He'd given away so much, he said, everything but his divine attribute: the nose that knew the good from the not good, the good from the great, the great from genius.

He mentioned his radiant Basquiat essay, the thing that had changed a young artist's life and his own. It had made him famous but only for discovering the boy genius. People forgot the other things he'd done, the film and the poetry. They forgot the others he had championed. Stephen Mueller, Brice Marden, Robin Bruch, Hunt Slonem, none of whom had seemed avant-garde to him because he saw the work as manifestations of the classical.

"And my great achievement," said Rene, "do you know what it is? The one thing that will prove to the future that I was indeed a poet, do you know?" Dismas shook his head. "My portrait by Alex Katz."

He didn't want to talk about Warhol, he said. There was no point. Rene was all talked out when it came to Andy. In any case all he ever did was work, work, work, and save up his money. He never spent a penny except when he took you out for pierogis and borscht and mined you for material. And for Andy everything was material, every little thing that came his way, gossip, a subway token, somebody's suicide, insanity, infinity, groceries, buildings, someone sleeping – it was all fair game.

Dismas said he had published a book some years earlier, a slim book with a descriptive title, *Twenty-Twenty Poems*. A poet, said Rene, looking at him as if he was a time-traveller from a future planet. Then he took a book out of the waistband of his jeans.

"In case I'm arrested," he said, "it helps to show the judge I'm not just another criminal and faggot."

It had a handmade cover with a gold border. The colour was teal or tealish, said Rene. It was meant to be Tiffany blue, a stipulation of his, the only thing he had insisted on, but they hadn't been able to do it, Raymondo and Francesco. They had only been able to manage a facsimile thereof. GOD WITH REVOLVER was printed in silver capitals above a picture of the poet in a Confederate cap and a Cuban revolutionary's wispy beard. His name was also in silver capitals, under the author photo captioned, 'Photo Booth Portrait, Penn Station Arcade, Spring 1988'. The title page informed the reader that the poems had been written between 1979 and 1982 and printed, astonishingly, in Madras by Hanuman Books. A thin plastic casing had been attached to the cover with a drop of glue on the front and back flaps.

"Hell to publish," said Rene, "the compositor knew no English. Each correction meant a bunch of new errors."

The copyright, dated 1989 and 1990, belonged to Rene Ricard and Hanuman Books. The volume was hand-stitched, the cream paper properly thick and heavy to the touch, the smell of the pages cool and woody. There was something old-fashioned about the way the words were arranged on the page. Spaciousness had been a consideration. Poem titles were in capitals and each full stop was followed by a double space; and if the punctuation was eccentric, it was consistent. Dismas opened at random to page 47, the last poem of the first section, and he read the opening of 'The Pledge of Allegiance'.

> Ah, Painting, my love is true
> Painters are so horrible it's amazing they come up with you
> And though the artists are all shits, I still love you

The poem went on to berate painters for a multitude of sins, chief among them the inability to resist wealth and stupidity. Yet, despite themselves, they made the work that would hum in the museums of the future. There was a blank page titled 'Lost Christmas poem 81' and a poem in Spanish. One, in its entirety, read:

> I wake up hallucinating
> I lock the windows so I don't jump out
> into this glorious view
> I've become so corrupt.

Dismas turned the pages and noticed that the poems were always about the same subjects, early and late trauma, the imminence of death, the futility and necessity of love inseparable from art. The tone was mixed tenderness and contempt, much like Rene's speaking voice. He noted the references to murder and suicide and the names of poets who had died unnatural deaths, many names, listed like some kind of crime-honour roll. He read and dozed and read again and toward morning he asked Rene if he had heard of the Indian painter and poet Newton Xavier.

Rene said, "Who?"

At seven a.m. they were taken out of the cell and escorted to police headquarters, which was already noisy with the first instalment of the weekend's business, prisoners and detectives finishing up paperwork, and because the officers were undercover you couldn't tell the cops from the criminals, they all had the swagger and the dead-eye stare. The detective assigned to them was a jittery man named Paolo who pushed them through to the front. Dismas was photographed first. They went before a judge and their cases were read into court records and in less than five minutes they were granted an adjournment to arrange counsel. Rita's bail was set at two thousand and Rene's and Dismas's at fifteen hundred each. They were dismissed and given receipts for money, keys, wallets, identification, and in a back room they stripped and turned their pockets out. An officer went from one man to the next, pinching seams, tapping shoes, flipping over underwear, and at last they were sent to the showers, followed by a visit with the medic. Dismas told the man he was not an addict and so he was assigned to the fourth floor, not the ninth, which, according to Rene, was the worst floor in the Tombs. All night you heard men screaming in withdrawal.

The thing that bothered him most about being arrested wasn't the way life stopped and started in reverse so he had to learn all over again how to shit (quickly, with other men in the room), how to shower (quickly, economically, with other men in the stall), how to eat (quickly, methodically), how to talk (without inflexion or expression, because you never knew who was watching), how to sleep (with your blanket over your head so when they put the lights on at the ass-crack of dawn you had another sweet minute of darkness). It bothered him that when Paolo said he was allowed to call someone – and it better be someone important because not only had he fucked up and got himself busted, he was an alien, an immigrant, which meant the Department of Homeland Security would be on his ass in a heartbeat – the only person Dismas could think to call was someone who had no reason to come to his aid. He made his phone call and settled into the routine decided by meal times, exercise periods, and work assignments, breakfast taken in the cell, lunch and dinner in the mess hall, and he swept and mopped, stacked blankets, and gave out toilet paper and soap. He and Rene met during the lockout periods from ten to eleven thirty in the morning, from one to four in the afternoon, and from six to eight thirty at night, when they had to vacate their cells and go to the recreation area.

But on Monday morning Rene was gone, bailed out by a friend.

It was Xavier whom Dismas had called. On Tuesday, his day in court, Dismas found him waiting on the courthouse steps in the company of an Indian lawyer. The lawyer was a nervous man in a new suit and loafers, who kept checking his nose in a tiny pocket mirror, the kind of Indian who made it a point to mention that he had never lived in India, he'd visited only once and felt no inclination to return. New York City was his home.

"Let's strategise," he said in greeting.

He asked questions and wrote in a notebook from which he distractedly tore out tiny squares of paper. How much heroin had Dismas been carrying when he was arrested? Was he addicted? What kind of work did he do? Had he published anything other than articles?

He said, "This judge is well read, mate. He's kind of a scholar and may be the only one you stand a chance with in all of Nu Yawk. It's a gamble, a gamble, but let's beat this thing. I'm going to get you a suspended sentence."

There was a crowd in the courtroom and when Dismas saw the prosecutors and defendants, the policemen and gawkers, he was struck by sudden vision. The enforcers and incarcerators were white men of a certain age and the offenders were black men and women. He and the lawyer balanced each other as brown men on either side of the divide. It was plain to see that America was in the midst of a race war and the prison system was its clearest reflection.

The lawyer put his mirror away and told the court it had no right to keep his client in a cell without letting him make a phone call, Nine Eleven or no Nine Eleven.

"As clear a case of civil rights violation as I have ever encountered," he said. "This is no way to treat the perpetrator of a victimless crime. I contend that NYPD overshot its jurisdiction."

The judge took off his eyeglasses and asked Dismas if he would like to address the court.

Speaking slowly and apologetically Dismas said what the lawyer had told him to say. He admitted that he used heroin but insisted that he was not an addict, he was a journalist and poet working on a book. He added that he was ashamed to be standing in front of the court and that he had hoped he would do better for himself in America. He had let himself down. The judge sentenced him to six months, suspended.

Outside, the lawyer shook his hand and disappeared and Xavier clapped him on the back.

When he went to collect his things the officer gave him a brown paper envelope on which someone had scrawled the name 'Dismas' in so extravagant a hand that he knew it was Rene. The tealish book was inside. On the title page, in the same spacious cursive: "For Dismas / Rene Ricard / no sloppy sentiments".

They walked to Christie Street and Xavier waited while he washed off the jailhouse stink one grateful inch at a time. In a café in the meatpacking district he had his first good meal in days, a breakfast-type event starring Eggs Benedict. Afterwards Xavier produced Cristos and they walked along the cobbled streets of the West Village puffing at the smokes. And this was when Dismas asked his friend if he had ever regretted telling the *Post* that Nine Eleven was an example of "the chickens coming home to roost", the quote that had made him a vilified figure in the city. Xavier said he regretted only the second part of the quote in which he had said that the old world order was kaput. In his opinion 'kaput' was a word that he should not have used under any circumstances. Then Xavier hailed a cab and went uptown and Dismas took a hurried walk to Avenue A where he paged Tony from a pay phone. He shivered sweatily for forty minutes waiting for his man and later he snorted two quick lines in a doorway.

Xavier did not go home. Dis's cold turkey spikiness had filled him with a craving he could not immediately identify. The cab took him to MoMA where he took his usual spot on a bench in front of *Water Lilies* from where he could also see *One: Number 31, 1950*. He looked at the paintings together and let his eyes unfocus and his vision meld. It was his habit and his pleasure to respond not to colour but to rhythm and sheen. He let his eyes rest on *One* and he let the *Lilies* crowd his peripheral vision. There was maintenance work going on in the museum. Men pushed handcarts full of paintings across the scarred floor, the room noisy with tourists and students. Xavier sat as if alone, as if time and the body had fallen away and he was returned to himself at last, visited by light. On the way out he stopped at *Starry Night*. He was always surprised at how small it was and at how much work was put in by each square inch of the canvas, how much toil toward how simple a provocation: that hallucination and vision were as one to the dislocated mind. Who would not rather die than look up at a sky so terrifying? He muttered some remembered or misremembered lines, "the day's on fire, a night glowing with birds", and he knew Vincent would have liked the workmen and the crowds and the idea that the museum was messily alive, not a hushed cathedral.

An hour later on the subway home he found himself squeezed between a man with an empty birdcage and a woman who got up and said, excuse me, honey. Her filled jeans were rolled to the knees and she wore clunky leather boots. When she saw him staring she pulled a joint out of her pocket and held it up and Xavier followed her to the street where they sat on a bench in a tiny park and smoked the giant spliff, expertly rolled in the reggae style. Her black lipstick left kiss marks on the filter. Near them was a trash can surrounded by litter and a basketball court with the hoop missing. Plastic bags blew across the gouged concrete. The weed hit him in an instant. His heart raced and the daylight shifted by a tone. The woman said, this is good hydro right here, baby, and all he could do was nod. She laughed at him and then she dusted her clothes and said she had to go to work, nodding in the direction of an outlet store on Lexington. Xavier watched her walk away, the rolled jeans and the sway, and a police siren swelled and was cut off and he flinched. He took the subway home and he waited, did nothing all day but wait with his stomach butterflying, timing it so he got there a little before she was done. They picked up a bag of McDonald's, because, she said, she needed her grease and they went to his apartment where she ate on the floor because he had no dining table. When she was done he moved the damp food cartons to the side and they fucked quickly and she made another spliff. He turned on all the lights because he wanted to memorise the deep colour of her and they fucked again, in his chair, slower this time.

As Xavier fucked the outlet worker whose name he would never discover, Dismas Bambai sat alone in his apartment. If we can separate for a moment a thought worth recording from the welter of junk, not yet junk, and future junk in his brain, then he was thinking of Q Ball Li, a seventy-two-year-old former junkie who had recently published his journals. Li's rent-controlled apartment on the Bowery was a lesson in how to live alone. There were hundreds of books but no clutter. In Dismas's opinion Li was a philosopher, an American mystic, a man who'd written of incarceration in relation to addiction and decided that the conditions were comparable but dissimilar because addiction was desirable, an exercise in joy, and incarceration was not, except in rare instances. In his sixties he'd given up heroin and focused the considerable force of the addictive brain, as he called it, on the smoking of a daily cigarette, always one cigarette and never two, taken with intense enjoyment every night after dinner. He spent all day in anticipation of it and he spent all night in the satisfaction that followed, and he received, he said, as much gratification from the single cigarette as from his six-bag-a-day heroin habit. As if, thought Dis, addiction was a human condition like parenthood or grief and everybody was addicted to everything or one thing, like a default setting, a given, and the only area in which free will played a part was in which substance or activity or adrenaline rush you chose as your personal Jesus. And Dis thought vaguely about the future, about whether he would have to find another job and what that would mean to his own habit. And he thought about Xavier and Goody and considered it likely that the reason Xavier had kept himself productive, if not prolific – periodically making art radically different in tone from what he had done before – was because he did not have to chase after instant gratification:

his emotional and sexual and artistic lives were anchored in the same person. He was one of those fortunate men whose partner was also his muse. They were complete, thought Dismas, a team, and his thoughts went to the Two Marys and when he touched himself he climaxed immediately, shudderingly, because he was low on H.

He saw the yellow I HATE NEW YORK T-shirt from half a block away. She wore it with a leather jacket and a boy's slouch and there was something different about her hair. Slung across her chest was a camera in a small leather case. She was looking at a phone booth plastered with the faces of the disappeared, on fliers that said LAST SEEN AT THE WORLD TRADE CENTER, and when she saw him she put her shopping bag on the sidewalk and made a quick shock face, eyes wide, mouth open, gloved fingers spread. They walked two blocks to a diner on Fourteenth Street and did not speak until they were seated at a booth in the back.

"Downtown?" Dismas said.

"I like it. I collect things New can use. Or I look for photo ideas. The fliers? I've been taking pictures of pictures of missing persons."

"Photographer."

"Yes. Just set up on my own. Journalism is how I met New. I interviewed him in Delhi for a magazine and we moved here when his Indian life fell apart."

"Must have been quite the interview, tell me more?"

"Another time."

The coolant-green sheen was gone and she wore her hair in a side parting, at a sharp angle, a look from old Hollywood publicity stills. She arranged the hair on her forehead and looked at him and did not smile.

"And what are you doing downtown?"

"Oh I work around here. This is my half-hour off from the Indian sweatshop."

"Which one is that?"

"*Indian Angle.*"

"You're kidding, right? With the halal meat and grocery shop ads?"

"That's the one."

"Holy samosas! But why? I thought people only picked it up for the classifieds. Hellish work, I'd imagine."

"The space between the matrimonials and lawyers' ads? That's where I come in. Among other things I'm Mrs Chatterjee, Agony Auntie."

"But that's fantastic!"

"Put it this way, the words 'Indian community' do not give me a warm feeling."

A girl came to the table with a pad in her apron. There was a tiny silver bone in her septum and a metal stud in her tongue and she wore a plastic tag with her name on it. June.

"A couple of aspirin for me, please, and an Americano and water? How about you?"

"Double decaf espresso and a scoop of vanilla ice cream. June?"

"Sure."

"Like your piercings."

"Thanks," the waitress said. She placed a cup of crayons within reach and nodded at Goody as she went away. It was that kind of establishment: patrons were encouraged to doodle on the place mats and selected doodles were posted on a communal board.

Dismas said, "Are you hitting on the waitress?"

"You're a druggie, aren't you?"

"Is that what he told you?"

"That's what you told him," said Goody.

"He wants to know things and I end up telling him," said Dismas.

"Everybody tells him things. There's no point resisting." She picked a red crayon from the cup and weighed it. "What's it like, heroin? Is it a comfort and balm to the troubled mind?"

"When Xavier told me your name I thought you were married to a Mr Lol. I don't know why."

"You thought I was droll Mrs Lol. It's my stepfather's name. More's the pity. He's a doctor and he really wants to be a spiritualist with an ashram full of young female disciples."

"And what's your good name, Ms Lol?"

"My good or better name is Maia. My mother named me after the goddess, which may be why I turned out so secular. She named me Maia and calls me Gudiya, Hindi for doll."

"Which makes you Doll Lol."

She scrawled a phrase on her place mat, 'Missing Person Last Seen', and a quick 'LOL' below it.

"My name is Goody Lol, daughter of Mrs Lol. In Kashmiri, Lol means love. I'm not married."

"But you're not single."

"Probably not. Does New miss India?"

"You're asking me."

"Yes. I'm asking."

"You don't know much about him."

"Who knows about anyone? Talking to you I get a sense of, I don't know, isolation fever. It's like you don't know anything about being with someone."

"Doesn't he tell you things?"

"He tells me and I listen."

"What do you tell him?"

"I don't. I try to protect him."

"From?"

She wouldn't say.

It felt like they were sparring, taking quick jabs at each other and flinching sideways around a still centre. He had to be alert to the swivel and he liked this. Her order arrived, three scoops of ice cream in a porcelain boat and coffee in a white cup and saucer. The waitress asked if there was anything else they needed and Goody said, no, thank you, you're very kind. She took the camera off her neck and put it to the side. Then she put a scoop of ice cream into her coffee and brought the cup to her lips and held it to her face and regarded him through the steam.

"Did you know that heroin was introduced to the world by Bayer? Your doctor would write you a prescription. All perfectly legal."

"Doctors were doing it for themselves too."

"American prescription meds are so great, Vicodin, Oxycontin, Demerol, Fentanyl. I don't know why you people bother with heroin."

"You people."

"What's it like, addiction?"

"You want the quick answer, you don't eat, sleep, shit, come. All the things humans do, you don't."

"What else?"

"A way of killing time. Time is stretched or compressed depending on how much you're holding and how much you've done. You're never bored, not until you quit, then all the time you killed comes back."

"So, time is elastic, you save up on boredom, and you don't come. This is supposed to be fun? Maybe you need to get out more."

"I joined a methadone programme three weeks after September Eleven. Not that it's necessarily connected."

"Methadone. Synthetic opiate, addictive, gets you off and you skip the go-to-jail option."

"You know your drugs."

"And anyway, everything's connected."

"Now you sound like New, I mean Xavier."

"Or he sounds like me. He's sixty-five, older than my stepfather. We've been together seven years, or six, and it goes both ways. He sounds like me and I sound like him. People think I've found an older man to take care of my every need. Except it doesn't work that way."

"How does it work?"

She took a sip of her coffee and said, "He needs to be looked after and I like that. He's a binger. When he's working he'll work for days at a time. If he isn't working, he drinks. A lot. We have terrible fights. He hides bottles around the house. If I tell him I'm leaving he won't get out of bed. Sometimes there's no money in his account, not a sou, and he'll borrow cash for a two-hundred-dollar haircut. My mother will send me a cheque or I'll borrow. But people see us together and create a fantasy in their heads. I want a drink, don't you?"

They were sitting at a table by the window and a slant of sun fell across her mouth and chin.

"There's a bar across the street but I have to be back at work."

"Well, have a quick drink and go."

"Or give me an hour and I'll meet you there."

"I can't give you an hour, is what. I can't give you any time at all. I want a drink before I go home. Come along or go and do whatever it is you need to do. It's simple, really."

Give me a minute, he said, and went through a pair of frosted swing doors to the restroom in the back. He took more than a minute, more than five minutes, and when he got back to the table she was gone. He looked at the place mat she'd been scribbling on. In a few lines she had sketched the figure of a woman between 'LOL' and 'Missing Person Last Seen', a woman viewed from the back, all full lines and falling hair, the face and torso hatched and cross-hatched: a self-portrait. At the bottom of the frame was a Union Square address and an arrow pointing to the portrait. He folded the place mat and put it in his wallet. Outside as he hurried back to work he glanced at the bar across the street. It was the usual Irish drinking franchise with green neon signage and dim interiors.

At six he punched out and walked to Union Square. The building had a uniformed doorman and an awning and from her window he could see all the way down the avenue to the exact spot where the towers used to be. There was no art on the walls and little furniture and the fridge was empty but for white wine, bottled beer, a jar of olives, and a dozen cans of film. She assembled items on a tray, Chivas, two short bottles of Cobra lager, water glasses, a bowl of ice. She put the tray on the floor of the room and placed two chairs facing the windows. He looked at the darkening skyline as she constructed the drinks, one drop at a time it seemed to him, first a cube of ice, then three fingers of whisky topped off with lager. She stirred with her finger and passed him the glass, the smoothness of the whisky coarsened by the rough beer, and he tasted sweat or hair, something raw and unwashed.

"Maybe I shouldn't be here."

"Maybe you shouldn't be a pussy."

They were high above Union Square. The windows were uncurtained and old snow lay on the sill. The park was a patch of forest green and the Virgin store a distant smear on the wedge between Fourth Avenue and Broadway.

She said, "Besides, Xavier doesn't care what I do with other men."

"You tell him."

"Sometimes I make up things to tell him."

"Will you tell him about this?"

"What about this? There's nothing to tell. I mean, what? We ran into each other downtown and had a coffee. You came by for a drink. We may or may not have sex. It's all so commonplace."

"If you tell him, mention it was your idea not mine."

"Maybe it's his idea, I come here with random men and women and he gets off on the details. Maybe if it's not your idea you should go home."

"Why are you so angry?"

Goody stared at him until something left her eyes and her mouth relaxed.

"He's always telling me to sleep with other people and it always upsets me."

"And yet."

"And yet here I am."

"Here we both are."

"Don't let it go to your head. It's got less to do with you than with me. I can't do meaningless sex the way New can. He's got a gift."

"Is this his place or yours?" he asked.

She got up and took her cargoes off, olive cargoes that stopped at the calves and hung in straps to her ankles. They were the seasonal variation. Women all over the city were wearing them in ways that went against the military meaning of the trousers, in lavender, pink, and black velvet, the fabric gathered at the bottom in pleats with ornamental D-rings and untied laces. She took them off and dropped them in a heap on the floor beside a blue vase and a camera. In a corner was a smooth sand-coloured rock the size of his palm. She dropped the trousers and picked up the camera. She wore white underwear that said 'Girl's' on the front and 'Football' on the back. She adjusted the hair that fell across her forehead and regarded the discarded cargoes. She had small bruised feet.

"Goody."

"It's his place but I live here."

"He never comes here?"

"Never. He says it's sterile and American. He's not about to walk in so why don't you relax? The one time he did come in unannounced he was more embarrassed than I was."

"And what about the guy you were with? How embarrassed was he?"

"So fucking typical, you old-school dudes. What makes you think he found me with a guy?"

Dismas walked around with the empty glass dangling from his hand and then he put down the glass and stepped out of his shoes. He knew what she wanted, a group of objects that would tell a story.

"The rock in the corner, is it a pet?"

"I found it in Delhi. I carry it around sometimes for protection. Never mind, long story. What kind of name is Dismas anyway?"

"Dismas, the good thief."

"Real name or you make it up?"

"Dismas the black saint who was crucified with Christ but without the fanfare."

"Answer, real or not?"

"My father's name was Mahi. He was an untouchable and a poet, untouchable twice over you could say. My mother was a Maharashtrian Brahmin, rendered casteless after she married my father. According to the holy books the offspring of a Brahmin woman and an untouchable man is a Chandala, the most degraded of all castes. We're not allowed to look at a Brahmin or wear anything other than the garments of the dead and the only property we're allowed to own are dogs and donkeys. I dropped the name Mahi for many reasons irrelevant to this discussion, and you're not interested anyway."

"It's good when you talk. It helps me get better pictures. Sit on the floor with your back to the window."

"Your hair, I like it."

"It's the boy cut, is what."

"Boy on top and woman below?"

"That's the idea."

"Ambiguous."

"Ambivalent, ambidextrous, ambitious, take your pick."

"All right then, ambiguous."

"Take off your shirt. Sit on the floor with your back to the window. You don't have to be clever. You don't have to talk at all."

He made himself another drink. Then he took off his shirt and sat on the floor with his back to the window. The apartment was heated but the window was cold and when he leaned against it goose bumps puckered his arms. They looked at each other. His eyes were level with her vagina and they looked at each other and already there was a sense of aftermath and separation, as if the act of sex would not bridge the distance between them.

"If it's okay with you," she said. "I'd like to tie you up. Hello, I'm talking? Look at me not my vajing-jong."

"Right," he said.

"May I tie you up? It won't hurt, I promise."

He thought about it. Tied up and photographed. What kind of tie, hog or dog? What difference did it make? In for a paisa, in for a pound.

"What will you do with the photos?"

She opened a closet stacked with coils of brown rope and chose a short length. It was soft on the skin, pliable and comfortable.

"Asanawa, natural fibre," said Goody. "I don't know yet. Show them in some way, I suppose. Just so you know, the tie and knot denotes the status of the model. The rigger decides."

"And what status am I?

"Not high, obviously, you're a man."

The coil dropped on the floor with a soft thump and he smelled oil and hemp. She looped the rope around his torso, a strand above and below his nipples, then around his belly and between his legs, a strand on either side of his penis and two more around his wrists.

"I'm using the classic single column tie and a lark's head knot. I'm keeping it simple," she said. "Make a fist."

With his hands tied behind his back he opened and closed his fists. He got down on his knees in his spot against the window and she adjusted the lens and fixed the shutter speed and shot three or four frames. She pulled her chair forward, scraping the legs on the floor until she was directly in front of him, and she took a picture from above, the lens pointing at his torso, shooting as fast as the camera's shutter allowed.

She untied him then and checked the rope marks on his skin. Satisfied, she took a last picture of his marked wrists and put aside the camera.

"I want to watch you do it."

"Do it."

"Get high."

"There isn't much to see."

"Show me. That's where you go, correct? When you disappear into the restroom?"

But when he emptied half a bag on his wallet and shaped it into two rough lines and rolled up a five-dollar bill, she wanted a taste. This is what she said, a taste. The apartment was dark now, the big window fogged at the edges, and she switched on a floor lamp that picked out the clothes and shoes and vase and made them elements in a frame. There was a hum of isolation in the room.

He said, no, can't do, but he thought, yes, I can.

She said, "I'm not going to sit here and watch you turn yourself on. Give me a taste or leave."

"Seriously, you don't want to."

"Why wouldn't I?"

And that was all it took. He gave her a line and did one himself and they lay on the floor and said nothing, they faded out and in. He turned on his side and took her T-shirt off one arm at a time. She pulled it one-handed over her head. There was a sound nearby of a helicopter thudding against the air. She unbuckled him one-handed and slid the belt off and went to work on his buttons, but there was no intention or urgency in her actions and he wondered where she was in her head. Was she with Xavier?

She said, "Don't take this the wrong way but it isn't drugs I want, it's money."

"Money."

"I'm a woman, you're a man. You give me money, I give you sex. Fair and unexceptional exchange, I should think. As conventional as it gets in the Indian context."

"How much?"

"How much do you spend on heroin?"

"Ten bucks a bag and I buy five at a time."

"Bloody hell, in that case give me a hundred dollars."

Yes because I've never done a thing like this before and I might as well do it right what do you mean you don't have a hundred on you okay fifty or no go that's my rock bottom going out of business cannot go lower price a girl has to keep her self-respect she can't be giving it away can she I've been giving it away since I was a child and I'm not going to do it any more it happens when your parents aren't qualified to be parents I should say parent since I only had the one my stepfather was pure predator nothing remotely parental about him people talk about bad fathers but they never mention bad mothers why is that listen you can't kiss me I'll save that for New I can't help asking myself what I'm doing here I mean what and why am I doing I'm such a mystery to me sometimes I asked Garima my therapist if mothers were to blame for everything because they bring us here and abandon us and she said is that what you think and I said well of course that's what I think why else would I be saying so my mother should have had her parenting licence revoked she shouldn't have been given a licence in the first place I mean you know what I mean listen this is new for me I wasn't always so easy but I caught on I did he goes off on his trips and it isn't like he's sitting in the hotel all evening watching television I counted the condoms in the bedside drawer I spread them out on the bed and he said they were all there but I told him to check the dates there were new ones and he certainly hadn't used them with me and I knew I'd crossed that line into crazy lady territory I knew it and I stopped and now it's sauce for the goose and sauce for the gander hey ho how do you do listen do you hear that like a foghorn like a big ship sailing up First Avenue looking for port I heard foghorns when I was in college in England foghorns in the night and it always made me lonely made me want to find a warm bar where people talked in the gravest of tones as if they were discussing confidential information but they're not they're not sometimes a guy tries to pick me up and he tries so hard I can feel myself losing interest I tell him listen the more you talk the less I want you shut up and fuck me fuck more talk less I like that about you you don't talk but I can't help asking myself what you're doing here and what I want from you and what I'm doing here at least I question myself I weigh the answer I allow for the possibility of doubt I mean no man ever does that does he and I can't help feeling sorry for myself sometimes this is super stuff it is God I'm stoned what's your name anyway your real name you can tell me I'm discreet like that I won't tell call me what you want Sakina no Saki Candy Lucky Lucky yes I like that too we could all use a bit of lucky but first can you give me the money how much is this baby forty is this a first instalment do you want me to take off my bra or leave it on what am I doing I don't know I don't know I'm so stoned on this super shit I can see why you do it the lure it makes you numb and beautiful invincible would you like me to suck your cockadoodle let me suck you don't have to do a thing or do you want to fuck me when I'm asleep I'd like that give me more money later okay I'll run a tab for you wait don't unhook I'll just push it up so you can do my breasts with my bra on that's what you want I know do you like them you don't think the nipples are too big they're huge they've always been huge how come you don't want to suck on this one I'll tell you because it's smaller all the boys go for the other one girls aren't so mammarian they're into pussy New is obsessed with tits big bigger biggest sometimes when he's off somewhere and I don't see him for days and then we meet and he isn't grabbing me I know he's been fucking stands to reason how could he not and if I look for it I find it dyed hair on the couch or the smell of perfume always some telltale cheap thing that's the kind of woman he goes for or I'll smell the funk on his beard I mean I'm queer you hear I know the smell of pussy take this off no oh okaay you want to fuck me with your trousers on you want to put your nice cock into me without taking off your trousers Jesus this is good shit but it makes you talk oh I'm going to shut up for a minute while I use my mouth on you I love boys they come so easy you don't need to work your arse off like with a girl suck on him a bit ride him and he's done it takes a while with this fabulous shit but you will come yes you will you'll have an insect orgasm that's what junk does right makes you an insect or an ant or something an insect getting its cock sucked sexistential insect oh nice do that I thought you said you don't come with this stuff do that and I'll come a hundred times I'll have an insectile multiple I will we're all insects some of us look humanoid is all but I'm not going to touch myself you know why I'm going to wait for you I'm so so stoned ducky and wet not feeling sorry for myself now am I you can't kiss me you can slap me but you can't kiss me you untouchable Chandala son of a bitch why why don't you fuck me I want to be fucked on my hands and knees it's my second most favourite position in case you didn't know or whatever you want I'll say yes I said yes I will yes

He was paying her. He owed her nothing, no pleasure or consideration; and he didn't get on top of her until she asked him to, asked once and then again. He searched her face as he pushed into her because he wanted to see some expression of cynicism or pain but she was absent from herself, passive, the aggression gone. He could do anything and she didn't mind; and though he lunged at her for hours until the movement was meaningless except as parody, for hours, she didn't complain or turn away but lay with him, breathing and solemn.

Early the next morning Dismas stood naked at the big window and sipped from a glass of whisky and water. On a desk he saw pens in a jar and a bottle of black ink and a magnifying glass and a Polaroid print of Goody in a sari, a black and white image out of Bollywood that she was turning into art in the style of Xavier, with pen and ink. He remembered seeing the image in the apartment on Central Park West and thinking it was Xavier's work and his heart jumped as the meaning of it came to him.

She slept on her side, slept right through the racket he made getting dressed, but opened her eyes when he unlocked the front door and looked at him and went back to sleep.

At the end of the month she moved back to the apartment on Central Park West and that was the end of the affair with Dismas Bambai, though affair may be too weighty a word for an entanglement that ran its course in a month or two. She'd moved in with Newton, she told Dismas, and they were thinking of visiting India, maybe staying for a time. New had been offered a retrospective for his sixty-sixth birthday and he wanted to make it definitive, the party of the decade. She said, why don't you come? It will be fun. It was said casually and he wanted to respond in the same way, make an off-the-cuff comment about the weather or popular sport. But when he spoke it was to tell her that he had enjoyed being tied up, it felt like freedom.

3.

This is the way the future arrives, flying low and fast, on silver wings that set the sign of the cross flickering over the business district. On a day like any other, a day like no other. You are one of the hundreds, one of the thousands hurrying to your place of employment. Above you the tower warms its skin in the falling sun, its steel core braced, the tower and its parallel twin built a segment at a time to withstand history. So when the plane appears the mind perceives it first as art. There is no other way to understand the images that follow: the clear blue sky, the clean line of flight, the way the plane tilts in the final seconds, the inevitability of impact. Later he will mark it as a premonition, the starting bell of the twenty-first century. And he will talk about eyewitnessing two kinds of terror, Islamic and white American. What he won't talk about is the woman, because it makes him ashamed that he could not save her.

From a walkway by the river Amrik sees smoke high on the north tower and then he hears the crash and a cloud of fuel boils into the sky. People stop moving, unable to supply a thread of logic to the scene: a plane-shaped hole in the side of the building. The first news van and television crew have arrived, a local station, and a police cordon is up, but where are the fire trucks? When the second plane appears the cameras are ready. He watches the aircraft's path into the new world, the scorched unstoppable gleam of it. Around him people are trying to get away or they are frozen in place, their heads tilted at identical angles, and he reverses direction to skirt the block. He's pushing his way through when the first tower comes down and people start to run.

The crowd is roiling off the buildings, the helter-skelter office workers in suits and dress shoes, the restaurant workers and tourists. He sees two men in running clothes standing frozen in place. He sees discarded backpacks and a pair of high heels and a single sneaker. A man takes off his scarf as he runs and the length of white wool joins the other detritus on the sidewalk. A delivery bike lies on its side, its rear wheel spinning.

The woman is the only one who isn't running, that is the first thing he notices. Hold this, she says, one second, and she hands him a small camera on a strap. Her eyes are lined with black and there is a leather tote on her shoulder and she's reaching for something inside when he hears a roar of bass that builds and holds and builds again. Advancing up the street is a solid cloud of smoke twelve storeys high, the colour of dirty snow. A heavy underground thump shatters glass all around them and the woman loses her footing and in an instant he loses sight of her.

Someone screams in short evenly spaced intervals, a woman's voice screaming, Mara, and there are shouts and sirens and his lungs are on fire. It isn't easy to absorb the moment: people concentrated on one task, the pumping of legs and the taking in of air and the deflection of thousands of arrows of information flying in from every direction.

This is how the future arrives, out of the bright blue sky. He knows this is the future but he cannot hope to understand it, not now, because something is about to yank him out of the moment and reduce him to a question of headgear. Across the street someone's yelling at him. Where did the guy come from? He is not a hardhat. He is not working in construction or any conceivable Wall Street job. He is a hooded sweatshirt and painter's jeans and he's saying something unbelievable.

"You, motherfuck terrorist, take the rag off."

Amrik's reflexes take a moment to kick in. The guy is still far enough away and the street is full of people moving in a jerky headlong rush, not a stampede or a migratory wave but a race kicking against oblivion, a collective hyperjump made up of many smaller ones. These are New Yorkers running for their lives and what he wants is to run with them, but he goes the other way, south, away from the two men, there are two now, who are following him.

"Yo, Ali Baba, wait up!"

The sky is overcast but the sun is there too, or a simulacrum of the sun inside the thunderclouds that have landed on the street. A hawk of some sort flies across the avenue in a rough diagonal only a few inches above the crowd. The bird too is headed north. Somebody's mail whips by, and more paper, stapled pages and newspapers blowing down the street. The air is full of grit and Amrik puts his handkerchief to his mouth and turns west on the zebra at the end of the block. He heads south then west again and when the two men start to run he does too.

When they were picked on at school his brother's response was to say God-bless, if you say God-bless they will leave you alone. But his brother is a cut Sikh whose kesh is gelled to who knew how many points, a kid who gave up on the five Ks in college because his dream was bhangra. Amrik's dream is all-American. He is Brooklyn-born and Brooklyn-bred, a New Yorker with a doomed love of the Red Sox, and none of it means a thing because today he is nothing more than an animated logo. He is a running turban.

Above him the great buildings of the business district appear stricken, block after block of dead air, the city under attack. Within that attack another is taking place and Amrik is the sole intended victim. He unwinds his new turban as he runs, a length of crisp black cotton as stylish as anything in a midtown store. He will take off his turban and stuff it in his satchel and he will tuck his long hair into his collar and run.

This is an American, a New Yorker, on the day the new century arrives. See him ducking into a subway station. The ticket booths are empty. On the platform people carry breakfast bagels and unread financial papers and dead cell phones. Some have just exited trains from Uptown, from Bronxville, White Plains and Riverside. He sees a tall blond man whose khaki shorts are wet with piss and the man makes no effort to hide the stain. A chain wrapped in blue plastic hangs from his fist.

The crack of the train comes scraping off the tiles.

When his pursuers jump the turnstiles their boots make a single whump on the sticky platform and such is the strangeness of the morning that no notice is taken of them or of the way they are walking through the crowd and scanning heads.

Amrik sinks into himself, becomes smaller, becomes absolutely still. He's taken off his turban and his jacket and tie but there is nothing he can do about his beard and skin colour. He is the only person in the crowd who is not black or white but an unrepresented brown, provenance unknown, from some place off the census grid.

The air smells funny, thick with exhaust and rust and a metallic residue he can taste on his tongue. The doors ding open and he enters a car and goes to the far end where he leans against the connecting door. A woman in a blue jumpsuit and hardhat is watching him. She is big and dreadlocked, the colour of black coffee with a drop of condensed milk, and he's the only one in the car, on the train, on the entire subway, whose colour is off the grid. The woman takes off her hardhat and hands it to him.

"Put it on," she says.

He can see the two men on the platform and he can taste the metallic residue in the air. He notices the camera in his hand, the brand name inscribed in silver, the name rhyming with leaker or liker. He puts on the hardhat and waits for the doors to close.

"Philomena Debris," the woman says. "What I do all day? I ride the rails. I ride and watch. That's my name and job description. Philomena Debris, rider-watcher."

The name on her overalls is De Brie.

"My advice? Keep your head down. Don't look up, not now."

He keeps his head down; he doesn't look up.

Saturday morning. He and Sukh were on the 6, *on the sex*, his brother called it, up in the first car because that had been their ritual when they were kids, up in front in sight of the motorman. There were seats vacant but they were standing, his brother hunched like he was already downtown at the Basement Bhangra spinning Punjabi remixes in his white K-Swiss. Amrik asked him once, how d'you keep them so white? He said, every night, before I sleep? I pray my *kicks* to keep.

"I were you I'd cut my hair," Sukh said. "Lose the turban, stop being stared at by the average white man."

"Turban's our pride," said Amrik. "I take it off, they win."

"Win? Shit," and Sukh laughed, "you can't win against a lynch mob."

"I thought about it, get a haircut and a shave. But racists see race, they don't see anything else."

"At this point and the historical process, race is everything."

"Why join them?"

"There's a war in America and like it or not you part of it. You being too idyllistic."

"You remember any Punjabi at all?" said Amrik.

"Bro, the pic, you want to or not? Gimme a peek? So I know what you're saying to me?"

"What I should be asking, you remember any English?"

"The pic, the snap, the grainy, you know, image."

Amrik dug the *Post* out of his briefcase, already folded to the page. Sukh stayed with the picture for a while, two white guys pointing at a word in red capitals on the front of a garbage truck, the guys wearing reflective sunglasses with straps, like they were on a skiing holiday. On Sixth Avenue.

The caption said: 'MAKE THAT DOUBLE FOR US. After more than three decades on the job, NYC sanitation men Phil Manzanera and Rick 'Raucus' Honeycutt (right) retire this week. After the catastrophic terror strikes of 9/11 they spray-painted their city vehicle with the motto above: REVENGE!'

"You sure these are the guys?"

"No question, wearing the same clothes."

"Same clothes when they're chasing you all over the subway system?"

"Yeah."

"Hoodies and Tims. White guys dressed like brothers. You in your Brooks Brothers and the towers collapsing."

"Sums it up."

"Amrik, their names are in the paper. You know we can find these guys and show them what the pagri stands for."

"I thought about it, got to admit."

"Bro, puttar."

"Turn the page."

Sukh turned to a double spread datelined Mesa, Arizona. He read the headline: *Trial Dates Set in Alleged Bias Killing of Sikh Immigrant*, and then the article quickly through to the end.

"Sukh, you get it?" said Amrik. "The bias killer shot him because he thought he was Muslim. It's happening all over the country."

"See what I'm saying? Lose the turban."

"No."

"What is it you're trying to sell me here?"

"Come to Arizona. The guy who did it, the bias killer? He's pleading not guilty due to insanity. I want to meet the family, show some solidarity at the trial."

"You see my new Ks?"

"I see them."

"You know what they are?"

"I know you'll tell me."

"Custom made. My K-Swiss with a upgrade on the classic style. All leather. See the one-piece rubber outsoles? Reinforced toe, five-stripe band, D-Ring lacing system?"

"What did it cost you?"

"Always with the most *un*important question."

"Okay, but what?"

"Senty dollars for the basic shoe. The customising? Off the grid. Check the laces and the gold eyelets. Not available online, not available anywhere. And the straight Lydiard-type bar lacing, see that?"

"Yeah."

"Okay, but do you see the main thing?"

"Which one, there are so many."

"Don't belittle, bro, don't be little. Check the sleeves on the laces."

"The sleeves."

"The metal tube at the end of the lace, holds it together."

"Okay."

"Yeah, gold plated."

"I'm finding this hard to believe."

"And the colour on the uppers, see how it's a different white from the shield on the tongue there? See how the toe and heel are a different white from the stripes?"

"Yes."

"Now look at that monogram there by the heel."

"What's it say? Sorry if I don't examine your sneakers up close on the subway."

"DJ Suki."

"Right."

"What I'm talking about. Customised. I'm not taking no three hundred dollar Ks to Mesa, Arizona, get my ass shot at by some alleged *bias* motherfucker."

"That's what I thought you'd say."

"And Rik? You ask me you shouldn't be going either. Who do we know in AZ?"

"Sukh, take a look at the picture of Balbir Singh, the gas station owner who got killed."

"See that double beard and jumbo turban anybody be scared."

"Funny."

"I'm on in thirty minutes, regular gig two nights a week. I'm getting it to work. I'm being responsible, unlike my older brother."

"I heard you."

"For real."

At City Hall the train's antique brakes shuddered and the crowd thinned out and Sukh picked up his CD cases.

"I'm supposed to be the rebel in the family but look at you. Quit steady high-paying job, check, try for job with reclusive artist, check, and now? You're taking off for Arizona just because you can."

"Balbir had just been to the local church. He made a Nine Eleven donation and he was planting flowers at his gas station when the guy shot him. Five shots from a car."

"Not now when my career's in take-off position."

"An hour earlier killer's sitting at Applebee's and laughing with the waitress. He tells her, I'm gonna go out and shoot me some towelheads."

"Mesa, Arizona. What d'you expect? Tolerance and understanding?"

"Family man, Balbir. Who does he look like?"

"Who?"

"He could be anybody, could be Papa, or Jarnail Chacha in Amritsar. You see what I'm saying?"

"I see what you're—"

"Listen, put an ad in the *Voice* for me. Here's the copy."

Sukh read from the notepaper his brother handed him, "'Seeking pinstriped woman I met on September 11. I'm the turbanned guy. You gave me your Leica to hold.' Yeah, okay, I can take care of it."

He jumped off the train at Spring Street with the cases clutched to his chest and Amrik noted his brother's unique running style. Sukh's upper body and thighs did little work; like a cartoon character the movement was all in the feet, it was all in the K-Swiss. No one on the platform gave him a second glance, just another city kid going about his business. Amrik would have been stared at because he had stayed loyal to the five Ks. Not that it was a flaw in the faith. How could Sikhism's founders have anticipated the ways in which their innovation would be viewed in the new world?

He found a seat and the compartment filled up again. The connecting door opened with a heavy crank and a man stepped in carrying a clutch of flags and baseball pennants.

He said, "Push in, push in, we're all American here."

Which wasn't necessarily true. There were several nationalities and races and combinations thereof. This was New York. The guy barrelled down the aisle and stopped in front of an old couple with a Chinese newspaper spread on their laps. They were reading together, reading the same article and possibly the same sentence.

He said, "Be American, buy American."

The woman looked up and inspected the man and his flags and went back to the newspaper.

A bearded guy in a camouflage jacket nodded at the flag-seller.

The flag guy said, "Fight the Taliban. Buy American, be American."

The bearded guy said, "Buy the blood of Jesus Christ."

"Say what?"

"The blood of the Saviour redeems me."

A ripple of movement, people looking for possible routes of escape, and the flag guy planted himself in the aisle two seats from the bearded man and three from Amrik. He looked at Amrik in his black suit and black shirt and black shoes with side buckles and his eyes lingered on the black turban and he offered a tiny pin, stars and stripes waving in an invisible wind.

He said, "Be American."

And the words shook Amrik out of his subway persona, the *don't make eye contact, don't talk, don't smile* shield he wore like armour.

He said, "I am American."

The bearded guy said to Amrik, "If thou has run with the footmen and they have wearied thee, how canst thou contend with the horses?"

The flag guy said, "Horse what?"

The guy with the beard said, "Old Testament."

Amrik said, "He's saying there's no point engaging with fools."

The guy with the beard said, "You think it didn't have fools in the time of our Saviour?"

The guy with the flags said, "Fucking city, everybody's got a mouth."

But he went to the connecting doors and left the compartment.

Amrik thought, New York, where racism is an equal opportunity enterprise. It wasn't the first time he'd been sniped at by a black man, but it was certainly the first time he'd been defended by someone white.

You blurt it to a nut on the subway, but you don't articulate it otherwise. You are an American with a job on Wall Street and an apartment in Park Slope. People give you their money and you knead it like dough: you supersize it. You run in the park in a warm-up jacket with headphones strapped to your arm. You don't take sugar in your coffee. You don't eat white bread or potatoes. You don't drink beer. You have a body mass index calculator on your computer and it tells you your weight, real and ideal, in relation to your height. You take your coffee black. In your office there is a leather couch and two leather armchairs and a framed lithograph of the Brooklyn Dodgers signed and numbered by the artist. You are an American: a New Yorker: a Brooklynite. Then the towers come down and you find yourself on a plane headed west. It is 2003, wartime in America. You have to be wearing a turban and sitting on a plane to Arizona via Texas to understand the meaning of this.

They made him take off his shoes and socks. He placed his black leather Cordovans in a tray and stepped through a metal detector. They made him do it three times. He retied the laces the first time and then he left them untied, slipped on the shoes, slipped them off. Random checks, but he was the only passenger who had to remove his footwear more than once, who had to unwind his headgear. It was embarrassing. Also, downright fucking humiliating.

On the second leg, a small jet from Houston to Mesa, he was the only passenger who was not white, who was brown, hairy, gym-fit, and it made him wonder, what happened to the melting pot, the salad bowl, the mosaic? Fly out of JFK and the United States was a foreign country. You found ancient race anxieties. You found extreme weather and isolation and brutal long-distance terrain. All the way on the short flight he was aware of the other passengers' awareness. He was sitting in the front row and this too seemed to him a misfortune: he could feel them staring. He was happy his brother had not come with him. If one Sikh could be the cause of so much dismay, the two brothers would have caused a stampede. Out of his briefcase he pulled a copy of Newton's first book of poems, the cover a painted cross, chipped and blood-spattered. The title, *Songs for the Tin-Eared*, appeared above a banner that said POEMS, and he hoped it would occur to his fellow passengers that a man reading a book of poems in English would most likely not be planning to blow them out of the sky. He held the book high and buried his face in it, but the man beside him did not seem reassured. He seemed as nervous as when he'd first set eyes on his turbanned bearded seatmate. Soon Amrik put the book away and pulled out a copy of the *Wall Street Journal*.

He took a taxi from the airport to the hotel and kept it waiting while he had a shower and washed his hair and changed his clothes. He hung his suit in the closet and put on a short-sleeved white shirt and sandals and when he got back to the taxi the driver had a cigarette in his mouth and the radio tuned to death metal, a bottomed-out voice shouting GowBowBowBowBangBangGang into stop-start guitars. He killed his cigarette and flipped channels to a soft rock station. He was wearing plastic sunglasses turned the wrong way around and there were empty food containers on the dashboard and bits of debris on the front seat.

From the upholstery a smell of antique smoke and dirty clothes. But the guy was helpful enough, he knew where the courthouse was, and he didn't mind waiting.

"Thanks."

"Hey, you're welcome. Where you coming from, you don't mind me asking?"

"New York."

"The big bad city."

"Not so bad any more."

"How's that?"

"The mayor did some housekeeping."

"Rudy Giuliani. Did a good thing, right?"

He drove with one hand on the wheel, his eyes squinted against the glare and his shades perched on the back of his head, twitchy and dry, with a reedy country-western voice. "Depends who you're talking to. I'm not complaining."

"You're here for the trial, I'm guessing."

"That's right."

"It's all over the news, radio *and* TV. They're pleading insanity."

"Guilty except insane."

"Crazy like a fox. Guy knew what he was doing."

"Yeah, probably did."

"Are you a lawyer?"

"No, I'm here for the solidarity. See what happens."

"Right."

"Because I'm a Sikh, like the guy who was killed."

"Balbir Sodhi."

"Okay, you know his name."

"Hey, I've been to his gas station a few times. Ask me they should hang the shooter no questions asked."

"Maybe they will."

"They're calling him the American murderer. What he's doing, he's giving Americans a bad name."

"And Arizonans."

"Guy isn't even from here, moved to Mesa from fucking Alabama."

"Can't hang a man for moving here. Sodhi came from the Punjab."

"Shoot a guy in the back? Dude *deserves* to hang."

The driver introduced himself as Charlie Moon, Mesa born and bred, driving now for three years. He handed out a card with the name and number of the taxi company. Amrik sat back and watched the city go by. Even the sun fell at an angle that felt strange to a man just arrived from a fortified borough on the coast. The streets were calm and orderly, raked gravel and wide sidewalks and no trash blowing against the storefronts. The desert was everywhere. On the traffic islands and street corners were stands of saguaro, stoic stumps reaching upward. Everything was beige or pink, the houses, the saguaro, the gravel, even the animal figures in people's yards: a hundred shades of pink and five hundred shades of beige.

When you are displaced in the world, displacement is its own reward.

He began to enjoy riding around the foreign city and looking at the sights and talking to Charlie Moon. Then they turned a corner and he saw a group of Sikhs in blue and red turbans. The headgear was vivid against their white clothes. A dozen men and women dressed in the Hindu colour of mourning. Amrik stepped out of the car and a guy with a chest-length beard extended his hand and introduced himself as Lakhwinder, brother of Balbir. He said, welcome, from where are you coming? The Punjabi-accented English sounded strange in the American desert and then it didn't sound strange at all. Others came up to introduce themselves and shake his hand. There was a television crew and a woman who asked if she could speak to him later to get a comment about the trial, but he didn't get a chance to reply because now he was entering the courthouse at the head of a crowd of people he had never before met and he fitted right in with his saffron turban and white shirt.

The guy in the video is having a bad day. He argues with his wife, his lawyer, with law enforcement officers of various ranks.

He tells a policeman, "I didn't do it, man."

The cop just looks at him and nods.

He says it again, "I didn't do it."

The cop asks him to state his name.

The man says, "Frank Roque."

The cop wants to talk about his mood on September Eleven. Was he emotional? New York attacked, the Pentagon attacked, aeroplanes hijacked and thousands dead, the world trade tower down. How emotional was he?

Frank snaps at him, "Towers, man, two buildings. Get it right."

"Okay, towers, what were you thinking right then?"

"Ask the people who died what they were thinking. I don't know."

"Sure you do."

"I don't. How would I?"

"You told everybody how angry you were."

"Who's everybody?"

Frank takes a breath and looks past the cop. You can see it in his eyes, the hurt and indignation.

"If someone were to shoot somebody of Mid-Eastern descent."

"Yes."

"Why arrest *me*?"

Now the cop takes a breath and looks Frank in the eye and holds the look.

"Frank."

"I don't get it. What?"

"Frank?"

"What?"

"The guy? He wasn't Middle Eastern. He was an Indian from India."

In the next scene Frank is talking to his wife.

He says, "Wait, Dawn," says it like he's at a diner and calling the waitress to return an order of bacon and eggs because the eggs haven't been done to his liking. "Can't you figure it out? You need to be careful with these guys. They'll get you to say something against me. They'll use you to send me away. It's how the legal system works, see? They turn people against each other."

He's explaining the legal system to the woman who turned him in.

He says, "Everybody hates me, that's why I'm here."

Now, two years later, immobile in the defendant's chair, Frank doesn't look much like the man in the video. There's a family resemblance, sure, but he's got less hair and he's put on weight and he does not come across as drunk or belligerent. The indignation has been replaced by extreme stupor. He's so still he could be comatose and when he does say something the people in the courtroom lean forward in their seats. He rarely blinks. He never looks at himself on the video monitor. One morning he takes a piece of hard candy from his pocket and pops it in his mouth and for a few minutes he works his jaw, his freshly shaved chin sunk into the folds of fat on his neck. Then he swallows and takes a sip of water. It is the only time he shows any animation. When the jury comes in he is motionless again, a sad bland man with a heart condition.

They are trying to determine whether he's insane or faking.

It's a Tuesday in August and Frank is wearing a pressed short-sleeved shirt and tie. Under the shirt he wears a stun belt set to administer a wake-up jolt to the left kidney, fifty thousand volts of jumping juice if he makes a run for it or grapples with the bailiffs or whines one too many times about the colour of the jumpsuit they make him wear when he's not in court (orange). The belt is black and charcoal with Velcro D-rings, cable reinforced so you can't cut through it, primed to set off a siren that will stun you with electricity *and* sound.

Frank's lawyer is a man named Stein whose long hair bounces on the shoulders of his sharp suit. His domed skull is shiny in the courtroom lights and his bow tie is orange. He wants to talk about the drug Frank is taking.

Zyprexa was the first atypical antipsychotic approved for use in the treatment of schizophrenia.

He is reading from a printed sheet and Amrik can tell he likes the sound of the phrases. He is projecting, putting in some special rhetorical emphasis that he hopes will carry to every seat of the packed courtroom.

For the long-term treatment of schizophrenia and acute mixed episodes of bipolar mania. To treat the symptoms of psychosis such as hallucination and delusion.

Stein paces the courtroom with his hands in the pockets of his trousers, a dapper man on a stroll. He stops in front of the jurors and gives them a good look at the suit.

"Acute bipolar mania. That's the currently popular phrase for manic depression. Bipolar mania is manic depression is schizophrenia. It's a medical term for clinical insanity."

He waits a beat and looks around at Frank who hasn't moved, who's slumped in his seat.

"If they're giving him medication for insanity he must be insane."

A bearish blond guy with a biker moustache, Stein's partner, lists the side effects of Zyprexa: drowsiness in the day and insomnia at night, depression or agitation plus hostility, weight gain, constipation, blurred vision, stiffness in the fingers, skin rashes, difficulty in speaking.

Before lunch the prosecution produces one of the many mental health experts who will appear before the court.

"What would Zyprexa do to someone who was not schizophrenic?"

"It would leave the person wooden and sedated, his eyes at half mast," says Dr Scialli.

All heads turn to Frank, who doesn't look up.

Stein has made no mistakes so far but a wrap-up question at the end unravels much of the work of the morning. He asks Dr Scialli if Frank's courtroom demeanour indicates a man of normal perceptions.

Dr Scialli says, "The four-hour interrogation video shows his state of mind more clearly than any amount of conjecture at this stage."

By now it is clear to Amrik that Frank will be found guilty in a trial that will be known for its brevity. Sitting in the third row with the rest of the Sikh contingent he can see that Frank is uncomfortable in his own skin. He has exiled himself from his life by moving to a new town. It would have happened anyway. Even if he had stayed in Alabama the world would have changed around him. A sense of pity stays with Amrik through the day.

He is invited to dinner at Balbir's son's house where the extended Sodhi clan has congregated and the men stand around drinking beer.

"How come you came all the way from New York?" Lakhwinder asks.

"Well, Lakhwinder, it's a long story."

"Call me Lucky. Tell me anyway. We have time."

"Lucky, something happened that made me examine my life as a Sikh man in America."

"Yes?"

"I used to work in finance. My office was four blocks from the World Trade Center. I was on my way to work when the towers went down."

"Okay."

"I was chased by two men."

"Chase you, where did they chase you?"

"Through the streets and into the subway."

"Yes? Why?"

"Same reason they attacked your father. They saw my turban and figured I was a terrorist."

"That's it? Some guys chased you into the subway? That's what brought you here?"

"That's why you came to Arizona?" says Balbir's son, a quiet overweight boy who has started working at his father's gas station.

"It made me think about what it means to be a Sikh man in America. It made me want to do something."

"Okay, anything, it's good you're here."

Lakhwinder says, "More of us, more chance they hang him."

And Amrik's saga is dismissed. He had wanted to tell his story and share something of himself but he might as well have been talking about turbulence on the flight out from JFK, airline food, jet lag, weather, whatever.

"For Frank Roque? Not life sentence, he should hang. Eye for eye," Lakhwinder says.

"Death is too easy," says Balbir's son.

A man in a white parka, his belly a small boulder, says, "For my community it is a slap in our face. Our brother was murdered and if they don't execute his killer they are insulting us. They're giving life to the man who took my brother's life."

He blinks rapidly as he drinks from the Budweiser in his fist. His eyes are wet. The last thing Amrik wants to see is this mountainous Sikh bursting into the weepies. There's enough emotion in the room as it is, enough bravado for a mid-size Bombay blockbuster.

The men are heavily built, the dress code American casual, pressed jeans and collared shirts, parkas and sneakers. Within the basic armature there is a great deal of individual difference. Balbir's son has a turban shaped like a ship's prow. His beard is moussed and kept in shape with a net. Lakhwinder's untrimmed beard spreads across half his chest and his turban is wound sloppily around his head. The wet-eyed Budweiser man's bushy beard is separated into two long points, a sight that must strike terror into the local populace.

Amrik's father wore a netted beard and elaborate turban, a soft-spoken man whose ambition had been to get out of the Punjab. He would have gone anywhere, Iceland, Argentina, Papua New Guinea; but he had relatives in Queens who found him work in a grocery store in Jackson Heights. He married a girl chosen by his uncle and named their son after his adopted country. Amrik's mother wanted a traditional name, something Punjabi, but his father got his way with their first-born. With Sukhwinder his mother got hers. His father became a Republican, because the elephant reminded him of India, and he stayed one all his life. How hard his parents worked, how happy they were with how little, and because they had been poor they did not take money for granted. They lived small lives with few comforts and thought themselves fortunate. Back home they were success stories. Even after all these years his father thought of the Punjab as home. He wore his Sikhism lightly: he said faith was a private thing and there was no point parading it on the streets for the world to see. He would as likely have talked about his wife's lovemaking habits as he would the nuts and bolts of his faith. What would he say to these men?

He'd say, *Eye for an eye makes the whole world blind.*

The Court TV crew has also been invited to dinner. People leave their shoes at the door and sit cross-legged on the floor to eat – black daal, rotis cut into wedges, tandoori chicken and fish kebabs that are a bright unnatural shade of red. The Sodhis provide a quick house tour and Amrik understands that they are being savvy, working the media. Over dessert, the reporter asks Amrik what brought him all the way from New York to Mesa.

He answers truthfully that he has no idea.

"I guess I'm out of my mind," he says.

"Well, that's something. I think you should talk to me, tell your story to the world."

She gives him a card, *Cassandra Bird, Assistant Producer*. Call me Cassie, she says, her voice with a drop at the end. But Amrik does not want to talk.

He says, "And what brought you from NYC to Mesa?"

"I did a bunch of stories after Nine Eleven about people suffering from post-traumatic stress without knowing it. I interviewed rescue personnel at Ground Zero who suffered from insomnia, respiratory problems, anxiety attacks, and they wouldn't take sick leave. I spoke to a woman who'd lost her husband and her father. She was camped out there. She wouldn't go home. I kept meeting survivors who didn't come across like they'd survived, who—"

"Right."

"I met a woman who was riding the subways all day long. She was a senior custodian in Tower One and lost her job, obviously. Rode the subways in a blue jumpsuit—"

"Wait a minute! What was her name? Black woman?"

"Don't remember the name. Big woman, black, gave great sound bites."

"That's her, Philomena Debris! I met her just after the towers went down. She gave me advice that maybe saved my life. Hey, this is fantastic!"

But Cassandra Bird isn't impressed.

She says, "That's what she does, she rides the subway and talks to people. That's her disorder."

She takes a sip of sweet milk tea and coughs.

"How does all that bring you to Arizona?"

"Tell the truth, I needed to get out of the city. I was tripping on other people's disorders. I'd done so many stories on trauma I was traumatised myself."

On the way back to the hotel his cell phone beeps with a text message from Sukh. *No need 2B a hero ok?*

Amrik asks Charlie Moon to pick him up early the next day. He won't go back to the courtroom. He can already see the outcome as a ticker on a screen. Sentenced to death. Balbir's family telling reporters that only partial retribution has been achieved and the debt will be paid in full when Frank is hanged, electrocuted, lethally injected, clubbed to death, executed by firing squad, lynched in a public square.

On the American flight out of Mesa he stands with his hands on his hips and examines himself in the toilet mirror. He looks at his careful clothes and groomed facial hair and tries to see himself as a stranger might. He understands that he is permanently displaced in the new America and the new New York.

The return trip is worse. The other passengers' stares are more pointed and the stopover in Texas is much too long.

He orders draught lager at a sports bar and grill and flips through a bar copy of the *Texas Times*. His eye, newly sensitised to *turban* and *Sikh* and *terrorist*, finds an article about the Sodhi trial. *Victims of Mistaken Identity, Sikhs Pay a Price for Turbans*. It opens with Frank Roque's contention as he's being arrested, "I'm a patriot. I'm a damn American all the way." The phrase plays and replays in Amrik's head and coalesces into a chanted anthemic *damngoddamnAmerican, allthewayAmerican*. The article is a piece of subtle alarmism. Sikhs are being singled out because they wear "distinctive turbans that resemble the head wrap of terror chief Osama bin Laden". Sikh temples and homes vandalised nationwide. A gasoline bomb tossed into a window and a three-year-old hit on the head. A woman arrested for trying to pull the turban off the head of a man at a highway rest stop. The attendant wrestles her down and his explanation coins a phrase. "Turban rage." The article ends with the following paragraph.

> An intense debate has begun among Sikhs. Should they shave off their beards and cut their hair? Should they differentiate themselves from Muslims? Or is this an act of cowardice?

Amrik reads slowly and sips his beer and orders another. The aquarium light of an airport bar in the middle of the day in America. No conversation. TV bolted to the wall above the counter.

There's no way to justify it, warriors making a virtue of fear to explain themselves to white Americans.

Don't shoot me. Shoot him. Shoot the Muslim.

He likes the way the lager is working on him. He takes a roast beef sandwich and another beer. Then he gathers his bag and newspaper and sunglasses and heads for security check. He takes his shoes off with a smile, and what's this, the security woman, is she giving him attitude?

"Sir, please don't take off your shoes until you are requested to."

"You're kidding me, right?"

"Sir, do not address me."

And there are three of them now, two men and the woman, suddenly there, all heavy in the same way, bulk without muscle or tone. And it could go any way. One word, a moment of unthinking loudness or annoyance or anger and the whole banal exchange will implode. He can see it in their faces, how pumped they are. This is what they've been training for, the chance to take down some belligerent Middle Eastern dude, take him down and put his lights out. He'll end up on the floor in a chokehold with his hands cuffed behind him. He'll end up in a room waiting to be processed, waiting indefinitely, nobody the wiser.

This is the new America. Except it isn't America at all. This is Post America, After America, the dream of equality curdled into race paranoia. Rights if you're white, otherwise you take your chances.

He weighs his course of action. He thinks of Philomena Debris and the way she moves through the world, self-contained, graced, a black sailing ship, black dignity intact in the face of whiteness, accommodation without servility. And he's thinking of a story Sukh told him about a young software engineer waiting for a flight to Boston, detained at the airport because he was speaking Tamil to his wife on his cell phone. The story ended with the software engineer in tears, saying he wouldn't do it again, would not speak to his wife in any language other than English.

Amrik apologises and puts his shoes back on.

The small shop is wedged between a florist and Joe's Pizza and the only thing that marks it is the candy stripe.

He's putting on a little weight. He hasn't been running for a few weeks and already he can feel the difference on his belly. His legs are still skinny but his stomach mirrors every questionable decision about food.

In America weight is readable and quantifiable, a system of classification.

He is wearing his navy linen suit and walking east on Twenty-Third Street toward the Flatiron. Near the Chelsea Hotel he falls into step beside a blonde woman in faded overalls and floppy hat, oversize tote hanging off her shoulder. She is immediately familiar as a figure from Somewhere, the movies or the tabloids, and she has the hipster fray and druggy sidestep waver. At the pedestrian crossing on Eighth he remembers her name is Love and just then she looks at him and he smiles.

And that is all he does, he smiles, but the effect is immediate and perilous. It cannot be taken back. It's as if he has spat on her or said something unforgivable, the way she flinches and dives into her bag. She steps off the sidewalk into the street and punches numbers into a cell phone. She is asking for assistance, for some solid buffer against the man who's probably maybe following her. A man in a turban.

He hurries on and he won't turn around to look at her. He wonders if her reaction, her rage, is purely because of his skin colour and turban in combination. His foreignness. If he had been a black man or a white man or a turbanless brown man, what would she have done with his smile?

He is on his lunch break, in search of a smoothie, no sugar, and maybe a tuna ciabatta at Zoop Soups. But he walks past Zoop to the shop at the end of the street with the revolving candy stripe. Inside he looks around as if he's never seen a barbershop in his life, and it's true, he has not.

He tells the hairdresser, short back and sides, and the entire shop watches as he unwinds the turban. There's a discussion in Russian between the hairdresser, a tall blonde in a black leather coat, and an older man working with scissors and comb on a customer. The man leaves his station and comes to stand beside the woman, his arms crossed, angling sideways to examine Amrik's hair. He and the woman speak at some length and the man offers what may be technical advice if only Amrik could follow the flat uninflected monotone. The woman shrugs extravagantly and says a single breathy word and smiles at Amrik in the mirror.

She picks up a comb and a pair of scissors and gets to work.

Just then Amrik's phone begins to ring. He checks the name on the display and holds up a finger to the blonde. For a moment, as Goody reminds him about the opening, he thinks, I forgot. Wahe guru, I forgot.

"I know it's tomorrow," he tells her. "Of course I'll be there."

4.

66 opened in Chelsea at the Gallery K. Hardesh with a party that came to be remembered as the night Xavier fell off the wagon after three and a half years of unhappy sobriety. There were girls in striped leggings and boys in short shorts and oversize sunglasses. There was a small army of older men and women in black and a contingent of Indians unique to North America, who called themselves desis and seemed out of place with their straightened hair and pressed office clothes and leather satchels. The deracinated desis were office-bearers of the South Asian Journalists Affiliation. They asked Xavier if he would appear at a panel discussion in an Indian restaurant the following week where the topic would be the emerging profile, or not, of Indian art in the United States; and meanwhile would he consent to a quick interview for the website? He agreed to everything because he'd got quickly drunk and in the photographs taken of the event he could be seen holding various drinks, some with umbrellas and some without, a rum cocktail in a long-stemmed glass, two shots of tequila (one in each hand), a short bottle of beer, and a glowing bottle of absinthe that someone had given him, possibly for promotional purposes. He had not planned to drink; that evil thought had not crossed his mind. He hadn't planned it but in the evening after some last-minute points had been cleared up with Clare – no, there was no need for a microphone or a stand because Xavier would not be making a speech; no, he would not be giving interviews; yes, it would be nice if Clare and her staff were at the door to welcome guests; no, the photographer did not have to stay all evening – after some clarity had been achieved, Goody went home to change and Xavier stepped out to smoke just as the setting sun turned the neighbourhood orange. For just one moment he felt as if he were *in* place, not out of it, and that was when someone from the catering staff asked if he would like a glass of champagne. Xavier had been asked the question and questions like it many times over the years since he had quit drinking, and he had always declined; saying no had become automatic. But this evening for the first time he heard and considered the question the young woman had asked. Would he like a glass of champagne? At the entrance to the gallery was a poster, a graphic modernist interpretation of the numerals 66, and it occurred to him that *66* might be the last show of his life, and he looked at the sunset glowing like it was the last sunset on earth, and he saw that the guests had begun to arrive with smiles on their faces and hope in their hearts, and he knew the answer to the question was yes, he wanted a glass of champagne more than anything. He picked up a flute from the tray held smilingly toward him and toasted the server and took a small deadly delicious sip.

Later in the evening because the toilet was occupied (possibly by anxiously primping desi journalists) he went out of the gallery and around the corner and urinated in an alley. When he returned the doorman wouldn't allow him in. Xavier had a cigarette in his mouth and a glass in his hand and he was fiddling with the zipper on his vintage zoot suit trousers.

"No," said the doorman.

"Is it because I'm brown and this is a respectable Caucasian gallery?"

"Sir, because you're drunk."

"My good man, do try and pay attention. If you take the Asian out of Caucasian all you're left with is cock."

And that was when the young woman who had offered him a glass in the first place – the glass that would send him spiralling toward a place he knew too well, the padded anteroom some called rock bottom – that was when the young shaman turned up at his side and took his arm and told the doorman he was the artist Newton Xavier whose work was being celebrated that evening. He let her take him up and deliver him to the Goods, who did not make a scene because she was on the phone. The scene would occur later when they were alone. For now she said something about India and passed the phone to Xavier.

"National Gallery, Delhi," said Amrik. "Confirming that they will host a retrospective three-month run with shows to follow in Bombay and Calcutta."

"Indeed," said Xavier, "but we'll fly into Bangalore and we'll travel economy. I want the difference added to my fee. First stop of the *66* tour: Delhi. Then we take Bombay, Calcutta, Madras. I want a final blowout before I retire."

"Wait a minute," said Goody, grabbing the phone. "He hates to fly and he really hates to fly economy. This is a long flight."

"He wants . . . to India," said Amrik, his voice dropping and restarting mid-word, as if he were inside a wind tunnel. " . . . ing to go there and this way he doesn't . . . to pay for it . . . you?"

"You're breaking up," said Goody.

"On my way," Amrik said, suddenly clear.

But when he got to the gallery Goody had disappeared and Xavier was at the bar drinking methodically from a bottle of champagne. The journalist Dismas was there and so was Clare from the gallery.

"It's me," said Amrik. "Back from the wilderness. With a haircut."

"Rather extreme, don't you think?" said Xavier. "You cut the hair but you left the beard. A job half done, I'd say. Alas, the . . ." He didn't finish.

Clare's words were for Xavier but she was looking at Amrik: "We've been following the reviews. There was something in the *New York Observer* this morning. The reviewer says your relationship with colour is 'contention without revelation' and some other things I honestly couldn't understand."

Xavier said, "When people comment about art they're only citing themselves, they're making, you know, allusions to their own crisis. Colour is irrelevant. Talk about terror, laugh or weep or be silent, this is when you get it right."

Clare said, "Terror."

Xavier said, "Or holiness. If neither is on offer all you're left with is boredom and that is the world of art in one good word."

He placed the half-empty bottle of champagne on the counter.

Amrik held Clare's gaze. He noticed a slight frown and laugh lines.

He said, "Newton says if the artist isn't ready to pick up a weapon he has no place in the modern world."

Clare smiled; the frown disappeared.

"Now that's the kind of news newspapers should carry," she said.

"We aligned ourselves against the Romantics," said Xavier, "against the early nineteenth century, against Shelley, 'I fall on the thorns, I bleed!' We called them effete because they were lost to ideology. We denounced their daffodils and clouds. We congratulated ourselves for not getting caught up in causes, but look at us now. After all, where has it brought us?"

Dismas watched him reach for the bottle. His fingers grazed the label but he did not pick it up.

Dismas said, "Where's Goody? I thought she'd be here."

Xavier stared at the matt wall behind him.

"She was. She isn't any more," he said.

Then he took his champagne and disappeared into the inner room.

"Do you think I could talk to you for a minute?" Dismas said. "I'm compiling an oral history of Newton and the Bombay poets and I'd love to get some input."

"What does that mean, input? One of those words," Amrik said, "I can never understand. If you ask, I'll answer, sure I will."

Dismas noticed that his suit and shirt and tie were all the same colour, charcoal grey.

"Excuse me," Amrik told Clare, "my guest has arrived."

It was Cassie Bird, resplendent in a scarlet and green cheongsam.

They had business to discuss but first things first.

"Amrik, Amrik, thanks for the photos. One minute. What happened to your hair?"

"I took some advice, I guess, went to the barber."

"You look like ten years younger."

"That's good, right? This is usually considered a good thing."

"I don't know. I have a weakness for curls. You kept the beard, I'm glad. Why trim it, though?"

"Hair grows back, Cassie."

"Not for months and years."

She checked him out, circled him and came back around and stood with her arms crossed. Given a push or a gentle nudge he thought he could fall for the way her sentences dropped into inaudibility – and the swell of her hips under the silk.

"I printed the photos and showed them to my boss and we want to run them. But we don't have a name. We don't have a thing about her."

"I didn't get a chance. I told you, she gave me the camera to hold and next thing she was gone."

"You tried to reach her."

"I tried to reach her. I put an ad in the *Voice* and in the *Times*. Nothing, not a bite, and the thing is, if she were to walk in the door I don't even know if I'd recognise her."

"We'll tell the story just the way you told it to me. The images are addictive, almost pornographic. The stalled traffic, people running for their lives, panicked cyclists and tourists and behind them that mountainous white cloud. Not everybody's running though, some people are frozen in place, talking or staring and there she is in the middle of it all, taking pictures."

"I wonder what she was looking for in the bag."

"When you look at the photos serially? There's a kind of a charge, like documentary footage, war photography, something."

"The day the twentieth century ended."

"Do you think it's true that the first year tells you what the rest of the century will be like?"

"Let's see, mass murder as national narrative, earthquakes, the global rise of the racist right. What else?"

"Violence as performance art, the Chinese revolution and the Russian, technology that will help us know everything and live for ever."

They heard an aeroplane, too close, the ocean paying a visit. Amrik examined the scuffed panels of the floor, intently listening.

"We'll run the pictures and make an appeal. You could try talking to a sketch artist. Try and remember what she looked like. We'll run a portrait of her too."

"What I remember, she was there and then she was gone."

"The lost photographer of September Eleven."

"The loss photographer. And listen, since you're here."

He gestured at the profusion of styles around them – mixed media nudes, self-portraits, landscapes, cityscapes, line drawings, colour field abstracts, heads, still lifes, crucifixion studies, portraits of saints – and led her to the wall he loved the most, taken up by a single oil on canvas, *Man and Woman Dreaming*, the faces like giant African wood masks, the bodies flat planes of colour against a sky of blue rust, the necks punctured by ornate daggers plunged to the hilt; but there was something in the way the palette knife and the brush had been used that pulled away from the violence of the painting toward serenity or understanding, something he could not put a name to and would never speak of with Xavier.

"Always working, right?" Cassie said. "That's me too. Now tell me something, how does a lady get a drink around here?"

He could not move or speak or place his glass on the floor or ask someone to help him to a chair. His bones felt loose and his thoughts were ponderous and blurry and pleasurable. This was the point of drink, to be a two-legged ape leaning against a wall, all faculties lost except the mixed blessing of hearing. And because he was unable to move out of earshot he was captive to a conversation among the desis. A woman with a pair of chopsticks in her hair said it all came down to the silly question of us versus them. South Asians did not try hard enough to be us and so they stayed them. It was the permanent foreigner syndrome, she said, drawing quotes in the air. It was their mistake; they needed to make sure they were on the right side of history. A tall woman with animal print horn-rims said there was a hierarchy of belonging among Asian-Americans. Even if we're not bigots we all of us attach scripts to people, she said. It's true, someone else said, like if I've had a good meal at a Chinese restaurant I'll tell my Chinese friends about it. The woman with the chopsticks said, what I hate is when some fresh-off-the-boater asks where I'm really from. From here, where else? I'm from Brooklyn or the Bronx or Queens. I'm from Jackson Heights, that's my answer. You mean Jaikishen Heights, said the woman with the horn-rims. That's the oldest one in the book, said a white man with eyebrow piercings, but seriously, immigration shaped this country. We should welcome immigrants with open arms. Not always, the woman with the chopsticks said. Some people shouldn't be allowed into your home or your country.

They don't integrate. They don't assimilate. There is a hierarchy of belonging even among immigrants. The question is, do you as an immigrant know your responsibility to your host country? Your host country has responsibilities too, said the man with the piercings. Did you know South Asian prisoners are the fastest-growing community in American prisons? The Patriot Act is racist legislation at its most overt. What has it done, other than the masculinisation of Giuliani and Bush? What will the Coalition do in Baghdad, other than the masculinisation of Cheney and Bush? Oh, said the woman with the horn-rims, you finally said the four-letter word. I was wondering how long it would take. The man said, this is a critical moment. It's not an adequate defence to say I'm not Indian, I'm Caribbean, don't shoot me. Or to say, I'm not Muslim, I'm Hindu. But, said the woman with the chopsticks in her hair, I am Hindu. I'm not Muslim. I have nothing against blacks or Muslims but the fact remains that I am neither. Check who you're shooting at before you shoot. The man said, I can't believe you just said that. And they all started to speak at once.

Much later he sat at a table in the gallery's private office. People went in and out of the room. Someone had put a plate of pasta in front of him and a glass of red wine and when he took a sip he felt every drink he'd taken that evening settle like metal in his legs. He would have trouble getting up. In for a centime, in for a franc, he said aloud, and drank the wine and asked for another. Goody was nowhere to be seen and neither was Amrik or Clare or even Dismas. At the table were people he didn't know, among them a blond man in a blue blazer and a woman with a veil. Although the veil was sheer Xavier could make out little of her features, other than the fact that she was pretty or had been pretty. When she started to speak the room fell silent. She was from an Emirate in the Gulf, a society lady whose charity events were reported widely in the local press. When she mentioned the name of her father's scandal-ridden bank some of the people on the table looked at her carefully because they had heard that it would soon close down. Her sister had married a sheikh, she said, a man whose passions were falconry and racing, a man who already had six wives. The lady's sister became the seventh and youngest. The wedding was held at a fashionable London hotel, the grounds of which the sheikh had transformed into an Arabian desert with sand trucked in from Cornwall. Here he raced camels imported to London and jockeyed by Bombay street boys, also imported. Before the wedding the sheikh's wives and wife-to-be were prepared by a hair-and-make-up man whose two female assistants were expert manicurists. The make-up man was a Pakistani, London born. He touched the lady's sister's hair and lips and cheeks. He looked in the lady's sister's face, though he didn't see her true image but her reflection in the make-up mirror and when their eyes met, he flinched. During the ceremony the young Pakistani stood in the front row with his arms crossed. He stared at the sheikh's seventh bride with such an imploring look that she left the celebration early and told her husband she was tired and she would wait for him in their suite. Late that night the sheikh's second wife came to the lady's sister's room and escorted her through the service section of the hotel to a suite she had never before seen, where the fittings and furniture were similar to the items in her own suite but soiled somehow. The older wife was a Bahraini woman in her fifties and she motioned to the lady's sister to be quiet. They were in a kind of anteroom and by parting the heavy drapes they could see into the suite, which was full of the sheikh's security staff who took turns to sodomise the make-up man. The Pakistani lay across the arm of a couch while the men waited in line to rape him. After each man was done, he wiped off, zipped up and left the room. The Pakistani's shoulders were pinned to the couch and he was stained with blood and semen and he seemed to be unconscious. The lady's sister watched the rape of the only man to look into her eyes other than her father and her husband and she felt a terrible stirring that she did not recognise. It was late by then, the celebrations were over and the guests had left. The lady's sister thought about her room at home and wondered what her sisters were doing, whether they had eaten, whether her father was silent and anxious as usual, or in a happy mood and optimistic about the future, as he had been when she was a small girl and her father had seemed to her like a god capable of anything. Then the Bahraini wife took the lady's sister back through the hotel's secret inner passageways, unventilated corridors that the guests never saw, where the walls were scarred unpainted concrete and the light was dim, by the service elevator to the top floor and from a service entrance into another suite, her husband's bedroom, where the older wife left the new wife alone. When the sheikh arrived the lady's sister was waiting for him on the bed and they made love until dawn, when, exhausted, he fell asleep. There was blood on the sheets and her husband's penis was smeared with blood and semen and she thought of the men who had raped the Pakistani and she woke up her husband so he would take her again.

The lady looked around the table for a few minutes. Then she said, the question I wish to ask you is why my sister stayed with the sheikh. Why didn't she escape? After all, her father was an important man who would have protected her at any cost. At this the man in the blazer said the lady's sister was biding her time because she wanted to wait until she had accumulated the resources she would need to escape her powerful husband. The lady said nothing. She looked at Xavier who sat motionless, the pasta untouched on his plate, a thin sheen of sweat on his upper lip. His eyes had not strayed from a portrait of a woman in a burkha on the floor of a room lit only by oil lamps, *D_____, Bombay, 1982*. It had not been offered for sale. The woman in the picture was smoking a pipe that was also her penis.

Why didn't she leave? the lady asked again.

Because, Xavier said, even if by some slim chance you escaped your husband and went to a country where nobody knew you, your father, who lost everything in the crash of his bank, would offer your sisters to the sheikh in your place. But that isn't the only reason you stayed. The real reason, the important one, is this. When your husband came into the room and took off your clothes you understood that the thing you felt when you watched the rape of the Pakistani was desire, not for the Pakistani but for your husband, for the power he held and for the way he desired you, and you wanted him to do to you what you had watched his men do to the Pakistani. That is the reason you stayed and continue to stay.

The lady laughed and gathered her things but the blond man in the blazer was too angry to move. He said Xavier treated the world as if it was insane because he saw himself in everything and he was undoubtedly out of his mind. For the first time since the lady had begun to speak Xavier's eyes slid off the picture on the wall and came to rest on her.

He said, "If you ever want your portrait painted, do let me know."

Of the forty-one pictures exhibited at the opening thirty-six were sold, said Amrik on the phone the following day. Xavier was subdued, nursing a hangover that had left him mute and susceptible to religious trembling. It was good that the paintings sold quickly, Amrik said, because the reviews had started to come in and they were uniformly negative except for the desi papers whose articles weren't reviews as much as ecstatic notices of 'South Asian' achievement. The blond man in the blazer, it turned out, was the art critic of the *New York Times*. His review, titled *Portrait of the Artist as an Old Skell*, accused Xavier of engaging in the kind of street-corner hustle that had become obsolete in Rudy Giuliani's New York, the kind of hustle New Yorkers had devised multiple strategies to identify and bypass. The critic ended his three-paragraph report by saying Xavier's years in the wilderness famously suffering from artist's block or alcoholic dementia or just plain laziness had ruined him for good, had wrung out of him whatever talent he'd had as a young man, had left him old and used up and as dead as his work. *Time Out New York* didn't bother with a review but had an item in the listings page, without an image, that described the show as an Indian eccentric's last huzzah. The *New Yorker* carried a mention on its website though not in the print edition. It was a studiously non-committal paragraph that said nothing, positive or negative. Only the *Wall Street Journal* carried a review longer than two hundred and fifty words. The reviewer seemed knowledgeable about Xavier's career and asked whether the paintings were clever forgeries made with the connivance of the artist. He said they had no artistic merit or interest, except to scholars of the art of forgery. And after all, this is what it was, an art, though whether it was one of any value was a question that would have to be decided by art historians and philosophers. As far as the reviewer went – and it wasn't far because unlike his colleagues in the *New York Times* and the *New Yorker*, he was not ideologically committed to everything Newton Francis Xavier produced simply because he had at one time been part of the Trotskyite-Anarchist Bombay collective that called itself the Progressive Autists Group – as far as the reviewer went, *66* was a future virus that signalled the end of honour. He said the show was an act of violence by a master criminal whose own talents had long been squandered in the pursuit of wine, women, and vertigo, whose contention that art cannot save and pure art was impossible made frightening sense in a world where the pursuit of purity had led to endless bloodshed. It was an important review but no one in the art world or at least no one who mattered read the *Wall Street Journal* and even if they did they would not admit to it; and so the most potentially damaging accusation aimed at Xavier during this period went unremarked.

One evening in the fall of 2003 Xavier sat on the stoop of a converted storefront on Christie Street. His skin had a grey tinge as if he had not washed in days. He leaned against the railing and slept for some time but he opened his eyes when Dismas Bambai said his name. He pulled himself up. Ah no, thought Dismas, here we go. He's come to have it out and demand an explanation or a duel. Speaking in an exaggerated nicotine whisper Xavier said that Goody had kicked him out of the house. Could he trouble Dismas for a place to stay? Inside the apartment he asked for beer. Do you like them, he said, handing Dismas his sunglasses. His eyes were bloody and pouched in black silk.

"I gave myself a treat," he said. "Would you like to venture a guess as to how much?"

"I don't know. Forty dollars?"

"Try two hundred and forty!"

Dismas only shook his head.

"Forty is a knock-off from Canal, my good man. Does this look like a knock-off? Well?"

"Sorry but it does? Some of those copies are pretty real."

"Some copies are real. Truer words," Xavier said. "Now then, to the news of the day. She's had enough, says she can't take it. Told me to come back when and if I got sober. Hellish scenario if she's serious. I mean, beyond disastrous, a complete fuckaroo. All my work is there and why wouldn't it be? The apartment is mine. I shall have to evict her or patch it up and both options strike me as decidedly hard work. Quelle horreur!"

Dismas went to the Spanish grocery on the corner and bought some long-necked bottles of beer and a carton of milk. Xavier drank the beer like medicine, all four bottles, while telling a story about Goody's parents.

He had met them once in Delhi. Goody's stepfather, a retired doctor, suffered from a mysterious bronchial ailment that no physician had been able to diagnose and he spent several weeks of the year in a hospital unable to breathe without a machine. Stepfather Lol made it plain that he didn't approve of his daughter's much-married lover – he always called Goody his daughter, while Goody insisted he was her stepfather and her real father had left when she was little; all she remembered about her father were inconsequential details, for example that he wore white kurta-pyjamas – and Stepfather Lol took pains to mention that her lover was older than he. On his way out Xavier took Lol by the elbow and told him in a confidential tone that sex was the thing that kept men and women together. He said there was a reason why he had a young girlfriend and Lol did not.

"I can fuck," he said, "and you cannot."

He told Lol that his *step*daughter was a student of the human impulse, her subject being men and women, and women and women, and men and men, and the prodigious thing they had in common. He said that he, Xavier, had made it his subject too, or one of his subjects, which is why he and Goody got along as well as they did and why their sex was nothing less than incandescent. But why was he saying all this to Lol, who knew his stepdaughter's sex? Lol, said Xavier, was a tall man with a full head of white hair and a pale Brahmin face. Xavier could see the effect of his words, though the man's expression was mostly hidden behind a beard. I lost it, Xavier told Dismas. I admit it freely, I lost it and I was ashamed of myself. I called and apologised but the incident has somewhat coloured our subsequent interactions. He's never forgotten.

And what I'm saying, Bombayman, the point I'm making is that I didn't forget either. Her stepfather, I have to say, is a prick! You've heard the saying, if you want to know what a woman will be like take a look at her parents? Well, let's hope Goody turns out like Mrs not Mr Lol, Xavier told Dismas as he finished the beer and went loudly to sleep.

The next morning Dismas went to work and when he got home that night Xavier was asleep again. He'd changed into a pair of kurta-pyjamas and tidied the house. He had arranged the books, sending fiction and poetry to separate shelves. In the morning Xavier was deep into *The Prison Journals* by Q Ball Li and he was unusually communicative.

He said, "And where, pray, did you pick up this bit of social history?"

"Old Li? He's a Chinatown figure, a living Bowery ghost. I met him back when he was using. He's part of the lore of downtown and he gave me the book in lieu of a debt."

"I find it somewhat difficult to trust junkies as a rule but I must say there is something about these journals. I've been looking at them all morning. The best chapter for my money is the one composed entirely of food entries, what he ate at which time of day and what he drank, each item recorded like an entry in a cash ledger. It seems to me a kind of aphoristic spiritual text, if you see what I mean. Because it hints at the meaning of life without being didactic and much like life each entry ends the same way."

"With a ritual."

"For example,

13 October.

8 a.m.: 2 corn fritters, 2 eggs scrambled in bacon fat, instant coffee with milk.

11 a.m.: Glass of cold lemonade from a Mason jar, the bluish quart jars they no longer make.

2 p.m.: Green apple, half a farmer's loaf & avocado with olive oil, lime juice, salt & pepper.

4 p.m.: Black tea with milk, 2 squares dark chocolate.

8 p.m.: Goat cheese on rye, sliced tomato with salt & olive oil.

8.30 p.m.: Cigarette."

That evening Dismas found the room had been vacuumed and Xavier's sleeping space cleared. His towel was in the clothes hamper and his toothbrush removed from the communal bathroom down the hall. There was a note on the fridge. "Thanks for the hospitality. You may treat this note as an IOU redeemable the next time we meet, the note, that is, not you, or, for that matter, yours truly, X." A postscript had been added in pencil: "She isn't YOUR wife! You're off your onion & the poem sucks bollocks!" In the closet was a parting gift. A plastic bag with two empties of vodka and half a dozen bottles of beer, also empty, and a set of kurta-pyjamas streaked with shit and vomit. Also in the bag was the poem Dismas had not intended anyone to see. How had Xavier located it in its hiding place deep in a shoebox of printouts? How much snooping had the old man done?

Written in rhyming couplets reminiscent of a ghazal, though without the ghazal's formal complexity, the poem's narrator was a man who lived in a watchtower on top of a cliff. From the watchtower he had a view of the ocean and the rivers that fed into it. He watched the slow boats that travelled from town to town. Some of the riverboats had lights strung across the top deck, coloured lights that blinked on and off in a monotonous distracting pattern; and if the night was calm the narrator heard tiny music made by toy instruments, no melody or harmony but notes that followed one after the other without urgency or emotion. He grew to despise the music and on some nights he shut his ears with cotton wool, which served only to heighten the general agitation of his nerves. Then he would apply himself more intensely to the duties required of him: to warn the townspeople of any changes in the patterns of water and air and to look for unusual tidal formations or anything that might appear as a portent.

As time passed he did his job to the exclusion of everything else and soon he became convinced that a great upheaval was coming. He felt sorry for those who would be swept away. Often he slept in a room at the top of the watchtower and his wife brought him food and if sometimes she forgot he would go hungry for a night. With no one to talk to, his eyes were his only source of contact with the world and they provided him with the sounds and images he substituted for nourishment and his wife's companionship.

That year the monsoons failed and the comings and goings of the boats became more frequent. He could see the people of the towns gather along the coast and the riverbank. There was general distress among them and he knew more privations were ahead. The fishing boats went out even when the seas were rough. More items were shipped in from other towns, often at substantial cost. The farmers were the worst hit. They lived from hand to mouth in any case and the loss of their yearly crop meant a season of hunger was on its way. Some killed themselves in the hope that the government would give their wives and children monetary compensation that would last until the next monsoon. Sometimes entire families poisoned themselves, parents, grandparents, and small children. When the authorities came they found a room in which there were so many dead the officials had to put handkerchiefs to their noses and take shallow breaths. All the while the government's advertising campaigns continued to talk of the giant strides the nation had made in global business. It had become, they said, a beacon of light, a leader in the field of ideating, making, and spiritual technology.

When it happened, there was no warning at all, unless you took into account the agitation of the birds. From his lookout point at the height of the tower he watched the crows fly in circles as if they would dash themselves against the trees. The dogs began to whine and run inland. He took the plugs out of his ears and shouted for his wife and he kept his eyes on the horizon. He saw a hole in the ocean that seemed to fill and swirl. He saw the water recede from the shore and the townspeople run after it to retrieve coins and photographs, lost engagement rings, the bones of drowned friends, a car that had rolled off a ferry, a piano, a small aeroplane. As they crowded around these objects he did what he'd been trained to: he set off the watchtower siren. But by then there was too much commotion and not enough time for the warning to make a difference. And in any case the townspeople had forgotten the meaning of the siren. It had been too long since they had heard it ring.

In the last couplets of the long poem the narrator leaves his post and runs toward the ocean. The water keeps receding and the people keep running, idiotically, picking up whatever treasure is left in its wake. He sees an old woman fill the skirt of her dress with the fish that flop on the dry ocean bed. He sees a group of boys playing on the hull of a long sunken submarine. He shouts the name of his wife.

Goody, he cries. Goody.

But the wave gathered into the shape of a giant fist; he wept when he saw there was no one he could save.

One morning in the late fall on his way to work Dismas Bambai descended the stairs to the subway and caught a sharp stink of funk and urine. He walked past a man drinking beer from a tall can, drinking deeply, his hoodie pulled low. His wet parka sported lighter burns and black grease streaks but his sneakers were spotless.

"A quarter for a phone call," the man said. "I mean, a dollar, a dollar's what I need."

His voice was hoarse and papery with smoke and when he laughed his gums showed pink against the ash of his skin. Dismas envied the man. At eight a.m. on a weekday morning he was taking pleasure in a beer. The day was ahead of him to do with as he wished, to destroy or repair or fritter away; and not once would he have to gaze upon the cadaverous face of Mrs Merchant.

A sunless morning, sky the colour of smudged kajal, already cold though it was only October. The city had just had the shortest summer on record. In May there was old slush on the streets, July and August were hot, and now a chill was in the air. It seemed to him that winter had stayed all year round. And it was only a matter of time before the immigration authorities came to collect their debt.

At Madison Square Park he saw a man sprawled on a bench with coffee and the day's newspapers and he experienced another jab of envy.

He took the elevator up to *Indian Angle* and punched in, hoping to slip out as soon as an opening presented itself. But it was production day and he had to send off the Immigrant Agony page and the Immigrant Lawyer page needed to be formatted. The editor also wanted a quick story on an actor who had a role in an upcoming Hollywood movie. The actor played a cabbie and had one line. "Everything all right with you, my man?" But such was *Indian Angle*'s excitement that the story rated a thousand words on the front page.

"But he plays a Pakistani," Dismas told Mrs Merchant.

"I don't care if he plays the ukulele. Try and do a decent job. His parents are friends of mine. Nobody else is here, that's why I'm asking you."

Pereira arrived late and as soon as he was seated he picked up the phone and called Dismas. They sat at adjoining desks but Mrs Merchant did not allow employees to talk among themselves.

"Chinese?" Pereira said. "You go. I want Kung Pao Chicken and spring rolls!"

One of them would go first and order a meal for two. They would eat together but return to the office separately. The editor didn't like to see her employees going out for lunch. What if they talked about her? Worse, what if they enjoyed themselves?

Pereira hung up first and cradled his head in his hairy hands. The walnut skin on his hairless skull gleamed with oil and his fingernails were scored with diabetic ridges.

Dismas Bambai's hand was still on the phone when it rang again, Mrs Merchant with a summons, and when he looked up he saw her signalling urgently through the glass.

She had a lot to say and most of it concerned herself.

"I am shocked and disappointed, obviously," she said, applying moisturiser on the webs of her bony hands. "Shocked. Disappointed."

For some reason she smiled, showing yellow teeth in which the fillings were of a different, whiter colour.

"I should have known better than to hire someone without references. If nothing else it shows an appalling lack of honesty on your part."

She had had a call from the police about Dismas's arrest. The officer said the drug bust was fairly minor and Dismas had received a suspended sentence, but his work status would have to be reviewed.

Mrs Merchant shook her head slowly, a dreamy look on her face.

"You can continue here until the end of the month but after that we'll have to let you go," she said. "I can't afford trouble with immigration, I can't, cannot."

She applied a minuscule amount of moisturiser to each finger.

"I keep telling myself it could be worse," she added, "it could be the tax guys. Compared to them immigration's a walk in Madison Square Park."

Pereira and Dismas had lunch at Hong Kong Best Taste on Sixth Avenue. Because it was the end of the week they had beer. The small table wobbled when Pereira picked up a spring roll with his chopsticks and dipped it into the chilli sauce. He held the roll in front of him, his hairy blunt hands only slightly unsteady.

"Let us take pleasure in this good spring roll fried deep and fast, as Chinese as anything you may find so far north of Chinatown and so far west of China," he said, before taking a bite.

He chewed happily with his eyes closed.

He swallowed, smiled shyly, and said, "Kung hey fat choi."

"Kung hey fat choi to you too," said Dismas. "But it isn't New Year just yet."

"You know," Pereira said, taking a deep draught of his beer, "I wasn't always a journalist. There was a time I wanted to be a playback singer."

Here he broke off to sing, softly and tunefully, a Hindi song from the hit seventies movie *Sagar*.

Sagar jaise ankhon wali,
Yeh toh bataa tere naam kya?

"I had an idea. I thought I would do an album of Hindi movie songs translated into English. I'd keep intact the melody and the rhyme and all of the jauntiness. For example, the *Sagar* tune would go like this:

You whose eyes are like the sea
Tell me what your name might be."

"Fantastic," said Dismas, clapping softly.

"It's not bad but I had enough sense to know I was not a brilliant singer. So I wrote about singers instead, and movies, and Indians dead in America. Not that I'm complaining. It's a better way of making a living than being out in the world."

Dismas took a sip of his beer. There would only be the one and then they would rush back to work, returning separately to their desks.

"Now, you," said Pereira. "You are a different story entirely."

"What do you mean?"

"Can't you see?" Pereira said. "Can't you see into the future?"

"No," said Dismas, taken aback. "I'm trying to keep my head above water and I'm not doing a very good job of it."

Pereira looked carefully at Dismas and nodded.

"You're doing fine," he said. "And you really don't know about yourself?"

"Know what?"

"Since you ask, let me tell you. You are a writer. You were always meant to be a writer. All of this," he waved his chopsticks around the restaurant and toward the street, "this is your apprenticeship."

The noise of the lunchtime crowd quietened and Dismas saw himself for a moment from the outside; and the restaurant he was in, the job he held, the city in which he lived, all of it receded to a distance he could not bridge.

"It's a vocation and a curse," said Pereira, lifting his glass once more. "Full many are called but few are chosen. When it brings you fame and riches, when that happens, remember who said it first."

They touched glasses and drank deeply and then Pereira sat back with his eyes downcast and finished his meal in silence. They said no more about it but for years afterwards Dismas remembered what Pereira had said; and though it brought him no second sight, no snapshot of the future, it revealed to him the deep seam of unhappiness in his friend's heart.

When he returned to his desk Pereira was bent over his keyboard, already working. Dismas stared at his computer screen, blank but for the single sentence he'd written that day. He could see Mrs Merchant in her cabin gesticulating at Sheri-from-the-Islands. The end of the month was three weeks away; suddenly it seemed a long time to wait for the small paycheque he would receive. He printed out an email from his office account. He picked up his backpack and put away the books on his desk – travel guides to the United States and India, Xavier's second and last book of poems, *Saint Me*, a new biography of Dr Ambedkar, a small pile of Moleskines. He packed his Cross chrome ballpoint, the PalmPilot he had splurged on but rarely used, and a bottle of Eternity stashed in a drawer. Everything else he left untouched; he left the computer running; he spoke to no one.

From the deli he picked up a sandwich and a bottle of water and walked to the park. The man he had seen that morning was on his knees on the grass, feeding the squirrels with crumbs collected in a Burger King bag. Dismas found a bench not far from him and ate his sandwich. Later he walked to Union Square. He bought Fruit of the Loom T-shirts and a pair of black and chrome Air Jordans. They would be the last purchases he would make for a time. He drank an espresso macchiato and ate a croissant at a counter from where he watched the workers hurrying to and from their jobs, and he had a long overdue insight. He understood that leisure was the most expensive commodity on the planet, so rare a thing that the wealthy could not afford it. No one could, except the homeless and the deranged. He remembered Pereira's words.

This is my apprenticeship.

What would he write? He would work on two books simultaneously. He already had a title in mind for the first, *The Loathed*, about the poets of Bombay in the eighties and nineties. It would centre around Nissim Ezekiel, Arun Kolatkar, and Dom Moraes. The other book would be an oral biography of the painter and defunct poet Newton Francis Xavier. He would use the interviews he had conducted years ago in India and the new information he had uncovered. He would conduct more interviews and update the material. It would be a biography like no other; he would make of his subject a window from which to view a broken society and a vanished literature. That night he turned the alarm clock off and slept ten hours. The uninterrupted sleep and the morning sun made him hopeful. He made a phone call and took the subway uptown.

Xavier came to the door wearing a Burberry trench over pyjamas and a new pair of dark glasses.

"I came to say goodbye, I know you'll be leaving pretty soon."

Xavier nodded, distracted, a man with important things on his mind.

"I have a message for you from an old friend. First things first, you never told me if the Marys are yours or not. I mean, I did bring them all the way from India."

"I didn't, did I? Well, so it goes."

"Aren't you going to let me in?"

"I think not."

"But why not? You're leaving soon. I thought I'd come and say goodbye. I'm trying to make the appropriate noises."

"Everybody leaves. I've been making periodic trips to India mostly for art-related reasons. Lately they've been few and far between because I do hate to fly. It seems to me this is as good a reason as any for an extended visit. In any case, I've never been appropriate. Goodbye is a bit excessive, if you see what I mean."

"X, you're a cold bastard."

"I am cold to the cold-hearted. What message?"

He looked like he'd just woken up. Clearly he would keep Dismas waiting at the door like a salesman. Why had he come?

"A message from Benny Time, the televangelist?"

Xavier took off his sunglasses and put one end to his purple lips. He looked past Dismas into a distance.

"He saw my interview with you in *Indian Angle* and got in touch the old-fashioned way, by handwritten letter."

"Benny's not an old-fashioned fellow."

"Actually it wasn't much of a message. Says he's been trying to contact you and you don't answer emails."

"Goody's supposed to do that but she forgets from time to time."

"He didn't say what it was about. Mentioned that you were schoolmates. He was your agent for a bit in London and you painted his portrait."

Dismas gave him the email he had printed out and Xavier folded it and put it away without looking at the contents. He put his sunglasses on and searched the pockets of the trench for a cigarette.

"Super, and what's old Benn up to these days?"

"He's on the road a lot. He has the look of a man who relies on tanning salons and well-paid personal trainers, or at least that's what he looks like on the Internet. He's famous."

"He always did have that look. Benny has been famous, you see, for a long time."

"He read that you're going to India and he wants you to come to his event in Bangalore. He wants to see you in person. His contact details are in the email."

"Good. If he's in India I might have a job for him. Perhaps I'll ask him to stage the *66* opening party. He's rather good at that sort of thing."

He patted his pockets once again and turned around to look into the apartment. Dismas wondered if Goody was inside.

Xavier said, "I suppose we are old friends, the operative word being 'old' not 'friend'. Benn's friendships are need-based. He commissioned two paintings from me, portraits of himself. One official and one secret."

"With clothes and without?"

"Well done. Now, if that's it."

"Don't let me take any more of your time?"

Xavier shrugged exaggeratedly.

"There is one more thing. I've been thinking of writing your biography. I want to ask your permission and make it official."

"No, thank you," said Xavier, without so much as a moment's hesitation.

"It might be worth your while."

"I can't stop you from writing whatever you wish to, but let me be clear. The answer is officially no."

They stared at each other for a moment. As Dismas turned to go, Xavier unwisely spoke and in time the speech would find its way into print.

"One last thing," he said. "I wouldn't sell those paintings if I were you. Authorised forgeries are a separate category of artistic endeavour from fakes. They have nothing in common with mere copies. A forgery takes skill and imagination to execute and is usually made by a good artist, though perhaps not a great one. A forgery has its own value quite separate from the value of a fake. What I mean is that even after it has been unmasked a forgery carries some intrinsic value for a collector. I'd point you toward certain well-known individuals who collect forgeries and whose collections are enjoyed only in private. Such a collector will pay a substantial price for a forgery, much more than the inconsequential sum you paid for the Two Marys. Why do they collect forgeries? For one, they do not buy all forgeries, only those they recognise as exceptional, that is, a forgery in which the artist has painted something new, something that did not exist previously, and painted it in the style of a master who may or may not know about it. For another, I really must be going."

Dismas remembered the Polaroid picture in Goody's apartment, the intricate work she had done, the way she had inhabited Xavier's style. And who had painted the Marys? Xavier had hinted but he had clarified nothing.

At no point in the conversation did Dismas mention that he had left his job and would be returning to India.

Fireflies appeared the week he was leaving, fat city fireflies lit up like ocean liners. He went for long walks and in the evening he would see them cruising the avenues. Some afternoons he started at the Bowery end of Spring Street, the Chinatown end with the lighting and signage and restaurant supply stores; from there he walked to West Street by the river. He liked Spring Street because it was short and manageable: you could go from one end to the other in twenty minutes. He walked past the boutiques and galleries, past the Fire Museum, past Balthazar's red awning, past stolid cast-iron buildings and the modest James Brown House, which was not named after the singer and was loomed over if not cowed down by a giant glass structure; and for much of the walk he was accompanied by fireflies, pinpoints of yellow light that did not dance away when he approached. At Lahore Deli, a Pakistani cabbies' hangout, he took a seat at a plastic-topped table and watched Hindi movie songs on television and ate kheema-roti. The kheema was covered in a deep layer of golden-brown oil. When he stepped out of the restaurant the fireflies were gone.

One night he carried his writing desk to the street. He placed it on the sidewalk against a tree and placed a chair in front it. He brought down a box of odds and ends and put on the desk. Then he returned to the storefront studio he'd occupied for two years. The view from the window did not alter whatever the season, a stretch of dirty sidewalk, cars and litter blowing on the road, a few silent pedestrians, and on the weekend young drunks and the chaos they loved. It was difficult to think of it as a street in a first-world city. He watched a couple stop by the tree. The man wore the straw cowboy hat fashionable that year, curled at the sides and dipping deeply at the brim. Without exchanging a word, he picked up the desk and the girl took the chair and they were on their way. The furniture had been on the sidewalk for less than twenty minutes. Next came a man walking a bicycle, which he leaned against a no-parking sign. He went to the box of household discards and opened a bottle of olive oil and took a whiff and returned it to the box. He read the label on a bottle of mango pickle and he examined a bathroom rug and a box of detergent and shower curtains, but he took only a bottle of Ayurvedic liver medicine, which he placed carefully in a pocket of his cargoes. Though it was late in the evening he put on his sunglasses, and he climbed on his bicycle and rode away. Then Dismas saw a tall figure in a thick Kashmiri shawl, a man who looked like a professor at a North Indian university. By then nothing was left of Dismas's belongings except the box of discards. The professor took off his glasses to read the label on the bottle of pickle. He sniffed the contents. He examined nothing else but he took the box. He was seventy at least, tall and stooped and embarrassed.

Years later when describing the evening in the overly eloquent and sentimental style he favoured, Dismas wrote that he had been "overcome by the anxiety, the sadness, the grip of first-world poverty, the loneliness and lack of certitude, the hooded figures and blank winter-bitten faces, the week of work and the waiting for the weekend, the misery of New York City, the misery we carried like birthrights, all of us who were adrift in America and aching for the world".

BOOK THREE

Of What Use Is a Poem that Cannot Pick Up a Gun?

Saint Gandhi

of Porbunder; in darker South Africa,
saw the light when travelling by train;
wore only homespun;
gave up salt & sex; so tragic a

man, who split a nation
in two; befriended apocalypse;
died with the name of God on his lips;
shot by a man with God in his name.

Saint Arun

the Comeback Kid; of Colaba,
undisputed master;
patron of pi-dogs, disaster,
kittens & ogresses; of gulab, a

scholar; economical with pages;
advertising man; joined no schools;
wrote in two languages,
bhakti & the blues; did not suffer fools.

from *The Book of Chocolate Saints: Poems* (Unpublished)

Rama Raoer, former professor of English Literature, Bombay University, interviewed by Dismas Bambai at Dolly Mansions, near Dadar Station, March 2005

I'm sorry, I forgot. Give me a moment. Yes, yes, coconut oil, I cover myself with it and leave it on for a few hours. Old age is an indignity. That's the main thing. Indignity and humiliation and the stripping away of everything that makes for individual personality. It is as if you're part of a psychological experiment by the CIA and the KGB working together. And on that happy note I will take your leave. I'm going to have my bath and then we'll have tea on the balcony in the heat. Fine? See you in a minute, meaning half an hour. You can dip into the books; you can dip but you can't borrow.

Right then, let's start. I don't mean to be a diva but what to do, I am what I is. Doss and I went drinking one day, first to Turquoise, the dance bar on Grant Road, and then to White Horse in Tardeo and finally we landed up at Café Royal opposite the Regal. You must know the place. Now it's all respectable tablecloths and subdued lighting but back then it was a dive. It was rough and rumble tumble and the quiet fellow at the next table could have been a hit man for the Dongri mafia or a real estate tycoon or an accounts executive with a Nariman Point ad agency. I ordered the Mahim Creek, which is a big mug of strong beer, Khajuraho or Cannon or even Gurkha if you can get it, and into the beer you drop a shot glass of DSP or Solan or some other whisky, any whisky so long as it's cheap. A bunch of those and you're killed. You're gone. You're maroed. It's the old three-step. Ao. Bajao. Jao. That day I introduced him to the Mahim Creek and soon he made it part of his image as you know. Those pictures of him at the Casbah with a shot and a beer, that was me, I taught him how to do that. And it was thanks to me he came up with the name for the anthology. Not that I'm expecting any credit, however delayed and denied and deserved. I'm letting you know and that's all.

I liked him, Doss, and it's possible I was trying to impress him. I've always liked the awkward young men and I'm no casteist, god no. I like boys, circumcised, uncircumcised, washed, unwashed, touchable, untouchable, straight, bent, curved, I mean, it's all love, isn't it, in the end?

After a while I told Doss my Allen Ginsberg story. I met Allen when he read on a terrace in Cumballa Hill with Gary Snyder and Peter Orlovsky. Afterwards we walked to Nissim Ezekiel's flat and some of us Bombay poets read our work, Ezekiel and Adil Jussawalla and R. Parthasarathy and Lancelot Ribeiro and yours truly. We read our poems – in English, what else? – and then it all went to hell. Ginsberg and his company of Beats thought we were terrible. Conventional and derivative, they said. Harsh words and untrue, for what work of art is not derived from another? Which Ginsberg is not derived from some Whitman? Allen – I think I can call him that, after all he did make a pass – was visibly unimpressed by our efforts and this disappointed us no end. Especially because after us some of the Urdu poets read and that was another story entirely. Allen and Peter, his lovely boy, they sat at the feet of the Urduwallahs, oohing and aahing, ready to kiss the hems of their pyjamas. Of course they didn't understand a word of Urdu. Except maybe for, Wah! Oh, and the references to Marx and Chaplin, references our Beat judge and jury did not approve of either. Not exotic enough for them. This was the secret of the Beats. Inside the scruffy lazy bullshit bohemianism they were blatant Orientalists. Hypocrite moralists. The western gaze at its creepiest and most wide-eyed! They were full of compliments for the Urduwallahs and for us they had only insults. Peter leaned toward me and said, if we was gangster poets we'd shoot you dead, man! Allen took me aside and said the world had changed too much to be writing old-fashioned colonial pomes in English. Then, as if it was the most natural thing in the world, he took me back to the lavish Malabar Hill apartment he was living in. The King of the Beats living in the lap of luxury! I use the word 'lap' advisedly. For a long time after that night I considered making a T-shirt with the slogan, 'ALLEN GINSBERG SUCKED MY COCK, AH!' But I decided against it. Somebody in the university would have objected. Not the students, obviously, any mention of sex pleases them no end. I'm talking about the administration and the teachers, repressed homophobic cocksuckers, all of them. Anyway, so much for the Beats in Bombay. Some accounts will have you believe it was a watershed moment for Indian poetry, while others will insist it was a low point that set us back. These are fabricated reports by people who weren't there. The truth is the Beats were irrelevant. They had nothing to do with us. They were nothing more than a passing entertainment. Some months later I bumped into Allen and Peter in Calcutta. They'd just run into the Bengali poets who were so excited to be meeting the Beats they wanted to start a new movement. Allen suggested a name, the Hung Realists, because he thought those boys were real well hung. He was making a joke, is all it was, but they misheard. They thought he said the Hungryalists and that's how a movement was born. Of course it died almost immediately and was forgotten until Narayan Doss came to Bombay and started a poetry group that met once or twice a week in some bar or other and then one afternoon at Café Royal I told him the story about Allen and he said, the Hung Realists, that's a grand name! And it became the name of the anthology he and Xavier put together. When the Bengali Brahmins heard that their name – and it was never theirs to begin with – had been corrupted to the Hung Realists by some low-caste Bombaywallah, they raised a godawful clamour. They told Doss the name belonged to them, both names belonged to them, the true and the corrupted, and they started the hungry movement and now there are the websites and books and the name is everywhere. Do you see what I'm saying? The Bengalis know how to validate their history. Why don't we? Hum kisse se kum hain!

Would you like more tea? Or a glass of wine? I can't drink it any more. The acid reflux destroys me but I can certainly offer you some.

You must imagine if you can. A beautiful young man arrives in Bombay with a beautiful book of poems. Imagine. He's an untouchable. His grandfather cleaned toilets in the village, but he has an impossible wish. He wants to be friends with the beautiful people of the city. He wants to know the glamorous women with their fair skin (his skin is dark), their silky hair (his hair is like coir), and their beautiful clothes (his own clothes are cheap and faded). They are beautiful but so is he and unlike them he is talented and he knows it. He wants to dazzle the editors and proprietors of the television stations and news services. He wants money, enough money so he never again has to worry about paying for a meal or buying books. He wants the entire city to be in thrall to his talent and ambition and beauty. He knows it is audacious to have a name like Doss and want these things, to be so dark and want these things, to want what a Brahmin wants. He knows it is audacious, irresponsible, unrealistic, but this is what he wants and he wants it so badly it is a hole in the pit of his stomach. It will not let him sleep at night and it fills his days with schemes and emptiness. How do I know this? Because he told me and I'm telling you, against my better judgement I'm telling you. He said to me, this is the open secret of Bombay. Whoever you are you can come here as long as you have talent or money or beauty. Bombay will take you and make you. He made no mention of the other side of the equation, that the city will chew you up and spit you out while you are still getting your bearings.

And where did young Doss come from in any case? Don't you want to know? Kuch to bol, yaar.

The name of the town hardly matters. It was a town divided by a river and the river was also divided. A place of endless division. I visited it recently. Nothing has changed for a thousand years. On one side of the river live the castes. On the other side the untouchables live, if you can call it living. They are only allowed to take water from a specified place downriver. After they collect the water they are only allowed to take a specified route back. They cannot go upriver, for that would pollute the water for the Brahmins and other castes. They cannot walk home past the homes of the Brahmins, lest their shadow falls where it must not. These are strict immovable specs. Everything is specified and that is the meaning of caste. Each profession, each article of clothing, each item of food, each action and thought, each name is specified by the great books and the law of the true gods. And none of it can be changed or only at great danger to those who wish to question the old specifications. As you've guessed by now Narayan Doss's intention was to interrogate. You could take it a step further and say Doss *was* an interrogation, a question with no answer. Jawab hum denge.

You have a question too, I know. Why did I appoint myself the historian of Doss and the Hung Realists and the other poets who dominated those times, Ezekiel and Moraes, Kolatkar and Ramanujan, all dead now, every single one of them, but particularly, of all of them, why Doss and Xavier? The answer is obvious but only to someone like me. I am the historian of the outcaste poets because I am a homosexual Indian man. I know how it feels to be an outcaste. I have lived here all my life and before I became a Hindu activist I was a gay activist.

My question is this: what happened to Narayan Doss's last book? I hear that a Swiss woman is translating some of the poems but is this not too little too late? Why did it take so long? How did the painter Xavier write two books of poems in such a prolific burst? How did these poems by a neophyte author become an international phenomenon and how did they make their author so much fame and money? Did no one notice that the friendship between Doss and Xavier resulted in oblivion for one and glory for the other? Did no one see their friendship for what it was, a play of caste and class, the latter a result of the former? Doss, outcaste, was not translated or celebrated while Xavier who was from a prominent family found fame and riches. What does this say about our literary culture? Why has nobody asked these questions? Is it that such a mode of questioning is not relevant? Or is it that such questions are inconvenient to certain powers that be, certain powers that would do anything to prevent an untouchable author from receiving his due in the world? These are questions to which I expect no answers because there are no answers, which is a reason, perhaps the only reason, to believe in God.

Farzana Amanella Kaur, arts activist, interviewed by Dismas Bambai in Lado Sarai, New Delhi, October 2005

We all know how crazy it is now that the right-wing and the capitalists are running the world. But we forget how it was when we were in charge. Let me tell you it was crazier! Everything was ideology and ideology was everything. Words swam around us like phosphorescent deep-sea fish glimpsed for a moment and gone. We lived with a constant sense of obligation. But how can you be obligated to abstraction? That's the question I want to pose to my younger self. How can you let yourself be hypnotised by those whose loyalty is not to language but to the party? The one-point agendas that dominated every student meeting and coffee house discussion from Calcutta to Mysore. The idea that all language was ideological in nature and therefore poets and novelists had to ensure their work had a discernible revolutionary moral. A childish idea lacking in complexity and nuance, but it affected everyone, lawyers, doctors, teachers, and journalists included.

I tell you what, the genius of the Hung Realist anthology was the way its editors used ideology against ideologues on both ends of the spectrum. The right and the left both got played. They had no idea that the anthologists' only loyalty was to the anthology. They should have known. Players only love you when they're playing.

Do you know the painter J. Swaminathan? I worked for him when he was running Bharat Bhavan. Swami was a crazy man, absolutely stoic and tortured and he drank himself comatose every night. Always in a lungi and smoking a beedi. He was showing in Bombay and he wanted poetry at the opening and I asked Newton and Narayan if they'd be interested. Narayan said yes and Newton said maybe. Maybe, I said, why maybe? Swaminathan is the real thing, I said. Xavier said he was real but only in a topical sense. Narayan said, come on, Newton, don't be difficult. You don't have to be difficult about every little thing. Just say yes. So Newton said yes and they read some poems in Marathi and English and Swami made a speech and later we all piled into a rented car that would drop us to our respective homes. Narayan was in front and Swami and Newton were in the back with me. The talk for some reason was about whether or not it was morally correct to produce art and poetry when just a few feet away was someone who did not have enough to eat and could not afford to buy medicine and in any case the nation was made up of peasants who could not be saved by art. Swami said it was not morally defensible to be an artist in a country like India.

Doss in the front seat laughed. He said Swami only said such things because he was privileged in every way but most of all in his caste. He was a Brahmin and could afford to talk about art, whereas the hungry and the illiterate could afford only to labour for their daily bread. Swami said he had seen enough difficulty in his life to feel a kinship with the peasant. His art, he said, was anything but elitist. It drew from the soil and the air of rural India. Again Narayan laughed. When he was drunk his laugh became high-pitched and manic. It was the kind of laugh that put your teeth on edge. He laughed for a long time and then he said, Swamiji, you will forgive me if I take your savarna pronouncement with a pinch or two of sea salt. And the high-pitched laugh issued again, but it was cut abruptly short because Swami reached over from the back seat and slapped Narayan so hard that the sunglasses went flying off his head into a corner of the taxi. Narayan said, when the upper caste resorts to violence that is when you know you have won the argument. Then he started to laugh again, and again Swami raised his hand but this time Newton grabbed his wrist. He sat calmly in the back seat, looking straight ahead, with Swami in a death grip. But it ended there. He let him go and the rest of the ride passed in silence.

I thought to myself, in vino veritas. Narayan when drunk became reckless to the point of suicide. When Swaminathan was drunk all his lungi-wearing peasant-loving speechifying fell away and he became a patriarchal upper-caste landlord. And Newton? In vino caritas. The more he drank the nicer he became: wine revealed his charity. The curmudgeon's mask slipped and the true face was revealed.

Rama Raoer, former professor of English Literature, Bombay University, interviewed by Dismas Bambai at Dolly Mansions, near Dadar Station, March 2005

Do you know why I drink vodka in the daytime? Because it mixes with everything including hot milk tea and it doesn't smell, or it doesn't smell much. That's why it's the choice of professional drinkers and melancholic alcoholics like me. Did you catch that? Joke maara, main!

When a man makes light of his alcoholism as I just did most likely he is not one. Sabko maloom hai main sharabi nahin. It is the silent solitary ones you must watch out for.

I met Doss in interesting circumstances to say the least. According to my mother, a goonda-type fellow rang the bell first thing in the morning. She thought it was the milkman or the pauwallah but it was a roadside Romeo with his collars turned up. He looked like he hadn't slept in days. He didn't introduce himself to my mother when she opened, just glared at her with the most ferocious scowl on his face. She said she wrapped her housecoat around herself and glared back at him. She isn't intimidated easily. After all she's my mother, but the fact is she'd never seen the man before in her life and she was not reassured by the expression on his face, which was an expression of hostility or suspicion. I'm looking for the poet Rama Raoer, the man said in English. Is he here or not? And now my mother smelled the alcohol on him, a powerful reek of stale liquor and beedis, and she noticed that his shirt was bright green and a red hankie had been positioned between collar and neck and on top of the shirt was another, a khaki cabbie's shirt, and she saw that he hadn't shaved or bathed and though he was short, or at least no taller than she, the hallway had become dim and claustrophobic. It was as if his presence had blocked out the light. My son is not home, she said, he's out on some work. Tell him this, the man had said, tell him Narayan Doss called and will call again. Then he turned and left without another word. My mother was hoping he would not return and that I would not entertain him if he did. When she told me the name I recognised it just as he knew I would. I knew it from poems that had appeared here and there in Marathi journals, poems you could not ignore, strange beasts full of defecation and sex and caste rage. I hadn't decided whether they were any good or whether I liked them, but I had read them with interest because they were unlike anything I'd seen in Marathi or Hindi or English. And my mother's description of the man sounded nothing if not promising. I told her the usual thing. Don't worry, Ma, I can take care of myself and anyway he probably won't be back. But I wanted to meet the ruffian and when the doorbell rang that evening I opened it and before I'd properly looked at my visitor's face I made my famous proclamation. I said, from those to whom much is given, much will be taken away. Narayan Doss said, and those to whom nothing is given, what will be taken from them? Only then did we shake hands and only then did Doss enter the house and take his seat in the visitor's chair (there was only one) by the balcony where the sparrows are fed daily, the feeding of birds being my only gesture at the correct life. Jaisi karni vaisi bharni.

Doss looked around the room, which was tiny, at the paintings, which were numerous, at the books stacked in uneven towers on the floor against the wall, and his gaze came to rest on his host, who asked if he wanted tea. Doss didn't reply or he took so long to consider his reply that I went to the kitchen and returned in some time with two cups and a pot of strong Assam chai. I poured the tea and added sugar and apologised for the fact that there was no milk and that was when Doss said, look, thanks for the tea, but do you have something stronger? I said that I did not, that I lived with my mother who was out at the moment and didn't take kindly to alcohol in the house. Doss said this was understandable. After all it was a woman's duty to position herself against those substances and ideas and persons to which her son was drawn, because she knew these were the things that would take him from her one day. He said he had come by the house earlier and met my mother and liked her and I would do well to obey her and keep no liquor within easy reach. But since we were in fact two young poets in need of refreshment, he had an idea. Chalo dost, he said, come with me. I'll show you where I live.

He drove a taxi in those days, one of those khatara black and yellow Fiats. I remember the bench seat in front had collapsed and there were deep depressions where the springs had caved in. He told me to sit in the back but I refused. I wasn't going to lord it over the back seat like a paying customer. I wanted to sit in front with the driver. Solidarity among the working classes, yaar! Doss started the engine and a couple came to the window and asked if he would drop them to Dongri, an older couple with a suitcase. He flagged the meter and we set off with Hindi movie music playing on the radio. There was a robotic voice saying the words, disco crazy, uh-huh, uh-huh. He smoked beedis and drove badly, a terrible driver, the kind who made you fear for your life and the lives of anybody who had the misfortune to be on the road at the same time. He drove and smoked and hummed along with the disco tune. Also he managed to provide a running commentary on the state of the roads and he gave us a brief lecture about luck. He said it was luck that we were all going in the same direction. Not that he would have refused to take the couple but this way no one was inconvenienced. Luck was preferable to coincidence, said Doss, because with luck you felt as if you were blessed, whereas coincidence was random happenstance. There was no blessing involved. The old man in the back said he preferred coincidence. At least coincidence could not be evil. At this his wife laughed. You're so wrong, she said, coincidence and luck are the exact same thing. In the same way that there was bad luck and good luck there was bad coincidence and good coincidence. This was an example of good coincidence and it was entirely possible that good could turn bad, for example if the taxi got into an accident. When she said the word 'accident' she stopped speaking, as if she was afraid she had jinxed the ride. We had now begun to enter the innards of the city, the neighbourhoods most Bombayites avoid. We passed the station and a wide avenue with covered pavements and then the passengers asked him to stop. Doss said he was sorry if his driving had worried the lady. He knew he was not a good driver but it was the only work he could get. It bothered him sometimes, he said. If he was being honest it bothered him a lot. It drove him crazy that he drove badly and had to drive for a living. By now the couple were anxious to be on their way. The old lady said, beta, never mind, at least you got us here in one piece. She even gave him a tip.

From there it was a short drive to the heart of the red-light district, Kamathipura 11th Lane. He parked near one of the numbered brothels and didn't bother locking the cab. From the moment we got out of the busted Fiat and all the way to his door, which was on the second floor of a residential chawl, people stopped him to talk. A boy asked if he could keep the Ambedkar book he had borrowed for a little longer. Yes, said Doss, but he wanted it back sooner not later. A man asked to borrow money, a guy who smelled as if he'd spent his last penny on hooch, and country hooch at that. Doss gave him some notes and they had a short conversation about the stock market, of all things. Then there was a woman who wanted to show him a prescription for antibiotics. Her daughter was down with something and Doss had told her which doctor to see. It went on like this, all kinds of people stopping to exchange a few words about everyday matters. The pimps and pickpockets wanted just to greet him or be greeted by him. After a while I began to see him as a kind of local politician, corrupt and popular at the same time. Don't get me wrong. Woh kavi tha. That much I'll say about Narayan and Xavier, they were poets through and through. Unlike some of the others of their generation at least they didn't change their poetry to suit whichever wing of the communist party was currently in vogue.

I stood there listening to these banal and moving exchanges and thinking about the unlikely connection between Narayan and Xavier when the strangest thing happened. I noticed a figure coming toward us through the dust and cookfires. A figure all in black, black kurta, black jeans, a black sling bag, black hair down to his shoulders, and for a moment I thought Doss was in two places at once because it looked so much like him. Somebody said, aa gaya, chanduli aa gaya. I thought, yes, this man could very well be a chanduli, he had that air of boredom, the stone-faced boredom of the opium smoker. Narayan and the chanduli shook hands and it was like seeing mirror images touch each other, two long-haired fellows in black shaking hands on a street crowded with every kind of humanity except the law-abiding. The chanduli was introduced as Newton Xavier and then it all made sense to me. I knew who he was, the poet who'd given up London and Paris and returned to Bombay, the poet who had given up poetry. And now I knew why: he had become a chanduli.

When Narayan managed to shake free of his constituents we went upstairs to his living quarters. It was nothing more than a single room, although I'm sure there wasn't another like it in the district. A mattress on the floor that served also as a workspace, and an entire wall covered with books of poetry and fiction in Hindi and Marathi and English. I picked out a few volumes by poets who were familiar to me and found they had all been signed by the authors. I wondered what Doss's visitors thought of those books, the pimps and prostitutes and criminals who came to see him, what did they think of the books that lined the wall? The whole Clearing House backlist was present and accounted for but also preserved were obscure Writers Workshop and Mouj and Newground and Praxis and Pras Prakashan titles by vanished authors. And then it struck me, the most notable thing of all on a day of notable things. The shelves were custom made and the collection had been arranged alphabetically according to genre and language. A meticulous arrangement! You would never connect such organisation with such a poet, an outcaste legend of the red-light district. And as you stood there looking at the books your view also took in the facing buildings with the saris and blouses hung out to dry on the balconies. And there were the women hanging out of the sills, smoking and laughing and beckoning to you and shouting jokes to Narayan and Xavier who had returned from the kitchen with a bottle of Solan No. 1 and ice. We drank out of chai glasses and we toasted the women of the numbered brothels, who toasted us too. After the second drink and before the third and fourth and fifth, Xavier went to the shelves and retrieved a slim book of poems. It was my own lost volume from a lifetime earlier, a book they presented to me with a ceremonial flourish, and Narayan produced from the pocket of his khaki cabbie's jacket a Parker ballpoint and they said, maestro, please, your signature.

I'm an old man and I'm entitled to my peeves. The writers of today are as conservative as novelists or bankers. Terminal affability. Addiction to approval. What will Auntie think? What will the neighbours think? This is the neurosis of the middle-class Indian. But for a moment there we cared less about the relatives and the neighbours. We were devotees of anarchy and marijuana. We made our rhymes to a soundtrack of R. D. Burman, Waterfront, Ji Whiz, Human Bondage, Synthetic Frost, Savage Encounter, The Voodoos, The People, Tryst, Bharat Mata Nach Kud Bajaa, Kosmic Junk, and the mother mushroom of a hundred psychedelic Indias, Atomic Forest. Why has no one made a movie about that time, or a play, or book? We live in the moment. We have no talent for history and we are unable to adapt to modernity. This is the true reason. And I'll tell you one last thing. If a nation does not care for its past it does not care for its future; and if it does not care for its poets it does not care for anything at all.

Subir Sonalkar, journalist, interviewed by Dismas Bambai at Gokul Permit Room, Colaba, Bombay, July 1998

I believe the Bombay poets had a knack for cruelty. And if they didn't they developed it pretty fucking fast. They were masters of the number two trades, petit bourgeois petty criminals, habitual drunkards and fornicators, lone wolves and seers, desperados to a man, and they were all men except for the formidable Ms de Souza who had a kind of honorary status in the boy's club. It was a club, no question about it, women not welcome, nobody welcome except the six or seven founder members who appointed themselves dictators for life and locked the door behind them.

Do you know the London-returned boy with the long hair, the architect who gave it all up to write poems? Yes, well done, Adil Jussawalla. Do you know his second publication, which was not a collection but a single book-length poem, a clenched fist or raised middle finger in the face of Indian poetry? Do you remember the title? Of course you don't. *Missing Person*. In my opinion it is compulsory reading for anyone interested in the poets of Bombay. And never was there a more bitterly self-aware title, because that's what they were, missing persons, every one of them. They took pride in not publishing and not writing. One book and then nothing for a decade, just disappear off the face of the earth. Hole up somewhere nobody knows you and drink yourself to the third bardo or the seventh circle. If you wanted to meet them you'd have to lurk on a street corner in Tardeo or New Marine Lines or Santa Cruz or Colaba. You'd have to lie in wait like an assassin at Saint Michael's Church or Babulnath Mandir and they wouldn't come, they'd never turn up, because they were missing fucking persons AWOL for all time, and what I want to know, what I'm dying to know is, what the fuck were they hiding from?

I was a young poet in the eighties, age twenty-none and counting, which makes me not so old now, to address your great surprise. Well, watch and weep, my young friend, you age fast in the fucking po biz. For a young poet writing in Marathi and English it was a rare thing to find a poet you wanted to emulate. Plus, like all young poets I resisted the easy influence. I cherished the difficulty. And despite my wilful nature and my immense shyness, despite my youth and my arrogance, for there is nobody more arrogant than a young poet, despite my tremendous fucking handicap, I found two names worthy of the role of master, two names I hoped would consider me a worthy student. As luck would have it the masters I chose were drunken modernists, which says something about me. Perhaps I should have been less eager to approach them, perhaps it's a better thing to let one's heroes remain on the page, perhaps, as Ms de Souza says, it is "Best to meet in poems".

The first master I approached at a play he had written or directed or acted in, or all of the above. I took a bus to the theatre in Matunga where it was playing and because I could not afford a ticket I loitered near the entrance and looked at the posters and then I went over to the café area. I helped myself to a glass of water and sat at a table. I was carrying a volume of Mallarmé's selected poems in English and because I was young and hopeful it seemed the correct companion for me in my state of solitary and unintoxicated pennilessness. I read and sipped water and read some more and after a while a small crowd of people exited the theatre and stood around smoking and discussing the play. I saw Mr Oak sitting by himself at the farthest table and I gathered my Mallarmé and my courage and introduced myself. I was overjoyed when he asked me to take a seat. How naïve, how grateful is the young poet for the smallest gesture of kindness! We talked about the play, a Marathi adaptation of Ionesco, a comic adaptation that made much use of slapstick and a fellow in a rhinoceros suit, and then we talked about Brecht and Artaud and the sacred quest to eradicate the proscenium and make obsolete the division between audience and performer. There was a silence, a short silence, as occurs between people who are meeting for the first time and then Mr Oak got down to business. Would I lend him a few rupees, he said, and that was the amount he asked for, a few rupees. I was a goddamn student, a goddamn poet nursing my glass of water at the Matunga theatre café because that was all I could afford. I remember I had just enough money for the bus home. I had no lendable rupees. When I told him I was dry as a bone my master Mr Oak could not hide his disappointment. He sat completely still and stared at the ground. Minutes later he left on an errand, never to return.

That was my experience with the first master. With the second I decided to be more circumspect. I had heard that Mr Kolatkar liked to hold court on Thursday evenings at a café opposite the Jehangir Art Gallery. I think it was called Woodside Inn or Wayside Inn, a restaurant and tea shop with a grandfather clock on the wall and checked red and white tablecloths. It was there that Mr Kolatkar took his customary table under the clock and entertained his many visitors. By then he was no longer drinking whisky. He preferred copious draughts of water and cups of strong tea. He lived in a small apartment crammed with books, so small that when he had a visitor they had to go to the balcony to sit and talk. Not that I was ever invited there. These are stories I heard from those who had been allowed to meet the great man, the great poet in his poetic abode.

From my nondescript suburb it took more than an hour in a train to reach Churchgate. From the station I crossed the road to the Eros cinema and gazed for a moment at the building's art deco silhouette and signage, a sight I had loved as a boy, and for a moment I wondered what Arun Kolatkar would make of it, such was my devotion to the idea of the poet Arun Kolatkar who worked as an art director in the hallowed world of advertising, the glamorous world of copywriting and marketing, who must have walked by the Eros cinema many times in his wanderings around the city, whose understanding of the sign's art deco lineage was so much deeper than mine. What did he see when he looked at the Eros sign's whimsical onomatopoeic curves and the bespoke orgasmic O with the dot at its centre? What were the poetic or prosaic or aphoristic thoughts that occurred to him? These were the questions that came to me as I stood on the broken sidewalk outside the cinema, the storied sidewalk broken by the roots of an immense banyan, roots that broke to the surface like a sea serpent's limbs, and then I crossed the street to the

Oval Maidan, where of course a cricket match was in progress. I stopped to watch the game that had just begun and I took careful note of the opening batsman's stance, which was just a smidgen short of elegant. I watched the game for the space of an over, noting the paceman's line and his persistent forays into the corridor of uncertainty. I noted the placement of the fielders and came to certain conclusions about the players, because I too had played cricket. After all, I had been born and brought up in Bombay, how could I not? And then I thought of Arun Kolatkar walking across the Oval Maidan and I wondered what images came to him as he watched a game of cricket and how those images would transpose into the playfully poignant yet meticulously crafted lines of verse associated with his legend, or the mysteriously apt covers he created for poetry books, or the powerful yet subtly dissenting art he made for the clients whose products he sold in his endlessly creative advertising life. From the Oval I walked to the Madame Cama Road and then I walked past the YWCA where my mother worked from time to time as a receptionist and I came at last to the Regal Cinema. I stopped to admire its art deco sign, not as famous as the Eros sign but a significant fact of city life nevertheless, and of course I thought about Arun Kolatkar and his poems about Bombay, specifically the poem set in a modest tea shop, and I thought about the way the poem used the demotic and I thought perhaps one day I too would write a poem with just such a quality of informed insouciance, a poem that did not care what you thought of it, an untouchable poem that didn't seek your approval or understanding. I knew Arun Kolatkar had gazed at the same scene many a time and I wondered what thoughts would have passed through his distinguished head at the sight of the Regal's not-quite-imposing art deco sign. Almost immediately I knew the answer. He would redesign the sign in his imagination and he would improve it. He would make it a subtly transcendent work of art and a homing beacon for the city's movie-starved multitudes. From the Regal I went to the Jehangir Art Gallery, which was my favourite part of the walk because I passed Elphinstone College on my left and the Prince of Wales Museum on my right and I did what I always do when I pass the museum, I leaned in for a glimpse, which is what anyone who walks past it must do for it is one of the sweet sights of the city, the old white dome set in a formal arrangement of palm trees and framed by a cluster of smaller domes and pinnacles. For a boy like me, a poor poet from the city's Marathi interiors, such a sight exalted the difficulty. These were the thoughts that occurred to me and I remember with some embarrassment that I even spoke my thoughts aloud. The difficulty, I said, exalt the difficulty! When I finally reached the Woodside or Wayside Inn I was drenched in sweat and my shirt clung to my back. It was a humid day as only the city of Bombay can be humid. Rather than rush into the restaurant in my dishevelled state I waited on the pavement until I had cooled down a little and just when I had steeled myself to go in the door and introduce myself to the poet Arun Kolatkar, the great bilingual poet Arun Kolatkar, just then I saw him stepping out of the restaurant, the Wayside or Woodside Inn, what does it matter? He was alone. But there was a look in his eyes, his piercing eyes hidden under the bushy white eyebrows and long white hair, an eloquent look that I understood immediately. It said: I know you know who I am. I know you are a young writer and I know that you have read my work and admired it. I know too that you would like to come up and speak to me but I implore you, do not do it! It is not that I do not wish to speak to you in particular. The fact of the matter is that I do not wish to speak to anyone. I wish to take a small constitutional unmolested by the young and the importunate and I would be most grateful if you would allow me on my way. His eyes made this small speech and then he walked past me and of course I did not disturb the great man, for after all, who was I but a small, a meaningless speck on the vast page of poetry? He was a paragon, a Hector, a goddamn Samson, and I a mere Phoebe. I let him pass.

Keki Katrak, accounts executive, interviewed by Dismas Bambai at the India International Centre, New Delhi, October 2005

The woman said, they're not ashes, they are flowers. She spoke the words as if she were reciting an old poem in the correct way, from the stomach, and her voice carried across the water from her riverboat to mine. She gripped the urn as the boat pitched and she spoke with such yearning that her husband flinched. She said, raakh nahi, phool thi. My Hindi has never been good enough but that is what I heard. And because the future is always with us and because we carry our death like ghost marks on the skin, at the very moment that she spoke to her husband of ashes and flowers I had a vision of her in a kitchen lifting her arms to protect her face from the flames. I watched her tip the contents of the urn into the water and I saw her being emptied from her own urn into the same river at a future moment. I admired how calm she was as she turned over the urn. And then I saw her husband glance at his watch and make a gesture of impatience.

That is my clearest memory of Benares. Of course I remember the poets and the conference, but it's the river I remember best. I was a poet myself in those days. I hadn't yet come to my senses. I thought the poet's life was the way to live in this world. These days I write copy for butter and fizzy drinks and ice cream. I came up with a line that the agency guys consider a classic. "The snappy, zappy, slap-hap-happy apple drink!" You can smile, I don't mind. The fact is I'm happier now than I ever was then.

Benares works in mysterious ways. First you check into your flyblown hotel and look around your flyblown room and then you run to the river. I have an affinity for water, even toxic water, even the toxic Ganga. For me it was a river out of mythology and therefore it was more real than the conference where I first met Doss and Xavier and where the idea for the Hung Realist anthology and manifesto came to life.

This was in January. I had taken one of those small Indian Airlines planes from Delhi to Benares, so small that it shook each time the stewardess walked the aisle. My seatmates were new to air travel. However, I am certain they were veterans of the railway journey. They carried their own snacks and they had no idea how to fasten their seatbelts. But they did not grip the armrests during take-off and landing as I did. As soon as the plane was in the air my neighbours wrapped shawls around their heads and fell asleep and the smell of lunchtime whisky was so ripe it made me retch. Thankfully it was a short flight and we landed near a concrete shed on the edge of a field. I had no luggage and went straight through to the taxi stand.

Later I walked to the ghats from my hotel. I put on sneakers and a low cap and I walked by the river. But it was twilight, a night without moonlight, and all I could see were oil lamps in the water and floating bodies freighted with stones. I saw them go by and imagined their names. Alone and floating, I thought. Bodies added hourly, a thousand bodies of the recently alive covered by the river in a sticky green mist. I watched until full dark. Then I walked back to my hotel and sat in a hall where tables and chairs were grouped around a dead fountain. People drank tea and ate fried sweets, their faces watery in the white tube lighting. I went early to bed and was woken before dawn by shouts and the sound of blows. There were men in the hallway whose voices carried straight into my room. I woke exhausted and got out of bed.

This was the sight I saw in the hallway. Two men had taken off their shoes to beat a third man who lay on the floor with his arms around his head. They beat him in turns and they aimed for his head or back or groin. The man on the ground was a cook and the two men hitting him were waiters. The cook had mixed up an order and the waiters had called him a sisterfucker, a standard insult heard in the kitchen a hundred times a day. But in return the cook had called them gandus and practitioners of gandugiri, insinuating that they had been born of the anal passage instead of the vaginal passage, which unnatural birth made them predisposed to the practice of gandugiri. This was a grievous insult and it had resulted in the beating that was being administered this morning many hours after the initial offence. The two waiters were breathing heavily and though the cook was already bleeding from his nose they did not stop hitting him with the heavy heels of their shoes. Whenever one stopped the other lifted his shoe and brought it down on the now unconscious cook, on his hands or his head. After some time the two waiters were no longer looking at the cook but at each other and when they stopped the beating they appeared embarrassed and spent, as if they'd been fucking instead of fighting, as if they'd been doing exactly the thing the cook had accused them of doing and that had driven them to fury in the first place.

I had a shower and changed and left the hotel in search of a boat that would take me to the conference venue. It was to be held in an auditorium at the other end of the ghats. The riverbank was packed with extended families washing with bars of Hamam soap. They scrubbed head, armpit, groin, and feet, in the precise prescribed order, and shed their sins together. Considering the state of the water I thought to myself that they were exchanging new sins for old. There was a sandbank on the far side where the water was cleaner. But here where the bathing took place the river was a drainage canal for sewage, household refuse, toys and plastic bags, and unidentifiable partially submerged fleshy remains.

I negotiated with a boatman whose wide-bottomed boat sat low in the water. I agreed to his second price. Slowly he poled. He squatted on his high seat with a beedi cupped in his hands. He took long pulls at the smoke and he let the boat drift in the slight current. There was a breeze mixed with stink. A boy of about sixteen drew alongside us in a sky-blue plastic armchair made of mineral water bottles that had been sliced open and melded together and lined on the inside with canvas. He sat back as if propped on cushions and examined a plastic syringe he'd fished out of the water. Throw it away, my boatman said, it will make you sick. Reluctantly the boy let the syringe go and we watched it float toward the bathers. The breeze fell and the sun dimmed to a deep glow. I pulled my cap low on my face and let the heat build on my arms. The ghats receded in tiers planted with beach umbrellas and painted gods. On the Babua Pandey Ghat I saw an Islamic sickle moon inlayed in Hindu saffron and elaborate Buddhist pagodas. On the Vijayanagram Ghat someone had built a model of the leaning tower of Pisa. The landing was candy-striped. I saw a sign on a burning ghat, FOR TUNA TEARE THE PEOPLE WHORESIDE ON THE BANK SOFT HE GANGA, and I could not unscramble the words or the images around them – the way everything tumbled together, the light, the pictures, the smell of smoke, the sound of water and voices. There was a sudden traffic jam. Two riverboats were going in opposite directions and our small boat was in the middle. We passed a skiff with a couple sitting apart. The woman carried a small clay urn and they argued about how much further they would have to go before she could tip the ashes into the water. The husband was in a hurry to immerse the ashes and leave. The woman wanted to find running water. And that was when I heard her say what she said.

Woh raakh nahi, phool thi.

Farzana Amanella Kaur, arts activist, interviewed by Dismas Bambai in Lado Sarai, New Delhi, October 2005

Do you know X was twenty-three and living in London when the Indian government annexed Goa? Portugal stole Goa from India and India stole it back. You would have to be a pretty disaffected Indian to say it belonged to Portugal. Or you would have to be from Goa, whose people were constitutionally recognised Portuguese citizens as long ago as the early 1800s. The point is Xavier was Goan before he was Indian and as far as he was concerned the annexation was a clear instance of post-colonial imperialism by the formerly colonised. He said so! Publicly! He criticised the government in the press and then he went a step further and said there should be a plebiscite for an independent Goa. He said the caste elites of Delhi were also its political elites and therefore they were stakeholders in the idea of empire. He said their real reason for wanting Independence was not to overthrow the British but to become one with them at least in terms of status. You can imagine what kind of response that suggestion evoked in newly independent India. X should have let it blow over because it would have blown over in time. Instead he wrote an opinion piece for a London newspaper in which he said he was ashamed to be Indian. He appeared on the BBC's *Tonight* programme and an Indian guest on the show called him a traitor. They burned his effigy in a public square in Bombay. There was talk that Nehru would withdraw his passport. X applied for a British passport and was granted one. It was all extremely dramatic, a political crisis.

Really, it was X acting up as he liked to do. They should have humoured him but they turned against him. Even the poets turned against him. When his enemies really wanted to score a point they would describe him as a British writer. It was the worst insult of all. This is why you never saw him in the anthologies, why he was excluded from Eng. Lit. courses, why there were no scholarly studies or monographs or critical evaluations of his work. X was Indian, absolutely Indian, and he was a real poet unlike the frauds ranged against him, but you wouldn't think so by looking at a school curriculum. I didn't know him then. I met him much later. I read about this in the newspapers like everyone else.

Goa was the source of his material, the Christ material and the saints, all of it was rooted in the churches of Goa and it was a mutual kind of connection. Some years ago I was at a literary festival in Dona Paula, a small festival but absolutely chaotic and mismanaged. I went because an old friend was speaking. At the last minute her panel was cancelled or rescheduled and when I reached the hall where her lecture was to take place she was nowhere to be seen. Instead there was a discussion between an African-American writer and a rapper from Staten Island. They were talking about outsider art, a shambolic conversation in which each speaker's only goal, it seemed to me, was to generate more words than his opponent or co-panellist. The audience drifted in and out like schools of shy fish. Near me were a group of schoolchildren, freshly washed boys and girls who had travelled from a village several hours away by road. They were in their uniforms and they carted humongous backpacks full of books. The event they'd come to see had been rescheduled at the last moment and they too had been forced to attend a talk between two writers concerning a topic about which neither knew a thing. This is the kind of festival it was. Chaos made banal. When the audience was invited to ask questions one of the schoolboys got up and raised his hand. Someone gave him a microphone. Apropos of nothing that had been said by either of the self-involved panellists he declared that he read only two poets, Henry Louis Vivian Derozio and Newton Pinter Francis Xavier. Then, his voice dripping with sarcasm, he said the genius of first-world literature was much too exalted a quality for a place as backward as Goa and a venue as modest and broken as the Goa International Centre. The poets of Goa, on the other hand, were as degraded as the broken mother tongues of their native land. This was their strength and their secret blessing, he said, and for a moment his voice stopped sounding angry and became almost kind.

I listened to this boy, this teenager, and thought, my god, there's hope for us after all. Perhaps the young will save us from ourselves. To contextualise, this was during Newton's dry phase, when he had stopped writing poems. I think it had been more than a decade since he had published anything. It didn't matter to the young man. He was shaking as he spoke, as if he were suffering from delirium tremens or a high fever, and after his outburst he apologised and took his seat. I thought, yes, this is the kind of boy who reads Newton, a boy who takes pride in his wilful nature, whose fuel is hunger and anger.

Keki Katrak, accounts executive, interviewed by Dismas Bambai at the India International Centre, New Delhi, October 2005

How foolish I was to go to Benares on my own money to attend the World Poetry Conference, a misnomer considering the world was represented by all of four nationalities, mostly Indians, plus one Colombian in a beret, two Czechs based in the United States, and two Russians, a drunk who knew all his poems by heart and the one who knew everything about everything. Personally I've never trusted poets who memorise their poems. In the same way I don't trust poets who drive. It's a bias but there's nothing I can do about it. The drunk Russian was a world-famous dissident who stood with his hands behind his back and shouted at us. He was as intractable as a house and he had no interest in anything other than food and drink. A big man with a big voice and the more he recited the angrier he became. You didn't have to understand a word to know it was poetry. What else could it be? Poetry or religious threats or blind rage, nothing else has that quality of extreme duress.

I wasn't particularly interested in the conference to tell you the truth. The official events are never as interesting as the things that happen in between and around. Mainly I was happy to be among poets I'd been reading since I was twelve or thirteen.

That first morning I went to a discussion about poetry in translation moderated by the Czech poet Agata Jagr. I came in late. At first, I had to stand because all the seats were taken. Onstage Doss was saying that poets should write in their mother tongue if they were concerned about being authentic. Authenticity was the first thing, he said. With fiction it didn't matter, after all it was fiction. Xavier, he said, should have been writing in Konkani not English. Xavier replied that Konkani was his mother's tongue not his mother tongue. His mother tongue was the language they were speaking, English. He knew no other. He said he was willing to learn Konkani but only after he had acquired English, the mastery of which seemed to be taking somewhat longer than he had anticipated. I noticed that his views were unpopular. By then he had already acquired the upper-class British accent that made his reply more annoying than it might otherwise have been. Doss said nothing and he didn't need to. Between the two of them he was the sympathetic figure, the crowd favourite, whereas Xavier's manner and accent made him the caricature of a Bollywood villain. Then Jagr said to Xavier, but hello, you are Indian. Why do you write in English? And Doss said, perhaps learning Konkani will make your poetry better. And Xavier said, you mean it will become more authentic, like food, because the ingredients are locally sourced? At which, Jagr laughed and said, on that note, shall we break for lunch? And Doss said, no, let's finish this. I'm throwing this question open, this is a question to everyone. What is depression? Is it a feeling of sadness or a feeling of emptiness? At which point Jagr said, wait, this is a discussion about poetry in translation. But that's exactly what we're talking about, said Doss, poetry as a translation of feeling and my question is, what is depression, a sense of sadness or a sense of nothingness? Xavier said, only someone who has never known depression would ask such a question. Doss said, finally. Finally you're saying something worth saying. Sadness, continued Xavier, can be pleasurable. Who does not enjoy the pain of melancholia? Emptiness, on the other hand, is intolerable. There is nothing pleasing about it. Doss said, now you're speaking the living truth. That was when I put up my hand. After all, how could I be silent? This was my topic. When the moderator pointed at me I stood up and said that sensation is sweet even if it is the sensation of misery. Only the absence of sensation is unbearable, for emptiness is the sister of suicide. I don't know why but Jagr took this statement personally. Her face changed colour and she started to make her closing remarks but all she could manage were disjointed phrases that had no bearing on the discussion we had heard.

When the panel ended I made my way outside and lit a cigarette. I watched the Colombian being photographed. He had the look of a man whose eyes were on longevity and legacy. He never took off his beret and he posed only with his left side to the camera and if the angle wasn't to his liking he refused to be photographed. Someone came up to me and asked for a light. It was Xavier. Soon we were joined by Doss, who lit up a beedi. The two poets said they were going to walk to their hotel at Assi Ghat and I said I was going the same way. It turned out we were all in the same sorry hotel.

As we started to walk I realised I hadn't eating anything all day except for a banana at breakfast. I'm type two diabetic. I said I needed a minute and sat on some steps leading to one of the ghats. It was full of people. We were upwind of the smoke from the central platform. Then I realised we were at Manikarnika, the burning ghat, and that four bodies were burning and others waited their turn. There was a heavy smell of ghee. No colour or women, only men in white kurtas come to perform the last rites. They were impatient to light the pyre and crack the skull and let the trapped spirit ascend.

I noticed that the sky was full of paper kites. It was strange to look up and see hundreds of bits of happy colour bouncing on the breeze while near us the dead were burning. I noticed Xavier was drawn to a particular pyre on which a slender body lay wrapped in muslin. The fine cloth was transparent, wet against the face of a young woman. Her features stood out in sharp relief and I could see the down on her cheeks. Xavier stared at the face as if he knew her from somewhere, as if they had been friends once and he was surprised to see her in this place lit by the fires of Hades.

I felt anxious and confused at the same time, a blood sugar condition that happens when I haven't eaten. But when I looked at the pyres my problems seemed to be nothing more than a small mind's small matter. I thought, you are meat and you will be cooked. This is all you know and all you need to know. At which Xavier said, yes, you are quite right, and moreover intimations of mortality have a way of clarifying one's mind.

I realised I had spoken my thoughts aloud and this made me more disoriented. I needed food but the thought of eating made me feel sick.

A group of men arrived to light the young woman's pyre and soon the pouring of ghee began and the speaking of incomprehensible words that sounded to me like curses. I imagined them saying, go, wife, you are no longer of use and for each moment you wait you will have to give an accounting. Do this last thing for your husband: burn quickly. The smoke was heavy, a dense white fog that issued from a spitting core, the human fuse, it seemed to me, and for some reason my morbid thoughts gave me some comfort. Then Doss materialised before us. Where had he come from? It gave me a chill the way he appeared out of the smoke like a djinn and I think he was well aware of the effect.

"Shall we find some lunch?" he said. "The smell of burning flesh always gives me an appetite."

We walked into an alleyway. Buildings crowded round on all sides, the old wood houses whose façades were brown from years of smoke. We went into a small place with a shaded portico on a street of firewood merchants. A man behind a desk gestured for us to sit and we ordered tea and pakodas that a boy brought from a kitchen in the back. A woodcutter split and stacked logs in a rough pile against the wall of the alley outside. He wore a lungi and a T-shirt with a slogan: 'Sorry I've not contacted you but I've become a secret agent'. He was small and tightly bunched, drinking whisky from a tea glass, and at each swig the sweat dripped from his face into the drink. He didn't look much like a secret agent.

Doss asked him how much wood he cut in a day.

"Depends how many dead people come," he said, and laughed.

"How many will this pile of wood cremate?"

The man put down the axe.

"This pile? Maybe forty?"

The man behind the counter said, "This is eight hundred kilos of wood, eight quintals. Fifty people, no problem."

They were bragging. The merchant grabbed a small bottle from a cupboard behind his desk and replenished his glass and the woodcutter also took a refill. I worked it out: eight hundred kilos for fifty bodies meant it took only sixteen kilos of wood to reduce a man to an urnful of ash.

"First the body is washed in the Ganga," the merchant said. "Then the butter and sandalwood powder must be bought. You can get it over there in the shop next to the cigarettewallah."

The woodcutter said, "Or you can bring it yourself. Cheaper."

The merchant said, "You put the butter and sandalwood on top of the body and a special agni below it."

The woodcutter gulped his whisky and said, "But the most important thing is the spirit." He used the English word, spirit.

The merchant laughed, "You put newspaper under the logs and light it and squirt the spirit all over to make the fire catch."

The woodcutter said, "Everything's available on this same street. Spirit, kurta, agarbatti, talcum powder for a quick beauty treatment for your grandma."

And the merchant said, "Grandpa too. Men and women get the same treatment over here."

The woodcutter said, "Except in the fire."

"Yes," Doss said. "Yes, yes."

"They burn differently when the fire takes them," said the woodcutter, finishing his drink. He spat on the ground and picked up his axe.

We listened to the sound of splintering wood as he lifted the axe and brought it down and steadily the pile of logs grew taller.

Xavier went to where the woodcutter was working and offered the man a cigarette. He asked him something in a soft voice. The woodcutter hammered iron wedges into a piece of wood that he split with a single blow. His words acquired the rhythm of the axe.

"The fire moves into the bones when the flesh turns into water and disappears in the flame. The chest-bones of men don't burn, only the chest-bones of women. The spines of men will burn but not the spines of women. Only the chest-bones of the men and the spines of women remain."

When they gave us the bill Xavier insisted on picking it up. I offered to pay my share. I didn't have much money and my offer may have been made half-heartedly but at least I offered. Doss didn't even try. It was not that he was broke. He did not believe in paying. We walked along the ghats to the hotel and I realised I was feeling better thanks to the food. The morbid thoughts that assailed me earlier now had no hold on me. Doss talked all the way and when he wasn't talking he was singing. Xavier was silent for the entire length of our walk. It's a funny thing that their friendship took shape in Benares. They knew each other from Bombay, but the translation panel was the first time they had interacted professionally. In other words their literary association began with an argument. I always wondered how they got along. But maybe it's like that thing people used to say, different and the same.

At the hotel Xavier clapped me on the shoulder. He said, would you care to join us for a drink, dear boy? It was the first time I had heard him sounding cheerful. One of the Russians, not the drunk, the other one, he was there as well and the four of us went to the bar. This was a corner with a counter and a few bottles placed against the wall. Xavier asked if I was old enough to be served alcohol. I said I was eighteen, old enough to drive and serve in the Army, which meant I was old enough to kill someone in the name of my country; and though I wasn't of legal age to drink, in a moral or logical universe I was certainly old enough. That is more than adequate for me, said Xavier, ordering whisky and beer. And for the first time that day, with a glass in his hand, he began to talk. I don't remember all of it but I suppose I remember enough. I understood that he needed whisky to come alive. Until then he had been grouchy or sullen, the kind of guy who wouldn't say two words when one would do. He'd say, hungry. Or, water. Now you couldn't shut him up.

He said, if you were to ask me why men and women burn differently I would likely say that it is because we are differently inclined and our differences cannot be resolved to our satisfaction, not by time and not in death. Time heals nothing. Those who say time heals and death resolves are speaking falsely or thoughtlessly or without the experience of loss. They are making up easy iterations that dream the dead, all the dead that ever died, packed in neat horizontal rows or stacked in pyramids of pyres that reach the sky, stacks so tall it takes all of one's strength merely to ask, how can there be so many?

He went on in this vein for a time. Then the talk turned to Rimbaud, as it does among poets of a certain age. There was a discussion as to whether his death was due to gangrene or cancer. Doss said cancer but he didn't seem convinced. He had a book open on his lap and he was making notations in the margin and talking to himself the whole time. The Russian poet said he wanted to procure some of the local marijuana and Doss burst into a song about the colours of various intoxicants. The song compared bhang to charas and charas to ganja. It ended with a couplet that compared opium and alcohol:

Afeem rang bhootiya,
Sharab rang chootiya.

The Russian poet said he was a disciple of Pushkin and a close reader of Tagore. This is when the conversation became a little heated, as I recall. The Russian, Nikolayev, said Tagore may not have been a great poet but he was undoubtedly a genius for there was a certain kind of clarity in his thought that illuminated his life and times. Doss or Xavier, I forget who, or maybe it was both, they were unnecessarily dismissive of Tagore. Xavier called him a professional mystic. He said it was his white beard and sadhu's demeanour that had endeared him to Yeats, who was a sucker for all things mystical. Doss said Tagore was the first Indian poet to understand the importance of marketing one's self and one's image. He said Tagore's true mastery was public relations. It gave me a bit of a shock to hear all this. I suppose it still does. It seemed to me a cold-hearted way to talk of one of the great figures in our literature. Whatever you may say about him he was the only Indian poet to win a Nobel.

Xavier said he was tempted to stay in Benares, perhaps on the steps of Assi Ghat. He would grow his own beard to Tagorean length and resume his thwarted saintly destiny. He would give up art and focus on the real, on self-denial and vision, on fasting and mortification, on saying the ten thousand and one names of God until he forgot the meaning of language and no longer knew his own name. He would become Saint Francis of Assi or Brother Ass and he would speak his poems to the burning dead.

This was some time after the publication of his second book, *Saint Me*, and I couldn't tell if he was joking or if he was articulating a fantasy. We had all heard that he had writer's block but only when it came to poetry. Only Doss had anything to say in response.

"I have a better idea, Brother Ass," he said.

And that was when he came up with the idea of the anthology. He knew how many poets, sixty or seventy, no more, and he knew how big the book would be, five hundred pages, with poems, essays, and drawings, edited by the two of them, Brother Ass and Brother Doss, and he had the title too: *The Hung Realists: A Subaltern Manifesto.*

Philip Nikolayev, poet and editor, interviewed by Dismas Bambai at Ramanna Ashram, Rajouri Garden, New Delhi, October 2005

Is that what he told you? Not true, absolutely off the mark! In fact it was I who was critical of Tagore! The Parsi boy was much too young to catch the nuance of the conversation. As far as I remember he sat glued to his seat and sipped his beer or whatever it was he was drinking. I remember he wore his hair in a Prince Valiant bob. Obviously he drank too much because he got the main points backward. I am a believer in and student of Bengali culture but I am able to maintain some distance from the kind of adulation that Tagore elicits. It is true that Doss and Xavier were critical to the point of rudeness but that's a story for another day.

It was 1984, a big year for me though I didn't know it at the time. I was spending more and more time with the poet who would become my wife. At the time we were friends and nothing more. She was some years older than me and already famous in Russia. Six years later we would leave the country separately and soon the USSR would no longer exist. But I had little inkling of the future in 1984, the year of my first visit to India. I went to as many places as I could. Bengal, Bihar, Kerala, New Delhi, Benares, and in the last named city I discovered that an event grandly billed as the World Poetry Conference was currently in session. Of course I went and introduced myself and the organisers were kind enough to include me on the programme. I read some poems and I talked about Mandelshtam. After my lecture there was a question from someone in the audience. Why did Mandelshtam criticise Stalin? It was a young student from the Benares Hindu University. He seemed genuinely distressed that a poet would criticise Stalin. He was of the opinion that poets should not be reactionaries. These are the kind of questions you get in India. I said Mandelshtam criticised Stalin because he was a poet first and it was the poet's job to ask the questions no one else had the courage to ask.

After my reading I walked along the river to Assi Ghat where my hotel was situated. I saw oblong shadows under the skin of the water, moving shadows that rose in steps to the surface. I was subject then to an odd vision. I felt I was looking at myself looking at the water and I saw myself from a far distance and I did not know who I was. I remembered my name, my circumstance, my history, but I felt as if that particular name and face and history had no connection with me. It was an accident, nothing more than a random aggregate, and I, the true I, was separate from my body. I suppose I should mention that I was feeling a bit poorly. It was my first visit to Benares, a place with which I felt a profound connection. Yet I had spoken to nobody since my arrival. I felt as if nobody knew me or wanted to know me. They flocked to the other Russian at the festival who was famous all over the world. Me they ignored. So I was feeling sorry for myself. But then I walked into the hotel and was approached by one of the Indian poets, a well-known painter, though in my opinion the poetry is superior. He wanted to buy me a drink, he said, in recognition of the poetry of Mandelshtam and my own poems. And then he quoted from memory one of my Calcutta sonnets, a stanza that begins, "A million poets have lived here, small and big," lines that embarrass me now, but not so much. We drank rum and water because in India the rum is good and the whisky terrible. We ate Indian Chinese, the cuisine they call Chinjabi, and then we recited poems from memory.

That night I felt a kind of transference or transfusion or transmission. Trust me, I would never talk like this in Boston. In Boston I'm as American as a Smith & Wesson Saturday Night Special. It's only in

India and in Russia that I allow myself such liberties. Let me rephrase. I received a message that night from the vast partially charted forests of Indian poetry and it was only correct that it should happen in Benares. Where else can you find death, fear, and acceptance together in one place? I still felt the sting of separation from myself but now I knew what I was. I looked around me and I knew. I was one of a lost tribe of brothers and sisters marked by ink and drink, wanderers who find each other wherever in the world we may go.

Aruna Dangle, social theorist and critic, interviewed by Dismas Bambai at Café Noz, Malabar Hill, Bombay, March 2005

First of all I'm always happy to talk about the eighties. Most people tend to denigrate the music and hair and fashion because it makes them feel better about themselves and the desolate modernity in which they live. They don't see that everything is circular. I take the longer wider view. You can do that when you are old. Baggy goes out, skinny comes in. Skinny goes out, curvy comes back. If you wait long enough everything comes back. I'm a sixty-two-year-old woman and I wear Hawaiian shirts and baggy jeans. I've been doing so for thirty years. Why change now? I still listen to 'When Doves Cry' and 'Let's Go Crazy'. The hell with it, I still play 'Wake Me Up Before You Go-Go' and 'Footloose' and 'What's Love Got to Do with It?' Now that's music, my friend. It makes you want to get up and shake your bees' knees. It's not trying to bludgeon you into submission. How can you listen to the new without hearing a soundtrack for the dungeon, music for the mean marquis while he dissipates the young and corrupts the innocent and scars the beautiful? Okay fine, let's get to specifics.

I came to see the anthology as a kind of hand-grenade. Those chokras lobbed it into the drawing room of the academy and everybody had to run for the exits, even the poets who were included had to run. It was a stun grenade. We had no idea! When Doss and Xavier asked for poems we didn't know we would be part of a bloody palace revolution. I thought, right, another anthology, here we go again. I suppose I wasn't paying attention. I suppose I should have known by the title, *The Hung Realists: A Subaltern Manifesto*. Of course, by the time you got to the introduction you knew exactly what was coming. You knew from the first para about the corrupted religious orthodoxy that determined our cultural lives and the idea that religious merit was nothing more than mere observance. Go to the temple or the mosque or the church and your duty was done and for the rest of the time you could be as immoral as you wished. It was fiery talk for a conservative god-fearing nation. The literary orthodoxy was most annoyed by the accusation that it had drawn up divisions between writers of different castes that were as rigid as the divisions between men and animals. Brahmin poets had arrogated to themselves the position of gods on earth and passed their privileges on to their descendants as a matter of course. After centuries of such abuse our poetry was crippled and mute. It had been bled unto death. People have been saying similar things since 1850 at least, when the Marathi social reformers began to publish their views in privately circulated journals. But nobody had said such things in the context of our literature.

They positioned themselves those two. They thought it through and the end result was a grenade, I say. They even looked alike with the long hair and black kurtas and black jeans – as if they were in uniform. A Dalit and a Christian, brandishing an anthology everyone wanted to be in, an anthology that excluded the dozen or so names on which the upper-caste anthologists had always relied. Adil Jussawalla, Arvind Krishna Mehrotra, Keki Daruwalla, R. Parthasarathy, A. K. Ramanujan, Dom Moraes, Nissim Ezekiel, Arun Kolatkar, Vikram Seth, Jayanta Mahapatra, K. D. Katrak, Gieve Patel – they were all out. Only Imtiaz Dharker and Eunice de Souza from that lot were included and I'll tell you why. Instead of picking the usual names these crazy fellows packed their book with poets who had been overlooked, the untranslated and untranslatable. More important, at least for me, they included women. Not that these choices were unjustified. They were completely justified. I suspect that gender may have been a guiding principle and why not? For how long had we been excluded for reasons of gender, women poets from all over the subcontinent, from all over the world? I say women poets not poetesses because I prefer not to use the detestable words. Eunice and Imtiaz were included because they were real poets – that goes without saying – but also because they had always seemed to be temporary members of the other club. Besides, Narayan considered Imtiaz a friend and that's one thing in favour of those two. They believed in their friends. When Doss was poor and homeless she helped him out. She published him and paid him. She introduced him to the poets and expected them to treat him as an equal. He never forgot. Xavier also liked her, and Eunice, but for other reasons. I always thought the Mehrotra headnote in which he referred to Ezekiel as endlessly or hopelessly or perennially priapic applied just as well to Xavier.

Between those two my sympathies were with Narayan Doss as you can see. Xavier is a man deserving of no sympathy. I think his silence was a mask and in truth he had no fellow feeling. Empathy and charm were beyond him and this was especially noticeable when he and Narayan were together. Narayan was charming, effortlessly charming, and Xavier was effortlessly unfriendly. Yes, quote me on that.

Sahej Singh Rana, trustee of the Sikh Museum, interviewed by Dismas Bambai on a bench on Platform Two, Churchgate Station, Bombay, March 2005

It was the last day of October 1985, one year after the assassination of Indira Gandhi, one year after the state helped murder more than three thousand Sikh women, children, and men in the nation's capital. This is another way of saying that it was the first anniversary of the worst time in our history. No, not true, one of the worst times in our history, because there were others. Let's not forget 1947 and 1992 and 2002, the days of blood and feasting, families murdered in their homes because of faith or lack of faith.

31 October 1985. A group of us had gathered to remember that miserable day. We were melancholic Sikhs transplanted to Bombay from Delhi. Some of us were born here because our parents or grandparents

could no longer bear to live next to friends and neighbours who had turned on us in the moment of our need. They say some things must be forgiven if they cannot be forgotten. But there are things that can never be forgiven.

We gathered at Café Britannia in the Fort area and had a dismal meal. We were sitting around with our milk teas when Xavier came in, followed moments later by Doss who had stopped to pick up whisky. They were the only ones there who were not Sikhs and this matters a lot. For them it was a question of solidarity among poets, though I hardly thought of myself as a poet in those days. Also it was an act of solidarity among those who did not belong to the overclass. I believe they were already thinking in terms of the subaltern manifesto.

From Britannia some of us went to Ankur, a divey permit room where the poet Manohar Shetty was tending bar. This was before his Goa avatar, back when he'd published just one book, *A Guarded Space*. Or it might have been *Guarded Space* without the article, I'm not sure any more. To tell you the truth I remember the title because I thought it was an accurate description of the city at the time: a safe space for all faiths, for women, for the homeless, for refugees. In less than a decade that would change but we didn't know it then. It was strange to think that a poet who had been published by Newground, one of the hot presses of the time, was working in a bar. The thing is he was a Shetty and the bar and restaurant was part of the family business. He wasn't exactly a hired hand.

He gave us a booth to ourselves and joined us and because of the nature of the remembrance by then the conversation had turned to brutality and blood lust. As I remember Xavier was silent during this, though he'd drunk as much whisky as anyone. Shetty preferred feni, in my opinion the stinkiest drink in the world, the kind of drink that exits through your pores and makes a man smell like a distillery. All of a sudden two bottles of Launi cashew feni appeared on the table. I don't know where he'd sourced it or why he decided to share it with us, but we each had a shot followed by sips of whisky. This is not the best mix in the world, and meanwhile the conversation or argument was still raging. After a few hours Xavier stood up holding a shot glass with both hands as if he was about to bless us or consecrate the drink or sprinkle it on the gathering like holy water.

"I would like to toast the Indians," he said, "the most bloodthirsty of all races on this sad and benighted," and he didn't finish because he fell headlong into a table thick with bottles and glasses and plates. There was a big sound of breaking, the sound of heavy table glass shattering and more delicate cut and blown glass smashing into the floor tiles, and in the midst of it all the poet Xavier moved his two arms as if he was swimming on a broken sea of feni and whisky, and by some miracle nobody was hurt, not even Xavier.

After this the party drew to a close and everybody dispersed. I found myself walking with Xavier and Doss toward Churchgate Station. I don't know where my friends had disappeared but they were gone, vanished into the moisture of the city in October. Doss asked if I was a writer. No, I replied. I didn't have that luxury although I had written a memoir that was looking for a publisher. What was it called, he asked. *My 1984*, I replied. He asked if I wrote poetry. I said I had started as a poet and published a slim book that was no longer in print. None of our books are in print, Doss replied, this is what it means to be an Indian poet. All this while Xavier was a little ahead of us, walking or staggering with the bow-legged gait of a sailor. I told Doss what I had been thinking about during the conversation at Ankur. For whatever reason I had not felt like articulating it then. Blood lust, I told him, was something only humans enjoyed. It was a pleasure, I said, like anger. No other animal killed for the pleasure of killing, No other animal let the wash of blood go to its head in such a way that it could only be assuaged with more blood. I said this and when I looked around I noticed Xavier had disappeared. Where did he go, I asked Doss. Oh, X has a tendency to disappear when he's drunk, he said. He's not one for goodbyes. When we got to Churchgate we found we'd missed the last train, which in those days left at a little past midnight. I was living near Opera House and I knew I could walk or take a taxi home. Doss had to go up to Grant Road. I assumed he was living in Tardeo or up near Chowpatty Beach around Wilson College. I told him I could give him a lift up to Marine Lines or Charni Road, but he said he would stay right there and he pointed to a bench on platform two, this bench, the last on the platform. It was dark and he would be able to sleep until the first train arrived at five. He said he liked the bench, that he would use his shoulder bag as a pillow, that it wouldn't be the first time he had spent the night on platform two.

A year later or maybe two years later I read a poem in the Sahitya Akademi newsletter. It was titled '31 October 1985', and in it he told a coded version of the events of the night, coded but faithful, as I recall. After I left he had fallen asleep and woken up when the first train trundled in at five. He opened his eyes and realised he could not see. His first thought was that he had gone blind, or partially blind, because he could see movement and shape without definition. Was this the meaning of blind drunk? He feared the cashew feni had been adulterated with methyl alcohol and had destroyed his eyesight. And then he realised that he could see after all, that someone had stolen the spectacles off his face as he lay passed out on the bench. The glasses were a foreign make worth a hundred rupees on the street. The poem ended with a list of the stations from Churchgate to Bandra on the Western Line. The narrator was a thinly disguised version of Doss. He disdained buses and refused to take taxis if he could help it. He'd driven a taxi once and he would never willingly sit in one again. It was all about the trains for him, the times, the Western Line versus the Harbour Line, the names of the stations like mantras, or madeleines, and each assigned a musical note:

Churchgate | Sa
Marine Lines | Re
Charni Road | Ga
Grant Road | Ma
Bombay Central | Pa
Matunga | Ta
Mahim | Ni
Bandra | Sa

Churchgate and Bandra, according to this system, were the same note occurring on different octaves. The poem also assigned a sea to each station:

Churchgate | Red Sea
Marine Lines | Adriatic Sea
Charni Road | Mediterranean Sea
Grant Road | Black Sea
Bombay Central | Caspian Sea
Matunga | Persian Gulf
Mahim | Arabian Sea
Bandra | Red Sea

Later, as we know, the poem became one of the founding tenets of the Hung Realist movement and it came to be permanently associated with the Bombay poets. The reason I brought you here is because this is the bench on which he died eighteen years later, just as his poems were being studied by a new generation of writers. This is the bench he liked to sleep on, this is the platform he knew best, this is the name that begins the list of Western Railway stations in his poem. The corrugated roof up there must have been one of the last views of his life. I thought you'd like to see it.

Farzana Amanella Kaur, arts activist, interviewed by Dismas Bambai in Lado Sarai, New Delhi, October 2005

I became a kind of rakhi sister to those boys. I always had a job, which meant I always had a bit of cash. Through most of the eighties I was working as a liaison at the British embassy in Bombay. It led to the usual jokes. Are you a spy, Farzana Amanella? What does a liaison do, Farzana Amanella Didi, other than liaise? Do you tell them what we say and do and think and drink? In that case could you give them a message from us, Farzana Amanella, tell them the Raj is over and they can fuck off back to Blighty. And before they fuck off how about an apology from the Gateway of India for the two hundred years of plunder and famine? I gave it right back. I had to. It was the only way you won any respect from those rascals. I could tell you the answer, boys, I said, but then I'd have to leave you floating face down in the Backbay. Another time I said, even if I were a spy, which I can never admit, do you think MI5 is interested in what poets think?

I knew Lula from the movies and I met her when she hosted a panel for a British Council event and asked for an assistant. Someone suggested my name and I went over to her place a couple of times. Later when she started to edit *Turnkey*, possibly the shortest-lived literary magazine in the history of short-lived literary magazines, she asked if I would help and I said yes. Lula was the managing editor, not that she did much managing. Mostly she was photographed at the offices in one of her beautiful saris and she would perch elegantly on an armchair or a desk. She was the face that would launch a thousand sponsorships. I was supposed to help with correspondence and press. It was easy work. I turned up for a few hours on Saturday and that was that. It wasn't because I needed the money. I was a devotee and she recognised that right away. She was the same.

I asked her once if she wrote poetry.

She said, darling, pottery? No, thank god. I'm a reader not a writer and it is a far far happier place, if you ask me. Don't you wonder why these poor souls do it? There isn't a sou in it and hardly any fame. Or there is a bit of fame but only when you're too old to enjoy it. And it's hard work, sweetheart, seventy drafts for a tiny page of print and for what? What do they get other than a bit of love from the likes of you and me? Is that the only reason they do it, do you think? For our love?

On Saturday Lula was in the midst of preparing one of her elaborate French meals with the linen and cutlery and individual servings, everything except a nice wine for each course. Vodka was the drink in that house and by then it was the only thing she and Xavier had in common, Indian voddy just this side of rotgut. We sat in the living room and every once in a while she'd toddle off to the kitchen – she never drank in company, she was too much of a lady – where she'd down her voddy and come back loopier and happier. And while in the kitchen she'd also supervise Newton's favourite bacon-wrapped prawns or scallops in cream or beef stew in red wine, always preceded by a green salad and always followed with dessert.

My desk was on the enclosed gallery facing the garden. She toddled in wearing that famous smile that was a little blurry at the edges and getting blurrier. She said, Farzana, darling, I've had the best idea. We have a hole in the magazine this month, sweetheart, so I used the old noggin and came up with a deliciously naughty notion. Why don't you interview Newton? I said, me? I might have blushed. But I've never interviewed anyone, I told her. Darling, Lula said, it isn't like pottery. Anyone can write up an interview. Besides, once Newton gets going you can't shut him up.

That's how the interview took place. The final version had little to do with my original questions. He insisted on writing it himself and said he wouldn't agree to it otherwise. Nothing came of it. *Turnkey*'s proprietor made Lula drop the whole idea. He said there was too much sex in it. As the publisher he would be charged with obscenity and there would be a lengthy court experience. I have possibly the only existing copy. Xavier gave it to me and forgot about it. For the record the questions about the woman and the sari and so on aren't mine. He added most of it later. It wasn't an interview as much as a self-interview, a way of fleshing out his old obsessions. That was the only reason he agreed.

Philip Nikolayev, poet and editor, interviewed by Dismas Bambai at Ramanna Ashram, Rajouri Garden, New Delhi, October 2005

I went back to India in 1990. I flew to Bombay via Calcutta and Delhi. From there I thought I'd go to Madras or Cochin but it never happened. I came down with a fever, a stomach bug I picked up on my travels, and a doctor diagnosed it as paratyphoid. I told him I'd never heard of it. What, I asked, is paratyphoid? He fixed me with a look and wrote out a prescription. I was staying at the Sea Face Guest House, a dump near Wilson College. There were no amenities, no minibar, no room service, not even a chair, but it was cheap and close to everything. And it was only going to be for a night or two, I thought. Of course not! The dump became home. I stayed for months.

The Sea Face logo was a kind of seaside fantasy, the 'S' with its elaborate curlicues and tropical colours wedged between air-conditioning ducts and exposed wiring. It made me laugh. Sometimes I didn't laugh, I smiled in a bitter self-deprecating way. The Sea Face Guest House. Even now the name is enough to bring forth a paratyphoidal churning in my bowels. It was within spitting distance of Chowpatty Beach, which was not a beach for swimming. You sit on the sand and stare at the water and I did a lot of that in my first few weeks in Bombay. Every evening I would have a low fever but by morning I'd be well enough to go out for a small walk.

I spoke only Urdu. This gives you some strange looks from Bombaywallahs who speak only Bombay Hindi. Urdu is comparatively classy and it might even be considered elitist. I smoked charas at an adda near the temple in Babulnath and I spoke Urdu. I found the charas medicinally helpful in that it settled my stomach and made me feel better generally. First thing in the morning I went to the temple of Babulnath and smoked a chillum and then I went back to the guesthouse to rest. I napped or worked and sat on the beach with a book for an hour or two. Once I started to feel better I'd go back to the temple at night for a last chillum. Even a newcomer to the city would know that it wasn't the best charas, hard as stone and that smell of boot polish. Classic Bombay black! But it helped me sleep and in a week or two I found I was regaining my strength. I'd go to Babulnath and sit and listen to the bhajans, and one day, purely as an exercise, I started to transcribe the melodies. I found it was a calming thing to do, because I thought about nothing except the music. Sometimes it seemed to me that I was trying to transcribe shadows or the notes between the notes. And it seemed to me that this was a pertinent quest for a Russian-American poet in Bombay. To be a shade, a shadow man in search of the shadow notes of typhoid bhajans. I searched and did not find and after a while I felt I was turning Indian. This is what it means to be Indian, I thought. You are forever in search and the search becomes its own reward. First I gave away my trousers and switched to pyjamas. Then I took to wearing a dhoti, the only type of garment that was comfortable in that humidity. And I realised I was wrong: after all, I wasn't turning Indian, I was turning into a Bombaywallah.

After two weeks of living like one of the sadhus of Babulnath I began to feel almost normal. I telephoned Xavier. It's Philip Nikolayev, I said, do you remember me? The Russian poet! That was his immediate response. He welcomed me to Bombay. He said the anthology we had discussed all those years earlier had been published at last. I said I already knew that because he had mailed a copy to me in Boston. Forgive me, he said, my memory isn't what it used to be. He said it was something about the water in Indian taps. The river that supplied the water must not be the Ganga but the Lethe. This was the true cause of our collective amnesia, he said. Then he laughed and said he was living in Colaba. He invited me to visit him the next evening.

I took a number 123, the red double-decker BEST bus that ran all the way from Chowpatty to Navy Nagar. I sat on the top deck with my feet on the big open window in front and I enjoyed the breeze blowing in from the Arabian Sea. From there you watch the lights of Marine Drive on your right and the water-stained art deco buildings on your left. The night is warm and from your position on top of the bus you are willing to concede that the Queen's Necklace may be a cloying colonial nickname for that stretch of sea-facing road but it is not entirely inaccurate as a visual or poetic marker. A Russian poet in India may even burst into song as he watches the waterfront lights and the hundreds of people going about their business. He might feel a sense of hopeful oneness and sing a few lines from 'Awara' or 'Pyar Hua Ikarar Hua' or some other Raj Kapoor classic. He might even forget his illness for a few moments. You never get an experience like that in a car, however nice your car might be and however well your chauffeur may drive. On the top deck of a Bombay BEST for the price of a two-rupee bus ticket you will be rewarded with a sense of accidental luck.

I found the address without much trouble. It was off Electric House on the second floor of an old redbrick building called Sargent House, the last building at the other end of Allana Marg. The elevator was a cage-like antique that rattled and shook all the way up. I was shown in by a thuggish fellow, some kind of major domo, well-spoken English but cagey. Not the kind of guy who reassured a visitor. He told me where to sit and brought me a glass of water and wanted to know all about me. What was my name? Was I Christian? Which country was I travelling from? How long would I be in Bombay? Was I staying for dinner? He was unshaven and broad of face and he had a way of licking his chops after asking a question. I never saw any sign of Xavier or his wife although every once in a while I heard shouting from inside the apartment. The major domo, the old Bombay apartment, the shouting from the other room, the fact that Xavier was nowhere to be seen, all of it struck me intensely because I was still a bit sick. I felt as if I had walked into an Indian version of a gothic horror tale and in the next room was Jane Eyre grown old and angry.

I waited but the major domo made no move to find Xavier. Instead he sat on the couch and asked all kinds of questions, as if it was he I had come to meet. After about forty-five minutes of this I gave up. I left and had tea at an Irani restaurant before taking the 123 back to Sea Face Guest House. There was a phone on the counter of the restaurant and on a whim I asked the proprietor if I could use it. He said yes in British-accented English, an accent I hear only in India. It always amuses and dismays me at the same time. I thanked the proprietor and dialled Xavier's number. The major domo answered and I refused to hang up. After some time Xavier came to the phone and apologised. He had been asleep and if I didn't mind would I please come back? I paid for the tea and the phone call and walked down Colaba Causeway and turned left on Allana Marg. The major domo let me in again and I found Xavier on the couch where the major domo had been sitting just moments earlier. There was no sign of his wife, an actress who had worked in some of the better Indian movies. Then Xavier asked if I would care to join him for dinner. We talked about Narayan Doss and his disappearance from the Bombay scene. I had heard it was because of alcohol but Xavier would neither confirm nor deny this. We talked about Benares, my travels, Thom Gunn and the poetry of Aids, why Elizabeth Jennings had been forgotten, Elizabeth Jennings's considerable bust-size, the sodomites of Cambridge and the demonstrable connection between homosexuality and espionage. Dinner was pork and chicken, heavy food, especially since I'd been on a mostly vegetarian diet. By now exhaustion was beginning to creep up on me and I said I better go back to Wilson College. I explained that I hadn't been well for some time.

Before I left he took me to a room off the balcony where he had stacked some of his more recent canvases. It was around the time of his Kanheri Cave series. Do you remember the five-line stanzas painted on colour field caves? I remarked on one in particular, *Kanheri Caves No. 9; Black, Blue, Black*, because there was no black or blue in it, only purples and reds and anyway it was nothing like a cave. He pointed to a smear of crimson at the centre of the painting. The stupa, he said.

"Like a red phallus in a purple yoni," I said.

"Caves are about sex. But sex is not the point."

I admitted that I had never been to Kanheri and he suggested I make a trip if only to get a sense of the destruction wrought on a first-century monastery.

"Look for the delicate defacements," he said. "Be mindful of the dexterity it took to cut off the tiny noses and breasts, quick careful work with the tip of a sword."

Suddenly I heard a woman's voice shouting in Hindi. The voice came from somewhere close, the next room perhaps. Xavier excused himself and I heard him speaking to someone in an undertone. Then I heard the woman's voice again and her words were absolutely clear and I felt on my skin the words she said.

"Oh Newton, how do you keep going from day to day? Why don't you give up?"

Again Xavier spoke in a barely audible voice.

And again the woman spoke, her voice louder. "What? What will you do? You know you'll never leave me."

When Xavier came back I could tell he wanted to be alone. Soon the clamour started again from the next room. She was shouting at the downstairs neighbours because they had left garbage in the stairwell, or at least that was what I understood from the little I heard. I took Xavier's hand and wished him well with the cave series. I had wanted to ask about the poetry. Was it true he had stopped writing? But the major domo appeared out of nowhere to show me to the door.

On the bus back to Chowpatty I didn't feel like sitting on the upper deck. I got off at my stop and went directly to my room and tried to sleep. Paratyphoid is a strangely proprietorial ailment. You become detached from the functioning of the body. You are fatigued but the fatigue belongs to someone else. You feel as if you are not body but mind. Today, so many years later, I still associate with Bombay the feeling of physical detachment and separation.

I waited a few days until I felt better. Then I packed water and a bag of nuts and a couple of boiled eggs and took a bus to Grant Road. From there I boarded a local train to Borivali Station and took a cab to the national park. When I got to the entrance of the caves I had to sit down. The climb looked exhausting and I was already tired. I peeled an egg and realised I had forgotten to bring salt and pepper. I chewed slowly and drank some water and then I started to climb. I counted the steps and each time I came to fifteen I took a short rest. There were fifty-two in total. At the top I bought a ticket and walked past a gauntlet of vendors, women selling bruised fruit out of baskets, bottled water, packaged peanuts, and uncovered cooked food. Everywhere in the caves I would find the results of their venture – plastic bags, empty wrappers and bottles, layers of rubbish like alluvial deposits.

I had been thinking about the first time I saw Xavier's illustrated poem 'Kanheri Caves, No. 9' in a literary magazine run by a Russian poet I know, a friend and rival who lives in Brooklyn. I remembered the disembodied genitals in the picture and the stanza embedded in it that began with the lines, "Giant Buddhas wait their crash, / The stone worn smooth as flesh." Caves are about sex of course, he was right about that, but at Kanheri this is both true and false. Kanheri is about the expression of sex and the denial of it. You only had to look at the voluptuous wall friezes of men and women with noses and breasts lopped off. Everywhere in the caves were male and female embodiments of early earthy Buddhism. Some of the figures were so tiny it would need a certain delicacy of touch and, yes, a certain dexterity to cut off the tiny noses and breasts. Every figure in every cave, even the third and central cave with its echoing chamber of stone and towering three-storey Bamiyan-like guardian figures – one on either side, the lineaments distinctly Greek – even these had body parts missing.

The invaders had gone from one joyous human figure to the next and worked with the tip of their swords, as Xavier had said. And what had this painstaking work achieved? The missing parts made the sensuality of the figures more rather than less vigorous: it made the thought of sex inescapable. As a viewer I was as affected as the defacers had been. Affected, afflicted, whatever it was, I felt like a defacement addict visiting beautiful amputations. Were they everywhere in India, I wondered, these mutilated figures? Was it similar to learning a new word? Once you saw it somewhere you saw it everywhere.

Sex emanated from the mutilated cave figures and entered the visitors, the Indian tourists who were uninterested in the site and ignorant of its meaning, who lounged against the wall and gazed at each other or blankly into the distance. Small armies of monkeys loped around them, expert foragers who knew how to intimidate and steal. Near the central cave two women in bright fitted salvaars sat on a low wall. The taller one brushed her hair. They were time-passing, grooming, taking their ease at an ancient cave formation and watching the monkeys. A large male, his erection sharp against his fur, dipped a lazy finger into a smaller female and pulled out a sticky white rope of fluid that he touched to his tongue. Then he was into her from the back and done in a few quick strokes. The women watched expressionlessly, without embarrassment, and the one who brushed her hair, whose gaze was direct and unnerving, for a moment or for two moments moved her hand in the exact rhythm of the male monkey's denuded buttocks as he pumped disinterestedly, briefly, into his partner.

As I made my way back to South Bombay I knew I was ready to leave the city. I missed my books, my work, my wife. I missed my life. There's nothing more to tell. That was the last I saw of Xavier. I returned to Boston and finished the book I was working on. We had a baby. I became a householder. From time to time if I felt nostalgic for that impossible country I dipped into the subaltern anthology. It always cured me of any lingering false sentiment.

Farzana Amanella Kaur, arts activist, interviewed by Dismas Bambai in Lado Sarai, New Delhi, October 2005

Newton's version was different to mine. The last thing he seemed to be concerned about was veracity. Reading it now, I see what he was trying to do. He wanted to tease out a set of private obsessions and use fiction to tell the truth. I think he had a compulsion also to be entertaining, or to not be dull. He insisted on calling the interview a collaboration, which I don't think it was. And he insisted on sharing the byline, which was generous of him and misleading. Here's the full transcript or whatever you want to call it:

Q: Shall we begin?
A: How did you find me?
Q: Not very well by the looks of it. Do you mind if I use a machine?
A: You are already using a machine. How did you find me?
Q: Tracked you down.

Q: Let's talk about the woman. Tell me about the first time you met her. Tell me about the . . . room.
A: Always the same room on the first floor of a numbered lodge on Shuklaji Street. She is standing in front of a mirror dabbing at her face with a hankie. I note that it is a clean embroidered hankie and the streetlights have just come on.
Q: What else is she doing?
A: She is not looking at me. She puts her handbag on the windowsill. The handbag is one of those cheap plastic jobs, so cheap it looks like imitation plastic. I know what's inside because I take a look when she goes into the bathroom. Item one: a second hankie, also cheap. Item two: a pair of bus tickets. Item three: bright red nail paint. Item four: lipstick of the same shade. Oh, also a box of Ship matches and two cigarettes, make them Gold Flakes. You've got to understand that she matches things in the most vulgar way. Today it is red, a red plastic comb in the hair, red slippers, red lipstick and nails. She thinks she is being

fashionable. She is not. She is being a Bombay whore. No, that's not good enough. She is being a Shuklaji Street whore or a Falkland Road whore or a Kamathipura whore.

Q: Right. Right. What is she wearing?

A: Peach coloured panties, a bruised peach frayed at the edges and much the worse for wear. 'SWEETY' is embroidered in black thread on the left just above the thigh. Add a white bra. Preferably the incomparable Sona brand with the medical straps and stiff pointy cups and multiple rusted hooks at the back. The important thing is that she is embarrassed about the underwear. She has no idea how desirable ugliness can be.

Q: Is this a turning point of some sort, even if it's a bit ambivalent?

A: Nothing if not ambivalent. Put that down instead of staring at me with your microphone. Put it down as my epitaph. Of course it is a turning point.

Q: Why?

A: This is when I understand what I am feeling. I love and I long to suffer.

Q: Is that all she's wearing, underwear and a blouse?

A: No, no. She puts a petticoat on. She smiles at me as she ties the cord. She says, what are you looking at? Never seen a girl dress? And then it begins. She picks up the sari.

Q: What colour is it?

A: Changeful like thought or water. Conceals more than it reveals and reveals more than it conceals. She could be bare-breasted and bare-bottomed and you wouldn't know, such are its voluminous, luminous hiding-places. The colour doesn't matter.

Q: Can you describe it?

A: A shiny synthetic sort of turquoise. Awful really. She tucks in one end and the rest is a bright puddle on the floor. She is twisting around to look at herself. The fabric follows like a dog. She does not look at me.

Q: Is she being coy?

A: Certainly not. She couldn't be bothered.

Q: What are you doing?

A: Sitting on the bed with a book in my hand.

Q: Which book?

A: Who knows? The Bible, maybe, or some detective with a drinking problem, or the biography of a dead Englishman. What difference does it make? A book she bought from the raddiwallah. She is teaching herself to read English.

Q: Could we talk about your book?

A: Which one?

Q: The first, *Songs for the Tin-Eared*, and the award.

A: What about it?

Q: There's a description of Holi repeated throughout: "Tell about the game you play / O toreador, you skintight tease / tell how you feint & sway / the image that lies at ease / down, a dream in friendly dust / as chalk outlines your silhouette."

A: That was a long time ago.

Q: But aren't you contradicting your stated Hung Realist position regarding the modernist's floating identity and the cultural placement of Indian iconography?

A: I try not to think. I prefer to drink.

Q: Are you a plagiarist?

A: Who isn't? Or to put it another way, wouldn't you? Which itself is a plagiarism. I told my friend Tom that good writers steal and bad writers borrow. He stole it immediately. Everybody is a plagiarist.

Q: What is she doing now?

A: Tying tight a white cotton cord and hooking the sari into her petticoat.

Q: Tell me about priorities.

A: Priorities are subject to circumstance. They are rearranged according to the critical faculty.

Q: What happens when priorities are rearranged by the critical faculty?

A: Madness is a rearrangement of priorities.

Q: What about obsession?

A: What about obsession?

Q: Do you think you are obsessed?

A: If I thought I was obsessed I wouldn't be, would I? I know what you're getting at.

Q: What is obsession?

A: The hair in the reel, the milky drop oozing out of the single eye and so on. I shall tell you what obsession is, the name of a perfume.

Q: Do you want to take a break?

A: No, do you?

Q: What's she like?

A: She's my favourite whore.

Q: Jealousy?

A: Of course.

Q: You said, "Life imitates Hindi movies," but you also said, "In the word lies the seed that is treason to the flesh."

A: Mumble. Mumble. Mumble.

Q: May I ask why you drink so much?

A: Such a question, useless and terrifying.

Q: You mean there's no reason why you drink so many vodkas and beer chasers?

A: Yes, there's a reason. Someone has to do it. Someone has to drink as much as can be drunk.

Q: Do you have to drink as much as can be drunk every time you drink?

A: I have to.

Q: Why do you have to?

A: It's better than being a banker or a chartered accountant or a chime lesser.

Q: Sorry?

A: A chile Melissa.

Q: Child molester! Right!

A: It's the only possible act in a world where all action has been stripped of meaning.

Q: Would you like to comment on the recent criticism of your work as "prodigious feats of twisted sexuality"?

A: All non-adult behaviour is labelled childish by the simple-minded. If you are tagged as a child prodigy every thing you do will be seen as prodigious. Speaking of which, although I have reached my prodigious capacity I do believe I shall have another drink.

Q: Do you mind that we're sticking so rigidly to the Q&A format?

A: I mind only the secret life of colours.

Q: The streetlights were on.

A: Her eyes – the cupboards of her soul.

Q: She left at dawn.

A: All she took was rainy day money.

Q: No bodies abroad.

A: I remember . . .

Q: Nothing.

A: . . . splattered on the wall and across the dresser there was indeed . . .

Q: Nothing.

A: Her secret colours.

Q: No bodies abroad.

A: I let her go.

Q: She left at dawn.

A: I remember . . .

Q: The streetlights were on.

A: I remember . . .

Q: What do you remember?

A: Dimples.

Q: Are you comfortable?

A: Are you an imbecile?

Q: How does she look?

A: Bored.

Q: What is she doing?

A: Walking away from the mirror and looking over her shoulder. She wants to get the fall of the sari right and tuck the bra straps out of sight.

Q: Black bra?

A: No! I told you, white with conical cups. A sense of the hospital, of something old-fashioned.

Q: Old-fashioned?

A: Unyielding, uncomfortable, too wide in the middle.

Q: How does it look?

A: Beautiful.

Manoj Patel, artist, member of Progressive Autists Group, interviewed by Dismas Bambai at Pocket 17, Artists' Colony, New Delhi, November 2005

I count myself as one of the few friends he had among the artists. We started around the same time. Once we painted together in a gallery. Ten-foot canvas in one hour and ten minutes and we went home with sixty thousand in cash. Each. This was in the eighties when sixty K was not bad at all for an hour's work, but Newton said we'd been cheated. He said it was robbery. I think he was short of cash. He wouldn't have said such a thing otherwise. He didn't know what to do with money, other than to spend it.

I knew he had a separate life in poetry but I didn't know much about it. Of course I heard about the prize and I remember the headlines when he protested the annexation of Goa and announced that he was a British citizen. You see, I'm a Gujarati speaker. I had to teach myself English by watching television. Even now English is not my most fluent language. Better I don't talk about poetry, but I can talk about the art and I can tell you something about the kind of man he was. His strategy from the first was to make enemies not friends. He wasn't interested in being liked. For some reason he considered me a friend or he thought of me as someone who was not an enemy. I don't know why.

I want to talk about the night of Ram Khanna's party. Xavier happened to be in town and I asked if he wanted to come. He thought about it for a long time, long time, weighed it over as if it was the most important decision of the year, and then he started to ask a lot of questions. How many people would be there? What kind of guests, from the art world or the real world? Would there be dinner? I said, yes there would be dinner and there would be a lot of people. He thought about it some more. Then he wanted to know how much talking he would have to do. I told him he didn't have to talk if he didn't feel like. He said, not at all? I said, no, not at all. Finally he consented as if he was doing me a personal favour and I called for a taxi. I didn't want to drive because I knew some moderate to heavy drinking would be done that night. Ram Khanna lived in one of those old Delhi houses with a lawn and a driveway, landscaped bushes in the shape of dinosaurs and pterodactyls, the whole Lutyens thing. It was a cold night, Delhi in January, and there were wood fires in braziers lining the way to the front entrance. I saw Ram Khanna and his wife standing at the front door and greeting guests with folded hands. Then I noticed the strangest thing. When he saw Xavier, Ram Khanna's face collapsed into lines and caverns. He looked very old. He clenched his teeth and said something I couldn't hear. Of course he regained control in a few seconds and remembered his role as host and greeted Xavier in a polite way. I should mention also that they knew each other's work but it was the first time they were meeting.

Xavier didn't say hello to Ram Khanna. He launched directly into a lecture or speech. You don't know what to put in and what to leave out, he said. And if you don't know that, how will you paint a still life? For example, you cannot put a telephone into a still life and you cannot put a computer into a still life. Do you see? Then he nodded at Ram Khanna and went into the house. I apologised though I had done nothing wrong and I went inside too and got myself a drink.

Friends were there. Manjit Bawa, Manu and Madhvi Parekh, Vivan Sundaram. I think Arpita Singh was there, though I might be mistaken. On a stage on the lawn were dancers from Mizoram. Waiters in white served bamboo-smoked pork and the bar had a lawn all to itself. I lost myself for a while saying hello and making chitchat. A Delhi winter party can be fun if you know what to expect. Everybody dressed up, the braziers glowing, a bar that never runs dry. After a while I ran into Ram Khanna. He took me aside and said, why didn't you tell me you were bringing Xavier? But it's a party, I said, why would I tell you I'm bringing somebody? Ram Khanna looked at me for a minute with his arms crossed. He was in his horn-rims phase and he looked a little bit like a tall owl. He said, why would you bring him here? You wouldn't invite him to a party at your house, would you? I said, of course I would. What kind of man do you think I am? He gave me another of those looks and I decided the only way to get through the night was to tank up at the bar. Vadra was there. He had an idea for a show he was putting up at the National Gallery. Political appointee, crony of the chief minister, but he's been running the gallery for so long he learned something by accident, maybe by osmosis. He was planning a retrospective of the Delhi school and he wanted my Kashi series. We talked about it for a long time and I gave him plenty of ideas and then I got bored and walked around and saw Ram Khanna again. He said, where is your friend? He said he hadn't seen him since we arrived. I realised I hadn't seen him either and I thought I'd better look for him, but first a stop at the dinner buffet. It was the usual Ram Khanna spread, North Indian winter food, several kinds of rotis, mutton and chicken, two or three types of daal and sweets. I was in the buffet line serving myself kadai paneer when I realised that the woman next to me in the low-cut blouse and sunglasses was my former wife. I shouldn't have been surprised. She's a Delhi art critic and of course she would be at Ram Khanna's annual bash. We exchanged a few words for politeness' sake but I couldn't take too much of it. Whenever I see her all the old feelings come back and it makes me confused. Worse, it makes me sober and the whisky I'd taken burned off in a flash. I'd worked hard on getting a buzzy buzz and it had gone out the window. I was annoyed and I put my plate down and decided I would find Xavier and go home. First I checked the outer area, then the rooms, including the kitchen and the bathrooms. I went upstairs and worked my way along each floor and stuck my head into each room. I felt as if I was in a studio set and there was a different movie being made behind every door I opened, including a soft-core featuring a former Lucknow courtesan and one of our better-known arts impresarios. I was thorough about it and in the end I had to admit he was not in the house. He had left without saying a word to anyone. But this is Xavier after all, a man who had made a cult of listening only to his own counsel. I went downstairs and told Ram Khanna that Xavier had left. I told you, said Ram Khanna, I told you he is a man who cannot be trusted with the basic courtesies. Is that how you say hello to a man in his own house? You don't know how to paint a still life? The more Ram Khanna warmed to his subject, the more people gathered around us. Then Ram Khanna started to tell a story about a friend from his college days who was newly arrived from the boondocks. Xavier sold his friend a painting by Raja Ravi Varma that turned out to be a fake, an original Xavier fake. There was silence for some time and then somebody said the painting was probably worth something today. It was a skinny woman in a striped sari. Her hair and jewellery were the same shade of silver and she had a way of holding her cigarette, like it was a fountain pen. Ram Khanna was about to make some cutting remark about the way his poor friend had been treated when one of the houseboys came running and whispered something in his ear. Ram Khanna motioned to me and we trooped after the houseboy who led us to the top floor. The woman in the striped sari followed. We found a crowd spilling out of one of the rooms. The boy took us through to the balcony. I took a deep breath and looked over and I already knew, a part of me knew what I would find. He was fast asleep on a narrow ledge and it was a long way down, believe me. Ram Khanna turned to me with a strange smile on his face and said, you brought him, you take him. I leaned over the balcony and touched Xavier's arm and he came awake instantly, that was the funny thing. The other thing was that he hadn't been drinking. He'd just decided to take a little nap on a ledge four floors above the ground and when he opened his eyes he found a crowd of faces peering at him. Give me your hand, I said. He waved me away and grabbed the balcony railing and swung over easy as you please. Ram Khanna clenched up like he was going to punch him or grab him by the lapels, but Xavier didn't give him a chance. Thanks much, he said. I had a lovely time. Then he walked carefully down the stairs. I went with him of course, followed by the woman in the striped sari. On the way down she introduced herself to Xavier as the editor of a new magazine named *Closed*. She was a student of his work, she said. In the eighties she had bought a painting from his Chocolate Jesus Period, a tableau of Christ's brown body being lowered from the cross. She said she bought it for the quality of the tiny cuts criss-crossing Christ's legs and torso and arms. Cuts inflicted by the tip of a sword, careful lines that leaked black blood. Would he, she said, consent to an interview? She knew he was busy and she knew he didn't like interviews but she would send her best arts correspondent, a young woman who had studied at Goldsmith's.

For god knows what reason, maybe he liked the striped sari, maybe the nap had put him in a good mood, for whatever reason he agreed. The interviewer of course was Goody Lol and the rest is history or maybe biography or maybe a sexy soap opera.

Farzana Amanella Kaur, arts activist, interviewed by Dismas Bambai in Lado Sarai, New Delhi, October 2005

I heard he had left her and I went to see how she was. Kuthalingam let me in. Master gone, he said, shaking his head. She was sitting up in bed with a thriller. That hadn't changed: she was still addicted to thrillers, a leftover from the days of Newton. Come in, darling, she said. She had moisturiser on her face and she was reading and it seemed to me she was glowing.

And she was sipping from a steel glass. She winked and said, it's medicine, darling. At least she didn't pretend with me. She wouldn't use a real glass, that was unthinkable, but she didn't pretend. In the couple of hours I was there she rang the bell a few times for Amma, Kuthalingam's wife, who would bring more medicine. Kuthalingam came in at one point to complain to me that the financial situation was dire and he had suggested that she take a paying guest. That way at least there would be a regular income. Sometimes it seemed as if Kuthalingam and his wife were the true owners of that high-ceilinged old house in one of Bombay's oldest localities, and Lula was the paying guest who rented a room. Well, it was true that there was no income. I found out later that when she needed cash she would sell some of the art she and

Newton had collected on their travels, a painting or a bronze or one of the antiques. Kuthalingam would sell them and I can only guess at the commission he charged himself.

I'd brought along some periodicals, including a movie magazine in which there was an article about her, a speculation, what happened to Lula Xavier, you know the kind of thing, and it was headlined, *A Lifelong Battle Against Beauty*. The writer said Lula set no stock by beauty, that she had always been at loggerheads with Bollywood because she didn't understand them and they didn't understand her. She read it through carefully, right to the end. Then she said, you know I agree with almost everything here. I don't understand them and I never will. I said, that's because you were always beautiful, Lula, for you beauty was a given. No, my darling, she said, it's because I never thought beauty was any more of an attribute than one's blood type or the shape of one's feet. I saw no achievement in it. She was quiet for some time, flipping back and forth and looking at the pictures they had published, including pictures from the day she married Newton. Then she said, the only thing I don't agree with is the title. Darling, my lifelong battle wasn't against beauty, my battle was and is against stupidity. That is the true enemy! Look at what they've done to Bombay. Look at how violent they are, sweetheart. Isn't violence a failure of the imagination, after all? And that failure, isn't it stupidity?

I asked whom she met and whether she would like to go out for dinner one evening. On occasion, she said, she met her daughters from her first marriage, but those occasions were few and far between. She said, oh dear, what do you do when your daughter tells you to fuck off? What? You have to fuck off, darling, there's no other option. For me it was always a bit of a thrill and a shock to hear Lula talk that way. You never expected vulgarities to drop from her flawless classical face.

She was drinking too much and she kept falling and hurting herself. Once she needed eight stitches to the head because she fell in the shower. I went to see her and I asked her point blank, Lula, are you trying to do yourself in? She looked at me as if I had just put the idea in her head and she found it most alluring. Don't do it, Lula, I said, I shall miss you terribly. You know what she did? She nodded as if she were considering the idea, not doing herself in, I mean. She would think about it and let me know. She would weigh the pros and cons of staying alive.

When I went to see her the first time after he left and she was sitting in bed sipping from her steel glass? She told me she had been expecting it from the time he began travelling to New York and staying in the apartment his father had left him. She said he left for an extended trip in 1990. He had a new show opening, he said, and he left her alone for six weeks. Sometimes he'd be gone for weeks and months. So one day when he mumbled something about an affair she was not surprised. You do know I'm seeing someone? That was what he told her. Her reply? Well, I hope it's a psychiatrist, darling, because you know you need one. She expected him to leave but she didn't expect the notebook and the sketches, dozens of sketches of the same woman, Goody.

I asked her if she would ever forgive him. She said forgiveness didn't come into it. I'm grateful he left, she said. I only wish he hadn't taken so long to make up his mind.

Goody Lol, artist, interviewed by Dismas Bambai in New York City, November 2003

Everybody asks the same thing. How did you meet? I should think there are more interesting questions but apparently not. Is it the gossip quotient? Is it a way of keeping the social network oiled? Or some kind of leery male curiosity? I find it annoying, to be honest. But I've told the story before and I'm sure I'll tell it again. Be warned. It is longish and it begins on a foggy winter morning. Delhi fog, which isn't fog at all but mixed pollution and wood smoke.

The year I'm talking about is 1996. I remember because of the music, angst-in-my-pants from North America. Bands named after food items, pumpkins and honey and jam, suicidal white boys trying on grime like a flannel shirt. Newton was still in Bombay, living in Lula's Colaba apartment. I'd just returned from the UK. I was a student at Goldsmith's, part-time job, English boyfriend, moderate debt, the usual trappings. But you can't be a student forever and so I came back, boyfriend in tow.

I was fresh off the plane. Not acclimatised to Hindustan or Delhi or Vasant Kunj. I suppose I was floating toward decompression, working freelance for a magazine and floating.

If I considered my surroundings at all I imagined a place out of mythology. Say the Wild West or Afghanistan. It was the kind of neighbourhood where a chance interaction might take your life. The pub signs said patrons must leave their guns and ammunition at the door. The highways were dirt strips in the desert. You saw no life forms for miles. Sudden storms picked up handfuls of dirt from the road and flung them in your face. On the main road were camel-drawn tractors and horsemen among dust-laden trees. Villagers carried country-made revolvers that misfired and the security guards' weapons resembled flintlocks or muskets. Accidents were commonplace. Murder more so. Once I saw an old man in an autorickshaw being shot at by a chap in a car over some small traffic dispute. Instead of stopping, my taxi driver sped away. I saw four riders on a single bike and the last was a full-grown langur monkey holding on tight like the men. After some time I began to see the men of Delhi as monkeys or cattle, inarticulate and easily riled. In my first week a man on a scooter stopped on the other side of the street, rode across the road, and followed me against the traffic. I was walking home from the store. It's a long walk and he kept after me the whole time. I picked up a rock and told him calmly that I would kill him if he didn't go away. The man looked respectable, as if he had a decent job and a family with at least one female member. I could see him considering his options and then he turned and sped off without a squeak. I put the rock in my purse. I liked the crustiness of it and the roughness against my palm. I was floating toward decompression but now I was armed.

That morning I stepped out of Block A, Pocket C, and wound a scarf around my neck for the cold. Two men on a bike went past. They wore black jeans and black windcheaters and their helmeted heads were turned in my direction. The helmets too were black and they reminded me of insects, black two-legged insects riding an insect-mobile, predators from a far galaxy hunting for earthwomen to abduct and impregnate. Fucking gross Delhi men, I was covered up in two layers and an overcoat and still they stared. What did they see? Or was it the smell of clogged blood matter? Male animals are attuned to the scent of female menses, to female confusion, to any kind of female vulnerability. It's a bastardly biological imperative. Being chaps and sons of bitches they had sniffed me out from a distance on a windy morning. I watched the bike go very slowly up the street and I put my hand in my purse and I felt better the minute my fist closed around the rock. The bike didn't stop. I closed my eyes and an image flashed. Two helmeted insects bent over a tied woman. They would leave the helmets on, I knew, leave the helmets on and take turns and they wouldn't stop until I was dead.

People driving on the mud-made outer roads of Vasant Kunj would have seen a girl with a deep fringe, a forlorn figure speaking to herself, because I used to do that, I number-spoke. I remembered numbers like others remembered faces or scents. Twenty-eight, I said. And I said it three times rapidly, because three is a good number and the insect bike's licence plate ended in twenty-eight, unlucky twenty-eight, the date of my mother's birthday and my own.

I hurried on to the general store near the wine shop and grocery, the only businesses in that entire one-donkey outpost of an outpost. At the counter the proprietor drank tea from a thumb-sized glass. He'd just woken up, a plump man of about sixty, unshaven in an oversized wool sweater and too-tight monkey cap. The ensemble was so outré it was almost chic. I nodded at him and felt an impulse to reach across and squeeze his penis in greeting, because, don't ask, it was a vision I had sometimes. A world in which men and women fondled each other dispassionately when they met, as if they were handling fruits and vegetables at a store and deciding what to purchase. Except if someone tried that with me I'd bludgeon him, make no mistake. I picked up household essentials, batteries, light bulbs, a carton of milk, a packet of paneer, and the only unexpected thing in the entire establishment, Clarins sunscreen, SPF forty. Then I found the most essential item of all, at least for me that morning. Menstrual pads.

(Why is it that people never talk about periods? Why aren't a woman's periods taken into consideration by employers? Do you know that tampons are taxed like luxury items while men's razors are considered essentials? Do you know that male murderers get caught more often than female murderers? Women are used to getting blood off their clothes.)

I added the pads to my purchases and as the proprietor rang them up I saw it again. The first digits on the receipt were a two and an eight.

(My analyst Garima once called it the magical child syndrome. I heard the words and I recognised it as my own condition and before even Garima explained I knew it was a condition from which abused children suffered. Sometimes, in the privacy of my own head, I call it the digressionist's complaint.)

I walked home with the bagged groceries and, though the men on bikes and in cars turned to look me up and down and weigh each body part like meat at the butcher's, no one stopped. This was a good thing. My hands weren't free.

At the building I went up three flights and walked into the flat. The English boy was snoring gently. He wore a faded Air Force Academy T-shirt and his man breasts sagged. His boxers were open and I wondered if I might someday grow to cherish if not love his reluctant wrinkly penis. It seemed unlikely considering I never saw his penis or I saw it so infrequently it might have been a dream penis with no practical benefits. I made tea with milk and sugar for him and placed a cup by his side of the bed, doing my wifely Indian duty though there was no point really. Sam was not Indian and I was not his wife. There was little chance I'd ever be his wife or the mother of his children and yet I was the one who went out for groceries and I was the one who cooked and I was the one who worked and paid most of the bills. The worst of it was that I did it uncomplainingly, as if my expensive education and ongoing self-education mattered not at all. When it came to the important things I was as powerless as a village woman whose only purpose was to please the bastard man.

I had a shower and switched on all the lights. I found English pop from the eighties and turned it up loud. I like getting dressed to music. I would have been happy to be alone but Sam was getting up and the mornings were difficult for him, not that the evenings were better.

(Sam. What can I tell you about Sam? Let's just say he was in analysis too. We were two analysands living together in perfect disharmony.) I washed my face with an alkali soap and when I looked up Sam was leaning against the doorway with his milk tea.

"I dreamt someone was teaching me patience in a house that was on fire," I told him, because I like to tell someone my dreams. "It wasn't my stepfather. It was a man in white kurta-pyjamas, a man I dream about sometimes. I see him with my mother but I never see his face. The house was on fire and he told me to sit quietly in my chair. Just sit, he said, sit with your knees together and don't do a thing. This was when I knew he was not my stepfather. How did I know? My stepfather would never say those words to me. Sit with your knees together. The man in my dream shut the doors and windows and the room filled with smoke but he wouldn't let me get up. Don't move, he said. You must learn to be patient. If you don't know how to be patient you don't know anything in this world."

Don't get me wrong, I felt quite safe in the dream. If you tell a child everything's going to be fine she'll believe you. Children want to believe. For example, I always believed my mother however stupid her lies. I believed her but I didn't trust her.

The night before I'd been lying in bed looking at a men's magazine when the phone rang. I remember there was a photo of an Indian or Pakistani starlet on the cover, nude but for a bar code on her navel. And the phone rang and Sam said, go on, answer it or she'll keep ringing. I said I couldn't help her. I knew what she was going to say. She was going to go on about the dog.

"For god's sake," said our Sam and picked up just as the phone stopped ringing.

"I don't remember the last time we made love, do you? Is it because you're English?"

"Oh, please."

"Because if you're gay there's hope," I said.

The phone rang again and again Sam picked up.

"Hullo, hullo, yes, here she is."

Then he said no and gave me the handset.

"Why do you call in the middle of the night? Call in the daytime like everybody else," I said.

The voice was the same as always, heavy, sedated with alcohol or drugs, rusty with disuse.

It said, "I knew you would be awake."

"I'm not awake," I said.

"I can't sleep," the voice whispered. "I'm alone and I can't sleep and it isn't even midnight."

"I've told you before, take a pill."

"I took a pill, I took a few pills and they don't work."

"I don't want to talk to you."

"I know, but there's no one else I can call. Tell me, who can I call?"

I threw the magazine to the floor. I was cramping with pain on both sides of the abdomen, my fallopians most likely, and I had a sudden craving for prescription medication or codeine or Thai whisky (which is actually rum), something anything to take the edge off. But there I was comforting my mother when she should have been the one to comfort me.

I said, "If you need to talk to someone in the middle of the night call a professional. I'm not your therapist."

"Therapist, the rapist. Terror piss."

"What? What?"

"Thoreau pissed."

"Have you finally lost your mind?"

"I was thinking about the dog. If he hadn't made me walk the dog none of it would have happened."

When my mother finally hung up Sam was asleep. Or he was pretending to be asleep, because he was good at pretending was Sam. Whoever said girls are the great pretenders had no idea. Boys are better. It's the only thing they're better at. I went back to the magazine, the Pakistani on the cover who reminded me of a waitress at the Sliver where sometimes I picked up coffee. The waitress wasn't butch exactly. She wasn't your mama's dyke. She had the new look. She was wide open to the world in whatever shape or gender the world chose to manifest. On my first visit she had caught me staring and she'd stared right back. She had thin lips and badly made eyebrows, actually a badly made unibrow. But my nipples had hardened just looking at her. The waitress smiled as if she knew the exact effect she'd had and I remember wanting to reach across the counter and slap her face or pinch her or squeeze her until she yelped; I'd wanted to mark her in some way. The girl had a bone-shaped stud in her tongue and I wondered if there were studs in her labia. Then I asked myself why I was attracted to working girls, waitresses, salesgirls, beauticians. Because the lower a woman is on the social rung, the better the sex? Or was it simply a power thing, someone who can be told what to do? Lying next to the sleeping Sam, I touched myself without heat and fell asleep and dreamed of the man who taught me patience.

(By the way, I'm quite aware that I have a tendency to digress into thoughtful exegesis at inopportune sexy moments but there's nothing I can do about it. Blame gender studies. Blame gender. My generation and yours is of a more recent uncorking than Xavier's. We exchanged the intellectual tyranny of communism and existentialism – followed closely by modernism, with false starts in the general direction of deconstructionism, post-structuralism and semiotics, itself an offshoot of the older subjugation of symbolism – my generation exchanged these tyrannies for the new tyranny of gender studies. But the ends of tyranny are the same. If you are not up on Foucauldian biopolitics and heteronormative versus homonormative and the minutiae of the gender binary and the homoerotic subplots of Charles Dickens, if you're not up on the jargon you are not part of the discussion. You are a pariah. Your bark is irrelevant.)

That morning as I got ready for work Sam sipped his coffee and asked what I was doing. I was in the bathroom with a pump dispenser. What did it look like I was doing? I read aloud from the label: "Removes excessive sebum, dirt particles and dequamation without drying skin, supports the barrier function of the skin's acid mantle."

I said, "As far as I know, dequamation is not a word. Do you think they mean desquamation, the shedding of the skin's outer layers?"

Sam said I should look it up.

"I did. It's from the Latin and it means to scrape the scales off a fish."

I pushed the pump twice and spread the stuff evenly on my face. I rinsed with cold tap water and wiped with a tissue and said the words again, the skin's acid mantle. I soaked a cotton pad with alcohol-free toner to close my pores then mixed a bit of the no-nonsense Clarins sunscreen with a generous puddle of aloe vera moisturiser and dotted my cheeks, chin, forehead, and nose. I spread the dots evenly over my face.

"You look like you're getting ready for a date," Sam said.

"Sam," I said, "blimey, cor, cry-fucking-key, the twentieth century has left the building. Women have sex with men as anonymously as men have sex with men. You don't own me or owe me or want to make love to me. I wish I were going on a date."

"Sex without strings."

"The stringless fuck, yes, if that will get a rise out of you."

With a flat sable brush I applied a base for the concealer. A white soufflé-like fluid, its job was to deflect light and make it harder to spot blemishes, which I had my share of, alas, not to mention, alack.

"I discovered only recently that sable is made from the fur of a marten, a shy, slender, bushy-tailed creature that lives in the northern forests. Actually I'm not sure it's shy, though it is certainly all of the other things. This is a posh-ish brand and they say they don't test their products on animals but that doesn't mean a marten wasn't violated for my selfish ends."

I picked up a hairbrush.

"Cheap brush, some kind of fake wood. It does the job."

I was jabbering because I was nervous. My eyes didn't need much work. I outlined with kajal and highlighted with a coppery brown mixed with black. I skipped the lipstick.

"No date," I said. "I have an interview with a painter and I want to show him some of my work. See what he says."

I put on a skirt and slipped the hairbrush in my bag and the phone rang.

I picked up and said, "Now what? Why don't you give it a rest?"

But it was my analyst.

"Sorry, sorry, sorry, Garima," I said. "I thought it was my mother."

"Then I'm glad you're standing up to her at last. I'm calling to ask if we could reschedule tomorrow's session for the evening?"

I said yes and hung up.

I didn't have a date but I had hopes. The power failed just as I opened the front door. In the silence I heard Sam curse. It took ten minutes to find an auto. The driver was young, not more than eighteen or seventeen by the look of him and so new to the city that he didn't even glance in my direction, which, I have to say, was a nice way to start the day. I told him to take me to the Sliver and I took a table at the back. The shop had just opened and the waitress was alone. Good morning, ma'am, she said. We sized each other up and didn't smile. I want a double espresso and a banana-nut muffin, I told the girl, and don't call me ma'am. A television above the cash register was tuned to a religious channel. A bare-chested man with a bushy black beard and a lazy eye assumed a series of yoga poses. At the end of each asana he leered suggestively at the viewer. Utterly disreputable little man, I thought. When the waitress brought my order I asked her to show me where the toilet was and she led the way to the ladies' room. It adjoined a larger restroom with a wheelchair access sign. I pointed at it and said, after you. She didn't hesitate. That was something in her favour: she didn't hesitate. Inside she held her face up for a kiss but I stepped back and locked the door and put a finger to my lips. Then I reached into my purse and took out a five-hundred-rupee note, which I folded and tucked into the girl's bra. She looked at me as if she had expected more or as if money was the last thing she expected, but she didn't return the note. Her lips were small and bow-shaped and seemed to be smiling even when she was not. She smelled of fried food and sweat and her fitted black trousers were so snug it was difficult to push my hand inside. Obligingly she unbuttoned the trousers and pushed them down and started to say something. Don't talk, I said, reaching in my handbag for the hairbrush with its palm-sized round back. But I'd hardly begun when it cracked in two. The waitress moaned, her cries muffled, her dark ass red and marked; and I spasmed twice. I sat on the toilet and pulled the girl around. Her mound was shaved and hairless and darker than the rest of her.

There were no piercings in her labia but the clitoris was an anatomical miracle, a fleshy pink head buried in folds of dark flesh like a dwarf penis, visible even when she stood with her legs closed. I kicked her feet apart and licked briefly and tasted metal. Just as the girl began to tremble a response I stopped. I smelled menstrual blood and realised it was my own and I was afloat again, I was a floating head of air and light. On my skin the low hum of fever and my mind clear and emptied, perception narrowed to smell and taste and touch, the first time in days or weeks that I'd felt alive. I stood up shaky in my heels and took a quick look in the mirror. My hair was perfect. I pulled down my skirt and grabbed my handbag. Outside I ate half the muffin and took a sip of the lukewarm drink and left without checking to see if the waitress had returned.

It was ten a.m.

It took forty minutes to get to the offices of *Closed*. I met my editor and said I'd file a story in the evening in time for the web edition. Then I Googled the painter and blocked out more questions and printed out some of my own work. I had a smoothie at my desk and went to the ladies' room to change my sanitary pad and made it to the terrace of the café in Hauz Khas a little before two. I wrote the first sentence of the story before he arrived. "New York-based artist Newton Xavier is in Delhi for an exhibition of his nudes." The rest would write itself. He was about twenty minutes late and when he sat down I caught a whiff of something, unwashed clothes or some general dishevelment. He wore a fisherman's sweater and a duffel coat with a paperback stuffed into one of the pockets. I spread my notebook and recorder and pencils on the table and said something about the weather, always a topic in Delhi. I ordered coffee and felt a bubble of moisture or blood drip into my sanitary pad and I remembered that I hadn't let the waitress kiss me. The thought made me wet again.

I turned on my recorder and said, "Tell me something you've never before said to a woman."

His reply was immediate. "I do not want to sleep with you."

I said, "Is that a line that works usually? I want to sleep with you?"

"Not always," he said, "but this one does. Let me paint you."

He took off his coat and placed it on the back of a chair and said, "Speaking of which, perhaps you should allow me to paint you."

I noticed that he had an odd way of saying these things. It was as if he was mouthing lines he'd said many times before and didn't really believe, as if he was playing the role of roué with no real interest in the outcome. Later it struck me that it was an effective seduction technique. I thought I should try it myself.

I asked what he was reading and he pulled the paperback out of his pocket. It was an advance copy of a novel by a famous writer. What was his opinion of it?

"The hero's name is Ka," he said. "Say the name twice in rapid succession and that is my one-word review of the book."

I asked why he would read a novel he did not like. "Because sometimes I read for the opposite of pleasure. This book is an inadvertent lesson in how not to write."

The interview stretched to lunch and we went downstairs to the restaurant and took a table by the picture window. I remember there was a wide view of the city in all its haze and I switched to vodka cocktails because I knew where this was headed and I needed backup. He ordered black coffee – the former alcoholic's beverage of choice, he said, because he was newly on the wagon and a little push would send him tumbling off – and grilled fish, to which I helped myself.

I gestured to the waiter and pointed at my glass and used the universal code. "Repeat." When the cocktail arrived I drank thirstily and the sight of me drinking too much had an effect on him. He acquired the manner of a Jesuit monsignor, a type I knew from one of the schools I attended.

Was he a good Catholic?

"Catholics grow up in the sin house, if you see what I mean," he said. "We are always talking about sin or thinking about it or committing it. Then we confess. In return we receive just as much penance as we can handle, we recite sixteen Hail Marys, we put money in the poor box and kneel on the stone and beg forgiveness and then we do the dirty all over again. Sin is expiation, salvation is negotiable, pleasure is pain. I mean, who invented the communion of sadomasochism?"

I considered his pop eyes and white stubble, the air of disreputability, and mixed with all that some inescapable charisma, something in his self-containment you wanted to shake up. He was returning the scrutiny. He said later that he knew at the moment of our first meeting that I was capable of anything.

I said, "I'm not Catholic, thank god, but for some reason my notion of God is western. I experience guilt and shame."

"I would not have thought so."

"You mean I come across as guilt-free and shameless. That's a hell of a thing to be telling a woman at the first meeting. How old are you?"

"Fifty-eight, and you?"

"Twenty-six in September."

"I'm old enough to be your husband," and, realising what he'd said, "I mean, your father."

"Old enough to be my husband, old enough to be my father. But you're married."

"I am. And I live in my wife's house in Bombay."

And then he said the words that would determine the course of the evening and possibly our life together.

"Come to communion with me first thing in the morning, refresh your sense of shame. When God is in your heart I'll show you how to sin like a good Catholic."

The city lay before us, flat and vast. In the distance streaky lights flared from the haze of construction dust and dropped a layer of yellow on the tarmac of the old airport. Parakeets flew an erratic line to the darkening trees.

He said, "In fairness and as a countermeasure I give you two verses of John: 'Most assuredly, I say to you, whoever commits sin is a slave of sin. And a slave does not abide in the house forever.'"

I felt a chill on my neck and gathered my things.

"What are you working on now?" I asked. His blue notebook had been in his hands the entire time. I pointed at it. "Is it a poem?"

He said he liked to make lists because a list was a way of shoring up your ruins. He was making a list of suicide saints, he said, a partial list because a complete list would be endless.

"Where would you stop?"
"I'd like to hear it," I said.
"Are you sure? It does go on a bit."
"I'm sure."

He opened the notebook and said the list would begin at the beginning with the Book, because nowhere does the Bible condemn self-murder. How could it when martyrdom was an early variant of suicide? And if suicide was a religious act then suicides were the unacknowledged saints of the universe. Beginning with Samson under the pillars. Or Saul taking to his sword, his name cursed for all time, like Saint Judas, the second most famous Biblical suicide. Or Jesus himself, whose death was a pact the Son made with the Father, Jesus and all his apostles, self-made suicides to a man. He said he had come to the conclusion that a complete list was too difficult an enterprise even for him, akin to making a world sized map of the world. Instead he would begin with the poets and proceed not chronologically but sideways, starting with the earlier Romans such as Lucretius and Lucan and Labienus. Or Attila Jozsef who answered to the name of Pista, because after consultation with the neighbours his foster parents decided that the name Attila did not exist and when he found it years later in a story about the King of the Huns he threw himself on literature as on a sword. Mayakovsky the gambler, partial to Russian roulette, failed prophet whose gunshot was heard around the world. Sergei Yesenin's blood-written goodbye, his patent leather shoes and the handheld noose like a scarf around his neck because there was nothing new in dying or in living. And Marina, unable to work, penniless from slaving on the hard ship, her husband and daughter taken, abandoned by her lovers and begging in advance for her son's forgiveness. The pharmacist Georg Trakl, whose sweet secret was colour, the white sleep, the silver hand, the silver scent of daffodils, the red body of the fish, the red poppy, the red wolf, the purple clouds, the purple grape, the green silence, the green flower, the black rain, the blue grief, the soft blue footsteps of those who had risen from the dead. Gérard de Nerval, who told his aunt, this life is a hovel, don't wait up, and hanged himself with an apron string. Reinaldo Arenas sick in New York City, and his note, Cuba will be free, as I already am. Ana Cristina

Cesar harnessing the evil of writing to confront desire, who gave in on a London street. And Celan deep in the Seine, free to be Ancel again. And the outlaw poet Johnny Ringo, his boots tied to the saddle and horse run off, feet wrapped in his undershirt, dead in the fork of a tree from a gunshot to the head. Vachel Lindsay and Sara Teasdale happy in the wide starlight because the dead are free if only for a single hour. Sylvia, classic head on a kitchen towel in the oven. Assia, acolyte of Sylvia, also by gas. Anne Sexton in furs, sipping a martini in the garage. John Berryman off a bridge into the frozen Mississippi, whose last lines were, I didn't, and I didn't sharpen the Spanish blade. Randall Jarrell's dark overcoat stepping into night-time highway traffic. Lew Welch, disappeared into the wilderness. Hart Crane, disappeared into the sea. Weldon Kees, disappeared. Harry Crosby, priest of the black sun, who crafted images from the air and gave himself a twenty-five calibre black sun hole. Reetika Vazirani with a borrowed kitchen knife, taking her infant son first, in a house borrowed from friends. And after the poets, the others. Dhan Gopal Mukerji, pioneer writer in exile, never white enough or warm enough in America, never Indian enough in India, marginalised by preference, performed the rope trick at home. Hargurchet Singh Bhabra, in his leather and shades, smashed dinner plates to the floor of the lecture hall as a writing exercise and with the sickness upon him he changed the name of his novel to Faust. Andrés Caicedo on a failed mission to Hollywood, returned to Colombia to follow his own rule that young men should not live beyond the age of twenty-five. Géza Csáth, neurologist, violinist, music critic, painter, writer, seducer, wife murderer, morphine addict, whose study of pain led to brilliant complications and poison at the border. Jerzy, who wrote, I'm going to sleep a bit longer than usual, call it eternity. Virginia, bombed from two homes, left on the banks of the River Ooze her hat and cane and a letter to Leonard: everything has gone from me but the certainty of your goodness. Walter Benjamin in Spain on a trudge to nowhere, transit cancelled, delivered by morphia, whose friend Koestler borrowed some and tried it too, but failed, and tried again forty-three years later, this time taking with him a wife. Malcolm Lowry, buried in Ripe, dead by misadventure or alcohol and barbiturates, rich man's son who never recovered from early happiness, author of impossible instructions to himself: describe sunlight. The novelist Ryunosuke Akutagawa, who inherited his mother's madness, took Veronal for the vague uneasiness. Dazai Osamu, Akutagawa worshipper, five-time attempted suicide, thrice with women, who succeeded alone in a canal. Yukio Mishima's short sword on its left to right trajectory, then the difficult upward pull; two years later his friend Yasunari Kawabata, who for two hundred consecutive nights saw Mishima in his dreams. Harry Martinson, killed by critics in a Stockholm hospital, seppuku with scissors; Richard Gerstl, seppuku with butcher's knife raging against Schoenberg's wife; Emilio Salgari, seppuku in a park, raging against his publishers, to whom he wrote, at least have the decency to pay for my funeral. Diane Arbus who said if she had photographed Marilyn, suicide would have been writ plainly on her famous face, as it was on her own, Diane, with her downers and slit wrists and overkill. John Minton, friend, drinking partner, hoarder of Tuinals, painter at odds with an abstracted time. Ray Johnson's backstroke from the Sag Harbor Bridge, Frida's painkillers, Dora Carrington's pistol, Pollock speeding and the tree he aimed for, the miniaturist Daswanth's dagger, Witkiewicz tied to his lover, who revived, Arshile Gorky wifeless, studio burnt down, broke and yearning for clarity. Dalida and her luck the third time round. Richard Brautigan and Freddie Prinze and Leslie Cheung, who stepped from the Mandarin Oriental in Central, twenty-four floors to the street below. And the actresses of the Indian south. Silk Smitha, who took the poor woman's recourse and wound dupatta to ceiling fan. Lakshmisree and Nafisa Joseph, also Monal, also Shobha, all of seventeen. Fatafat Jayalakshmi's sleeping pills. Prathyusha's juice and poison in a parked car. Divya Bharati, fooling on the ledge under her window. And my old friend and collaborator, the poet Narayan Doss, dead drunk and dead on platform two of Churchgate Station, and if the cause of death was a heart attack the true cause was suicide by alcohol, the Bombay poet's recourse. And the list would end as it began, with a Roman poet, say Cesare Pavese on a hotel bed, writing, "Okay, don't gossip too much," because he knew that gossip would become part of his myth, the poet's suicide myth, which, as we know, is the most powerful of all suicide myths.

When he shut the notebook I told him to pay the bill and take me to his hotel. We held hands in the cab to Connaught Place and kissed in the lift. He told me I tasted nice, strange but nice, a taste he couldn't place. I laughed and told him it was the taste of clitoris. In the room I looked at myself in the mirror. I told him, take off everything except my panties and scarf. Watch, I said, and turned to lick his face. He stood behind me and watched the images in the mirror shift and coagulate. Squeeze my ass, I told him. I was cupping my breasts and he was too and it was hard to tell who was doing what to whom, there was so much going on, so many hands. My breasts were sore from my period but I squeezed them together and watched him stare. Never fails, I said, cleavage. Months later he told me that his future paintings flashed then in his head with such clarity that his erection disappeared. I didn't notice. I squatted on the carpet in my boy's shoes and guided his hand and came quickly because I'd been well primed. His hand came away redly smeared. But he was soft and would not be revived.

"No," he said. "I need control or the illusion of control."

"The illusion," I said. "Because you're not in control, I am."

I fell asleep and when I woke much later he propped me on my hands and knees. I told him it was my second most favourite position. When I started to moan he cupped his hand against my mouth because he was of the silent generation, uncomfortable with articulation, comfortable only when the sex was silent and furtive and conducted in the dark, neither party able to see clearly or speak or fully undress, a generation so far removed from mine they seemed like a species unto themselves.

I fell asleep again and woke to sheets marked with lines of red. Some lines were tiny and delicate and there were also solid clots of blood jelly. One side of the room was spattered, as if there had been a murder, and I found it hard to believe I carry so much unnecessary blood matter. Xavier slept facing away from me and this little thing made me miserable.

(I'm always surprised by my need for intimacy and that I expect it only from men. From women I want sex. So strange, don't you think?)

From his hotel I went to *Closed* and filed the story in plenty of time for the deadline and it was then that I realised I had forgotten to show him my own work and I had forgotten my appointment with Garima. I was sitting at my desk staring at the phone when it rang.

"I'm sorry, Gudiya, I should never have gone out to walk the dog. If I hadn't everything would have been fine."

"Why do you call so late?"

"I don't know why you came back to this country. Nothing works, nothing changes. I don't know. Gudiya, I'm sorry."

"That you certainly are."

"If I hadn't gone out everything would have been okay."

"No, it wouldn't have. He did it when you were there too."

"When I was where?"

"While you were in the house. You would be cooking and he'd be in my room with his fingers in my pussy. Do you know how old I was?"

"Stop it," my mother said.

"I'm not sure, but it goes back as long as I remember. I would have been two or three. Do you know he got into my bed and pretended to sleep? Every chance he got, whether you were in the house or not."

"Stop it."

I hung up and read the story through once more. It was good enough and I sent it to the editor.

I want you to know something. The story was no puff piece. I portrayed him warts and all. For example, I mentioned that every important event in his life seemed to have at its centre religion and women, and women came first. He said he had learned about colour by looking at flowers and women. He said the predominant subject matter of art and the only complete formal motif was the female form. He said the problem with Cézanne was that there were too many apples in his work and not enough women. I quoted all of this and I posed a question. How can we take such provocations seriously? Obsessives are divorced from reality, I wrote. When a man professes too much admiration for women you must wonder if in fact his true response is fear.

I knew he would hate the piece and I wouldn't hear from him again. But when the story appeared I found an email from Newton in my inbox. Was I free for lunch? I replied with one word. Then, for a year we communicated by email and telephone while he worked up the nerve to leave Lula. For a year he asked me to move to New York with him. He can be persuasive if he wants.

BOOK FOUR

X, 66

Saint Santosh

of runners, sailors, romancers;
voice of the robbed & drowned;
found himself in a foreign town,
distracted by the eyes of dancers;

enjoyer of denim & rhythm;
soccer star of the Republic of Kerala,
whose motto, Kiss My Posterior,
is repeated in graffito, lore, & drum.

Saint Dharini

of Noon Wines, Infantry Road, Bangalore;
a/k/a Ari; d/o Bhuvapathi,
student of planet, moon, & star;
her own arenas of study

were social science, fashion, the cosmos;
nimble with numbers; Internet savant;
kind child partial to the tearless rant;
tough enough to outlive the loss

of her father & of me.

from *The Book of Chocolate Saints: Poems* (Unpublished)

1.

Those who enjoy mental health turn away from the mad. An axiom. Those who are healthy turn from the sick. Another. Goody didn't think about Xavier's small eruptions until much later when they were impossible to ignore, when his broken nose sent a stream of gore to his chin and crisp white shirt. Broken precisely at its apex the nose would precede him for the rest of his life, a weirdly flattened appendage that reflected the untidiness in his head. But that was later. At the moment his condition, or one of his conditions, was anxiety rooted in the sky. He could not bear to fly, a strange problem for a man who had done so much of it. The longer the haul the more extreme his unease, and this journey was eight thousand miles across continents and time zones, an odyssey that made him re-evaluate his position viz. the world, made him feel like a stranger in evening dress wandering the streets of a foreign town, mute, without memory or personality, hypnotised by a shop window or the sight of a family having dinner in a restaurant. He told her he could not fly without his lucky boots of heavy pointy-toed leather, uncomfortable, yes, but they kept the plane in the air. He could not fly bootlessly and he could not look out the window, he said, and when the plane taxied into position for take-off he made the sign of the cross discreetly with his thumb, twice in rapid succession.

She said, "Admit it, you're scared and you revert. You go back to God by default."

They were flying Kuwait Airways from New York to Bangalore via Bombay because Xavier's research showed that the airline had never had a crash in this sector. But the service was no frills, no smiles, no nothing, and the aircraft was elderly and there was a seven-hour stopover in Kuwait, accommodation not provided.

"And, New, you're a famous painter. You're allowed to fly business once in a while."

"Might I point out that the flight isn't any shorter in business class? Also, exit row's in economy. In case something happens you are closer to the outside."

Kuwait International was a throwback, medieval, a quick return to the world that was Not America. Goody felt heat exposure on her skin. She felt unprotected, at the mercy of testicle soup and testosterone stew, a target of reptilian male psychosis. Everything gleamed with money but behind the gleam centuries-old tribal systems were in place. She folded her arms around herself and let suspicion show on her face. This was her new position: assume hostility at the outset.

She walked along the display aisles and stole a lighter, white plastic, a disposable artefact of international travel emblazoned with a slogan in red, I ♥ KUWAIT. She clicked the lighter and watched a group of young Arab women in one-piece leather masks, the peekaboo hoods and oiled straps a sexual signal in any language. Shepherded by a man in a white robe they left a heavy wake of perfume, and there were similar groups everywhere, three or four women guarded by a man. The men were bored and randy; they stared at other women, at Goody.

She told Xavier, "They're probably fucking each other, the women."

"One can only hope."

At the airline counter she picked up coupons for dinner. The attendant wore a short-sleeved shirt buttoned to the top. It was too hot for buttoned collars even in New York, never mind Kuwait. Maybe he was still living in the eighties when people wore air ties. Or was it the nineties? Goody had been too young to note the flannelled moment and there was no point checking with Xavier. For him the eighties and nineties were a single decade that blurred one into the other, a hyphenated intoxicated feast.

They wheeled their luggage trolley into a lift and went up two floors to the dinner buffet, a narrow amalgamation of generic colour and overcooked North Indian curry. The apples in lieu of dessert rotted in a bowl. Xavier looked seasick; he refused to touch any of it. The peeling paint, the dim deadman's light, the neglect and general decrepitude amounted, he said, to a preliminary taste of India. Even the weather had been adjusted: there was no airconditioning. He stared at the previous day's *New York Times* and noted that the weather forecast – "Hazy sun, mixing with clouds" – seemed already to describe a faraway country.

Goody said, "Pick it up, old man, we have a long way to go before you get to pack it in."

"Remind me, why are we making this desperate journey back to the land of our ancestors?"

"Because America is finished, history is moving backwards, and India is the future past. Quoting you. Also, you own property in Bangalore."

"Last but not least."

"Um, no. That would be *66*, your life's work, coming soon to the National Gallery."

They went to the main terminal to wait and Goody fell asleep in her leather seat. When the flight was called Xavier patted her lightly on the knee and she came awake in panic. He examined her eyebrows as if he had only just noticed that they were shaped differently, the left brow acutely angular in relation to the right.

She said, "I dreamt we were married. People on the street carried placards that said you were cheating on me. And the worst thing, the worst thing, they misspelled my name."

It was midnight when they took off.

Xavier had insisted on the aisle. He wanted quick access to the lavatory, quick access and return in case of turbulence. Goody sat next to a Punjabi woman whose kajal had smeared from tears. Of course she was crying, Indian woman flying alone from Kuwait to Bombay because of an emergency or family tragedy, why wouldn't she cry? Goody wanted to take her by the hand and weep in solidarity. How many weeping women in how many aeroplanes rushing homeward to the heartbreaking denouement?

The cabin lights dimmed but it was still bright. She felt Xavier's fingers tighten around hers as the plane gathered speed and tilted and became weightless, rubber wheels lifting unsmoothly from the tarmac. It shuddered and rose, rose and shuddered, and the light became brighter: the moon, fat and full and glued against the sky, an oversized dinner plate.

He gripped the armrests for the entire flight. The movie was a

Bollywood melodrama in which a woman was separated from her two small children and treated cruelly by her dead husband's family, and at the climactic moment when the widow beat her chest until her bangles broke and it was clear that she had lost or was losing her mind, Goody was surprised to see Xavier in tears. He had forgotten his fear for the moment.

New York–Kuwait–Bombay–Bangalore, so many flights the take-offs and landings merged into a single hum of engine noise and vibration, until they arrived at an apartment off Infantry Road, a yellow space in a faded beige-on-beige Soviet-era block, the small apartment that his father had bought for Beryl. She had furnished it but never lived there: she preferred the asylum. The building was badly maintained and gloomy but the second-floor apartment was full of light, the rooms furnished with items his mother had acquired on one of her furloughs from the asylum, heavy side tables and teak almirahs stocked with old-fashioned crockery and bed linen. There was a four-poster bed and no writing desk. In a tin trunk in the kitchen they found clippings of articles Xavier had written, as well as gossipy magazine items and interviews that spanned the decades.

They were close enough to walk to Cubbon Park, to the teeming mall world of MG Road and Brigade Road, but to walk was to risk one's life. There were no pedestrian crossings. The traffic was murderous and the air full of carbon. Goody felt it in her lungs, in her throat, in her eyes, the city bursting out of its skin and putting a new face on top of the old. The makeover wasn't working. It was still a toy town of toy cantonments, club architecture, good weather, and bad roads.

One night they saw a car brake to a stop in front of an autorickshaw. A ponytailed man exited the car and pulled the rickshaw driver out of his seat and bounced the man's head off his vehicle's windshield. The man cowered and the driver of the car slapped him, then dropped him on the road and got back into his car where classical music had been playing all along, a piano sonata nearing its climax of moonlight and grandeur. The ponytailed classical music lover bowed his head and paused a moment before he drove off and soon the rickshaw-wallah drove off too. Neither man had uttered a word. The sonata's muted notes hung in the air like the exhaust fumes that sat in layers on the street, visible only under the sodium streetlights.

The suicide capital of the country, said Xavier, if not the world.

"There should be a sign, with an arrow. You Are Here: Suicide World. That smell in the air isn't carbon or chemistry or emanations from the construction pit. No, Goody. What it is? Hysteria. Rilke was off point. Nobody goes to Paris to die. This is the place. Look around you, this is the place!"

They went to a wedding reception for the son of a state politician. The politician was the only Syrian Christian face in the Hindu national party's local operations. The man suffered from a syndrome that made him "anxious to please his captors", said a friend of Xavier's.

It was a fine day, cool and bright. Goody wore a dress and Xavier a stingy-brim black straw he'd found in the East Village. He trimmed his beard and put on a tie, a wide striped silk number.

Guests crowded the lawns of the bungalow and men in white walked among them offering trays. Goody took a glass of champagne and Xavier a Virgin Mary. He had assumed a strict non-alcoholic regimen since the Chelsea opening and Goody's two-word ultimatum: no more.

The luncheon party was in honour of the politician's younger son who'd recently married an American woman, a PhD student of divinity working on a dissertation about Islam. She was travelling to Hyderabad to study the city's mosques, she said. She was small-built and scrappy and she'd brushed her hair to a shine. She had a mind, which wasn't surprising, and she wasn't afraid to show it, which was.

"Do you like India?" someone asked.

But the divinity student did not make the expected reply.

"There's a lot I don't like. And there's a lot I don't understand."

It was clear to Goody that this was one of the things she was unable to understand, a lunch party that her father-in-law had insisted on calling a wedding reception although she and her husband had been married several months earlier at the Manhattan City Clerk's office. Goody liked the woman's seriousness even if it verged on the absurd. The American stood slightly apart, examining the crowd around her. She blinked in the powerful mid-morning sunlight as if all this had nothing to do with her, the three hundred guests sipping champagne at noon, the blur of faces and names, the rich array of appetisers, main courses, desserts, the white linen and silver cutlery, the waiters' formal white sherwanis and turbans – and the unimaginable tab for it all.

Goody told Xavier, "Like she's thinking, I'm a divinity student for god's sake. What am I doing here?"

They overheard heated conversation from a group of men who stood in a loose circle with glasses of whisky in their hands, conversation so loud you were obliged to eavesdrop.

"You're living in one of the best countries in the world." The man's accent was brittle, almost American.

"Easy for you to say, you're a NRI."

"And you? You are Sunni, Shia, what?"

"Like I always say, NRIs are more loyal than the king, more Hindu than the Hindus. Why is that?"

"What does it stand for anyway, NRI? Not Really Indian?"

"Answer my question, Sunni or Shia?"

"I am a peaceful person until provoked."

"We are all peaceful, babu. That's the problem with this country. Too docile we are, like cows chewing on grass. What we need is a dictator, someone who doesn't mind breaking a few eggs. With a corrupt system there's no other hope."

"The system is not corrupt. Our infrastructure is sound and the engine is running. It is the motorman who is corrupt."

"The motorman, conductor, catering officer, supervisor, passenger, all are corrupt."

"Sunni or Shia? First answer my question."

"All are corrupt. That is the first principle of democracy."

"Money talks, look at Japan."

"Yes, yes, exactly. Look at Japan."

"Look at China."

"What about China? They are corrupt too."

"Yes, but once in a while over there someone is shot. In public. And there's a big party, bigger and better than this one."

"Admit it, if you have money in this country there's nothing like it. The Indian middle class is king. We live much better than the middle class in the west."

"Where is the middle? Even our servants have servants."

"In San Diego, Sunday was laundry day. Full load, detergent, wash, dry, sort, stack. Here, throw it in the bin, finished, everything comes back washed and ironed."

Goody and Xavier wandered into the house, where a flatscreen television emitted a murmur of voices and theme music. She looked around for the remote. Where was it? Buried under the tidewrack of newspapers and magazines on the coffee table, but where? She gave up and raised the volume by hand. On the screen a coiffed man of forty held a cordless microphone, then the man disappeared and there was a photo of a floor lamp with an image of the coiffed one on the base. A rapid voiceover: *This beautiful earthenware lantern worth Rs 4,375 or more, now at half price. Let your loved ones share in the light of Benny Time.* A video followed of Time speaking to a sea of faces, his accent unidentifiable.

"New, come here," said Goody. "It's your friend Benny Time!"

Xavier crossed the room to take a look at the screen.

Time said, "In the midst of darkness, who will shine a light? Say Jesus."

It was like falling asleep, he told her, listening to that voice from the past, Benny sounding just like his old man, Father Time of the Church of Time.

A turbanned servant came in to say they were wanted in the dining room where toasts were being drunk to the bride and groom.

"I do rather want to watch this, don't you?"

"New, focus, focus, it's a social occasion and there's a toast being made. Come with me."

She led him to a room where a woman was saying, I'm Glory and I'll tell you a story. Glory told jokes at the rate of one a minute, in Goody's rough estimate. The laughter from the crowd was rude and knowing. She's done this before, thought Goody. She knows her audience, and what an audience, what a bunch of bozos.

Later Goody and Xavier stood by the unlit fireplace and examined the art, two large gilt-framed oils of a couple seated in leather armchairs, the man in a suit, the woman in a sari.

"Hideously perfect," Xavier whispered.

"If I'd known," said a voice behind them.

It was Glory, who had snuck up behind Xavier and put her hands over his eyes. Up close Goody saw laugh lines and expensive cleavage.

"Hello, Glory, nice to see you or not see you."

She took her hands away and spun him around.

"If it isn't the prodigal painter returned from his travails around the world."

"This is Goody."

"Nice to meet you, my dear. I'm one of the first women who ever posed for Newton. It was a scandal in those days. He painted my portrait and enhanced me."

"That sounds about right. New has an incredibly fertile imagination."

"He made my boobs much bigger than they are. Years later when I got married my husband was most upset. I thought, how sweet, retrospective husbandly jealousy."

"I hope you sold it for a lot of money."

"Sell it? Are you mad? I wouldn't part with it for the world. It's in the bedroom away from prying eyes and my husband's gotten to like it. Especially now, considering I'm old and grey and fighting the forces of gravity."

"But you're looking splendid, Glory, splendid. Not a hair out of place and that glint still in your eye."

"Newton, such a charming liar. And do you remember Nayantara, my maid? Her boobs were bigger than mine in your painting and in life. That one I sold."

Goody said, "Glory, you mustn't call them boobs. They don't look like mistakes to me. Knockers, mammaries, sweater pups, the twins – anything but boobs."

Glory put her hands on her hips and examined Goody.

"Oh Newton," she said, laughing, "I like her. Now come along and meet your host."

He was the suited man in the oil painting, Cherian by name, wifeless for the moment. When he laughed his eyes turned wet behind his tiny glasses and Goody saw that he was already drunk. He waved his hand and sloshed the beer in his mug and spread his feet and addressed his remarks to Goody and the ceiling. Glory had disappeared and Xavier was on a couch in the corner, sipping listlessly at his tomato juice.

"Only God knows what my religion is," Cherian said. "I go to church even though I'm swadeshi through and through. If I had my way our churches would be swadeshi."

Goody said, "Swadeshi churches."

"Yes," said Cherian, "Christianity is an Indian religion and English is an Indian language."

Goody watched Xavier get up from the couch. He turned in a small circle and sat down again.

"Be lee you me," said Cherian.

Goody said, "What about this televangelist, Benny Time?"

Cherian dropped his voice and said, "What about him?"

"He's here all week long at an airfield on the outskirts," Goody said. "I've been watching the news."

Cherian laughed; he too watched the news.

"Is it true," Goody said, "hundreds of thousands of people? And the rumours about mass conversions?"

Cherian stopped laughing.

He said, "This is the kind of Christianity that gives Christians a bad name. Why convert Hindus and Muslims? Worship and let worship, allow a million flowers to bloom in the house of God. It's a big house and there are windows and rooms for everyone."

He took another sip, his big-lipped mouth loose around the glass.

He said, "Mr Time is like a glutton in a restaurant who cannot concentrate on his dish because he's looking at other people's food."

He used his belly as a shelf for the whisky-soda and there were wet stains on his shirt where the glass had sweated through the fabric. Like the other men at the party, he wore a white long-sleeved business shirt tucked into belted trousers, but his clothes were stale and his shoes had mud and bits of grass sticking to the sole. As he drank his talk became pauseless and confidential. He said he'd studied divinity as a young man and spent a year in Africa working as a priest. Then, in a moment of clarity, he'd given up the priesthood for ever. Goody asked if he had left the church to marry.

"No, no," he said. "I left to join Lipton. In six years I became the deputy director. Now I'm starting a campaign against tobacco multinationals, big campaign for the economic wing of the party."

She noticed that he never referred to the party by name, as if there were only one party in the country or only one party worth discussing, and it was a matter of pride that he was its token Christian.

"I hope you know," he said, lowering his voice, "that I was living outside India when I turned swadeshi."

"Just like Gandhi," she said.

His smile vanished and he became serious, his eyes wet behind the small frames.

"Exactly," he said.

He collected suicide trivia and reeled off dates and figures from the top of his head. Immolation by kerosene or diesel, hanging by dupatta and ceiling fan, bloodletting by razor blade and box cutter and kitchen knife, the mixing of rat poison with Coca-Cola, self-murder by long-distance train, leaps from short buildings, drownings in restricted bodies of water, and the usual self-shootings, overdoses, and death by traffic. He said there were two a week on average, two successful suicides, usually women in their teens and twenties but also entire families who drank insecticide or set themselves ablaze; and the cause was creeping hysteria, the certain knowledge that the future had passed and you would never catch up. There were nets in the mall to catch the despondent; if they survived they were prosecuted, because attempted suicide was against the law. He took her to an office complex on MG Road and showed her the city's first suicide net, which had frayed alarmingly over the years. He explained with the air of a guide that it was the site of Bangalore's first jump *inside* a tall building. Goody looked dazedly at the patchy walls and broken light fixtures. I know it doesn't look like much, he said, but it is an important site. Think of the young woman watching the tower take shape as she walks past every day. She attends the official opening, the cutting of ribbons, the dedication, the speech by a minister or deputy minister, and back in her room at the hostel she calls her parents and describes the building, exaggerating its height, making it a story about the city's improbable growth. Then, days later, or weeks later, or hours later, she takes a lift to the thirteenth floor and stuffs a handkerchief in her mouth and throws herself into the atrium where she lands at the feet of a three-man string section, the cellist wondering for the rest of his life if the sound he heard when she hit the floor was really a one-word review: ugh.

"Would you agree," said Goody, "that your study of suicide qualifies as an unhealthy obsession?"

"There's a difference between obsession and awareness. How can you live in a place like this without thinking about suicide? Prediction, Goody, Bangalore's suicide rate will only increase. By 2030 all who live here will want to die."

She wondered if he was disintegrating, bits of his personality flaking off and slipping away. He spent hours sitting in a chair, doing nothing. He might have been asleep with his eyes open, but he was too anxious to sleep and he refused medication, saying, I've been crazy off and on for years, why fix it now? There were other symptoms; Goody made a list. He was moved to tears by tales of lost siblings and parent–child estrangement, exactly the kind of improbable Hindi cinema that he'd denounced to the press at memorable length; was claustrophobic, particularly in lifts, on aeroplanes, and in basements; was susceptible to irrational urges in the presence of high windows; was in need of anxiety medication when it came time to visit a dentist; was, if not a hypochondriac, certainly over-attentive to various workaday ailments including mild digestive disorders, small aches and pains, and a blood-sugar complaint; was susceptible to cross-referenced superstitions, the number 13 but only when written in blue ink, or a cat of any colour near a ladder taller than a man's head, or a hat placed brim-down on a double bed; was averse to the numerals 00 and refused therefore to date paintings he had made in the year 2000.

He said he was casting about for something to take his mind off the daily grind of not drinking, not working, no longer being a Hung Realist or Progressive Autist. Because he was not working he was vulnerable to superstition and doubt. He worried that his well had dried, had never been much more than a trickle, a cruel joke perpetrated by the hucksters who had lionised him to buy his paintings cheap and profit from the investment. *The man's a genius, buy his paintings. From me.* His true contempt was reserved for those who valued the visual art over the poetry. Did they not know that he'd been poetry-stopped for twenty years and that was why he painted, because he could not write? Here he would mention the Two Marys and Goody's unwise dalliance with Dismas Bambai. A week later when he was on the upward curve of his cycle she'd hear him proclaim it as Truth: *he* was a genius, certifiable, the greatest *living* artist. You could see it even in his worst pictures, hell, you saw it especially in the bad pictures; as for the poems, there was not a bad one in the lot. Once he was dead they'd all be saying so and he would be worth millions. What was the point? He wanted it now.

Then he would say, "Why don't I admit it? Time's up and I'm tired. I'm useless and it's time."

Or his talk became fantastical. One night at dinner he spoke excitedly about the Aztecs, spoke for half an hour about blood and mythology, an extempore comparative study of Tamil versus Aztec bloodletting rituals.

"The Tamils are as bloodthirsty as the Aztecs but Tamils are masters of presentation and they know how to hide their essential natures under layers of mumbo, not to mention jumbo. The Aztecs did not wish to conceal but reveal. The long hair matted with blood. The blood worn like ribbons of honour. The faces dyed black. They were addicted, if you see what I mean, vampires to the brightness arterial."

He spoke admiringly of the way they cut earlobe or tongue for the thin red sashes with which they draped themselves, comparing them to the Tamil ritualists who embedded hooks in their backs or killed a goat and licked its blood and walked the streets with their chests gleaming red.

"It is useful to compare because in the worship of blood they are certainly comparable. But, and this is the point, if there was a blood championship the Aztecs would win. Their goal was to appease god not worship him. The blood is key, the sacred colour of the sacre coeur, a petition of mercy to the supreme authority."

Then he took a breath and forgot all about the Aztecs. He compared the Roma songlines of North India and Europe to the Dravidian lines of Australia. And on he went, talking non-stop, dazzling a table full of people; only Goody knew he was out of his mind.

He was out of his mind and the days became unpredictable. She took to spending time on her own, walking around the neighbourhood or disappearing to a coffee shop. One Sunday there was no water in any of the taps and she discovered there was no water in the entire building. It happened, she was told by friends, it happened often and it would continue to happen until one day the water would stop for good. She went out, turned left past the shopping complex on the corner and walked along Commercial Street toward the old Russell Market. Here she found an elderly peepal tree where a man had set up a small shop. A rope was lit at one end and allowed to smoulder and it was used as a lighter by the men who bought single cigarettes or beedis and smoked them quickly, their eyes vacant. She took a beedi and lit it with the rope and smoked standing by the side of the road, away from the other smokers who stared because she was the only woman among them. The tobacco burned her throat and the leaf left a bitter taste on her lips. When she went to pay, the man who ran the shop asked her if she was unwell. She told him her throat was scratchy. The man said he also sold lemonade, cough drops, and paan, but it was the lemonade that would help her because he made it with black salt and soda water. He wore a khaki bus conductor's tunic over a collared white shirt. Reading glasses hung on a cord around his neck. She nodded vaguely. The man used a metal lemon squeezer to make a fizzy drink.

"This will make you feel better," he said.

They hired a box on wheels that Goody was convinced would tip over in the lightest wind and the driver took them to a disused airfield two hours from the city. On the way they passed crowds of protestors, Hindus of all castes shouting slogans in Kannada and Hindi, united against a foreign evangelist who had dared to fish in local waters.

"Bharat Mata ki Jai. Benny Time go home."

The driver stopped the car. A crowd of bare-chested swamis blocked the road, flanked by a wedge of photographers and journalists, the swamis wearing pressed orange robes and shampooed beards. When a photographer gave the signal their expressions changed, placards and fists waved in the air, the slogans began. It was craft and choreography, thought Goody, impressive to behold. She saw a fight between two photographers who wanted the same vantage spot.

"Girish, Girish, calm down I say," said a reporter to one of the men.

Girish was beyond calming. He grabbed his opponent in a two-handed wrestler's grip but was unable to gain the advantage and the altercation ended only when the other man pulled off the cell phone that dangled from a cord around Girish's neck and flung it to the side of the road. Girish had to give up his spot to retrieve the phone.

The car could not move in either direction: there was a crowd behind them and a crowd ahead. Xavier wound down his window and a blast of sound and heat entered.

"Bharat Mata Ki, Hindu Dharam Ki Jai!"

It took a good twenty minutes for the photographers to get their shots and for the road to clear, and when the photos were done the swamis climbed into an air-conditioned jeep and relaxed against the towelled seats and waited for the next call.

In a vast lot jammed with cars and trucks the driver parked and said he would wait. They walked to the airfield, a fenced-in grid of giant screens and plastic chairs.

"I want to surprise him. If there's a chance, I want to avail," Xavier said, stretching the last syllable and its suggestion of Old Testament rigour, of *flail* and *vale* and *prevail*.

In the centre of the field was a stage awash in white lights and flowers. There were no stars in the sky. They made their way through makeshift aisles and found seats and then the wait began. Around them was a crowd of thousands or tens of thousands, people drawn from every class and caste, believers who'd waited all day squeezed two or three to a chair. An hour went by, two hours, then a helicopter landed into a dust storm and a tall figure stepped out and made for the stage, the spotlights reflecting the white dazzle of his suit.

Now a choir of twenty singers led the crowd through a version of the national anthem. The names of the states were mispronounced but Goody had never heard the song sound so grand, all leisurely pauses and effortless harmonies. The music sounded like gospel from the American south, funky gospel in a rattlesnake church, and seductive too, because the female voices were orgasmic or pre-orgasmic. Two Pandits, Jasraj and Hari Prasad, vocalist and flautist, came up for a quick spot and applause swelled before they had made a note. Then the Pandits left the stage and here were two women in white saris, the sisters Mangeshkar, Asha and Lata, their lifelong rivalry set aside for the moment. And what must have been the cost of bringing them to Bangalore for a single duet, India's most famous singers, movie industry mainstays whose private lives were gossiped and speculated about as much as the movie stars who lip-synced to their songs? Each sang a verse of the anthem, Lata's shrillness a long way from the sweet aching timbre of her early years, and together in hushed accented voices the sisters introduced Time.

"Bunny Tame," they said, "welcome!"

He bounded onto the stage in his white suit, holding the microphone with thumb and forefinger like a nightclub crooner and the floods picked up the shape of the multitude in its hundreds of thousands.

"Hallelujah! The people of God said Hallelujah!"

The answering roar put the crowd on its feet.

"Are you ready to be loved?"

Another roar.

"India will be blessed, a great past *and* a great future."

He introduced the politicians and industrialists who waited in the wings, well-known names and faces with the hushed hypnotised look of men who had become as unto children.

"We have so many VVIPs, more stars on the ground than in the sky."

A stocky white-haired man in billowing white cotton tottered into the spotlight, how frail and odd he looked, in a gold-bordered lungi and gym socks bisected by aged rubber slippers.

"It's the Prime Minister of Karnataka," said a woman behind them as the spotlight slid off the elderly politician and went back to the man in white.

"And we are honoured to have the Prime Minister of Holland because we're all human and we're all hungry. Aren't we, Mr PM?"

The man stepped forward, smiling shakily and showing no teeth. There *was* something hungry about him, Goody thought, a hollow-cheeked something that belied the beautiful grey suit and the pearly gleam of the pin in his tie.

The woman behind them said, "Sthothram, sthothram." It was the Malayalam for 'praise', Xavier whispered to Goody.

A man behind them belched and said, "Halla, Hallelujah."

The Prime Minister of Holland said, "It is a pleasure to be in Bangalore with Benny Time."

"Sthothram," repeated the woman.

"Can't you say it quietly?" someone said.

"Bengaluru, Mr PM, that's the new name," said Time.

"Soothram, soothram," the woman said. It was the Malayalam for 'secret', according to Xavier, who prided himself on his language skills.

"Bengalwoowoo," said the Prime Minister of Holland.

But Time had lost interest in the Dutchman and he turned to work his ministry, healing his way through a queue of several dozen sufferers, a two-finger touch on the neck and backwards they fell into the arms of a waiting minder, or they winced and swayed and stayed on their feet.

"I bless you for the whole rest of your lives."

There were scattered Hallelujahs.

"If you can hear me, let me know."

Time waited but there was nothing.

"Let me know louder."

Now there was a roar from the crowd.

"Is that the best you can do?"

A girl was screaming, stopping only to draw breath. How frightening to be a child among a crowd of the deranged and the worshipful, thought Goody, as another roar erupted. The child shrieked again, her cry lost in an ambient forest of dislocated yells and whispers, the restless fidgety lowing of a herd. Goody looked for her but all she could see were their immediate neighbours standing on chairs. Above them Time loomed on a giant screen.

She felt Xavier's agitation. There were too many bodies too closely packed together. She told him to tilt his face but the sight of the open sky did nothing to lessen the dread that was accumulating, he said, in the exact centre of his chest. Goody thought, this is what it means to be a mother, this helplessness and anguish in the face of another's infirmity.

She said, "If you want to start making your way to the stage, I'll come with you."

"Nope, nope, let's see how it goes."

A woman in a housecoat and headscarf nodded at Goody. Tears fell to her cheeks and her lips said a silent prayer and though she cried without cease otherwise she was composed, her eyes calm and intelligent.

Behind them the now familiar voice said, "Gee suscom forts you. Heecom forts me too."

Time said, "I want to introduce a young man, shining Johnny Starr. Johnny, I got a Q for you. Is this your first time in Hindustan?"

"Yes, sir, it certainly is."

"And how do you like it, Johnny?"

"I love it, Mr Time."

"Believe me, guy, the people love you too."

The music changed, became faster, and Johnny waded into a cloud of smoke. There was a saxophonist and a big-haired man with a keyboard slung around his neck. The choir bobbed in the back.

> Jerusalem, Jerusalem.
> Hear the fearsome angels chime
> Hosannas to the King of Time.

Johnny wore a white silk T-shirt with a flannel shirt and torn jeans. Goody admired the way he threw his hand in the air and cocked a hip and held the pose. Then, unexpectedly, he stuck out his tongue at the floating cameras and pogoed in place. It was mid-career Elvis via Kurt

Cobain. It was rock & roll and Broadway.

And it was a fundraiser.

Time said, "I believe the Lord Almighty wants to bless your finances and not just your life."

"Here we go," Goody told Xavier.

"Cumshot," Xavier said loudly.

Time said, "We've spent a lot of dollars on this great event. Now we'll pass the bags through the aisles. Let the people of God give. I'm asking you to give freely tonight. The angels of Jerusalem need you. John?"

Now Johnny Starr took a solo, a cappella, his phrasing more Seattle than Las Vegas.

> Jerusalem, Jerusalem.
> Hear the chosen children cry
> Glory be to him on high.

A camera crane passed over their heads, the operator pointing his lens at the billowing white gowns and shiny dark faces of the choir. Johnny waited until the camera had floated to a stop directly in front of him before starting his big-voiced finale, an eight-second rendition of a single word, *Time*.

> Jerusalem, Jerusalem.
> Earth will open, dead will live,
> Open up your purse and give.

> Jerusalem, Jerusalem.
> Jesus says we'll all be fine
> If we follow Benny Time.

Time reappeared just as Johnny's last note belled into a hush. As a professional, Goody admired the technical finesse and for that reason alone she thought the Benn and Johnny show deserved six out of ten.

"Give Johnny a big god-bless-ya. This is the largest meeting in the history of Christianity: 2.3 million people here tonight! A golden testament to the glory of God. Go on now, give the Lord a hand and show him you believe in history tonight. And the people said Amen."

"Amen."

Behind them the woman said, "Bliss a balathoost."

Goody took a quick look. It was a family, a man, his wife, three children, and several aunts, eyes closed and arms raised, absolutely ordinary except they spoke in tongues.

"Holy species us, holy calebola velapana."

"Send your power maker, elapum elopum."

"Holy calaybalamalapum glory elabum."

A bespectacled boy of ten said, "Hiss, hiss."

The music stopped and for a moment only the woman could be heard in the silence, "Sthothram." Other voices joined in, "Sthothram, sthothram."

Time had returned: "Oh people of India, I've not come to tell you about deliverance. I've come to tell you about a deliverer."

The man translating his speech into Kannada imitated Time's tone and manner and at times Goody couldn't tell where the English stopped and the Kannada began and this too seemed like a speaking in tongues.

"People of India, I ask you, do you want a miracle from the hand of the maker?"

"Yes!"

"Then stand up and call his name. Stand up in the name of Jesus. You too will be healed tonight."

Three women appeared on stage. Time touched them and they fell together in a heap and he pointed at another, who cringed.

He said, "This woman had a gynaecological problem for thirty years. Come here, gynac." The woman fell without being touched.

He said, "This boy was deaf and dumb for twenty-three years." He clapped into each of the young man's ears. "Hello, hallelujah," he said. "Say Jesus! See the tears in his eyes!"

There were tears in many eyes, but when Goody turned to check she found the verbal family dry-eyed, alert with appraisal, looking back at her.

"This boy couldn't see from his left eye. Yes, now follow me."

Time ran around the stage followed by a small boy in shorts and stopped at the spot where the main camera hovered above the stage.

He said, "You in your homes, I speak to you."

He pointed at the crowd. "Who will be healed tonight?"

Me, said Xavier to Goody as he waded into the throng. She called to him but he was already too far ahead. She had to use her hands to push and because she was small she made little headway. The crowd was thick, thickest near the stage, and she shouted his name knowing he wouldn't hear.

Benny Time said, "Hey, muscular dystrophy, come up here, baby, wave for me. Who believes in history tonight? Who will be healed? We give you the praise, Lord, we give you the honour."

He ushered a woman and small child to the front of the stage.

"A mother and baby. Hello? Does anyone speak Hindi?"

A man came up to speak to the woman and translate for Time who relayed to the audience.

"This woman is a widow, her baby's father is dead. It has been two years but her baby cannot walk. How old is your child?"

"Two years old!"

"Let this two-year-old baby stand and let her walk! Give the Lord a mighty hand of praise!"

The baby tottered a few steps and was taken away by her mother.

Then Goody saw an old man with a faint stumble, his skin transparent in a nimbus of light that adhered to the white stubble on his cheeks, Xavier, approaching with his hands extended.

He said, "Benny, Benny, oh my fuck!"

And because there were microphones and cables everywhere Xavier tripped and fell at Time's feet. And because there were microphones everywhere his words echoed and rang in the silence that followed. Benny Time tried to help him up and Xavier grabbed Time's lapels and Johnny Starr grabbed him. Time tried to intervene, but Xavier, panicking, flailed his arms and Johnny head-butted him and a warm red stream fell to his shirt.

In photos of the event that travelled the world in an Internet second the blood gush was Aztec black, spectacular, full entertainment. It was how the poet slash painter Xavier acquired his famous broken nose.

*

In the green room with a bag of ice on his face and Goody in charge, Xavier was all forgiveness.

"Not your fault," he told Johnny Starr. "You were merely doing your job."

"I'm so sorry. I thought you were an attacker. Forgive me."

"Let me get you a shot of Macallan," Time said. "Settle you down."

"No, no," said Goody.

"I'm not drinking, if you must know," said Xavier.

"Never," said Time, "did I think these lips would utter those words. Macallan. Not even a little bite to stop the bleeding?"

He went to a minibar that opened to reveal a selection of champagne, beer, and whisky. On a table were more bottles, mixers, a stainless steel shaker, and an ice bucket that had supplied the bag resting on Xavier's nose.

"I thought you were a friend," Goody said.

"But, yes," said Xavier, "that's why he's asking."

"Not that I want to be the cause of marital discord," said Time.

Xavier removed the ice from his face and stared at Time and neither man spoke. Then Xavier shook his head and put back the ice bag.

He said, "As far as I remember you liked discord, sowed it even. If anything, marital status was a red rag."

Goody got up, pointedly, and went to find the facilities.

"Listen, it's good to see you, I didn't know how to get in touch. You look, I don't know, distinguished is the word. Back then you were only disreputable."

"Which I was and may be still."

Time's voice dropped a rung. "I'll tell you who I remember. Miss Henry. Are you in touch? Last I heard she was a cat burglar drifting around the British Isles in a tinker's caravan and writing her memoirs. A whole chapter was devoted to you, or was it two chapters?"

"Miss Henry is in no hurry to speak to me, you'll be surprised to hear."

"Oh, true, true. You left her saying you were stepping out for cigarettes, a dramatic climactic point in the book, the moment she wins the reader's sympathies despite the drugs and the jail time."

"Because of the drugs and the jail time, you mean."

"Why are you so cruel to the women in your life, Newton? You've always been nice to me."

"There's nothing I expect from you other than this, Benny, a bit of conversation once in a midnight blue moon, an exchange of pleasantries, some inadvertent comedy or blood spill. But other than that, no expectation, no disappointment."

"And Edna, the mother of Gillian, your only child. How is the lovely Edna? I liked her. She didn't let love go to her head. She knew you'd disappear sooner rather than later, she expected it and she didn't take it personal. She was English."

"Dead of cancer. Gill blames me and doesn't pick up when I call. Is this a recap of my failures? If so we'll be here all night and possibly half the next day."

He took the ice bag off his face and gently moved his head. A black drop pooled in his nostril. Goody returned to push his head back and replace the bag.

"Don't mind me," she said. "Ask about Lula. I know you're dying to."

Time said, "Newton, she's right. I'm holding my breath. What happened to Lula, who used to scream loud and long in the same high pitch as your mother? I remember how sensitive you were about a high mad woman's voice."

Xavier said nothing.

"Still is," said Goody. "That won't change."

"Lula of the proper place settings, never drank in front of the guests for some reason, always tottered off to the kitchen to take her medicine, in quotes. End of the evening, she was drunker than anyone and that's saying a lot. Four a.m. and we'd be around the dinner table, still drinking, food untouched, ashtrays full. Passionate gossip about Rothko and Bacon, or was it Spender and Auden? You were trying to write again and you were fully invested in the midnight oil. Once I saw fifty drafts of a single poem. When you were inside a poem you kept at it no matter what was happening around you. Couldn't have been easy, the place was a madhouse. Any kind of stranger was welcome. I remember a wheatgrass evangelist and young poets by the score and a couple who had to leave their house in a hurry and arrived with pots and pans and a miniature herb garden. You were no recluse then. Lula wore a housecoat and played the piano. One night she turned off the lights and crashed one demented chord into another to chase away a bat that had flown in the window. You don't remember? How? I remember all of it. I used to worry about her."

"I know the answer to this one," Goody said. "May I, Newton?"

Xavier moved his head in what might have been assent.

"He left a notebook full of sketches in a bill drawer he knew she'd open," said Goody. "Then he left on a business trip and never returned. A hundred sketches of a woman who clearly was not Lula, who clearly was me."

"Such cruelty," said Benny Time. "I suppose it's a talent like any other. Do you meet her at all?"

"She doesn't meet people," said Goody. "She's become a kind of Garbo figure. Tell me, what happened to the bat?"

"The bat."

"The bat lost in the living room, did the piano dissonance work?"

"Yes, she managed to chase it out," said Time. "I think I miss her."

"Everybody does," said Xavier. "Even Goody, even though they've never met."

He noticed that Time's hair was still thick. Like his stubble it was more salt than pepper. He looked designed. The spotless white suit. The buttonhole. The orange tan and air of wellbeing. The healthfulness that reminded you he was in the God business and business was good.

"I wanted to get in touch with you and I didn't know how. I wrote to Dismas when I saw the interview in the Indian tabloid," said Time, "I couldn't tell him anything except that it was a matter of some importance."

"Well, here I am," said Xavier. "A captive audience. Captive and bleeding."

"I even considered getting someone to stake out Koshy's. I knew you'd drop in sooner or later."

"Koshy's, is that the important matter you wished to talk about?"

"I knew you'd go and say hello to young Koshy and if I managed to get through to you then you'd hear what I had to say. Listen, it's been more than thirty years since you've published a poem. I think I know why."

"Do tell, the damn nation wants to know."

"You said art makes nothing happen and if it cannot pick up a gun it has no place in the twenty-first century."

"'Poetry makes nothing happen,'" said Xavier. "Auden to Yeats, in memoriam. It wasn't me."

"'What use is a poem that cannot pick up a gun?' That was you and this is what I want to talk about. The party wants to ban the Church of Time in India. We've been getting emails, mildly unfriendly, and some outright threats. We had to increase the security cover. Johnny has reason to be paranoid. We all do."

"If this is some kind of elaborate apology, I'm not going to sue."

"No, ha ha, I mean, I apologise but that isn't it."

"How do you know the emails aren't from a Muslim group?"

"I don't. It's a distinct possibility."

"Or loony Christians hoping to whip up sympathy and solidarity?"

"Like I say, it's possible. We haven't ruled out anything. I'm thinking of inviting the party to a sit-down in Delhi. We have a press conference about pluralism. We say it's possible for different faiths to coexist. I make it clear I am not interested in converting anyone."

"Sounds somewhat doomed to me."

"I've been saying the exact same thing," said Johnny Starr.

"I know you have. Still."

"Sometimes preaching only works with the converted," said Xavier.

"Right, but let's say I appear to lose the debate. I agree conversion is wrong. I even say the Lord Jesus Christ would not want such a thing. We strike a blow for peaceful coexistence."

"A blow," Goody said. "For peace."

"Imagine if they're successful in banning the church. You saw how many came tonight. What happens to them?"

"Where, no, why do I come in?"

"You're a famous Christian. You have the name of a saint and the temperament of one, you know, a taste for isolation and long periods of denial in pursuit of your art."

"Let's not bring art into this."

"If you were present the thing would carry some particular weight. You could mention that you've known me for years, which is no lie. We could make a joint statement and say religions can work together."

"Get a Muslim. You don't want the Muslims to feel sidelined. Or a Hindu, obviously, get a Hindu."

"Newton, look, I want you because you don't get out much. You don't do press conferences. That interview with *Indian Angle* was the first time you said anything in public in years. You out there talking coexistence will reverberate. It will travel out into the saffron void and the void will send it back enhanced with echoes. It's a way to put a gun in the hands of a poem."

There was a silence and Goody went to the buffet to pick at the cold cuts and fruit and bread sticks. The plates were white china with a close-up of Benny Time in the centre. She placed sliced strawberries on his eyes.

She said, "Your face on a plate? I know it helps to love yourself in this line of work, but really?"

"Johnny's idea, not mine."

Johnny nodded. "Helps to pump up the adrenaline before you go out in front of a million people."

"Let me put your mind at rest," said Time. "I don't expect a Church of Time endorsement or any kind of cheesy advertising. I will not tell you what to say. Tell them I'm a phony, I don't mind, as long as we do the important thing, you and me in a room speaking reasonably to a camera. Then we leave it to them."

Xavier put the ice bag down and wondered what would happen if you contracted a nosebleed that never stopped. How long before the blood loss made you pass out?

Benny was his friend and he was in need. Of course he would say yes.

He looked at Goody who was making her way to his side of the room. She put the plate on the coffee table and removed her shoes and put her feet up on the couch.

"And what are your thoughts on this pressing matter?"

Goody said, "God."

*

And what of God?

Confession: he is not the only digressionist in this tale.

Nor is Goody.

After all, what is digression but the story entire? Every story is a digression from some other, it is in the digression that meaning resides.

There's been some discussion as to why God created the world. Let me clear it up.

He made the world because that's what he does. He makes things.

A more pertinent question, though pertinence is hardly the point at this point: why did he make humans?

Now there's a question.

He made us as a bulwark against loneliness and boredom. Too late he discovered we were in fact the opposite. We augment boredom; we deepen loneliness.

In time we make boredom and loneliness preferable.

As I speak, the moon bides its time.

Because of orbital distance the moon appears to be exactly the same size as the sun. The fact that it appears to be the same size as the sun is no coincidence, whatever scientists may say. It is design. It is a way of telling us that we are guilty of a conceptual error.

The moon is male and female. It is the true husband, the first wife, the secret father and earth mother.

It tinkles a stream of warm yellow on the mountains of a city; it bides its time.

Soon, though, soon it will give up all restraint and urinate in abandon on a street many miles to the north, and a woman on the street, and a man in a car, and an uncertain feast.

It will urinate on an old man dying in an alley in the city to the north. No, that won't do. Be specific.

A city one thousand and eighty-four miles to the north.

The moon has questionable hygiene and indifferent health. His urine isn't yellow but a deep hepatitic honey.

The moon is a monomaniac, a piss artist, and peeper.

He does not care about us.

2.

You die. You get old and die. Your anger curdles, your grief dries, your talent fades on the page. Your cells metastasise into an army dedicated to the overthrow of you. You become dependent on paid strangers for the maintenance of your blood and your brittle bones. You understand that thought is the enemy, the source of all lesions, tumours, and sarcomas; then thought becomes flesh becomes the emblem of your shame.

In the mirror he examined the hitherto unsuspected reservoirs of gore between his badly bandaged nose and collaterally blackened eye. Every day there was a new colour or some unexpected new shading to an old colour. He had never considered how much the nose shaped the face and how much disrepute must accompany its disfigurement.

Thoughts plagued him like a head cold as he walked around Sankey Park, or, to honour it with its true name, Wanker's Park, a title it had earned after an incident involving Goody and an aged Indian patriarch. (More on said incident later.) Wanker's opened at six in the morning and closed, inexplicably, four hours later; it stayed closed all day and reopened briefly in the evening. Located between Brahmin Malleswaram and unBrahmin Palace Orchards, it was landscaped but a shambles. New pagodas and benches were being installed; plants had been uprooted; there was mud and rubble everywhere.

The city too was a shambles, accursed by the outsize nature of its greed, structures razed and reconstructed in front of your eyes, roads widened, flyovers erected, and none of it built to last. This was the new Bangalore, made with substandard materials sourced and maintained by a gang of men in white khadi.

Goody said, "I spoke to the doctor. He wants to see you next week. You can't keep putting it off, New, how long will you put it off?"

The walkway that bordered the lake was being resurfaced. Xavier stopped to watch as park workers placed the paving stones, laborious work, like fitting together the pieces of a concrete puzzle. The stones were of an unwieldy shield-shaped design and some had to be broken to fit the walkway's curving borders. The result was all gap and overlap.

"He was interested in your symptoms, seemed excited, actually. I think he's the right doctor for you if only you'd give him a chance."

The workers wore chilli red or turmeric yellow lungis over shorts. What language were they speaking? A high-pitched bird staccato of truncated vowels and hard consonants. They were always working, supervised by a fat man in a windcheater, who did nothing as far as Xavier could see except smoke and nurse his hangover. Meanwhile, the workers sat on their haunches, bird-like, and placed the stones in the intricate, self-defeating pattern.

"He says you have mild hypomania. It disguises itself well enough that you seem completely normal."

What an ecstasy of invention they were, the paving stones, in their unevenness and the intricacy of their design. How much misdirected energy, how much labour had gone into their execution, how many days and hours of work by the diminutive men in lungis.

"In any case at least you're off the booze," she said. "What a word. Booze. I mean, it has ooze in it."

He wanted to weep. One of these days I'll start, he thought, and I won't stop until I die.

At night Wanker's Park was a commotion of fluorescent light, the lake hidden under a layer of green slime. A group of boys clambered out of the water with a plastic bag in which a dozen fish floated belly-up. They took the bag to a man on a bench who bought the lot for fifteen rupees. When the boys had gone, Xavier asked the dull-eyed purchaser of the fish if he had bought them to eat or to sell.

"Selling no good, *too* small," said the man. "I fry and eat."

Xavier nodded in the direction of a large half-dissolved Ganesh leaking blue and red paint into the water.

"Thirty thousand idols were drowned here," he said, grinning. "The paint from the idols killed the fish. I do hope you will reconsider your dinner plans."

The man nodded at the brownly stained bandage that protruded from Xavier's unshaven face. He nodded but the gesture conveyed no agreement and after a while he lit a beedi and sauntered away.

In the water Ganesh shed his necklaces, bracelets, and jewelled headgear. He shed his skin. He shed four arms. Now he was an obese child, head sawn off and a shrunken-to-scale elephant's trunk sutured in place. Now he was a straw figure bound with string, grotesque and pleading, a repository for cruelty and pity.

The festival rituals were all oddity and creeping nuance and it had always been thus. The men placing the paving stones were tribals and the fat man telling them how to go about it was a highborn or higher-born official. The conversation between them had occurred many centuries ago and would continue centuries hence.

I am home at last among my people, thought Xavier. My men and women with their love of the lash and indifference to filth, whose cruelty and serenity is the source of my rich, my inexhaustible subject matter.

You get old and you die. Your enemy is the disintegrating face in the mirror and the heart that will attack you one day. I is the enemy.

Naked came I of my mad mother's womb and naked shall I return.

In his dream his father was on a beach. If you don't mind (he said), I won't share. I discovered it only recently and I'm making up for lost time. Xavier waited while his father – who had never smoked a joint in his life, whose pleasures had been alcohol and cigarettes, who had been the editor of some of the most prominent newspapers in the country – smoked the joint down to the butt. The sea seemed unnaturally calm, like a sea in a dream, or like a painting of the sea made by a child, or like something that looked like the sea but was really something else. He saw a white cloud shaped like a mastodon and another like a sleeping woman, a woman whose profile and rose-pink complexion produced a constriction in his chest. Who is it? My mother? My wife? Someone who left me? The answer was about to reveal itself, was about to drop from his eyes in slivers of salt ice. But Frank yawned and said: my role in your dream is small but significant. I'm here to provide a bit of preliminary context and to tell you that dreams are tenseless. They have no past or future. They don't predict, they are. They exist like stories, or, to be more precise, like manuscripts with no title, author's name, footnotes, or publication details. That doesn't mean the story is incomprehensible or that some of its pleasure is lost. On the contrary the story derives its power from incompleteness and from its partial and fragmented nature. Those who ask after its meaning are mistaken or they are being intentionally rude. Then his father lifted his arms in a gesture that encompassed the sea and sand and blue sky. There are at least five ways to experience the ocean without demanding to know its meaning. For example, you can touch it. That is, you can cup it in your hands or immerse yourself in it or you can stand at its edge and dip your toe, said his father. Another way is to listen to its music. Did you know that the ocean rhymes with itself in each of its manifestations around the world? Because wherever in the world you find it the ocean's sound is the same. It sounds like itself. A third way to experience the ocean is to look at the shape it takes and try to map its abundant architecture. Let its immensity seep into you. A fourth way is to taste it and take a sip of its salt. The fifth is inconvertible and extreme. It is a permanent solution to a temporary problem and there's no need to go into it now. Do you see? Your mother was insane but you don't have to be. Xavier nodded and said, may I ask you something? That's what I'm here for, said his father. You can ask me anything you want. Xavier said, what is it like to be dead? His father nodded and looked up at the sky. What's it like to be dead, he said, that's your question? Yes, said Xavier. I'm glad you asked, said Frank. Every morning the body and the soul are reunited. At night they separate and free associate. Sleep will teach you how to die. Look around you and don't be afraid. Then his father spread his arms and turned in a small circle. Xavier also spread his arms and turned in a circle. But when he came back around Frank was gone and the beach had disappeared. He was near a lake. In the sky was a sliver of moon. What kind of moon? A moon like a clipped fingernail, like a smudge of powdered sugar, like a yellow laddoo, like a shattered dinner plate, like the tusk of a wounded mammoth, like a scimitar buried in the enemy's skull, like a horned demon drowned in blood, like a fallen warrior's silver visor, like the prow of a ghostly mothership, like the smile of a giant black cat, like God's half-closed night-time eye, a low murder moon, the kind of moon that will soon illuminate a woman not alone, in a city to the north. Not yet, but soon.

Why hadn't he noticed it before? The lake was shaped like a death's head moth. As the Ganesh immersions continued it grew thick with sludge. One morning they walked to the quietest part where a bridge connected the bird sanctuary – behind a link fence, the smell of excrement high in the air, no birds or sanctuary to be seen – to a small lotus pond. There was a crowd on the bridge, police officers, some park employees, and a couple of morning walkers in sweatshirts and sneakers. They pointed at a figure wedged among the litter and purple lotus blossoms. Xavier saw a bubble of black cloth in the green water, a man's shirt, and he saw a body floating face down and a glossy fringe of hair.

Goody spoke to a policeman who did not respond. She made her intonation flat and rough.

She said, "Dead body."

She's turning Indian, Xavier thought. What happened to the girl with the London lilt? But the policeman understood her now.

"Dead body," he agreed, "came in the night."

They watched as park workers pulled the man out of the water. Clumsily they dragged him to the embankment and clumsily they turned him over. He was youngish, naked from the waist down, with a faded rakhee on one wrist. More people gathered.

"Dead body," said the policeman, looking at Goody, his hand near his khaki-clad crotch.

The drowned man was on his back, his arms stretched above him as if asking for help, a bit of lake slime on his knee. Nobody had bothered to cover him up. They had pulled him from the water and turned him over and their work was done.

How had he got there? Had he drifted across the lake in the night or was he dumped into the pond from the bridge? A reveller accidentally drowned during the immersions? Had he been murdered elsewhere and brought to the park? If so, how had he been transported past the guards at the gate and brought to the most deserted part of the lake? And finally, who was he? Nobody knew. When Xavier persisted they told him to make a complaint at the police station.

They put the man in a hand-truck and manhandled him into a van and the next day there was no yellow tape, no policemen, and no barricades. In the days that followed Xavier looked in vain for a mention in the newspapers or on television. A man's body had been fished out of the water and it had been removed. There was nothing more to it.

Life went on; it was the Indian way.

You are sixty-six, one six short of the devil's own number. Your years rhyme with the black river Styx. You are in a town in the south to which you hoped never to return and you cannot shake off the feeling that you are starting from scratch with nothing to show for your years in the mines.

"What about critical acclaim?"

"Acclaim. Say ecstatic attention. Say adulation. Oh, and two books of extraordinary verse, and while we're at it, half a dozen pictures verging dizzyingly on greatness, and shows on every continent except Antarctica, which isn't a continent, and—"

"I get it, acclaim doesn't help."

"Wrong, pointless, monkey chatter."

They went to a coffee shop where they argued about the future.

"I'm sick of this place," said Goody. "Wasn't Delhi the destination? Every time I try to talk to you about it you say tomorrow. I'm sick of tomorrow!"

"The idea was to get a feel of the property my mother left me, the flat in which we are living at the moment, rent-free, I might add. A crucial consideration since we don't know how long we intend to stay in India. The plan was to visit Delhi and make the appearance for Benny. I do feel obliged. We were in school together."

"You were in a lot of schools. That's not saying much."

"Either way, moving to Delhi was never part of the script."

"Listen, New. I'm sick of this place. The air is bad and water's scarce. You don't like it either. We should move to a city that works."

He said, "Maybe you're sick of being with someone and you want to go back to being single."

"But that was your idea. You were the one who didn't want commitment. You said, and I quote, monogamy is the defeat of love. You called it monotony."

"I'd come out of a dry marriage. I was penniless, paying all kinds of alimony and child support. I craved my independence."

"You wanted my independence."

"I suppose I didn't expect you to take to it with such gusto and flair."

"And by the way you're still penniless. Don't blame marriage."

More than the marriages it was the long aftermaths and the in-between periods that had depleted him.

He married Edna in the Summer of Love as the sounds of the electric guitar and the Indian hand cymbal wafted through the streets of London. He grew his hair and published his second book and the poetry slowed to a trickle. He started to paint. In 1972 a small gallery in the West End hosted his first show, *Haré Krishna, Haré Christ*, a suite of melting psychedelic oils on canvas: Christ depicted as an Indian sadhu meditating in a cave; Christ escaped from the cross and hiding out in Kashmir; Christ with wife and daughter. (Edna had just given birth to a baby girl.) It was his controversial debut and the critics were unanimous. Xavier was the tonic the British art world needed, they said, and for a year he was once more the toast of Soho. He was interviewed on television and in the newspapers. A tabloid offered its readers a dinner date with the artist as a prize. He showed all over. He sold twenty-three paintings in one good month and made a lot of money; and then, as suddenly as it arrived it was gone. He was in India, on commission to paint the prime minister. The Emergency had just begun and the canvas took on the heavy sunless hues of the era. This was when Edna chose to leave, finally showing signs of the temper she had managed to hide when they were married. She sued for divorce and the court liquidated his assets including his art. He was left with very little. When his lawyer advised him to leave town he flew to Milan, where he lived in the immigrant quarter and didn't paint. He went to the museums and wrote (prose) in his rented rooms. He became a man, as he wrote to his London agent, "who dines alone in restaurants". His landlady was a big-breasted Roman of about fifty, whose loud voice and no-nonsense manner reminded him of some Indian women he knew, among them his aunts and cousins. But in private she proved to be the opposite in temperament to what he'd expected; she was needy, insecure, satiable.

His agent lent him a sizeable advance and he moved to Paris, where he began to paint in earnest. He made the work that came to be called his Chocolate Jesus Period, Christ stretched on the cross and looking heavenward, a fairly conventional representation, except this was a dark-skinned Christ, a sun-stained Palestinian, a Levantine, a Nazarene, a Jew, not the blond blue-eyed man hung in the churches and museums of the west.

One day in a bookshop near the Notre-Dame as he gazed at the poetry shelves a dishevelled old man approached. In his arms was a Persian cat that seemed serene and perfectly groomed in comparison to its master. The man asked a one-word question. Goan? Yes, Xavier replied, so surprised to be addressed in this fashion that he spoke the truth, which in those days he was not always likely to do. Need a place to sleep, the man said, and it was a statement rather than a question. The old man looked like a hobo but was in fact the proprietor of the bookshop and he took him upstairs to rooms with books on all four walls from floor to ceiling. There were cots and a table but no doors. You can sleep here and there's a closet in the hall for your things, he said. In return you work in the bookshop for a couple of hours a day. What kind of work and how many hours is a couple, asked Xavier, suddenly unsure if he wanted to stay. The old man laughed and in his arms the cat twitched. Nothing strenuous, he said. You place or replace books in their correct positions, an hour or three of work at the most. My name is Walter Shelton and when I was a young man I spent a year in India travelling around with little money, without so much as a thought in my head. People took me into their homes, they were kind to me, they gave me so much that in my own way I try to help travellers in need. All this is a roundabout way of welcoming you to my bookshop. I hope you feel at home.

Xavier took the metro to Gare du Nord and retrieved his bag from a locker and went back to the bookshop and spent a comfortable night, though the big room was dusty from the hundreds of books that circled the darkness. That night his dreams were set in cities he had never visited, heavy dreams filled with colour and sound as if the words in the books around him had seeped into his head through his ears. He was on the cobblestone streets of an ancient European capital, drunk on wine and vodka, and he walked past a turreted house with small stained-glass windows, the street narrow and steep and leading inevitably to the broken cobbles of a Bandra bylane near Saint Andrew's Church and to the broken walkways he had known in other parts of the city, in Navy Nagar and Colaba and Byculla and Shuklaji Street.

In the morning there was coffee and fresh bread from a bakery. The work was not difficult. He took books from a trolley and stacked them with the help of a stepladder. The San Franciscan at the cash register wore a goatee and ill-fitting beret and Xavier understood that the man was enacting a fantasy of French raffishness. He was Xavier's overseer and he explained how to place the books on the shelves with, he said, minimum effort and maximum efficiency. There was plenty of time to browse. At one o'clock the shop closed for lunch and he wandered into a garden nearby, where he sat on a bench and drank cheap red wine and ate nothing. Some days he went to Pigalle, always in the afternoon, and he walked around Pig Alley and drew a map in his head of the studios of the artists. He envisioned a five-pointed star, Vincent on top, Picasso and Degas at the bottom, Manet on the left and Utrillo on the right.

He saw Shelton off and on, the old man always in the same ratty sweater and colourless corduroy trousers. One afternoon the San Franciscan told him he had been invited to dinner at Shelton's private quarters on the top floor. Brush up on your Poe, the man said. Xavier asked why he would want to do that. Because Shelton claims to be Edgar Allan's great-grandson and Poe is his only topic of conversation, he said. Xavier was deep into a paperback, *The Peoples of the Americas: Vol. III*, a brief blood-soaked saga of the Aztecs, and he saw no reason to put it aside for the sake of Poe. He spent the afternoon on a bench reading about burial rites and the step pyramids of the moon and sun at Teotihuacan. At seven he put on a clean shirt and his quilted black jacket and walked up to the old man's quarters on the top floor. As in the rest of the house, books covered every wall of every room, including the kitchen and toilet.

This is where I keep the rare volumes, Shelton said in the kitchen, pointing to signed first editions of Joyce and Beckett, Henry Miller and Anaïs Nin, to suppressed or disappeared editions of M. Ageyev and J. K. Huysmans, to *Thaw*, a lost manuscript by Anna Kavan, to a collection of aphoristic texts by Edgar Varese that contained, among other things, a transcript of a conversation with the star Sirius, a stilted, mostly one-sided exchange concerning the date of the true apocalypse, and he pointed to a volume of Victor Jara's lyrics, to a copy of *Les Chants de Maldoror* inscribed not by Lautréamont or Isidore Ducasse, but by Albert Lacroix, the book's second publisher, a man renowned for the coldness of his feet and the soundness of his taste, whose inscription in Spanish, *El Palacio del Miedo*, may or may not have been genuine, and then Shelton's hand described a wave around the main room and Xavier realised that every book on every shelf was either by or about Edgar Allan Poe. The little space that remained on the walls was taken up by portraits of Poe at different stages of his life, as a boy with a wispy moustache, as a young dandy with haunted eyes, and as a slightly older gentleman whose face seemed to have collapsed into itself. There was a framed notice from a newspaper with the headline, *The Poet Poe is Dead*, and below, *Beastly Intoxication the Cause*.

Assisted by the San Fransican and his wife, the old man served fish soup and melted blue cheese over baguettes, a dish he called Franco-Welsh rabbit. Xavier produced a half-bottle of whisky, which he offered to the table and drank alone.

Yes, Shelton said, I noticed that when I was travelling in India. You drink before you eat. I'm afraid so, said Xavier, it's one of the bad habits the British passed on to us. Shelton looked surprised, as if Xavier had suddenly materialised at the dinner table. Tell me some of the others, he said. Xavier said he didn't want to ruin dinner with a litany of woes and if Mr Shelton didn't mind he would mention only the top items on his personal list: 1) corrupt top-heavy bureaucracies, 2) malfunctioning municipal administrations, 3) outdated laws and legal machinery, 4) a collection of states linked by no common language, except English, 5) a sense of cultural inferiority so strong as to be permanent or at least several generations deep, 6) mixed race Anglo-Indians excluded from the power centres of both India and the United Kingdom, who claimed allegiance to their fathers but were unwanted by them, 7)—

In fact, said Shelton, you're right. Let's not ruin dinner.

Xavier refused coffee. He waited for the old man to bring up the topic of his ancestry but he seemed disinclined to do so; and finally Xavier mentioned it himself. I heard in the bookshop that you are a descendant of Edgar Allan Poe, said Xavier. My great-grandfather, said Shelton. Xavier said, not officially, Poe died without heirs. No, not officially, my grandfather was born in 1850, a year after Poe's death. Sarah Elmira Royster Shelton, my great-grandmother, was unable to speak of her son's true parentage. She would have lost the family estate. It was a stipulation in her first husband's will that she must not remarry. In our family, however, it is common knowledge that Sarah and Edgar were married secretly in the last year of his life. I am working on a family history that will clear it up, as well as the final mystery of his death. I argue that it was not a case of beastly intoxication as the newspapers alleged but brain fever. As you might guess my family has laboured under the poet's great shade. My grandfather wrote stories that were serialised in magazines and collected into books and none of them has stayed in print. He wrote a travelogue under the pen name of Ptolemy Hephestion, who you may remember was Poe's invention, a geographer who named and mapped the Eureka Ocean that sweeps men into nothingness. The travelogue too is out of print. My father wrote a series of sestinas in which the rhyme words are taken from the language of Poe. For instance, in the double sestina 'Facilis descensus Averni', the rhyme words are *fathom*, *simoom*, *Ashtophet*, *eidolon*, *farthingale*, and *ichor*, words that are devilishly difficult to rhyme, though *fathom* with its double meaning gives itself more easily than the others to the machinery of the sestina. Even among poets it was said to be an achievement. My father was also an essayist and editor and his innovations included putting bylines and photos instead of advertisements on the front page. His publications include five books of verse and a book-length essay about the use of ghee as a daily tonic for the digestive system, as well as the following unclassifiable works, *How to Talk to Azaleas, Rhododendrons & the Flowering Dogwood*; *Mating in Captivity: the Anthropology of Marriage*; *The Man who Stole the Rain*, and *Jesus: The Collected Works*. Of course none of this matters since he is remembered only for the book of Poe-inspired sestinas. As a young man I turned against what I saw as the dubious legacy of my great-grandfather. I decided I would not be a writer: I would be happy. I travelled the world and made friends wherever I went. I lived in India, Afghanistan, the Greek islands, Trinidad, and I returned to Europe in my late thirties and started a bookshop. I became a businessman and householder and I had children I did not neglect. I made a success of myself. Then, in my sixties I had a dream of my father. He was dressed in a nightshirt in the snow on the streets of Baltimore, a city I have never visited though I dream about it more often than I should. I say the name to myself in the dark and it never fails to bring me an image of a white gravestone and horses in the snow. In my dream my father's lips were moving but I could not hear what he said. I got down on my knees and put my ear to his mouth and realised he was not speaking, he was shivering with cold. When I woke I understood I was being foolish. After all, Poe is my heritage, my great heritage. I was wrong not to embrace him. What do you say to that?

I have no idea what to say, said Xavier, finishing off his whisky. But there is no genetic law that says a father's or grandfather's or great-grandfather's neurosis must become one's own. Your youthful self may have got it right. It is better to cultivate one's own obsessions than fill out second-hand ones, for the simple reason that one will never fill them to their original rounded dimensions. And who's to say your own obsessions, prosaic as they may be, are not as valuable as a dead poet's? Nurture your obsession slash addiction because it is – and forgive me for using such a cheap word – it is destiny. But this is only my opinion, and opinions, as the popular expression goes, are like assholes, everybody has one, which doesn't mean they must be aired. Or excuse me, since we are in mixed company, let me rephrase that. Opinions are like armpits, everybody has at least one.

Soon after making this speech Xavier thanked his host and left. Shelton said, that, friends, is an example of a bright and unsteady mind. Keep an eye on him. Make sure he doesn't steal my books.

Xavier decided to take a walk. He did not want to hang about the bookshop where he was the only non-white boarder, the shop staffed entirely by Americans, no Europeans, no Asiatics, no dark-skinned races of any kind; it was an outpost of white America and more than anything he was sick of the accent, the earnestness, the grating timbre of the voices. The dinner with Shelton had left him angry and tired. What's more, he was still hungry. For the first time in his adult life he considered the possibility of returning to India.

I've lived too long abroad and I'm turning into a brown redneck or a black racist, but who can blame me?

He exited the shop and rushed blindly through the twilight. When he bumped into other pedestrians he muttered rudely under his breath though it was his own fault. Some people smiled or laughed because they saw that he was drunk and out of his mind, but others glared after him and muttered curses in return.

When he became aware of his surroundings he saw he was at the Cimetière de Montmartre, a place his mother had loved and taken him to when he was a child. He had visited it soon after his arrival in the city so he could look at Degas's grave, not because he was a devotee of the work, but because he was moved by the thought of saintly Degas in his last years when he wasn't painting, when he was friendless and nearly blind, his deprivations caused by the idea that an artist should have no life, no wife or children, no common consolation except art. The idea was insane and admirable and worth a return trip to the cemetery but tonight the gates were closed. It was late and it had started to drizzle. He recognised the fine Parisian rain that had killed so many poets and painters, a rain Xavier had learned to treat with deference. He turned away from the cemetery gates and wandered toward a dark avenue, where he hurriedly took a seat on a bench at a covered bus stop and pulled a book out of his jacket and a notebook from his hip pocket, reading from one and scribbling into the other. He realised he wasn't alone.

Partly hidden in the shadows on the other side was a thin bedraggled Arab who held a bouquet of wilted pink roses. Had he stolen them from the graveyard? The Arab's other hand was clenched in his overcoat pocket as if he held a switchblade or a pistol. At first he stared at Xavier without speaking and then he asked which country he was from. Xavier shook his head and the man said, Indian? You don't look Indian. In my country you could pass for Kuwaiti or Sudanese, some dark-skinned Arab, said the man.

"What are you writing?"

"Writing, rewriting, taking notes," Xavier said.

"Are you a note-taker?"

"Not exactly."

"Are you a writer?"

Instead of replying Xavier continued to scribble in his book.

"I don't like writers," the Arab said, inching closer. "I don't like writers and I don't like painters."

"Well, perhaps they aren't fond of you either," Xavier said. Then, seeing the look on the man's face, he added, "Whom do you like?"

The Arab held up the wilted bouquet.

"I like singers," he said.

He explained that he had been a teenager when he heard a song called 'Salma Ya Salama' on a dance floor in Tangiers. He had been fourteen or fifteen and just learning about sex and music and where his own inclinations lay. Here he wiggled his eyebrows suggestively at Xavier. He heard the song first on the radio and then he heard it in somebody's car and probably on the beach, in fact definitely on the beach, and soon it was everywhere. You couldn't escape it. Everybody seemed to be whistling it or humming it and all the nightclub singers were doing cover versions. It was a hit, a genuine over-the-moon beautiful fucking hit. He loved to dance to it and so did his friends, a group of boys who wore outrageous clothes and make-up and went to clubs every night. There were girls in the group but it was the boys who were the real queens. Trust me, he said, boys are more queenly than girls, more dramarama, you know, whatever. The song was all over the place that winter and then all of a sudden it was gone and replaced by another, just as catchy, just as maddening. Total French disco, which none of us had ever heard before. And he knew immediately that it was the same singer, because it was a voice you heard once and didn't forget, a voice that put a chill in your bones because it seemed to emanate from a landscape devoid of life, the voice of the moon if the moon could sing, a voice that belonged to someone who had looked into the heart of man and seen his true nature, an inconsolable voice.

The man held up the bouquet and said, "Dalida."

"I beg your pardon?" said Xavier, thinking he was referring to the extravagantly moustachioed Spaniard or some kind of Gallic sex toy.

"That was her name," said the Arab. "Dalida. Such a musical name, don't you think? I learned that she lived in Paris and I took a ferry from Tangiers to Algeciras and then a train. I came to Paris to be near her, to be in the same city. I took jobs here and there and I ran errands for people. I got by, thinking all the time that in a few weeks or a few months I would go back to Morocco and this was my Parisian adventure, ça va, ça va. Then one day I went to a club and there she was. I heard her, I mean, I saw her. She was beautiful but it was a frightening kind of beauty. I knew she would not stay long in this world. How did I know? I'll tell you. At the club I stood at the edge of the stage clasping my hands like a typical fag and there was a moment, one moment I'll never forget, when she looked straight at me and said, 'Mourir sur scene.' She smiled as she sang but it was a reflex, a facial memory of a smile that had occurred a long time earlier. I knew immediately because her eyes told me. After all how could she not when so many of her men had killed themselves and she too had tried so many times without success?"

"How many men exactly?" Xavier asked.

"Three times at least. Once she was in a coma for days."

"I mean how many men killed themselves," Xavier said.

"Six, six men, imagine! Her first husband shot himself in the head when he failed to win a singing competition. He was just twenty-eight, an age at which the weight of the world sits heavily on a poor boy's shoulders.

He was dropped from the final round and when he learned this he went to his room, wrote a letter to the jury, and shot himself in the left temple. Dalida found his body. Think of it! They'd just been married and they had presented the song together. A month later she tried to kill herself but she failed. Years later the man who had discovered her, her producer and former husband, a man with a lovely name, Morisse, he too killed himself and he did it the same way, shot himself in the left temple, as if he wished to send Dalida a message. Then her close friend," here the Arab made quote marks in the air with his fingers, "leapt to his death from his apartment. He was the same age as Tenco, her first husband, and it was as if he too were trying to tell Dalida something. What was he trying to tell her, what were they all trying to tell her, these death-loving men she loved? You can guess that she heard their voices in the night, saying sweet things and beckoning to her. She did not listen, not then. Her songs grew darker and darker but she went on and then one of her last lovers – she had many, so many, Egyptian pilots, Italian doctors, French journalists – he sucked the exhaust out of his Renault and died in the garage. At least two of her fans did the same, leapt from high windows and sucked off cars. But she? She chose a better way. A much more elegant way, pills in a warm bed in a luxury hotel. And she did not do it for love."

Here the man stopped and waited for Xavier to ask a question.

"Well, why did she do it?"

"Because she was getting old and she knew her best years were behind her and she knew that whatever happened next, it would be a disappointment."

The drizzle picked up a little and the trees dripped on the roof of the bus stop. Xavier smelled a wood fire somewhere, though the street was deserted. The Arab said he came to the cemetery to stand by her grave and leave some flowers. Xavier asked what he planned to do with the roses since the cemetery was closed. The Arab sighed theatrically. It had happened before, he said. There was nothing he could do about his absent-mindedness. He was distracted by his fate, his loneliness, his poverty, and the fact that he was a foreigner in an inhospitable town where even the rain told you to go back to your own country. How could he go back when his country no longer existed?

His parents had died, his extended family didn't care for him, and his friends, his beautiful friends, had vanished.

He nodded and walked unhurriedly to the cemetery gates. On the pavement he arranged the long stems and broken roses into the letter D. Then he set off down the unlit street, a small hunched figure in a dark overcoat, hatless in the rain.

Soon after this Xavier left Paris but he never forgot the story of the singer in whose life suicide had become a kind of contagion.

He returned to Bombay on the day the monsoon broke. The Emergency had at last been lifted and Mrs Gandhi voted out of power. The plane descended bumpily through clouds thick with rain. Foot by foot it descended and the turbulence eased. Outside, India was reappearing.

He was alone and starting over, his mother in the asylum in Bangalore, his blacklisted father living in New York, the apartment in Navy Nagar long vacated. He moved into a hotel on Marine Drive and supported himself with journalism, embellished reminiscences of the painters and poets and writers he had known. He went out every night. At a party he was introduced to the actress Lula Nadkarni, a former Miss India who had been voted one of the five most beautiful women in the world by *Vogue*. But New, she said, we are childhood friends. Don't you remember? He said that he did, though he did not. He dropped her home and they met again the next day and the next and finally he said, Lula, I own three pairs of shoes, a typewriter, and two pairs of trousers. But New, said Lula, I can help you with your wardrobe. He tried again. You don't understand: I own half a dozen shirts, some books, and a few paintings. New, said Lula, it's simple, let's go shopping, I'll take you. When she understood that he was proposing to her she said he would have to ask her father and he did and in a month they were wed. It was her second marriage and his third. They checked into a suite at the Taj where one night the phone rang with news. His father had died of a heart attack. His father had died and left him an apartment on Central Park West, an apartment and enough money to set up a second home if he wished.

*

On the way back to the apartment on Infantry Road they stopped at Koshy's to pick up his birthday cake. It was still early, the restaurant just opened for business, and he walked into the mid-morning gloom and felt warm air pockets open in his head, as if the flu had decided to set up camp. The big room's train station echo was exactly as it had always been, and the discoloured walls and peeling paint, the smell of cigarette smoke and fried meat and beer; he took a sniff of the air and understood what was wrong with him, that it wasn't the onset of the flu. He wanted drink.

Koshy's was where he would take his first vodka of the day at a table by the cash register as far from the window as possible, because in those days he was always hung over and sunshine was the enemy. All these years later being in the old room made him yearn for the oblivion of drink and as always his craving for alcohol was mixed with cravings for sex and travel and physical risk. He wanted drink but Goody had put her foot down. His last binge had been a week-long blackout that had ruined his New York opening. Plus, she said, who knew what alcohol would do in his current state? One more binge and she was gone, it was a promise, she couldn't take the stress of wondering if he would drink himself to death. They waited in silence for the cake to be packed and that was when the idea came to him. The restaurant's senior manager, Kurien, was a convener of the local AA group and a crony from the days of whisky. He was standing near the entrance to the vast kitchen in the back and he didn't seem surprised to see Xavier or to hear that he wanted to attend a meeting.

"This evening at six thirty. Come along and you'll learn a new way to meditate. The nose suits you, brother X!"

"I've never been to a Bangalore meeting. Too busy drinking, as you know. And the idea of hanging around with a bunch of grumpy drunks – it's enough to make you hit the bottle. In any case I always thought AA was for quitters."

Kurien laughed. "So it's time you joined us. It will be my pleasure to welcome you to the quitters' brotherhood. And on your birthday too, auspicious!"

The flame-of-the-forest was in flower on the road in front of the apartment. There was nothing too remarkable from below, wide-spreading branches and shy fern-like leaves, but from a distance a great umbrella of saffron-scarlet flowers bloomed forty feet above the ground. He'd been feverish all day, tremble-handed and subject to visions, imagining a shot glass of whisky dropped into a schooner of beer. When the whisky leaked into the lager it turned the exact colour of the flame-of-the-forest's flowers. Then with no connecting thread he saw a Senegalese woman who'd posed for him once in London, her face framed by a stiff red wig, sweaty in the electric light. She wore a tight black skirt that peeled like a sock and her figure was identical to some Palaeolithic drawings he'd studied in school, voluptuous mother images that were all torso and curve of hip and breasts that hung to the navel. He saw the woman's face as clearly as if she were in front of him, the exact jut of the lower lip, the smile like a trace element, the serenity in her eyes; and he remembered the jolt in his belly when he saw her shaved sex, the bud in the great valley of her.

He got to the restaurant exactly on time and he imagined himself in the future, a punctual old man nursing a mug of lemon tea and waiting for the AA meeting to begin. Fifteen minutes later Kurien arrived, apologising, saying he was chairing Oye. Xavier wasn't sure he'd heard him right.

"Overeaters Anonymous. Now look, don't you worry, the boys will take you to the meeting and I'll come by when I'm done."

He waited at a table in the back and one by one they arrived, the boys, who were in their forties and fifties, old-time members of the local chapter, and they went across the road to an empty school where a pool of white light spilled from a classroom. A dozen or so men sat at desks constructed for children and on the blackboard in white chalk were the usual sobriety slogans. Xavier knew them all; they sounded to him like the battle hymns of a doomed republic.

At the teacher's desk was Vincent who introduced himself as a liar and good-for-nothing who should by all rights be in jail, or dead. It was only thanks to the fellowship that he'd managed to save his life, to let go and let God, et cetera, et cetera, and Xavier tuned out for a time, until finally the man called the meeting to order and asked if there were any first-timers. Xavier put up his hand, meaning it was his first time at this fellowship, but he was misunderstood.

"Hi, Xavier. Welcome. We're glad you're with us for your first time."

Vincent introduced a man with an accent out of Hell's Kitchen.

"Hi, my name is Keith and I'm an alcoholic?"

"Hi, Keith."

"Tell you what, I thought I knew everything, right? I went to meetings to learn the twelve steps, follow for a while, and go right back to drinking. I wanted to show the guys I'd given it a shot and it wasn't for me."

He was a small tense American with a weightlifter's upper body and he leaned forward with his elbows on his knees and spoke with long pauses.

"This is a big day, maybe the most important day of your life," he told Xavier. "Opportunities, right? You either take them or you don't. I used to let them go because they cut into my drinking life. Now I pick up on them."

When he stopped there was applause.

Vincent said, "Mike, do you want to share?"

On the street a car backfired. Nobody flinched except Xavier.

Mike spoke with his eyes closed and hands clasped, the picture of someone lost in prayer. He said his job was to be on the phone all day reassuring his clients and what he really wanted to do was to hurt them. He wanted to bitch slap them. One morning, after his usual quarter of vodka, he was leaving for work when he had an argument with his wife and blacked out for three minutes. He came out of it covered in blood, his wife and two kids screaming. He'd stabbed himself repeatedly with a pair of scissors. It was not easy to connect the calm look of the man with the chaos of his life.

"I started to write down my fourth step," he said. "A searching and fearless moral inventory. I should be in jail for some of the things I've done. My wife would leave me if she knew. I start writing and I look at the words on the page and I don't know who wrote them. Even my handwriting looks different. Been sober now for eighty-two days."

He too had been addressing Xavier, who began to feel like a fraud.

Mike said, "Another thing I've learned here is to keep quiet. My mouth has got me into a lot of trouble, I'm learning to keep it shut."

And he did; he said nothing more.

Xavier put his head on the desk and pressed his forehead against the gouges in the wood. Someone was addressing him.

"Do you want to share?"

"It's my first time here, I don't know if I have anything to say that will suit."

"That's okay," said Vincent.

"And I'm not sure I need a group."

"You can say anything you want."

"I quit alcohol without AA, may I say that?"

Vincent said, "Personally I don't think you quit, I think you're taking a break. Meeting makers make it. Let go, let God."

Some half-grunts of agreement and then a new voice, a man whose name Xavier didn't hear. Arrogance, he said, was the original sin. Only attending regular meetings helped him stay sober in the world.

Xavier understood that the men wore alcoholism like a secret identity only other alcoholics recognised. To the world they were ordinary men but in their own heads they were superheroes and saints. He imagined a halo two inches above the head of the man who was speaking, a dull oval glow the colour of dirty copper. They all had them, even Vincent.

Above my head there is no halo, only a hollow. They are the halo men and I am the imposter.

The meeting ended with a group chant, "Keep coming back."

Outside, the last man to speak joined Xavier and Keith the American. He said he had come to the meeting because it had been raining that day and whenever it rained and there was a cool breeze blowing he wanted a drink. Xavier knew the condition: nostalgie de la boue, de l'oubli, de l'oblivion.

As they walked to the street Keith asked how long Xavier had been sober.

"A few months. I'm not counting the days, if you see what I mean."

"And you don't get urges?"

"I don't know if I can call them urges, more like a false flu, some strange viral refraction. I wait until it passes."

"How come you don't take a drink?"

"Fear. If I take one I'll take a dozen and the next thing I know, three days have passed, and I'm in a town I don't recognise with someone I've never seen before in my life."

The two men looked at him seriously and the American nodded in a solemn way. Perhaps they had quit humour when they quit drinking and a joke was seen as some kind of gateway drug back into the big ooze?

Now Vincent joined them.

"Excuse me, Xavier, why you bother coming if you're against the fellowship?"

"That's a fair question. I don't know."

"You're the painter, right? Sit. Let's talk."

There was a bus stop and a bench and the men sat down.

Vincent said, "My mother named me for a painter."

"Oh, yes, yes," said Xavier. The man was named for one of the high ones and that had to count for something. He remembered his last visit to *Starry Night* on a Friday afternoon not long before the museum moved to its new location, the rooms full of crowds, locals, tourists, regulars, and he'd looked at the canvas of drowned stars, each glowing like an underwater moon, while people and workmen milled about, and he'd thought, yes, Vincent would have preferred a thoroughfare to a cathedral.

"I always wished my mother named me for someone different. Someone who wasn't famous for cutting off his ear and giving it to a hoor."

"That is not what he's famous for."

"Yes it is, trust me. The first thing people remember is exactly that, not his paintings, his life. And the first thing they remember about his life is his earlessness. I always wondered how he managed to wear his glasses."

Somebody laughed.

"Perhaps you should stop talking," Xavier suggested.

"I'm thinking of legally changing it, mate, my name. What happened to your nose?"

Then he said something that Xavier heard and immediately forgot, or he didn't hear because the nasal grating of the man's voice was too loud in his ear. With a firm two-handed grasp he grabbed Vincent by the neck. Why did he not stop talking, why? He'd asked the fellow to stop, asked politely, and now there was nothing for it but to get a little forceful with the fucker. There'd been too much talk in any case and words hurt his head. It was important that the man stop speaking, absolutely vital that he shut his lying mouth. If he said another word Xavier would have to crush his useless shit-clogged windpipe. But the others were crowding him now, giving him no space to move, grabbing his wrists.

And then Vincent said, I think you should let me up.

3.

There was no gentle build-up, two glasses of wine one evening, four the next and so on, exponentially into the dark. He went all out from moment one, bought a quarter bottle of whisky, a nip bottle, the professional's measure, and put a slug in his coffee first thing in the morning and got to work. He went from teetotal to alcoholic in one sip. It was possible that if he kept at the ooze he would stop working but this morning, whisky taken, he was high in the visionary company. He banged out two self-portraits before lunch. Mixing the paint may have taken more time than the actual work of brush on canvas. The portraits were variations on a theme painted on pages of ghetto porn. He gave himself an egg-shaped head and leaden eyelids and put bits of white paint around the eyes and mouth, the only white on the canvas, as it turned out. He used blocks of burnt umber and sienna for the body and head and left only one area unpainted, the heart, and – this was when he knew he was in the presence of God and all his angels – it so happened that the unpainted heart occurred on a high-res image of an ebony vagina, slippery and liver-coloured. All he had to do was pencil in a few quick lines to suggest the heart's rubbery tubing. No viewer would make out the background image unless he mentioned it, which he would to get a little buzz going in the right places and push the price up by a digit or two. The second portrait was faster and stranger, a humanoid blob of multicoloured oil spatters, and the two finished pictures put him in such a good mood that he took Goody to Koshy's for lunch. Before leaving he went to the bathroom and killed the rest of the quarter and brushed his teeth again.

They took a table by the window.

Xavier said, "Remember the waiter in the café on Greek Street who refused to serve you because he said you were too young? And we had to show him your passport? We drank all day and they gave us buy-back shots and I left the keys on the bar and had to climb in through the window to get into the apartment?" He looked around him at the photos on the wall, shots of old Bangalore when you could walk the length of the promenade in a leisurely half-hour and there was no traffic except the occasional Model-T import; sepia full frontals of the Town Hall, the Parade Ground, and the Victoria Hotel; royals and other notables, and the inescapable picture of the Mysore Maharaja unresplendent in his crooked turban. "Climbed in the living-room window and opened the door for you and we fell asleep fully dressed. I woke in the middle of the night because you had me in a chokehold and all I'd done was snore."

"It was a snore heard around the world, you were so drunk. I had a nightmare that you were trying to kill me."

"So you thought you'd kill me?"

"It was either you or me and I went with the devil I knew."

"Be that as it may, in New York the first time you left me I went back to London and tried to find that bar. I went up and down Greek Street. Honestly, I thought if I got drunk enough you'd come around and save me."

"You're a silly man."

"Went all over Soho and never did find it. But I sent you emails and a postcard and I didn't paint. I wrote sorrowful separation poems and felt drunkenly sorry for myself. I hoped you might turn up, you know, and surprise me."

"You surprised me. I had no idea you were so ardent."

"I was and I am."

There was a figure beside them, a squat toad-like man in starched white kurta-pyjamas, a gold ballpoint prominent in his breast pocket, who smiled at Goody and folded his hands in namaste. Xavier had no idea who he was until Goody said, Mr Cherian, how nice to see you. Newton, you remember Mr Cherian from the party the other day? Xavier remembered: it was the Hindu Christian Lipton man.

"Please call me Cherry. May I join you?"

Xavier said, "My pleasure. What are you drinking?"

Cherian called for a waiter and demanded beer.

"For everyone," he said. "Beeru."

Even Goody was agreeably smiling. And why not? A smallish glass of frothy lager, what possible harm could issue from so blameless a beverage? When it came, and was poured, glorious honey-bright refreshment, Xavier emptied his prettily sweating tankard and poured another and only then did Goody's face register some – what? – not coldness exactly but discomfort. Then more people came to the table, Keith and Vincent and the AA boys.

"I can see it's working for you," Keith said, "not going to meetings, I mean. Helping you stay clean and sober."

Vincent said, "Watch out, mister, keep talking that way and the man's liable to go for your throat."

Xavier said, "I'm sorry. As I said before and say again, I'm sorry and I'm sorry. I'm a sorry-faced sorry-mouthed bit of sorry business."

Goody said, "Did you attack him? My god."

And the swadeshi Cherian said, "Are you fellows from AA? You don't look like it, if you don't mind me saying so."

"We should go."

"Maybe I'll go with you," said Cherian, but he didn't get up. And it was Xavier who went with them to the door, to shake hands and make a last apology to Vincent.

"I mean it, forgive me, my mind's not well."

"I hope I'm never so desperate I have to resort to violence."

"You're right, you're right, there's no doubt in my mind that you're right."

"Yeah, well, looks like you got other problems, bro. Looks like the fat man's got his eye on your girlfriend."

Cherian was kissing her hand.

"And she doesn't mind, does she?"

Goody was smiling, and, dear god, did she just bat her eyelashes? Xavier hadn't seen that move in years. He went back to the table. She said, I mean, I enjoy beer, though really it doesn't have much effect on me, Cherry – other than to make me affectionate, that is. And she laughed. The smarmy swadeshi still had her hand in his and she made no effort to take it away. Of course it was entirely possible that she had a thing for ugly men: Xavier was no prize in the prettiness department. Maybe she had a thing for ugliness in all forms, human, divine, artistic, and maybe it was time to give in and confront the ghost who walks everyfuckingwhere. If nothing else it called for urgent measures, of whisky, beeru, winu, rumma. Xavier summoned the waiter and ordered a double Black & White with ice.

"Tu mettrais l'univers entier dans ta ruelle, femme impure!" he said.

"If that's French for I'm a complete fucking alcoholic and I can't wait to flush my life down the loo, you can say it again," said Goody.

"L'ennui rend ton âme cruelle."

"I say," said Cherian. "Who needs the French anyway? India is standing on her own two feet, mon ami."

"Two feet, do you really think so?" said Xavier.

"If you haven't noticed," Cherian said, "incredible new India, shining at last."

Xavier looked coldly at the man. When he spoke it was in a voice Goody did not recognise.

"What new India? This is the same old India, poor, poorer, poorest, as fucked up as she ever was and slathered with whore make-up to cover boils, moles, and warts, at least for the night."

Their voices had risen above the general Koshy's din, no small feat considering the level of noise in the restaurant. But Xavier was beyond caring and bad behaviour seemed to have its rewards. Cherian, being the oily Malayali that he was, decided it was a bad idea to be caught in the middle of a public marital spat and he scurried off, mumbling something about being late for a lunch appointment.

With his two hands Xavier held his whisky to the dim electric light. The liquid had turned the colour of smudge. Thank you, oh Lord, for your small mercy, he thought, and swallowed the drink and ordered another.

I am glowing in the flowing, high in the visionary company.

"Right, Newton, I think this needs to be said," said Goody. "You have a talent for forgetting, especially when it comes to those things deemed inconvenient. Thing is, I do not have this talent. I remember the New York opening and your insane suicidal binge. You disappeared for two days and I thought you were dead. They found you asleep in a doorway at Saint Mark's Church. I still remember the address, East Tenth Street. I'll remember it all my life. I'm not going through that kind of torture again."

"I have the solution. Drink with me and we shall together sail into the wine dark sea."

Goody left without another word, though she took her time gathering her things. Was she expecting mollification and coddlement? He was not in the market for Molly or Coddle; he was in for the conspicuous consumption of Choice Old Scotch Whisky from the twin barrels of the inestimable Dr James Buchanan and his company of knighted highland terriers. But there was a balance to be struck, a window of chance and opportunity before the ooze reinstated its depressive temperament. He needed to be at work because he had had an idea, a real idea, a flash of lightning type IDEA, and he lifted up the new whisky and said to the deserted table, Emperor Buchanan, to your incomparable malts and grains. Then he paid the bill and left a good tip and walked home, stopping at Noon Wines to buy cheap red plonk for a cheap red day. It's our honour to serve you, sir, said the shop owner's daughter. I saw your picture in the newspaper. You can pay later if you don't have money. She gave him change and a calendar on the house. She said, sir, we also have free home delivery. He said, good, good, now stop calling me sir. What's your name? Dharini, she said. Dharini, he replied, it's a pleasure indeed to make your acquaintance.

He hung the calendar on a bare wall near his easel. It was the usual devotional scene, a trio of gods in fleshy human poses. He poured himself a short glass of red and noted the absence of the Goody and tossed off the monumental mixed media nude that had been flashing in his head all day, hips so big they were a landscape of their own, boulder breasts, tree trunk legs, small delicate lovely head. He used a marker to draw a faint outline and filled the canvas with paint, two colours, no more, and then he used the marker again. In a closet he found a piece of heavy gold fabric inlaid with cheap gemstones that he shaped into a necklace and placed on the nude's neck and she acquired the unmistakable contours of the giantess of his youth, an image from a poem he'd once read that had filled his erotic life for weeks – the idea of living in the valleys and crevices of a big brown woman devoid of speech but flowing with tenderness. He was blazing. And there was time for one last drink before Koshy's closed for the day. They'd still be serving dinner, the waiters in a hurry to count their tips and be gone. The giantess was done. Anyone could see that he hadn't put much into it, the necklace awry, the colour flat, unfinished skin tones against pale yellow, but it didn't matter because the power was in the line, the Palaeolithic curves and the serenity of the lips and eyes. The giantess was done and so was he; time for a drop of red and into the night.

He took a rickshaw and told the man to wait. At Koshy's candles had been lit and there was music. Was it jazz, opera, heavy metal? Impossible to tell because the sound was so muddy; or the mud was in his head. John, eradu whisky kodu, he told the old waiter, who replied in English. Sir, we are closing, do you want food? Closing time. Dread words calculated to put The Fear into any man. He called for two whiskies, then made it three and told John to line them up on the table. Where was Goody? Where was the Goods and her odd singularity of eyebrow, the one on the left sharper, more angular? He should have checked her closets to see if she had decamped permanently, but no, it would take a day or two to move everything out, art, books, toiletries, the pots and pans. Where were Keith and Vincent and his AA chums? Where were all his friends?

Let the night be solitary and let no joyful voice come therein.

He went to a table by the window where a couple of middle-aged men worked on their rum and Thums Up.

"I say, do you think I could possibly" – Why did he get so plummy and English when he had a drop or two taken? He'd lived in Paris almost as long as London, but when he was drunk, or even just drinking, it was always the English who won – "possibly borrow a cigarette?"

One of them held out a damp pack of Classic Milds and he took one and thanked the man and went back to his table, suddenly reluctant to reach for the waiting whisky. He took a deep drag of the cigarette and held the smoke in his lungs and felt the nicotine kick in and still the drinks stood on the table and still he didn't want them. He had smoked too quickly and it had put a pint of nausea in his head.

Where are all my friends, my best mates, my bros? Ah, here they are, all three of them, waiting.

He drank two whiskies one after the other and someone joined him.

"Mr Kurien himself. How good to see you, dear boy."

"Mr Xavier, how are you? Looking a little the worse for wear, I'm sorry to say."

"I'd offer you a drink but I know you'd refuse. Am I correct?"

"With pleasure."

"Here's to you and your odd sobriety."

Xavier downed his third and last whisky and he felt the spirit percolate downward into his kundalini, felt the serpent goddess begin her ascent up his spine and just as quickly die; suddenly bereft, he raised his hand for the waiter.

"We're closed, at least to you. Go home, Newton, for god's sake. Do yourself a favour. Go home. Make up to your lovely lady."

"I think I've just seen everything, a merchant refusing to sell his merchandise. This is marvellously noble and all, but aren't you shooting yourself in the foot, old boy?"

"You have the trembles, did you know that?"

"Give me a drink, merchant, or give me the bill."

"Your money's no good here. Go home. And change the dressing on your nose."

But he didn't go home. He left Koshy's and found the rickshaw still waiting and took it to Dewar's, a bar hidden under flyover construction in one of the city's oldest cantonments. There they let him buy a half-bottle and sit at a table for as long as he liked. A boy put a menu and a bowl of peanuts in front of him and pulled the shutters and lit a candle in a saucer. Police, said the boy as he put off the lights.

What a toy town. After eleven you drank with the lights off because the guardians of the law preferred to shake down drinkers rather than do some honest work.

"How do you tell the difference between a cop and a crook?" he said to the boy.

"Ji?"

"Cigarette kodu," Xavier said.

The menu was a collage of old Hindi movie posters and there was the old Dev Anand–Zeenat Aman hit *Haré Krishna, Haré Rama* showing bell-bottomed lovers among hippies and the Himalayas. Goody, he thought, I miss you, come home. There was already so much to tell her, the three paintings of the day and the fact that he was feeling better, almost Normal, the drink had calmed him down and cured the hypomania. Was she gone with the oily Cherian to his sprawling bungalow where she would sip daytime cocktails with the city's VIP set? The boy put a pack of cigarettes on the table. Eyevathu rupiah, he said. When had he become a smoker and drinker? Already it seemed as if he had been in this life for ever, his days measured in whisky and nicotine; and he was dreading the hangover that would surely come. But he was afraid to stop because there was the possibility that the work would stop too and the craziness would return. He'd learned to see the patterns in his own behaviour, which he could no more control than he could control the wind or the rain. When he was working and drinking he was one with the world, otherwise he was nothing, barely conscious, with the sensibility of lichen or a piece of coral. When there was about an inch of whisky left in the bottle he put it in his pocket and checked his wristwatch, ten past three, time for a working man to get some sleep. He blew out the candle and in the sudden darkness the words came to him unbidden. Lift your face to the sky and unbefuddle yourself, Commander Xavier. A great and complex task awaits you. Lift your face free of its infirmity and find her, for she is rescue from the disaster that awaits. Lift up, Saint Xavier, son of Forgottem, lift up.

He opened the door of the bar and stepped out into the street but his legs didn't obey him and he had to bend from the waist to keep from falling over. Bent double, he walked toward the main road. There was nothing moving at that time of night and unable to walk any further he sat heavily on the concrete bench of a bus stop and felt the bottle shatter in his pocket and a painless jab in his hip. He picked the broken glass out of his trousers and tried to catch whatever was available for salvage, managing to transfer to his mouth a small handful of whisky. His eyes closed and he thought he heard a small bird somewhere close and when the bird spoke he was only surprised it was in English.

"The air has eyes. It sees everything we do."

Just then the sky began to lighten on a stretch of dug-up road where great shards of concrete pointed upward like glass. No wonder there had been no rickshaws: there was no road. He limped onward, his trousers wet with blood and whisky, and he came to a junction dominated by a Kannada film poster and there stood a man who was naked from the waist down, whose long hair was wet with lakewater, on his wrist a pink rakhee. The dead man said, why did you not ask yourself the obvious question?

"As in, who but a nutter would find himself in conversation with a dead one?"

"No, that question is not obvious, only uninteresting. The important question is, what does it mean when a drowned man is found without his trousers?"

"Ah," Xavier said, as if he were about to sneeze. "I don't mean to tremble so but I can't seem to stop."

"It means he was robbed and murdered. It means he did not drown himself as the police claim. It means he must choose someone in whom he can place his trust, some one person who will know the truth even if he or she is unable to act on it."

Without warning, the tears came to Xavier's eyes.

"I'm not that person," he said.

"I am Santosh, state footballer of Kerala and lover of life, now expired."

"Quite so."

"There is no peace in death, only restless dreams."

Then the dead man clasped Xavier to his wet black shirt and kissed him on both cheeks. As he walked away he pointed to a bridge.

"Go that way, you'll know where you are."

Xavier limped toward the bridge, which turned out to be a flyover, and beyond it was traffic and new sunlight and, most miraculous of all, a line of rickshaws waiting for business. On the ride home he wondered how it was that a hallucination had left such a genuine memento, for the dead man had been a creation of his mind but the wetness on his shirt was real. It was full day when he got out of the rickshaw and made a last stop before home. Hello, Dharini, a bottle of Grover La Reserve and two Khajurahos please, he said, leaning shakily against the counter. It occurred to him that he'd made a similar purchase some twenty-four hours earlier when all had seemed so hopeful with the world. How things had changed, in how short a span.

"Are you okay, sir? No, no. You're bleeding."

He was touched, there was no point denying that he was touched by her distress. It was a weakness: he missed the ministrations of women, the concern and the tears, even the contempt.

Dharini came around the counter with beer and wine and insisted on carrying the purchases home for him. She helped him up the stairs and found his key and opened the door. She found cotton wool and water and put antiseptic on his wound. Then she poured a glass of beer and helped him get comfortable on the sofa.

He took a long drink and said, thank you, I can't tell you what a day it's been, I—

And he was asleep.

4.

Dismas Bambai was in a restaurant on Saint Mark's Road. The building had once belonged to the Bible Society of India whose name was still inscribed in stone above the entranceway. The room had high ceilings and new spotlights that illuminated the work on the roof tiles, careful work that had lain unnoticed for more than a hundred years until an American restaurant chain decided to restore the building. From the arched stone windows he looked upon a traffic jam that took up every inch of the road and much of the pavement. For ten minutes at a stretch the traffic was completely stationary and then it moved for a few minutes and then followed another period of inaction. When the waitress appeared he asked for a newspaper and the bill and she returned with a small pile of English language dailies. He thanked her and she stumbled slightly as she walked away. He read in the *Hindoo* that one of the world's earliest television broadcasters was visiting India on a tour. The report quoted the broadcaster as saying that the standard of English had fallen on all programmes broadcast by the BBC, fallen terribly, to the extent that Indians and Irishmen spoke better English than Englishmen. On the edit page was a letter from a reader who accused the newspaper's editors of being allergic to Brahmins. Why else would they compare Brahmins to Germans? The reader said the comparison was "most inept, odious, inappropriate and doltish, for when one sees the Nazi atrocities on film, one does not associate the citizens of modern Germany, but only those that went the whole hog with that mad fellow Hitler". The reader's language skills seemed to contradict the broadcaster's opinion, Dismas thought, but perhaps not. The man's English usage was strange but the English spoken in Britain was probably stranger. Then Dismas turned to the *Hindoostan Times* and read about a swami who thought the Gangotri glacier was receding so rapidly that it would disappear altogether in a few decades. When the glacier disappeared the river Ganga too would disappear, in the same way that rivers were disappearing all over the nation. But such a catastrophe was only to be expected, said the swami, because the disappeared river was in keeping with the prophecies of the holy books. For much of his life the eighty-nine-year-old swami had lived near Gangotri, the origin of the Ganga. He had noticed many changes in recent years, he said, but the most unexpected was how dirty the river had become, how discoloured and thin. Nowhere in the holy books was it recommended that we throw our sewage into it or that we throw garbage into it or wash our clothes in it. On the contrary we were asked to worship the river, which was holy, the source of all life. But, as he said, it was only to be expected in the interminably sinuous Kali Yuga. What confused him was the discrepancy in time. The prophecies said the Ganga would disappear in five thousand years, not fifty or forty or thirty, and he couldn't imagine that the old ones would be so far wrong in their calculations. Then the swami smiled and asked to be forgiven for expecting God's conception of time to conform to man's. He posed a last question. What would be worse, death by water or the lack of water? The story ended with a phrase in Hindi, Ab meri Ganga maili, and Dismas turned the page. Between items about an actor's latest haircut and the Airbus acquired by the head of a local liquor conglomerate he found a photograph of Goody and Xavier. She wore a white dress and held a glass of wine and a cell phone; he sported a straw hat and a moustache. They were smiling. To Dismas they seemed unreasonably cheerful.

The caption said: "IN HAPPIER TIMES. The bad-boy-turned-grand-old-man of Indian art is back in Bangalore. Newton Xavier and his friend Goody Lol were spotted at a lunch reception (*see picture*). Once dubbed 'the 20th century's last whiskey priest', Mr Xavier has mellowed with time. These days he conspicuously consumes only water. How the mighty have fallen. Or have they? According to some birds in the know the X-Man was admitted to Asterion Hospital early this week following an extended binge. Watch this space for more details."

When the waitress brought his bill he asked her how long it would take to get to Asterion Hospital. Less than twenty minutes, she replied. Dismas thought her voice sounded off. If she was right it gave him just enough time to meet Xavier and pay his respects and make his train.

"Excuse me, I feel sick," she said. "It might take an hour."

It took more than twenty minutes and less than an hour. The hospital resembled a business hotel with 'Asterion' in blue neon cursive at the top. Clock-faces in the lobby gave the time in various cities of the world but the cities appeared to have been chosen at random. New York and London, but also Accra, Älmhult, and São Paulo. Dismas told a receptionist that he had come to see Mr Xavier. Visiting hours were over, she told him, but family members were allowed at any time. That's me, Dismas replied, family member. The receptionist told him to follow an orderly who led him down a corridor to an exit and through a covered walkway into a smaller building. Here they came to a room that the man opened without knocking. He showed Dismas inside and shut the door.

Xavier was sitting in bed watching television while a young woman fed him soup. She whispered something in his ear and he flipped channels to a wrestling show. She laughed and said, fighting. There were fruit baskets and ashtrays on the bed, and chocolates, magazines, and clothes on the floor. The room looked like a honeymoon suite. Velvety bags of insomnia grew under Xavier's eyes and his beard had filled out.

When he saw Dismas, he said, "What on earth."

"I happened to be in Bangalore, passing through. Saw an item in the newspaper. They made it seem like you were at death's door."

"Indian newspapers and the truth are far removed. If anyone should know that, it's you."

"There was a photo of you and Goody."

"Ah yes, that's a name not spoken round these parts. Dharini doesn't like it. Do you, dear girl?"

Dharini said, "It wasn't a good picture, out-of-focus."

Xavier winked at him, delighted.

He said, "Isn't she splendid? Dharini, dear, get up and show us your new sari. Do a little twirl."

The sari was sky-blue chiffon and she wore it carelessly, pallu twisted across her chest like a fat blue rope. She looked at Dismas through her fringe and shook her head. Then she shrugged and got up, full of misgiving. As soon as she had accomplished half a turn, awkwardly and without embarrassment, she sat down and primly she placed her hands in her lap. There was a small cut on her upper lip.

Xavier lit a cigarette with a disposable plastic lighter that said I ♥ KUWAIT. He sucked the smoke deep into his lungs and exhaled with a little sigh, but when a nurse came into the room his manner changed. I have to go up for an MRA scan, he said. Don't try anything funny, you pantywaist Bombayman. I don't want you speaking to her, you hear me? Where're you going? Stick around.

Dismas stuck around; it was Dharini who spoke first.

"He talks about some poets who died this year, three poets one after the other."

"That theory has been debunked. Conspiracy buffs said the killer was a poet who'd been excluded from their anthologies. Thoroughly debunked by the coroner's reports. Cause of death natural in all three cases. Not a bad scenario though, I plan to use it myself."

"He talks about death a lot. Sometimes he talks about you," she said. "You tried to kill him once?"

Dismas giggled. He said, "No."

"Mainly he talks about the party he wants to throw and of course Goody, says she's an incarnation of Kali and she wants to add his head to her collection. She told him she wanted his skull if he died. Only if you love someone you say that. He doesn't realise. It is love, but."

She sat with her legs crossed and spoke distractedly as if none of it had any bearing on her life.

"I feel I know her because we both live in the same dynamic bubble. Her things are still in the cupboards. Her dresses are there. I think so we have the same shoe size. He likes to think she's my enemy but I don't. I understand her."

She would not meet his eye and she kept adjusting the fringe that lay bushily on her forehead. For someone so young she seemed exhausted, beyond the reach of conversation or affection, and he noticed that the cut on her lip was fresh.

"Maybe you understand her better than you understand him. How long have you been together?" asked Dismas.

"Dismas and me? Not that long."

"I'm Dismas."

"Did I say Dismas? I meant Xavier, but. Obvious."

"Slip of the tongue. When you say someone's name like that it means he's on your mind."

"Don't fool yourself. Only thing on my mind is the universe, nothing else, and phones. I want a cell phone. What are you staring at me for? You think I'm pretty?"

"What kind of phone?"

"I don't care, a nice phone."

"Do you like my Razr? What do you think of the striking aluminium exterior? And the slim form factor, isn't it groundbreaking?"

"You think I'm pretty or not? Tell."

"I haven't thought about it."

"Yes you have. It's the only thing people think about when they see a woman. You see a man, you think about money. How much money does he have, how much power? But a woman, always, she's pretty or she's not. Do you think I'm pretty?"

"I think you're almost pretty."

"Almost."

"Let me ask you something: Alicia Keys or Aaliyah, what's your opinion?"

She pulled at her fringe but she could not straighten it to her satisfaction.

"For me it is Aaliyah," he said. "It's always Aaliyah."

She said nothing and stared at the television at the foot of the bed. On the screen was a documentary unlike any he had seen. Bound men and women walked on a beach and some of them had white crosses tattooed or painted into their foreheads. After a while Dismas said he had better go, he had a train to catch. She stared at the screen; she ignored him; she did not look up when he left the room.

In the hallway, accompanied by a nurse, was Xavier in a wheelchair, his smock unbuttoned to the sternum, showing a bony chest shaved clean.

"Where's Goody?" Xavier said. "Tell me where she is, you backstabbing git. I know you contrived the whole thing to run off with her and take my paintings. I have high-powered lawyers. I have more money than you. I'll make you pay. Bloody hell, I will make you pay."

It seemed to him that Xavier and Goody were made for each other, both obsessed with making people pay.

"Newton, I happened to be in town and I came to see you. I'm travelling around the country. I'm working on a book."

"Why? So you can write my biography and make more money out of me? Nurse, call the police. This man is in cahoots with my former wife. They are trying to swindle me."

The nurse said, "Okay, now, Mr Xavier, please calm down or I'll have to give you a shot."

"Look," Xavier said in a sudden whisper, "that girl in there is a stop-gap arrangement, my muse of the month, a merchant's daughter, heir to the Noon Wines fortune. She is pure random chance but she's all I can manage at the moment. I want Goody back."

"You want Goody back."

"That's right," he said, his voice suddenly very loud. He clapped himself on the chest. "*I* want her back, I, I, I."

People had stopped to watch.

"Go to Infantry Road and tell her. She has my legacy and I want it back. She *is* my legacy."

"I have a train to catch in an hour."

"I have a train to catch," he said, in a nasal effeminate version of Dismas's tone. "Look around you. This isn't a hospital, it's a loony bin. They're planning to electro-shock me, aren't you, nursie dear? You hear me, Bambai? This isn't art. This is life. There's no escape. Wait here."

The small group who had gathered to watch wandered off when Xavier disappeared into his room and the nurse pushed the wheelchair down the corridor. The blue ceiling lights flickered and stayed. There was a smell of antiseptic and something else, something older that wouldn't wash out. In a while he emerged in street clothes and led the way to the exit, Dismas warily following.

"I will talk to Goody myself. I may be mad but I'm no fool."

"And Dharini, what did you tell her? See you in ten minutes?"

"Twenty, twenty minutes."

"Bravo, a little variation."

"She'll recover. She's young, unlike yours truly."

"Newton, I've been wanting to tell you I'm sorry."

"No you're not."

"You were good to me in New York. You helped me out. I'm sorry I let you down."

"You didn't let me down. You betrayed me."

"Sorry, that's what I'm here to say."

"Finally an apology. Well, it's too little and too late."

They rounded a corner into the lobby. A male nurse at the desk got up when he saw Xavier.

"The doctor has not discharged."

"I'm discharging myself, old boy. Send my bill to the Department of Art and Culture, carc of Government of India."

The man picked up a phone. There was a form to be filled, he told Xavier. And his possessions, did he not want them back? Into the mouthpiece he said, please send Dr Virani to the registration desk. It stopped Xavier for a minute. What form? he asked the clerk. What possessions? The man put a printed sheet in front of him and slid a pen beside it. Registration form, he said. Xavier looked at it for a moment and took up the ballpoint and wrote very quickly. HOLY YS THE DRINKERE.

"Dr Virani," said the nurse.

"Do you think the word 'holy' in its earlier incarnations ended with an 'e'?" Xavier asked.

The nurse said, "Send Dr Virani, urgent."

Xavier resumed his scribble.

HOLYE YS THE VAGABONDE SAINTE!

He tucked the pen into his pocket. Outside was the street. Outside was humidity and night and freedom. Dismas followed him down wide littered hospital steps.

"Really, I'm sorry."

"Doesn't mean a thing, sorry, easiest word in the English language. Instead of mouthing the empty word, think. I'm escaping without funds, without a sou in the world. Lend me some."

"What?"

"Dosh, jack, cabbage, the wherewithal. Lolly, filthy lucre, the loot. Greenback, stack, rack, a peti."

Dismas had a backpack and a clamshell phone. He had a black hoodie and satisfactorily scuffed desert boots. He had a wallet with dollars and rupees, a train reservation, two debit cards, and a passport-size photo of Aaliyah.

"Uh, how much do you need?"

"How much do you have?"

"Twenty thousand rupees and a few hundred dollars," he said, regretting the words as they left his mouth. "I could lend you five thousand?"

"That won't help very much, I'm afraid. I'm skint, as in, there's nothing in the till. Give me the twenty, you can always get more at an ATM."

"I'm about to catch a train to Goa."

"You owe me. You owe me."

Dismas shook his head. He saw the nurse at the top of the steps. A rickshaw stopped near Xavier's outstretched hand.

"I'll send you a cheque care of the post office in Panjim. Give me the dollars too. I'm in need. I am dependent on your kindness."

"Newton, this is a bit much," he said, but he handed over the money.

"The inability to love."

"What?"

"Dharini. I saw it in her face, what it means to live without love. What does love mean when the world is ending? Twenty-year-olds feel the end of days. I do too. I mean, look at me. This is what happens when the void engulfs your brain. Inability. Your curse as well."

"It's time we ended this."

Coming toward them was the nurse and a man in a doctor's coat. Xavier laughed and climbed into the auto and Dismas realised that he'd never before heard the older man laugh. It was an unsettling act of aggression, like a monkey baring its teeth; there was no affection, only malice.

"It's not me, it's me," Xavier said.

"Either way, time to break up."

Xavier reached into the pocket of his ancient sports coat and brought out a sheaf of folded paper, which he presented to Dismas with a small flourish.

"Something I've been working on intermittently for decades, a book of poems about the black and brown saints of the world. Rather autobiographical, I must immodestly add," he said. "Consider it an advance payment against my debt."

Reluctantly, Dismas took the poems.

And as the auto pulled away Xavier said, "You can't break up with me, Bombayman, I'm unbreakable."

5.

On the overnight train Dismas remembered he knew someone in Goa, the defrocked editor of a Bombay men's magazine that went out of business when mass-market pornography arrived in the world. But it had been years since they met and he wasn't sure of the address. He also had the location of Xavier's boyhood home in Forgottem and a recommendation for a hotel.

Late at night he overheard the men in the compartment discussing a ghost ship. A bearded man did most of the talking, describing the ship in loving detail, how the night before she was to set sail a powerful current seemed to drag her keel this way and that. All night the vessel moved independent of the tides, as if a giant underwater hand were playing with her as a child might play with a bathtub toy. In the morning they found a dead dolphin near the stern, a young dolphin with a terrible gash in its side. When the first mate saw the dolphin his eyes filled with fear and though he said nothing the men knew he had seen a premonition and they too were afraid. Soon it was time to set sail and they weighed anchor. The mainsail filled and the ship rocked but she would not move. There were shouts from the men of awe and incomprehension. The sunlight seemed to darken by a shade and they saw mist wrap around the forecastle and spread from spar to spar as if they were far out at sea. Where had the sea smoke come from? The men, superstitious as are all seafarers, looked to each other for a sign that they had not drowned in the night. There were whispers among them that a ghost was on board, perhaps the ghost of the dead saint they were transporting to Spain. The saint did not wish to leave Goa, said the bearded man to the others. And here he quoted a song, or a proverb from a book, perhaps a yogi's biography or autobiography, or perhaps it was from a movie about a yogi, he couldn't remember. But how well the couplet fitted the tale of the saint who wished to stay.

His ship was set to sail for Spain;
Before it left, t'was back again.

You can still feel his power, said the man. This is why people take away bits of his flesh, to see for themselves if the body is still fresh. One of the other men asked if it was true, was it fresh? Yes, the bearded man said in a child's voice. It bleeds!

Dismas tried to sleep but images crowded his head and after some time he sat up on his bunk. Only he and the bearded man were still awake and when the man began to speak his words mixed with the sound of the wheels. He said he was a steward on a cruise ship and it was his first time home in more than a year, but he was in no hurry to return because he didn't know what he would find. His father had died and his brother-in-law had taken over the family home. This was the problem when you sailed for a living. When you returned it was as a stranger to a strange land.

He was silent for some time and then he apologised. It was late and he had been travelling all day, he said, and it was always in the final leg that exhaustion set in. He asked if Dismas was on work or holiday and when Dismas said he planned to visit the Basilica of Francis Xavier, the man closed his eyes for a moment. What a coincidence, he said, for that was the saint they had been discussing earlier in the evening, whose remains would not leave Goa. Dismas was in luck: the Exposition of the saint's remains occurred only once in twelve years and the next viewing was scheduled for the following week. An important saint, the patron of wanderers without destination, said the sailor, holding up the medallion that hung around his neck. There was a book by a former Jesuit named John Lobo that told the true story of what had happened to the saint's relics. Of course the church had tried to suppress it and some booksellers refused to stock copies but the Restoration bookshop in Panjim was worth a try, he said. And now, if you don't mind, I will shut my eyes and try not to dream.

Just then the sound of the train changed. Everywhere, in village and mangrove and level crossing, night was falling, and in the rough dwellings by the water the glow from the kerosene lamps joined the colours of the Christmas lights strung among the trees, a shifting wall of green that fell away as they pushed forward. In the shadows thrown by the train indistinct figures moved, emptied of colour and detail, and as one by one the lights were extinguished in the towns they passed the train also went dark until nothing remained but the dim blue of a night light in the corridor.

Living in Goa, even temporarily, even with your onward tickets booked, you thought about futility. The beach was everywhere and power failed for long stretches and from noon until five in the evening it was too hot to go outside. You ate big meals and took siestas after lunch.

His accommodation was a one-room cottage not far from the address he'd been given for the old Xavier house in Forgottem. He had expected some remembrance of the artist, a bust or plaque to mark the house where he'd been born, but the plot looked abandoned, its entrance marred by a thorny overgrowth of bush and a sagging padlocked gate. He tried the neighbours but the Ribeiro house too was empty: he would have to come back. His boots were wrong and his clothes were too heavy; grit settled like a new layer on his skin and he had to make an effort to walk to the beach in search of the ship he had been told about.

"It's the kind of thing you will see only in India, one of our specialities – dereliction," the Bangalore businessman had said, and pleased by the sound of the phrase, he had repeated it. "Dereliction is our speciality!"

Dismas had expected trance music and squalor, garbage strewn with marigolds, deranged tribes of long-haired legionnaires. But there were no reggae shacks selling sarongs and alcohol, no drug dealers and prostitutes, no parade of hallucinating tourists and vengeful locals; instead he found a narrow strip of clean sand and a shack and a fence of bamboo matting to keep out the stray dogs and cattle.

My River Honey dominated the view, a big ship stuck fast in the shallow water: the dereliction he'd been told about. Tourists walked on the sand or bathed, dwarfed by the hull of the crippled sailing vessel. They took snapshots of its faded insignia and the thick brown rust that leaked into the water. The ship was the subject of half a dozen legal actions and discussions in the legislative assembly and now it was part of local folklore, emblematic of the state's corruption at the highest levels. A British salvage firm contracted at great cost had tried and failed to refloat the vessel. Fresh tenders had been offered but nothing had come of them and in the intervening years *My River Honey* had become a part of the waterline, an iron reef that had changed the shape of the beach.

And at the far end of Forgottem bay, another oddity, a sixteenth-century prison fort converted into a five-star hotel. There was a sign with a list of partially crossed-out warnings. The first was untouched, 'Swim on this beach at your own risk.' The second and third had been painted over, but hastily, half-heartedly: 'Swimming here is like committing suicide', 'Many people have died here – please do not swim without supervision'. Careless as it was, the obscuring of the warnings had worked. Entire families were in the water, British visitors on a package tour, living in a refurbished Indian heritage site and swimming in its dangerous private waters.

He rented a scooter and took it on a road that was a thin strip of raised earth between coconut trees and paddy. He rode past egrets in a waterlogged field and a whitewashed church, and he stopped near a garage where a group of men worked on a motorbike. Across the road was a house so darkened by grime that it took a few moments to see the murals on its façade: a slender figure in a green waistcoat and hat, and a rooster in faded red, yellow and green, and a woman in a red dress holding a lacework fan.

He knocked on the door and peered into windows and trailed mud on the stained porch, but everything was dark and printed with dust as if the house had been unoccupied for years, exactly the kind of place in which he expected to find his friend. The men working on the motorbike knew better. Jacopo's house was next door and in any case he was not home, he had gone to market. They told him to look for the red scooter.

"Nobody else has one like it."

Dismas remembered passing the market early on the ride out. Now he reversed the trip and went back toward the beach with the sun in his eyes. He saw the egret, motionless among the paddies, and he parked in a gravel courtyard. The big church was empty but the fans spun on their long stalks and the floor was spotless. He sat in a pew at the back near a picture of Saint Sebastian, whose posture suggested his true identity – a saint of perpetual assent, his confusion and faith as clear as the sunlight on the gravel. Dismas was subject then to an old memory, a Bombay rave where Ecstasy mixed with orange juice had been passed around as fuel for the dancing. Half out of his head he had climbed a stack of speakers and waved to the crowd from the top. Jacopo had put out his arms. Jump, he'd shouted, I'll catch you. And such was the pull of the music and the chemicals that he had considered it.

The market was a flat-roofed shed in the main square. He found the red Lambretta right away, its licence plate and rearview missing, the machine in a state of advanced disrepair, and he found Jacopo in a market stall staring intently at the tomatoes.

"Been a time," said Dismas.

"Yes, yes," Jacopo bellowed in greeting.

They rode back to his home, which was in worse shape than the abandoned house with the murals next door. On the porch were puppies and half-chewed bits of bread and bowls of water. Jacopo fell into a broken rattan chair. His faded blue jeans were cut off above the knees and he was shirtless, his chest a mat of dark fur, leaner than Dismas remembered.

"Just sit anywhere," he said. "Later, we'll do some budding."

Birding. They would go birding.

Dismas cleared the debris from a low wall that bordered the porch. Near him was the cot on which Jacopo slept, surrounded by firewood, toys, bits of wiring, electronic components, odds and ends of mysterious provenance and purpose. On a stool was a pair of German binoculars in a beautiful leather case.

"I picked up something," he said, holding up a tube of hash. "A present, like."

He broke off a good chunk and held it to Dismas's nose. The smell was heady and unmistakable and it had an immediate effect: his arms came alive with goosebumps. A small joint was made and lit, in silence, the ritual protocol observed, and now an elderly man walked past the porch and Jacopo exhaled a cloud of smoke in his direction.

"My uncle," he said, gesturing at the man. "I'm the black sheep, like, they expect a certain kind of behaviour from me, can't let them down."

When he passed the joint Dismas took a cautious pull of unadulterated resin. The heat and ambition drained out of him in an instant. To smoke hash in Goa was to lose all interest in your surroundings. You let the sun work on your pores. You watched the puppies waddle and fall. You knew there was no reason to get out of your chair.

In the decade since they'd met Jacopo said it had become difficult for him to continue in Bombay.

"Everything changed. People I'd known for years, shop owners, barflies, layabouts, I realised I didn't know them any more, didn't trust them. The crazies were in our midst. Plus the drugs changed. Paranoia, I know ya. LSD-25 became -26 and -27, MDMA cut with mephedrone, and the Special K, yeah? Who decided elephant tranquilliser was a party drug for humans?"

One night, a month after the Babri Masjid was destroyed by a mob of Hindus, Jacopo took a taxi home to the suburbs. There were fires along the way, the city in flames, houses and shops put to the torch, and the strangest thing of all, no people on the streets. In Bombay! The taxi approached a police check post and an armed sentry gestured to the driver to stop. He sped right past. Jacopo ducked but there was no gunfire.

Minutes later they reached Mahim and the driver said, "Look, don't mind, are you Hindu or Mussalman?"

Jacopo replied, "Neither, I'm a Bombayite."

"It doesn't bother me but in case there's trouble I should know."

"I'm not Hindu or Muslim."

"Then?"

"I'm a Catholic. From Goa."

"Boss," said the driver, a well-built young Maharashtrian. "These days that's as bad as being Mussalman."

They drove in silence until Bandra. The driver said it wasn't safe to go further and Jacopo spent the night at a friend's house.

I came to understand the hold of fiction over the people of India, said Jacopo. I realised this was one of the last remaining places in the world where people killed themselves over invented stories. The riots had come to define the city. It affected everyone, even someone as marginal as he. And for some reason the city's madness came to him in the form of epiphanies that took place always in a Bombay taxi.

One evening he took a cab from the airport to his editor's house at Walkeshwar in the heart of the city. Because there were no shrines on the dashboard Jacopo assumed the driver was Muslim. Jacopo was travelling with a female colleague and he noticed the cabbie's eyes fixed on his in the rearview mirror. The mirror would slip and the man would tilt it up, positioning it for a view of the couple in the back. Then Jacopo noticed that the meter wasn't working. A wire had come loose, the driver said. He told the man to drop them to another cab, but at a traffic light on the arterial road connecting Worli to South Bombay the driver headed into a side lane. For gas, he said. The lane, Jacobo knew, was in a Muslim neighbourhood. His paranoia kicked in. Why couldn't the driver fill petrol on the main road? Because, the driver said, I need gas, not petrol. He meant the cooking gas cylinders some taxis used as cheap fuel. By now they were deep into unfamiliar streets and Jacopo shouted at the man to stop. As they haggled about payment two men in skullcaps came up to the driver.

Jacopo laughed soundlessly, exposing his black front teeth. "I knew it, Hindo's, Hindon'ts, Mozzies, city had gone to the dogs of god."

If his first two taxicab moments turned him against Hindus *and* Muslims the third turned upside down his view of the city and his place in it. He was on his way to the airport, finally making his move to Goa, and a woman approached the cab at a traffic light. He noticed that she didn't distort her face in the familiar dry crying. Her salvaar kameez was worn in the Muslim way, the pallu framing her face, and her glass bangles were a play of colour from elbow to wrist. Everything about her was tasteful but what held him was her face. He tried to look away.

"I am your sister," she said. "Don't turn away from your sister when she asks for your help."

She spoke in a quick rush timed for the traffic lights.

"You will go to London and Switzerland. Fortune will follow you like a bride. If you help me I will help my brothers and sisters."

Her hands were on the window frame and her face was inches from his, so close he could have kissed her. He gestured at the car ahead of them.

"See that car? Lots of money – try them."

"The rich are stingy," said the woman. "They never help the poor. Only the poor help the poor."

She was looking straight at him as she paid him this compliment. She had looked past their differences to the fact of their mutual exclusion from the city's citadel. Her eyes told him that nothing he might say or do would change her opinion about the connection they shared. As soon as he reached in his pocket and gave her a note she was gone.

These encounters were the three stations of his flight from Bombay. He was an outsider to both communities. In the long history of their hatred there was no role for a militant Catlick like himself. He kept his general hostility alive by taking paranoia-inducing chemicals and at those times, stoned, it was a source of anguish that he'd been forced to settle in Goa.

"That's what I'm doing here. I had to come back to my *own kind*, my *native place*, and start over."

But there was another reason for his return to Goa. The magazine he edited had shut down. Overnight he joined the ranks of the unemployed and then he discovered, by accident, that his family had been feuding over ancestral properties in Anjuna and Candolim and Calangute.

"I bump into this distant uncle, good old boy, at Churchgate Station, and he tells me, Jac, Jac, looks like your mother and brothers aren't any closer to working things out. Looks like it's going to be a long and bitter fight, too much cash involved. I didn't know what he was talking about. I didn't know my brothers and my mother had taken each other to court over property that belongs to me too. They didn't mention it. They wrote me off. So I came here to put a spoke, like, in their wheel, cause some trouble."

He appointed a lawyer who talked about the law as if it was something that could not be understood by ordinary men, as if it was a benediction, a mystery akin to the ways of God.

"There is a law within the Law," he told Jacopo. "Our work is to discern what this may be and to tailor accordingly our aspiration and our longing for release."

He did nothing for a year and more and Jacopo fired him and appointed someone else and while he waited for the case to work its way through the system two years passed. He found himself living like a primitive with few needs and possessions. He smoked and wrote articles on birds, identified two hundred and fifty of the four hundred or so species in Goa, compiled details about mating habits and diets: he went to ground.

"How do editors contact you?"

"They don't. What makes you think they do?"

"Well, how do you work?"

"I contact them, like. It's all fucked up," he said.

He had a way of stressing the last syllable of each sentence and the tic gave his speech an out-of-control quality.

"I like birds," he said, inside a heavy stream of smoke. "I like birds for the perspective they give. I'll show you."

He got up from the broken armchair and crossed the road to a steep hill fronting the house. As they climbed Dismas wished he had more water, stouter shoes, a wider hat-brim. They hiked steadily and stopped only to smoke, the effect of the hash cumulative, a slow expansion in the head and unease in the chest. But it wasn't unpleasant and the more they smoked the more he liked it. Sound deepened. He heard a hidden layer of detail behind the wind and the noise they made as they walked and he sensed the sea out there. Soon they came upon two motionless men balanced on sticks held to their chins. Small and perfectly still, they did not return Jacopo's greeting. They were men of the hills, tribals from Central India whose silence and stillness made Dismas feel like an interloper.

Heat, the occasional mouthful of water, the sound of insect life, the rhythm of the climb; Dismas felt his consciousness narrow to these elements. Jacopo pointed out a long-beaked bird so tiny Dismas would not have noticed him, a butcher bird busily hooking a piece of skink meat on a thorn for later eating. They saw barbets and bee-eaters and glossy raven-like jungle crows. They heard the complex and manic call of a nightingale. And then they crested a hill and came to a skeletal tree beside a garbage dump where Brahminy kites and golden eagles swooped for food or roosted amid great drifts of plastic and charred household waste. They were on a peak high above the Arabian Sea and the wind carried a stench from the dump. The Brahminys took flight, copper and white in the sun, or they waited, sentinel on the dead tree. Dismas held Jacopo's binoculars to his eyes and watched as a young Brahminy fell backward into the sky with a single flap of his wings.

They came to a headland and the sea came into view. The beaches of North Goa lay before them in a single unbroken curve of sand. Candolim, Calangute, Baga, Anjuna. Fishing boats and merchant ships crowded the water near the shore but further out to sea it was bare and tranquil, the sun beginning to set. Night falls quickly when you are on top of a strange hill in the middle of nowhere without a torch or supplies.

Jacopo went by instinct. He lost his way and found it again. He took a path and doubled back when he realised it led nowhere. It was getting darker from one minute to the next and soon it would be difficult to see. Dismas realised he was dependent on Jacopo to get them back to the road and the hash had made him paranoid. How well did he know the fellow after all? What manly ritual were they enacting on this remote Goan hill? What if he was deliberately trying to get them lost, what then?

Dismas took the lead and Jacopo said nothing when he blundered into undergrowth so thick it was impossible to proceed. They turned back, the path barely visible as they continued downhill, until, the sun gone and full night almost on them, they came upon a family walking in single file and a village with crying children and cook fires and sullen silent men. They emerged opposite Jacopo's almost exactly where they had set out. As they crossed the road the night turned featureless and Bible black.

The journey from Forgottem to Old Goa was only a few hours by road but it felt long and arduous. The bus bounced and swerved along unpaved country roads, braking only when it came to a village or small township. To take his mind off the bus driver's homicidal or suicidal tendency he paid close attention to the scenery as it blurred past, the gutter-spouts and eaves, the picket fences and peaked front porches, the whitewashed churches: a Mediterranean scene but for the scorch of sunlight and the corrosive sand.

He alighted at the depot and changed buses. Then, a different kind of journey – highways, regulated city traffic, frequent stops. The bus followed a river to the Basilica of Bom Jesus. There was a steep climb and the packages on the overhead racks slid to the floor. They passed the ruins of Saint Augustine's Church, the rafters overrun with moss and the walls missing but the windows and doors intact. For the final leg the passengers piled into a chartered van that took them to the church grounds.

It was a mela. Bollywood music issued from speakers attached to trees. Stalls sold paired links of chorise sausage and fizzy beverages in stoppered bottles. There were small hills of bruised apples and boiled sweets and cotton candy. He noted Saint Xavier dolls made of plastic and tin. The saint wore knee-length boots and a blue smock tight across the chest and hips. He had the wide-legged stance of a Jesuit superhero.

Dismas drifted into a church where people sat in small groups with plastic bags at their feet. They were staring at a tall oil on canvas that hung on the main apse. It was a representation unlike any he'd seen, not the gaunt haunted saint but a jollier man with a ruddy complexion and an air of well-fed bonhomie. A bushy red beard partially obscured his grin and jowls. Over the great stomach a rich surplice hung like the mast of a small sailing vessel. The artist had made solid areas of flagrant red out of the saint's cheeks and his hair was red and his eyes unnaturally blue. It was Saint Xavier as Falstaff, inviting the people of Goa to partake of the feast.

And though the picture was a falsehood it seemed correct in the context of the mela and the pilgrims with their plastic bags of food and drink. They posed in front of this or that reliquary and they stroked the empty Medici casket that served as Xavier's tomb, empty because the body had been moved for viewing. The casket's marble cupids and gilded Florentine pillars were open to the elements and to curious hands.

A woman, matronly, still young, placed her freshly reddened lips against the casket and asked her friend, "Removed photo?"

"Removed," her friend replied.

It struck him that they weren't pilgrims but tourists, holidaymakers in town for the opening of the season. The true pilgrims were in the pews and they carried no cameras or snacks, their eyes straying to the Falstaffian Xavier and to the tumult of tourists and cameras and to the sign by the casket: Please Keep Godly Silence. Don't Disturb Religious Feelings.

Outside on a raised stage a priest spoke into a microphone.

"How can we experience this god who protects us from bondage and slavery?" he said, showing the congregation the backs of his hands.

He was plump, with sharp sideburns and veined eyes.

"People say, 'I made love.' It means they had sex. Brothers and sisters, this is not love. Love is unconditional. God does not say, 'I love you, but.' To bear witness to God's love we must know the teachings of the church. This Exposition is not meant for fun. It is a catechism."

He asked the congregants to stand.

Anticipating him they said, "Oh Lord, hear us as we pray."

"To replace corruption with righteousness," the priest said.

"Oh Lord, hear our prayer."

Now it was time to collect money and women in blue saris went up the jerry-rigged aisles. Each carried a long stick with a pocket at the end, like a butterfly net. No coins were passed, only notes.

The priest began the communion service.

"We eat your body and drink your blood," he said. "Let this bring us health in mind and body."

More priests appeared, not as grand, in dirty white cassocks and worn rubber slippers. They walked the aisles and hesitantly handed out communion wafers. Pressed into Dismas's hand the communion was shiny and tasteless and slightly soiled. He touched his tongue to it and let it drop under the seat.

"Saint Xavier, your heart was burning with love. To proclaim this love you went from country to country and died. This is why God in heaven took you to him and kept your body uncorrupted on earth."

But Dismas had found the book the ponytailed man had told him about and he knew the body was corrupted and he would see it soon for himself.

The day before, in Panjim, he'd stopped at a feni bar near the canals to ask for directions. The auntie behind the counter pointed at a house that stood on its own beside a live oak threaded with pink ribbons. Inside was a high-ceilinged room that was more warehouse than shop. The light came from a single bulb on a wire caked with sticky dust. There were no customers and only one clerk. On the counter were CDs by local choirs and newsletters or homemade tracts or journals for the itinerant preacher and back numbers of *The Watchtower*, *Good News Journal* and *Awake!*

Dismas asked the clerk if the book was in stock and the man found a copy under the counter. It was as if he had been waiting for just such a request. Was it a popular book? The clerk said it was not; the author was a lapsed Jesuit. Dismas asked what this meant. The clerk said the author had given up the priesthood to marry and have children.

"But personally, I think once a Jesuit, always a Jesuit."

He put the book into a bag that had the name of the bookshop in Old Testament script, REDEMPTION HARDWARE. There was a line underneath in smaller print, 'Jesus saves and so can you. End of time sale: 30% off on all titles.'

It was a holiday of some kind. Children played cricket on the street, the wickets drawn in chalk on the wall. They used a lime-green tennis ball and a heavy bat and when the bat connected to the ball it sailed into the sky like a glowing green asteroid. He came to a canal where steps led down to a chapel or shrine, the water deep green and covered in moss.

On a bench he took the book out of the bag. *The Worldly Travels of an Otherworldly Man: Saint Francis Xavier's Hard Life and Difficult Death* was a handsome hardcover volume with cream paper and a silk ribbon bookmark, published in Bombay in 1982. There was a bibliography and index, transcripts from documents, photos and histories and colour plates. There was a list of recommended reading and thirty-four pages of notes. On the cover was an etching of the dark-skinned saint.

The author John Lobo may have given up the priesthood but his Jesuitic training was like a watermark on every page. He had compiled everything he could find on the saint into one orderly volume and evident in the crotchety attention to detail was his own astringent personality.

He wrote that he'd become familiar with Francis Xavier's style of letter writing and he could tell from the language when the saint was despondent and when he was elated.

> It will surprise no one if I report that the latter condition was rarer than the former. Key is the fact that he was seasick throughout the year-long voyage to India. Even then Xavier's was a remarkably sunny disposition and he was full of plans for the future, but only during the journey. As soon as he arrived at his destination, at any destination, how his manner changed! The Slough of Despond descended quickly. I learned some things about him. If he described a landscape as Indian you can be sure he was unhappy due to some imagined slight or inadequacy among the people he met. If he described a bird it meant he had been overtaken by joy.

But it wasn't Xavier's letters or the facts of his life that interested Lobo as much as the events that followed his death: the book was a meticulous documentation of the various exhumations and misadventures and mutilations that his remains had endured. It seemed like an eccentric way to compose a biography and there was only one clue as to Lobo's reasons. He began his introduction by saying that if hardship was an index of saintliness then Xavier was the prototypical saint, for death had put no end to his difficulties. Then followed the list of true-to-life indignities that his body had suffered at the hands of sailors, church officials, and devotees.

From an excess of devotion or bad luck his remains endured multiple exhumations and numerous acts of random mutilation. Two months after the burial on Sancian a sailor dug up the body and took as a souvenir a piece of flesh from his thigh. This is where the idea of his incorruptible body took root and spread. It began with the sailor reporting to his shipmates that the body was still fresh.

The saint's remains were transported to Malacca where they were reburied in a rocky grave. The difficulty of the burial is on record. His neck was broken to make the body fit into a space that was entirely too small to receive its guest. This assessment is built on the number and extent of injuries discovered on the body during the first exhumation: fractured ribs, a dislocated nose, a bruise on the left breast and another on the right cheek.

Two years later the body was exhumed once more and taken by ship to Goa. A medical examiner, who would contribute in no small measure to the saint's quickly growing legend, wrote, 'The body was incorrupt.' An English physician, who visited Goa in 1675, described the corpse as 'a Miraculous Relick of his better part, it still retaining its vivid Colour and Freshness, and therefore exposed once a Year to publick view'.

The body went on view and these yearly Expositions, as they came to be called, became further occasions for mutilation. An unbalanced Portuguese woman by the name of Isabel Caron bit off the small toe of his right foot. Instead of being punished she was commemorated and her name associated with Saint Xavier's in all subsequent histories of the saint.

Then came the worst cut. A lay brother who shall not be named cut off a piece of flesh from the corpse. Which piece? In later years he apologised for his action and attributed it to a kind of hysteria, but the facts of the matter are quite clear. He took a piece of the saint's genitalia and installed it in the reliquary of the

Basilica of Bom Jesus, where the corpse, separated from several of its extremities, still resides. The church has denied this terrible mutilation, but I offer the incontrovertible proof of mine own eyes. For I have seen the relic in question.

I am sorry to say that the Jesuits themselves were responsible for most of these unfortunate events. Of course, even in their depredations they kept meticulous accounts. The documents show that another toe of the right foot was detached – 'found loose' according to the account – and allowed to find its way to the Bom Jesus. Two joints of a fourth toe were added by order of the patriarch. These body parts did not travel far. Others did. Saint Xavier's right arm was sawed off from the shoulder joint at the request of the Jesuit Superior of the Society of Jesus. The hand and forearm up to the elbow were sent to Rome, where they lie at altar in the church of Gesu. The upper arm was divided into three pieces, one was apportioned to a Jesuit college in Cochin, another sent to a college in Malacca, and the shoulder blade to the former Portuguese colony and present casino destination of Macau. The corpse's internal organs from the chest and abdomen were removed and sent to various reliquaries in various countries at the request of Jesuit officials. But there were unrecorded mutilations as well. More toes were taken and between two official examinations, in 1932 and 1951, the left ear disappeared. The examination reports are revealing compilations of medico-religious prose. And by the mid-twentieth century there was a change in the terminology employed by the church to describe the saint's poor remains. The relics are no longer described as incorruptible.

Here Lobo quoted from one of the reports:

We can no longer speak of an incorruptible body – which is not necessary, for the sanctity of a person is not measured by the preservation of his body – but of the sacred relics of Saint Francis Xavier, for what we have today are mainly bones of the Saint

> . . . a shrivelled skull, two legs, the left arm and hand, and heaps of bones, loose vertebrae, ribs or fragments of ribs and pieces of skin.

"How meagre an inventory," wrote Lobo, comparing the list above to a report from 1782:

> He has the whole head with a great portion of hair. His facial features have deteriorated, but are covered up with skin, except the right side that has a bruise. He has both ears, and all his teeth visible, except one. He has his left arm with hand eaten up, he does not have the right arm . . . The body has everything save the intestines. There were legs with dry skin, the bare feet covered with skin, lines made by the veins as well as the nails could be seen. Only one toe on the right foot was missing, and had been taken off by a devotee.

Dismas closed the book and looked across the canal to the shrine. There was a white cross on which someone had placed a garland of marigolds. The sun was bright and the air had turned cooler.

Saint Xavier, it seemed to him, was the patron saint of migrants, of drifters and wanderers and those who were misplaced on the planet, those who were missing limbs and homes, those addicts whose addiction was movement without meaning.

No wonder X had taken his name.

There in the mild sunshine he felt as if he were in a world of cotton wool. It is no exaggeration to say that he entered a state of unthinking bliss. Of the many things that had happened to him he retained no formal recollection. He could not remember his childhood, his parents, the humiliation he had suffered as a schoolboy. All he felt was gratitude that he was alive and in possession of an imperfect but working body, for his feet that traversed the tiles of the road, for his lungs and eyes and ticking heart.

Xavier had taken his travel funds on a whim. For X the amount was little more than small change, but for Dismas it was a catastrophe. He would have to find work. Or cut short his stay in Goa and his travels around the country interviewing those who had known Xavier in his youth and middle age. Or he would have to sell the Two Marys, which were in storage. But what would be the point? Without authentication they were worth nothing. At least he had managed to keep his appointments in Forgottem and Mapusa; at least he had done that.

Now, at the Basilica, he bought a ticket for the audio-visual programme and joined a group of melancholy Malayali nuns. They entered a hive of connected rooms where viewers were shown an enactment of the life of Christ, an extravaganza of life-size moving figures and weeping violins and the kind of melodramatic score that accompanied early Hindi movies. They were ushered onto a sheet of blue-tinted plastic flooring and the music changed: there was a sudden burst of bhangra. Disco lights strobed under their feet; the floor started to move. How strange it all was. Then, in the next room, because he was a few minutes late the lights were turned off soon after he entered. In the sudden darkness he saw a figure triangulated in the yogic lotus, whose black eyes stared into his eyes, so close he could feel the static from the hair. It was a flesh-coloured likeness of Jesus as sadhu meditating in a Himalayan cave. The Christ wore a beard to his navel and a piece of sackcloth fastened over his shoulder, his feet hooked to his upper thighs.

It reminded him of something he'd read once about Xavier's first show in London, in which he had depicted Jesus as a Hindu holy man. Among the paintings that provoked Roman Catholics was a large oil of Jesus as a blue-skinned sadhu meditating in a cave, his doe eyes rimmed with kajal. The show was called *Haré Krishna, Haré Christ* and Dismas had seen a review in which the writer had used such words as 'genius' and 'iconoclast' but had tried to underplay his admiration.

And now, decades after the review had appeared, he was standing in front of what may have been the original inspiration for that picture, a piece of Goan kitsch that Xavier had transformed into art. And Dismas remembered something X had said, though he could not remember where or to whom. The point of art was not to imitate nature but to surpass it. Art supersedes nature, he had said, it reveals to nature how small are her horizons when placed alongside the imaginings of a superior mind.

After the state's elaborate preparations for the Exposition and a film festival that had opened at the same time – protests at the festival venue, residents complaining about the strain on the infrastructure – the actual Exposition was unexpectedly subdued. The tents were half empty and Dismas felt again that he was at the wrong place at the wrong time. A red-carpeted tented walkway led across the dusty grounds to where the saint's remains were displayed. There were signs advising pilgrims to rest frequently and to wait if they found too heavy a crowd. Millions had been expected but they had neglected to arrive. It was deserted but for Dismas.

And then he was under a worn chandelier in sight of the glass casket where Saint Xavier lay. Here the crowd was thicker, herded into an enclosure by policemen in plain clothes. Ahead of Dismas was an industrialist with a retinue of police officers and women in sunglasses, the industrialist in white shorts and a T-shirt, his face flushed red, his shorts too short. The man was a famous or infamous name in the nation's newspapers, a scion of liquor and air travel. But he too was asked to move quickly. A policewoman had been stationed at the casket, her only job to wipe the stains of spit and sweat left by the pilgrims who kissed the glass above the feet of the saint, who left small envelopes with printed prayers, currency notes, lockets, and bits of thread and fabric.

His sight of Francis Xavier was brief and unsettling. He saw a slender figure in a gown of gold and red brocade. The gown covered empty burgled space, he knew this, because there wasn't much left of the man, the skull, a hand, three toes. The bald head was textured like hide or parchment and there was flesh missing from around the mouth and he could see the incisors, which were stained a deep yellow. How far was the reality of the saint's remains from the romantic images of a tall white man with glossy brown hair and trimmed beard, eyes blue and soulful, a youth of strapping build and physical beauty. Here were the remains of the true saint, a small exhausted dark-skinned man.

He regarded the stunted trees laden with dust and the humid ocean-loaded heat that trembled on the flat brown land. Everywhere was salt and erosion. How easy it would be to melt into the air. He would not let it happen. He could not. He saw the finished book in his mind, the title and heft of it, two hundred and fifty pages of heft, and he saw the kind of blurbs that would populate the back cover. To feel better he bought things he did not need with funds he could not afford to deplete, white khadi kurta-pyjamas, a pair of knock-off Ray-Ban Aviators, and a glass pipe in the shape of a giant multicoloured mushroom.

And then, what did he do then?

He stayed true to his name, Dismas, the not-so-good thief. He returned to Bangalore and from the station he took an auto to the first guesthouse he found, a 'pure veg' hovel named Mr Majestic. The rooms were like boxes. There was a single cot and steel cupboard lit by the hospital glare of white tube-lights. There was no room service. He put his bag down and took a long shower and found a respectable collared shirt that made him look like a bank manager or journalist or young executive on his way up in the world. Then he went to Infantry Road, where it took less than twenty minutes to find Noon Wines. At the counter he asked for Dharini and when she appeared he asked if she remembered him. Yes, she said, greeting him without surprise. She let him buy her a cup of coffee: there was so much to talk about.

6.

She stared at the television at the foot of the bed. It was some kind of documentary, a group of men and women walking in single file on a beach. As they came into focus she saw white crosses painted on their foreheads and she noticed that their hands were bound. A tall photogenic minder accompanied each man and woman and a curious tenderness tied the minder to his charge. They walked toward a bluff where seven crosses faced the ocean. The camera panned from left to right across the crosses and then cut to the men and women walking one behind the other. There was a swell of classical music, some kind of opera, and there was a shot of the ocean and a bird far out to sea. There was a sense of something building. She opened a small refrigerator by the bed and poured herself a glass of water, her eyes on the screen. There was a close-up of a woman with fair hair and the cross on her forehead and another shot of the ocean. The sequence had been carefully composed and choreographed with three cameras if not more, the scenes cut with grainy footage of a surgical procedure involving the brain and another of a sexual act between bonobo monkeys, though the nature of the act was unclear. She picked up a nail file from the bedside table and worked on her nails as she looked at the screen. The animal documentary reminded her of the porn she used to watch in her teens when she had six or seven tabs open on her screen at one time. She remembered the first time she saw a dildo, purple and shaped like a sword. None of it was arousing but she found it impossible to look away; and for days afterwards the look on a young woman's face would stay with her, some inadvertent flinch or smile. The video went back to the original sequence, now nearing its end. The men and women who had walked as if strolling on the sand, who had uncomplainingly been lifted and tied to the crosses, began to struggle as their minders drilled nails into their bound hands and feet. In the last shot the camera switched to the point of view of the crucified men and women as the sun began to set into the sea and they understood that this was the last sunset they would see on earth. Instead of credits there was a slow dissolve. She watched it through to the end, without emotion and with no sensation other than tiredness. When Xavier came into the room to change into street clothes she was watching a Hindi music video, and here too as she watched a dozen white women in ghagras dancing on a lavish sound stage the only sensation she was aware of was tiredness. He said he was going out for cigarettes and would be back in some time.

"There are five packs of Wills on the table, but," she said.

"I like to prepare for every calamitous eventuality, as you know, and five packs of Wills is a mere fifty smokes, no protection at all," he replied. "More nicotine is the answer to most problems, at least in my experience."

"Don't leave out booze and sex."

"Yes, Dharini, worry not."

"Don't call me Dharini. I told you I hate it. My name is Ari."

"Ari, I'll be back in twenty, don't worry."

She had looked him up on the Internet's infinite stew of gossip, news, and innuendo; she knew some things about him; everybody did.

"Not worried, yaar, sceptical. Isn't that how you left your first wife? Going out for cigarettes."

"Not true at all, exurban myth with no basis in fact."

He laughed but the laugh trailed abruptly off into silence.

"Newton," she said.

"Listen, I must step out for a bit. Newton Xavier the saint manqué must head out into the night for a bit of solitude and leave this lovely room and lovely girl and whatever lovely thing he and the girl have been doing. He will take a small raincheck on the continuing saga of fornication amid catastrophe because he must, must, must catch up with his other life. He does have another, you know. Aren't you hungry? It's almost nine."

"Fuck off," she said, once and then again, anger resonating softly in her voice. "I'll cope up with my own mechanisms."

"You're a new kind of Indian," he said. "Your English skills are rather patchy but you are highly articulate nevertheless and there is even the flash of occasional verbal brilliance. Anyway. Goodbye, now."

She didn't get out of bed; she fell asleep watching American news. There was a story about three interplanetary events that had occurred earlier that year. Some scientists had identified the largest dwarf planet in the solar system and named it Eris. She knew there was nothing dwarfish about a dwarf planet, and Eris was a large dwarf, which made it a giant. There were many undiscovered dwarf planets, so many that eventually when they were all mapped perhaps astronomers would change the term from dwarf planet to half-planet. A week after the discovery of Eris, the space probe Deep Impact was launched with the intention of colliding with a comet, or sending an impacter to collide with the comet. And two days after Deep Impact impacted the comet another probe landed on Titan, Saturn's largest moon. It had been a busy month for space exploration, which made her think of her father, an amateur astronomer and former schoolteacher who had reinvented himself as a liquor retailer. She fell asleep and dreamt of two great planets that had somehow come loose from their orbits. When she saw the white hole of space dust that resulted from the planets' collision she whimpered so loudly that she woke herself up.

She came out of the shower and patted herself dry. She took a chocolate from a box on the couch and took a small bite and wound a towel around her waist and picked up the phone, but she could not remember why. It was late; she knew he was not coming back. The thing she would not forget about the whole Xavier episode, recognising him at the shop, getting to know him, looking after him, was that he had not even bothered to come up with a new excuse. "Going out for cigarettes." She put the phone down and heard a woman's voice say something about a stampede at a temple in which more than three hundred people had died. She looked at the screen for a minute but she could make no sense of the images. A crowd surging against itself. The pictures she had seen, the crucifixions, the surgical procedure, the sunset, the monkey sex, the stampede, the deep space probes, they were all of a piece; and, as always, televised evidence of the world's obsessions left her feeling grimy but untouched. It was all information and it was all the same.

She found her clothes and put on a black T-shirt, which she tucked into belted chinos. She found her shoes under a comforter on the floor. She put the sari and the box of chocolates in her laptop case and left the hospital. They stopped her at the exit and made her sit in the lobby while they checked Xavier's hospital bill. She was allowed to leave only after a senior administrator confirmed that they had his address and the hospital would contact a collection agency if necessary.

At home she let herself in quietly because her father would be asleep. There was a note on the dining table. Her father's handwriting was mostly unreadable, as if someone had pointed a gun to his head and told him to hurry; she had to guess at the meaning of the words. She understood that he had made patatas bravas and left a bowl for her. In the kitchen she took things out of the cabinet and the fridge one item at a time, feeling some pleasure as she handled spoon, plate, bowl, and jug, as if she had been away for weeks, though it had only been a day. She put the bowl into the oven and when it heated she put it on a tray and added a thick slice of bread from a box on the counter and a glass of cold lemonade and took it all to her room.

While she waited for the dial-up connection on her computer she took off her eye make-up and changed into shorts. She ate watching her new favourite webcam star, a Japanese girl who ate enormous meals alone. Solitary eaters around the world tuned in to allyouwhoeatalone.com to watch the girl eat breakfast, lunch, and dinner. Today she was wearing bunny ears and a plain black dress with primly rounded white collars. She used a soup spoon and a pair of chopsticks to prepare a mouthful.

When she was ready the girl held the spoon up to the camera and said, "Hey, would you like a bite of this delicious dumpling noodle soup? The ankake sauce gives it very nice flavour."

She slurped slightly and chewed a dumpling.

"Yes," Dharini said, taking a bite of her patatas bravas. "I would love to have some of your delicious dumpling noodle soup."

"Next we have this fried rice with meat sauce topping. When they call this a kaki sauce they mean I think sometimes oyster sauce."

She held up a spoon full of the meat sauce.

"The sauce is packed full of so good stuff. It got bamboo and wood ear mushroom."

The subtitles were mixed up but Dharini read them carefully. As always the Japanese girl sat in front of a table full of dishes and floating captions informed the viewer about how many calories she would consume. Eighteen thousand. She took her time but she finished every bite and she did it with a smile on her pretty face, and though the meals she ate were enormous they never seemed to show on her person, she was slender and willowy, which made Dharini wonder if she threw up after each meal and if the vomiting was as much of a ritual as the eating. It did not matter. Nothing mattered except the hypnotised feeling that came over her when she watched the girl eat and the comfort she felt when they ate together. The Japanese girl's meal would continue for at least two hours. Long after she had finished her own dinner she continued to watch and each time the girl took a bite of some raw fish or seaweed or pork, Dharini could taste the food in her mouth. After some time she began to feel uncomfortably full and she clicked off the channel and went to womenwhoweep.com. On the live cam two women held hands and cried endless tears. Whenever one of them stopped crying she would look at her companion and the tears would start again. One of the women said, you who have lost loved ones, you who are alone in your grief, it is for you that we weep. Now, said the other woman, we will take a request. This is for Miss T who has lost her beloved dog. And the women started to cry again. I miss you, Coco, they said between sobs, oh, how I miss you. Dharini watched the two women until the last tear had dried. Then she stopped in at a Bollywood chat room where a personal message was waiting for her from a regular who called himself M-Thug. (His real name was Muzamil.) They made small talk about cricket and a newly released Bollywood comedy that starred Salman and Bipasha. The movie was full of innuendo and double entendres. M-Thug said even the name of the movie was a reference to doggy style or missionary. Of course it was, she said, so what? That didn't make it a good name for a movie. They talked some more and then she shut the computer down and brushed her teeth and went to bed. She dreamt of her dead mother, Prasanna, and woke up giggling. She had a clear memory of her mother laughing in her dream, though she could not remember what she had been laughing about.

When she came out dressed and ready to leave her father was reading the *Hindoo* and drinking a cup of coffee. It was a memory from the mornings of her childhood, summer heat swarming in the window, the neighbour's dog barking, a big dog's perplexed day-long bark, and she would come into the kitchen to the smell of South Indian coffee decoction, idlis, sambar and chutney on the table, and her parents sharing the newspaper before they went to their respective teaching jobs. She made toast and a boiled egg and noticed that Bhuvapathi, her father, seemed to be ageing in front of her eyes. Just yesterday his hair had been black and full. Now most of it was grey and he seemed smaller, as if he was shrinking from the inside.

She asked him if he would be going to the wine shop that morning. She had to pick up a certificate from her college and would only be able to get to the shop at lunch. No, Bhuvapathi said, he would not be going to the shop. Had he given up on it, she asked. It wasn't that he had given up, it was just that he was busy with other work, he replied. After all he had not always been a wine shop owner, once he had been a physics teacher and according to his students a good one. He had been a physics professional and an astronomy amateur. The wine shop had started as a temporary measure, but they had become accustomed to the income and the temporary had become permanent. The shop had paid for her education and the house in which they lived and that was the only thing that could be said in favour of a business that counted alcoholics and thugs among its valued clients. It had been good for them but perhaps it was time to shut it down. What other work, she asked, looking at the *Hindoo* on his lap. Thinking, he said. He had been busy thinking.

"Do you remember something I used to say when you were a child?" he said. "About the sound the universe makes?"

She tried to remember but he had said so many things about the universe; it was a constant topic when she was growing up.

"You said universal vowel and first sound babies make are both same," she said.

"Not all babies, only smart ones like you."

"The sound of oh, this is what you said?"

"Better astronomers than me said it a long time ago. Now some gravitational wave theorists are also saying that the sound or vibration of space-time is ohm. Isn't that strange?"

He pointed to an article he had been reading in the newspaper. She moved around to read the headline, *What Is the Universe Saying?*

"I am opposed to the unquestioning acceptance of ancient teaching," Bhuvapathi said. "But this."

She put her breakfast plates in the sink and picked up the house keys and put on her shoes.

"I've been thinking about two things. One, ohm as a frequency or vibration may at last be measurable if the measurer knows what he is looking for. And two, some Arabic words in common astronomical notation reveal unexpected connections between civilisations and epochs," he said, folding the newspaper and putting it in her backpack. "Take this with you and look at it when you have the time."

But she took it out and put it on the table.

"I'll see it on Internet," she said. "There's never enough news in the newspaper. It's always less. There's never enough information to clearify my doubts."

"Clarify," said her father.

"Yeah, clarify."

At the door she asked if he had heard of the new dwarf planet, Eris.

"The goddess of discord. Also, 'sire' spelt backwards. If it is a dwarf, it's a daddy dwarf or mama dwarf. As large as Pluto. So the question is as many-handed as our own Hindu discord goddess. If Eris is a dwarf then Pluto is a dwarf. If Pluto is a dwarf we must remake the list of planets. Is it a dwarf or a full planet? Decide. And if Pluto is a full planet, then why isn't Eris the ninth planet in our system?" Bhuvapathi said. "Anyway they're always discovering new dwarfs. No reason to get excited."

She considered for a moment his solemn frown and lopsided glasses and faded Pink Floyd T-shirt and she went back across the room to kiss him on the top of his newly grey head.

It was a little after noon when she reached the wine shop. The new boy Arjun was at the counter and Mr Narasimhan was working the cash register. He had already taken out his tiffin box and placed it beside him. He ate lunch at the same time every day, twelve fifteen exactly, not at twelve and not at twelve thirty and she liked this about him. She decided to put off doing the accounts until the lunch rush had subsided and in the meanwhile she took over at the register and racked up sales, mostly quarters of rum and whisky; then it was all sound, voices in Kannada and English placing orders, faint traffic, notes counted and clipped, change made, coins dropped into the coin tray. A local beer manufacturer had delivered a point-of-purchase advertisement that was a life-size cutout of a woman in a bikini. She told Arjun to put the cutout next to the refrigerator so customers would see it near the chilled beer. Immediately beer sales increased.

Late in the afternoon she sat in the inside office with the accountant and went over the returns they would file the following week. The accountant had just had lunch and she could smell the spices on his fingers and the strong milk tea on his breath. She felt a little sick and hoped they would be finished soon because some college friends were planning an afternoon trip to Nandi Hills. The accountant began to itemise and double-check everything. He was annoyingly thorough and two and a half hours later they were still working. Every hour on the hour he would step out of the shop to light a cigarette that he never smoked to the butt. He took three or four drags, leisurely and with some surprise, as if he had only just taken up smoking and couldn't understand why it had taken him so long to get around to this essential pleasure. Then he flicked the cigarette on the street and came back into the shop. The accountant smoked Wills Navy Cuts, like Xavier, whose life had coincided with hers for a couple of weeks. She realised she did not mind that he had left as abruptly as he had. She had given nothing of herself to him, or nothing that could not be retrieved with a little effort. But he had picked her up and used her and dropped her like an empty bottle of whisky. Had he treated Goody Lol the same way, the woman she had heard so much about and looked up on the Internet? She and Goody were the same size and body type but Goody's clothes were more stylish and feminine, gauzy dresses, headscarves, hats, high heels. She knew how to be a woman. Dharini's wardrobe consisted mainly of jeans and saris. They had something in common though Goody would never know it: they were strong women drawn to rascally men. When the accountant left it was much too late for Nandi Hills. She stopped for take-out puffs and cutlets and took an auto home.

The house was dark and her father had gone to bed though it was still early. She put on the lights and opened the windows and put the food in the oven to heat. His morning coffee and newspaper were still on the dining table. She cleared the cup and sat down with the paper. Near the article about the speaking universe she found the following words written in Bhuvapathi's hurried hand:

AL KHWARIZMI = ALGORHYTHM
AL JABR = ALGEBRA
AL SUFI = AZOPHI
AL FERGHANI = FERGANA = ALFRAGANUS
AL BATTANI = ALBATEGNIUS = ZIJ

She put the food on a plate and took it into her room. She took off her shoes and dialled up the Internet and in less than ten minutes she knew that her father had made a list of ancient Muslim astronomers and attempted some kind of strange etymology, something to do with the migration of the astronomers' names and ideas into English and Latin. The discovery dismayed and thrilled her. She fell asleep wondering if she should ask him about it or if it would be better not to mention it at all and again she dreamt of her mother and remembered nothing of the dream when she woke. It was late and she went into the shower. When she came out he was at the window staring at the champakali that had not flowered that year. He had forgotten to make coffee. He had not bathed or shaved. He was talking to himself though she could not hear what he was saying. She asked him what was wrong and he lifted his index finger and nodded. She waited and when he still did not speak she went to the kitchen to start the coffee.

"Nothing wrong," he told her at the breakfast table. "I was going over something in my head."

"You're okay or not?"

"I'm okay."

"Means you won't come to the shop today also?"

"Dharini, Ari, crazy people do not worry if they are crazy. I worry therefore I am not crazy. I worry a lot so you should not worry."

"You're not crazy because you worry you're crazy?"

"Do you talk to her sometimes?"

"Who?"

"You know who. I talk to her every morning. Sometimes she talks to me."

"What does she say?"

"Just now?"

"Yes, just now."

"She said this country can be saved but only by those it is trying to exterminate."

She came home early that evening. Her father was out somewhere taking a walk or visiting the lending library. She noticed the house had been cleaned and the breakfast dishes washed and put away. His room too had been tidied. On his desk she found a small pile of handwritten notes, variations of the names he had scrawled in the margins of the newspaper. On the top sheet he had arranged the words in this way:

ALGORHYTHM = ALGEBRA = ALCHEMY
AL KHWARIZMI = AL JABR = AL KIMIA
ALFRAGANUS = ALBATEGNIUS
FERGHANA = ZIJ
AZOPHI = AL SUFI | ABOTANY = AL BATTANI

She tried to make sense of it. Had he put the words together according to category instead of meaning? Then why would Ferghana, a place name, equal Zij, a type of book? Where had Alchemy and Abotany come from? They were not among the first list of words he had made in the margins of the *Hindoo*. And what had happened to Al Ferghani? Why had only the Latin version of his name been retained? Why did Al Ferghani no longer fit into Bhuvapathi's overall scheme, if he had one? She hoped there was some kind of pattern in the way the words occurred and she looked up each word again in case she had missed a connection. Finally she gave up and sat with her head in her hands and then she switched to her favourite webcam channel. The Japanese girl sat before a dish that might have been dessert, small squares of yellow and red jelly over black beans and syrup the colour of menstrual blood.

In a while her father came home with books from the library. In her room he stood behind her chair and they watched the girl use a tiny silver spoon to eat the extra-large bowl of syrupy dessert. Lightly he caressed her shoulders.

BOOK FIVE

'I Only Know Beautiful When I Paint It Nude'

Saint Larry

or Lawrence, or Bantle the Man;
of Poona & Vancouver;
burned both ends before the ink ran
dry; of outsiders & the homeless, a lover;

precocious & precious, a prodigy;
patron of transmigrants, vegetable sellers,
men of spinach & tomato yellers;
rider on the tide of tragedy.

Saint Nissim

of Galilean oil-pressers
ship-wrecked off the coast
of Maharashtra
one hundred & fifty years
before Christ;
lover, bird-watcher, et cetera;
first of the comic confessors;

of Marathi-speaking
Bene-Israeli Jews;
lifelong Bombayman;
psalmist & palmist; beggar-king;
payer of latter-day dues;
'my backward place is where I am';
& the daisy's revenge: the forsaking.

from *The Book of Chocolate Saints: Poems* (Unpublished)

Beryl Xavier, mother, interviewed by Dismas Bambai at the Bangalore Institute of Mental Health, Bangalore, June 1998

It is a strange feeling to be released into the world after you've been confined for so long. How long I don't know, I stopped counting. I walked out of the asylum gates and discovered that everything had changed but only on the inside. The core had changed and the outer crust was the same. I was back in Bombay. Alone. My son had left his wife and moved to New York. My husband was dead. Everything had changed but still the world looked like the world. People went about their business. The weather changed according to the season. There were newspapers and cars. There were hospitals for people and animals. Façade. Everything is façade.

I went to live with my brother and his family in Bandra on the junction of Perry Cross and Turner Road. It was the house in which I'd grown up, in the neighbourhood where there is a park and a road and various other places of interest named after my family. Next to us was the Jogger's Park and next to the park was the sea. At first I felt like I was back in school. I was in my old room and some of my childhood things were still there, my globe, some photo albums, my collection of Miss Marple books, though my Sam Spades and Marlowes were missing. The other reason I felt like a schoolgirl was because they kept an eye on me. I suppose they couldn't believe a lunatic could return to the sane world and I suppose they were right to feel that way. A lunatic cannot unsee his visions however much he might want to – and me, I didn't want to unsee anything.

At first I felt like a guest, some kind of poor cousin from the hinterlands. I had forgotten how big the house was, especially when compared to my modest accommodation at the asylum. There were three floors, a lawn in front and a lawn in the back, and from the terrace a view of the Arabian Sea. As always there were more servants than family members. Let's see, two cooks, a bearer, a driver and a gardener, not counting the watchman and the tradesmen who came and went. One of the cooks and the bearer had been there since I was a girl. Then there was my brother and his wife who were both in their fifties, and my newly married niece – what a funny word, niece – and her young husband who was studying for a degree in hotel management. I thought, right, there will be no doctors in the next generation. And why should there be? I'm a doctor and look what became of me.

The first night we had dinner on the big table in the front room. The old cook Miriam made the kind of meal my father used to demand every day, mutton cutlets, mutton biryani, cucumber raita, noodles with deep fried minced okra, jaggery pancakes, sweet banana chips and fish pickle, and a bebinca for dessert. As a child bebinca was my passion. My brother had remembered and he had asked Miriam to make one for me, but it was different somehow, not so rich and the flavour too subdued. Or maybe it was me, maybe I was unable to taste complex food after all those years of lunatic fare. Still, it was a loud meal and a happy one, all of them talking at once and only my niece's new husband sitting quietly. I liked him right away.

The first night in my old room I had many dreams one after the other. Or it was one continuous dream with many parts. At the end I was in a forest at dawn and a pack of jackals had gathered around me in the weak light, slavering at me, each one laughing his head off. I can't describe to you what the laughter sounded like except to say that it sounded like the devil, whose multiple throats can produce simultaneous voices in different registers. I knew it was the devil laughing in layers at his own devilish joke and I knew what it was about. It is always a joke on me. When I woke it was dawn or getting close to dawn and I heard laughter coming from the road outside, voices laughing in concert. For a few minutes they would laugh loudly using all the breath in their lungs and then they'd laugh as if they were conversing in confidential tones meant only for each other and then there would be a whispery silence. I dressed hurriedly and left my room and walked downstairs as quietly as I could. It was still early. I encountered nobody as I left the house, only the watchman who opened the gate for me and saluted as I stepped into Turner Road and went toward the laughter. Of course he didn't know that I should not have been going out by myself. As I neared the park I glimpsed the sea beyond and just then the strangest feeling came over me, a sudden elevation of skin temperature combined with breathlessness and a sense of holy drift, I don't know how else to put it. My head felt warm but I didn't have a fever. I was dizzy and confused and for a moment I saw myself, my outer crust mostly unchanged but for the spectacles and grey hair, and my insides pinkly new. I saw myself on the curve of pavement leading to Carter Road, walking aimlessly in every direction as if I had picked up a virus or infection. That was when I understood what was wrong with me. Freedom. It was the first time in ten or twelve or fifteen years that I was walking in a city alone, unaccompanied by attendants. I could have got into a rickshaw or a taxi, there were several parked by the side of the road, and I could have asked the driver to take me somewhere. I could have gone to Bandra Talkies to watch a film or to Elco Arcade for ice-cold pani puri or to the station or to Poona or even Goa. I could have done whatever I felt like. The driver knew nothing about me. He didn't know who I was, who my husband was, who my son was, or what I had done to my son. As far as he knew I was just another old lady and the only thing different about me was that I was slightly less cared for than the other old ladies of Carter Road. He would gladly have taken me wherever I wished to go. I walked to the park thinking these thoughts that put a smile on my face and there I found a group of people following the instructions of a stout man in a white shirt and white trousers. Jumping laugh with mouth closed, said the man. Medium laugh, he said. Cocktail laugh, he said, and it sounded like a party at the Taj, such a sound of tinkling and merriment. One-metre laugh, he said, and how they laughed, so loud I'm sure it was heard even in Bandstand. Arm-swinging laugh, he said, and the laughers swung their arms as if they were marching. And now to end, said the man in white, silent laughter with mouth wide open. And that is what they did, laughed silently and heartily. And soon my shoulders too were shaking uncontrollably as I laughed. Oh, how I laughed!

When I got home I told my brother Denzil about the laughers at the park and he told me it was a club and they laughed for their health. I went the next morning too and the morning after and although it did no wonders for my health it helped in one way. Denzil and his wife were now quite comfortable with the idea of me going out unsupervised. My days fell into a routine. I woke up early as I always have and I went to the park unless I was feeling shaky or unfit for laughter. After laughter I would walk by the mangroves of Carter Road all the way to Khar-Danda until the smell of fish drying in the sun got too much for me and I'd go home for breakfast. Sometimes Patsy, my niece, and her husband, Olav, would sit outside if it wasn't too hot and he would practise scales on his guitar. He was teaching himself a song. First he would play it on a tape recorder and then he'd try to reproduce it on the guitar. When I heard him play the guitar it sounded like music but on the tape machine it was completely different, like traffic in a town that was falling into the sea or a sick animal fighting to the last, a death struggle that went on and on, more than ten minutes, more than fifteen. What kind of music is this? I asked Olav. He said it was a recording made by a saxophone player who had died. I don't remember the musician's name but I remember the name of the song because my aunt is also called Naima. Olav said he would change the music if it bothered me. On the contrary, I said, it made me feel better to think there were others like me in the world.

After lunch everybody usually took a nap, everybody but me. And in the evening Patsy and I would go to the market to shop for dinner. I got into the habit of going out for coffee at midday, sometimes as soon as lunch was over. I went to a small sea-facing café on Bandstand and ordered black coffee and a slice of chocolate cake. It was the best part of my day. I'd eat the cake and drink the coffee and listen to the conversations around me. If somebody said something interesting I would make a note of it. Once a bearded young man with an enormous backpack was deep in whispers with another young man who looked like his twin, except he had taken off his backpack and placed it on the floor. I didn't know what they were talking about but the words sounded to me like the old poem by the priest, the deacon, about men and islands and the prophetic sound of bells. I had started to carry an exercise book with me and I wrote down some of what the young man was saying. "Amateurs hack systems," he said. "Professionals hack people." And I thought of my son, of course, and the worst day of my life when I had tried to attack him with a knife. I started to cry but I made sure to cry softly so nobody would notice and the young man continued to talk and I continued to write. I wrote through my tears. "We used to think concealment was protection but it turned out exposure was protection," he said. And he said, "We're always one line away from being awesome." And he said, "Stay jealous." After some time I stopped crying but I kept my pen ready. There was a long silence and then the bearded young backpacker hit the tabletop with his hand and said, "Thursday's son I'm watching porn, you got your Friday duckface on, burn a U-turn to the john, moan the dawn we waiting on." Was it a message, I wondered, from my husband? But of course that couldn't be. It could not be. He was far away in some other café by another sea. And in any case there was nothing he wished to say to me. Or was it a message from my son? Some afternoons the conversations were in Hindi, Marathi, and English, people speaking three languages at the same time. Sometimes every conversation was work-related and it seemed as if everybody was there for a business meeting. A woman in a suit said, "Everybody is a customer." Immediately I wrote it down. She was speaking to a man who nodded eagerly. He was hanging onto her words. "Some happy customers become distributors." I was beside myself. Goodness, I thought, how could there be so much business in one city? Was everybody engaged in commerce of some kind? It seemed to me there were a thousand ways to make money and ten thousand ways to spend it. Perhaps it had always been this way and I had not noticed. One Monday early in the afternoon two men wandered in and ordered black coffee and when it came the one with the bald head and glasses produced a hipflask and added a shot to both their cups. The other man had a full head of hair streaked with grey, a handsome man who smoked incessantly. The smoke bothered me and I thought of changing my table but the tears were upon me again and I didn't want to attract unnecessary attention. So I sat and waited for the woe to stop and meanwhile I listened to the young drunkards, the happy drunkards sipping whisky at noon. It goes without saying that I envied them because I was not allowed to drink. Alcohol reacts with my medication, I fall asleep. The drunkards were discussing a magazine that lay on the table between them and they seemed fascinated by the cover photo of two middle-aged men in suits sitting at an outdoor table. "I thought they hated each other," the one with hair said. "Newton hates everyone," said the bald one. "God only hates Newton." And then I realised that one of the men they were discussing so intimately was my son. I took another look at the photo as the tears continued to fall. There was a title I could not understand, MEETING IN NEEMRANA. But there was no doubt that it was my son in the picture. Now the tears came in an unstoppable flow. I felt so humiliated. It was my son they were talking about. I had been disgraced in front of the world. I had been crushed. I told myself to breathe and I remembered the laughers in the park and I thought about the one-metre laugh. I took another look at the magazine. The caption said the other man's name was Naipaul and when I saw his face, the deep furrows, the downturned mouth and pouched eyes, the cold, absolutely cold and ruthless eyes, I knew God was the correct name for him. If God were to take human form he would look like this.

Farzana Amanella Kaur, arts activist, interviewed by Dismas Bambai in Lado Sarai, New Delhi, October 2005

The last time I met him? That would be the late nineties, probably around 1997 or 1996, around the time he left Lula and moved to New York. I went to a reading at the Jehangir Art Gallery and he was one of the featured poets. I was a Bombay girl for many years before I moved to Delhi. I'd been to a few readings but never one like this. It's probably best to describe it as a kind of avant-garde event, which was common enough in the world of visual art. The poets were considerably less experimental in my opinion. I don't know why, I really don't. It might have had something to do with the time. The years of planned socialism had just come to an end and India was stepping slowly into its future of unplanned capitalism. Maybe this had a reverse effect on the poets, what with the exuberance of the seventies and eighties unravelling into caution. So it was a bit of a surprise to stumble into this thing. There were six of them, Dom Moraes, Adil Jussawalla, Ranjit

Hoskote, H. Masud Taj, Newton Xavier, and a poet whose name I can never remember, skeletal fellow, strung out or drunk, who put together an anthology some years later, *The Bloodshot Book of Contemporary Indian Poets*, or something like that. Anyway the idea was the poets would stand at a measured distance from each other and recite simultaneously for half an hour. The audience was invited to walk from one poet to the next. You could listen to a poem and move on as if you were walking around a poetry bazaar and sampling a taster. Wonderful idea, I thought. The listener or viewer became a participant in the process rather than a passive recipient of the mercy or vitriol of whoever was reading. Unfortunately, the only people present were the poets and yours truly. This was before the age of self-promotion. They thought all they had to do was read and the audience would come. Three or four people did come but by accident, students and housewives on their way to the Samovar for a cup of tea or a beer, and they found themselves in the midst of a piece of literary history or performance history or art history, and of course they had no idea. The poets didn't care to notice and it occurred to me that they had never been in a room together before. Once they started it was obvious that they were reading to each other and not to the handful of people who drifted in and out. They were responding to the pitch of each other's voice, to the timbre and the rhythm. I listened in the same fashion. I put my mind aside. I knew it was not a question of understanding but absorbing, through the skin if necessary. Moraes was the first to take a cigarette break and when he returned he asked someone to bring him a stool. He was shaky on his feet, he said, and he preferred to be seated. I thought he read too softly, as if he was speaking to himself in a language he hoped no one would understand, or not understand too easily. Jussawalla started with a joke. He said the old rule about poetry readings was that as long as the audience outnumbered the poets you were doing okay. Then he looked around, shrugged, and read a poem called 'Land's End'. Hoskote and Taj struck me as the only ones who took the event seriously: there were no jokes, only earnestness. In Hoskote's case this was understandable since he was the youngest poet there. Xavier said he had written nothing new, or nothing new that was worth reading. Instead he would read some pages from his notebook, a list of words and phrases beginning with the letter D, words, he said, that might evoke some particular meaning for the Age of Rage. I made a note:

Despair
Disease; dis-ease; deceased
Destruction (see Self-)
Dropsy & dengue
Dukkha
Disgust (see Self-)
"Dark street by which once more I stand"
Decadence & the dandy
Disturbance, thy name is
Doomsaying the doomsayer
Daft, doped & delirious
Depressives against depressants
Dumb as in deaf & dumb as in dim
Diabolic, a daily diet of the
Die if you do, die if you don't
'Dilrubba O Dilrubba'
Degeneration; degradation; derangement
Dolor's delinquent daughters
Decrepitude & defeat
Dawood, the don of Dubai
Disaster the master
Distress the mistress
Damn the diminuendo
'Dulce et Decorum est'
Delhi dour ast
'Dum Maro Dum'
Dimple
Devilgod
Drowsy dullness
Drowning, the song

He went on but I decided thirty was a good number at which to stop. Meanwhile, the skeletal poet whose name I can never remember appeared to be nodding off, or he might have been speaking with his eyes closed and his mouth stuffed with cotton wool, or perhaps he was speaking in slow motion and the words were out of sync with his mouth. I don't know. He too had decided against reading poetry. Instead he improvised a lecture about *Nosferatu*, starting with the Murnau version and ending with Werner Herzog's, which he said was a secret portrait of the junkie as vampire, not as a caricature of evil but as an addict filled with self-loathing to the point of paralysis. Afterwards they gathered on the front steps of the Jehangir, those famous steps that seem so wide in our imagination but in reality were cramped and narrow. I noticed that they didn't meet each other's eyes. They said a few words, one-syllable salutations or off-hand farewells, and then they slipped into the moist Bombay night, the same night that had swallowed so many lost poets. They each went off alone because they were always alone, those boys, they had no talent for companionship. They were martyrs to a cause and for that if for nothing else I will always be devoted to them.

I believe Xavier's obsession with saints is in reality a bewildered or vengeful or helpless nostalgia for the poets of Bombay. In certain ways the lives of the poets and the lives of the saints are similar: the solitary travails, the epiphanic awakening and early actualisation, the thwarting and the mercy, the small rewards, the false starts, the workaday miracles, the joyous visions and fearful hallucinations, the flagellation of the flesh and the lonely difficult deaths. I don't mean to be a psychologist but it seems fairly clear to me that his saint obsession also had another source. His mother.

Beryl Xavier, mother, interviewed by Dismas Bambai at the Bangalore Institute of Mental Health, Bangalore, June 1998

Wait, before you go I want to tell you about my last conversation with the writer known as God. It wasn't long afterwards that I came back to this place. I wasn't sick or hallucinating, that's an important point. It was not a hallucination. Call it a visitation. And remember I'm a doctor, I know how to stay calm when I'm examining someone's internal organs, I know how to be precise and economical with my hands, I know I'm at the institute of mental health and I know I'm mad, but I can't be completely mad, can I?

I thought it odd that God chose to appear in the guise of the writer, the Hindu writer with the name of a Christian saint, Nai Paul or New Paul. I made it a point to note every small thing about him in case it came up one day. I noted the old turtleneck under his denim shirt and the fact that he was still handsome in a tired sort of way. I noticed his teeth, which were small and so pointed I thought of injections, and his eyes, which were full of exhaustion, and his fat stomach and dark skin and shaped goatee, so different from the ragged beard my son wears these days.

The writer sat at the counter of a bar in a high-ceilinged room and I took the stool beside him. I noticed he was making a face. It was difficult to tell what kind of face because the corners of his mouth were always pointed down. A man of constant sorrow, I thought to myself, with the face of an ancient sea turtle.

I said, "There's something I'd like to ask you."

"If it isn't the recurrent dreamer, in which case I must be the recurring dream," he said.

"I wasn't dreaming then and I'm not dreaming now. May I ask you something?"

"As you see, I'm at your disposal. One thing." He drummed lightly on the counter. "My boredom threshold has fallen to zero, so don't ask the standard question because then I'll have to give the standard answer, which is breathe. Or with my customary bis, which is breathe, which is breathe. Or in Persian, zhivaya zhizin. Zhivaya zhizin, do you see?"

All I saw was the lumbar back brace he wore over his denim shirt. I remembered the bad back he talked up in interviews, the heroic bad back he blamed on the hard labour of making the world. I understood that the wearing of the brace was a kind of vanity. He would not wear it under the shirt. He'd wear it for the world to notice and admire.

I said, "Are you having fun or is it just work?"

"Let me answer your first question first, for if we do not proceed chronologically we do not proceed. I can tell you that the next to be taken will not be you. That is what you wished to know, is it not?"

"Who will it be?"

"Don't ask questions if you don't wish to hear the answer."

"Newton? Do you mean my son?"

He shook his head. Did he mean no or did he mean he would not tell? There was no point asking. He would not reply; he would outwait me; his patience was endless.

"How do I protect my son?"

"You do what you know you must."

He raised his hand and the bartender tripped over with two purplish drinks in tall glasses. Japanese umbrellas floated among blue cherries, seaweed, stinging nettles, and assorted psychedelic morels.

"Sir," the bartender said, beaming, "your usual."

I looked at the identical drinks and said, "How did you know I wanted one?"

The writer said, "You do? Bartender!"

He took the umbrella out of a glass and took a sip. He liked it; he didn't like it. It gave him pleasure; it gave him none. He wanted another; he did not. When he put the glass on the counter it was empty. Immediately he picked up the second drink. The bartender appeared bearing two more purple cocktails. Putting on a pair of horn-rimmed sunglasses the artist known as God slid one to me. I noticed he was wearing a Panama hat and a neck brace. Where had they come from?

"The point about boredom is," and he paused to slurp at his second drink and order two more, "the point is, boredom is necessary to give time its forward momentum and springy, bouncy rhythm. Time moves in direct relation to the proportion of boredom it moves against. The more boredom, the less movement; the less movement, the more give. In short, it is a productive and calming condition, if you get my historical-continental drift. I knew this from the start and used it to my advantage, to my advantage."

"Advantage in what, though?"

"The genre-spanning work of my middle period, of course, after I announced the death of the novel and before I, the writer, brought it back to life with my late master fictions, master fictions. Exile, home and the world, post-colonial post-caste anxiety, the backward society and the centre, shabbiness, the arrival of enigma, these aren't empty slogans for me; they outline the inescapable map of my world. Let me ask you something, one minute."

The bartender placed more cocktails on the counter.

"Okay, but this is most def the last one or there's going to be a tsunami." He took a sip and set the empty glass down. "Let me pose a lickle question. What do creation stories have in common other than sex?"

I took a cautious sip of the drink, which tasted of fish and molasses.

I said, "Nothing?"

He laughed and all conversation in the bar stopped. The laugh was famous, heard a thousand times a day or a thousand times a minute, simultaneously in every corner of the world, a thick laugh, the laugh of an army riding into town to murder, rob, and rape.

I felt the hairs rise on my upper arms.

He said, "Let's consider some of the newer stories, only because the older ones will be incomprehensible to you. Here's one. The earth emerges from chaos fully formed, the earth and all her amenities. She lies with a god who gives her six sons and six daughters, not counting the last, the thirteenth, for important reasons that I'll get to in just a minute. One of his sons castrates the god and throws him into the sea. How is the castration accomplished? Who is the son's accomplice? Is it his mother, the earth? These questions are not answered. However, some facts are knowable. A god has been murdered who engendered all mankind. Foam appears from his mutilated testicles and from the foam the thirteenth child is born, a daughter who will continue her father's interrupted work."

The bartender approached but the goateed writer waved him off.

"Interrupted, as I was saying," he said, "always interruptus. Then there's Tem, alone in the vastness, so bored he creates the world from his copious seed floating among the stars like interplanetary battleships. Or to take another story from around the same time, god – and this is god with a lower case g, unlike yours truly who is always upper case –

gives birth to a hermaphrodite, a she/he in one capacious form (they are difficult to create, by the way, because of the intricacy when it comes to nerve endings and hormonal redistribution, and because an overabundance of sensitive orgasmic instrumentation must be compensated for with an overabundance of anguish). In any case the hermaphrodite – interesting, do you think, that Aphrodite occurs in a word for a two-sexed being? I digress, I digress, but it is my prerogative, how do you think you were made? – the hermaphrodite fertilises him or her self, the male part fertilises the female and they have a brood of sons and daughters. The children proceed to destroy each other or sleep with each other, which, as you know, may be one and the same thing. And then? Well, then they populate the earth with life forms, stunted and not, followed by the usual denouement. There you have it, two versions of creation. There are others. For instance, a goddess, one of yours, I believe, masturbates the universe into being and her masturbations, in their frenzy, in the froth of their ovulations, are so violent that the universe appears where before there was only silence. As a complement, she invents language. Think of it, a world and a language in one masturbatory moment. How ambitious if not foolishly taxing for any god. Language, not for communication or expression or to articulate the great conundrums, et cetera, et cetera, but purely as foreplay, pre-orgasmic utterance, alphabetic sex toys, not the twenty-six letters of English but the fifty-two letters of Devanagiri, and she inscribes each one on a skull, fifty-two skulls in all, which she wears around her neck like a rosary. All of which brings me to the question that is the point of this explication. May I?"

"As if I could stop you."

"Right. Why are you lot so preoccupied with masturbation? Somewhat childish, don't you think? Excuse me. Bartender, two more Purple Mandragoras."

"What do the stories have in common?"

"Cruelty, the twin of boredom."

"I think you answered the question as to whether you're having fun. What else?"

*

He said: the mindful killings, that which was then, this which is now, the self-murderers, the dogs of instruction, the teachers, the torturers, the ennui sold as spirit food, the cyclic insurrection of the will, the red leaf sap of tomorrow, the old toads of fervour and patriotism, the renegade eels, the death's head moths, the spastic drool of words, the succubus in the shape of a child bride, the infant's wild goat cries, the mother's curse, the broken sea shanties, the one-celled spasm, the premonitions of the crow, the immortal armoured cockroach, the unrenewable planet Teegeeack, the northern haar's thin tempests, the blood nozzle, the sleep abortions worse than waking, the artery spout sold as art, the multiple hunter's moons, the tree virgins' song of succour, the angular nymphs of paradise, the rapist in the family, the illegal migrant youth, the tubercular smell of poverty, the hymen smears on hemp, the midnight screes, the unilluminati, the ti guinin, the gris gris, the coco konkon, the serried enemy encampments, the precipitous inducements, the staged ferocities, the prayerful lords of mayhem, the fleet angels of misrule, the black arts or kala kalaa, Theos the rainmaker, the sick ships trailed by phosphorescence, the white plague rats, the frozen, the furious, the plundered, the numb, the suicide's retched tongue, the shamed archer's lost thumbs, the sea's sucked bile, the slop buckets of fortune, the reptile skull, the feast liver, the starhead nails embedded in his breastbone, the entrail filth of mortal birth, the malaria kiss upon waking, the spouse who waits, the wine dark, the decking fitted to ribs, the long gunwales of longing, the interlocked joints, the black ship's blue prow, the white sails, the halyards, the braces, the sheets, the white-armed woman, the leather sacks of barley, the mill-crushed grain, the water skins, the mixing bowls of true wine, the Wain Harrow, the Bear always to his left, the eye holes shaped like ears, the craven foetus underfoot, the bliss sale, the adulterated habit-forming poisons, the absent cave fathers, the prideful lobotomists, the no gnomes, the trickster, the raven, the white-faced bear, the rattlesnake husband, the coyote dances, the first woman's twinned twins, the hummingbird's fearful trembling, the hero disguised as demon, the demon disguised as angel, the angel disguised as human, the dumb instruments of no change, the catastrophes, the misfortunes, the false feasts, the friends felled in battle, the unending books of the dead, the libations to the dead, the mist-wrapped rivers of ocean, the sixth of seven oceans, the sea of milk, the second son tied to a stake, the sons exchanged for cows, the three-headed son whose middle head sips liquor, the temptation disguised as birdsong, the creator for whom no temple is built, the god disguised as nymph boar man-lion dwarf, the thousand years of prayer and penance, the air for food, the standing on one leg, the cunning supplicant, the vengeful sage, the outcaste curse, the horse sacrifice, the horse stratagem, the fever born of the great god's anger, the vow, the silence, the boon, the desert loo, the ticking heart of empires, the stumble fugues, the eaters of paper, the insect brain in wait, the nocturnal machinery of dismay, the committed whoredoms, the whoring after the heathen, the bruised breasts of virginity, the multiplied fornications, the broken wedlock, the shed blood in fury of jealousy, the prophets of vanity who see nothing, the lying divinations, the filled cup of astonishment and desolation, the old hatreds, the furious rebukes, the warm rivers of blood, the frogs, the pestilence, the lice, the flies, the festering skin eruptions, the rain of hail, the locusts, the darkness that can be touched, the deaths of the firstborn, the blood cities, the untempered mortar daub, the abominations of the fathers, the high tree brought down, the low tree exalted, the green tree dried up, the dry tree made to flourish, the abundance as long as the moon endures, the darling delivered from the power of the dog, the old men full of days, the remembrance of things to come, the aleph, the beth, the gimel, the divided tongue that walks in the world, the fool clothed with skin and flesh, the fool fenced with bone and sinew, the scent of water, the genealogy that is not to be reckoned, the sacrificial bull, the ram, the heifer, the calf, the thigh bones wrapped in fat, the forty days and forty nights, the flood, the ark of the horned fish, the dismantling of venerable archetypes, the bulbous protuberance, the carven substitute, the atrocities disguised as reason, the lost hallucinate prophecies of a race, all that is ruthless, solitary, and inseparable from insanity.

I've forgotten some of it but you get the idea. You get the endless murderous drift of the conversation. Then the writer said, and now I must be off, I have a chapter to finish. I'll see you again I'm sure. Then he picked up his cane and walked away. I noticed he was steady on his feet, absolutely steady. How could he be so unmoved when my own world had ended?

But I heard the message and I took it to heart. My son was in danger. In his anger and wisdom the writer known as God had told me what to do. I must take matters into my own capable doctor's hands as I had always done. That is why I had picked up the knife all those years ago. I wanted to save my son. I wanted to keep him safe from harm. And so I knew I had to return to the asylum and the company of my lunatics. And here I shall stay. Tell him that.

T. J. S. George, author and editor, interviewed by Dismas Bambai in Palace Orchards, Bangalore, September 2006

When I think about it now what strikes me about the whole unlikely story is how much of a role chance played in the way it unfolded. It strikes me too that Newton was a magnet for chaos and magic and he seemed to invite these kinds of unlikely occurrences. I was editing a newspaper in those days, the summer of 2003, and one morning I received a phone call on my personal line. Somehow the caller had managed to get past the switchboard. He said he had been trying to contact Newton Xavier and somebody said I might be able to help. I wrote a Sunday editor's column, 'Memory's Parade', in which I'd described meeting Newton and his father. Frank and I had known each other in Bombay in the fifties when we were both active in different ways in journalism, and I'd known Newton from the days when he was writing cricket commentary. It was elegant commentary for a teenager, or a writer of any age. Years later we were employed by the United Nations at the same time and we renewed our friendship. I mentioned all this in my column, which the caller or a friend of his had seen. He wanted to know if I was still in touch with Newton and his father. He didn't know that Frank had died soon after the Emergency of a heart attack, exactly the thing that took Newton some thirty years later at around the same age. Strange, is it not, how our longevity or lack thereof seems to be wired into our genes? I told the caller that I might be able to find a contact number for Newton and then I asked the man his name. He said he was the superintendent of the Institute of Mental Health in Bangalore and that Beryl Xavier, Newton's mother, had died there the day before. I was distressed to hear this because I had had no idea that she was living in Bangalore, not so far from my own home. If I had known, my wife and I would have visited her. What, I asked, was the cause of death? In an apologetic voice the superintendent explained that she had stopped eating and this had led to heart failure. He said Beryl owed the institute a certain sum of money and they were unable to release the body until the dues had been paid. It was a question of procedure. Further complicating matters was the fact that there had been a power failure at the institute and it was the height of Bangalore's summer. You see, the morgue at the institute was somewhat basic and the refrigeration wasn't working. There was the question of a health risk. Could I contact Mr Xavier and ask him to claim his mother's body at the earliest? I agreed without hesitation. I put a reporter on it and she found a telephone number for Newton, who, it so happened, was in Delhi on one of his annual Indian visits. It was around noon when I called. I have bad news, Newton, I said. He took it well or I think he took it well. He is not one whose emotions are immediately apparent. He thanked me and said he would make arrangements. I think he spent the afternoon trying to book a flight. When he got to the institute it was very late and then he had to wait until dawn to take the body to a crematorium. I learned all this from my reporter, not Newton, who returned to Delhi without getting in touch. I think he was embarrassed by the whole episode and I don't see why. Years later I saw poems by him in a magazine, his first poems in twenty years. There was a sonnet about his mother, about how much the body stank, forgive me, mummy, staring down from your heavenly asylum, and so on. Disturbing work, not for the faint of heart or stomach. And sad too, I mean, why was the son asking forgiveness? Considering her history of violence should not forgiveness have travelled from child to parent? In about a dozen lines he encapsulated mothers and sons, and madness, and the loss of a parent, and the corruption that is death. More than a sense of loss it was repulsion that the poem conveyed. But I'm a journalist, I'm no interpreter of poetry, thank god. Please don't take me at my word. Read for yourself.

Manoj Patel, artist, member of Progressive Autists Group, interviewed by Dismas Bambai at Pocket 17, Artists' Colony, New Delhi, October 2005

I went through that phase. I tried to give it up for the usual reasons, fear being foremost. That morning I was sketching around the idea for a painting. (I do this thing when I'm stuck, automatic hand exercises where I let my fingers move with no interference from the mind.) I drew a paper cup and then I started to fill it with ash. I thought if I completed the sketch I wouldn't want to smoke. But I did, I still wanted to smoke and I thought it would help to get out of the house. Newton was in town, staying in Chattarpur, of all places, at the house of a mutual friend. I asked my assistant to drive me there. You go past the metro station and take a left after a building called the World Centre for Energy and Consciousness – where do they get these names? – which looks like a cross between a cowshed and a spa. When we left the main road it felt like we had entered a forest. The house was behind a high wall. We parked and Newton came out to meet us and I told him I was trying to stop smoking. I told him about the drawing of ash in a paper cup. He laughed and offered me a cigarette and of course I accepted and of course it disgusted me. I felt like taking a shower but I smoked the cigarette to the end. My assistant was not happy. She likes to mother me. You know how conservative the young can be. Watching me smoke had made her go long in the face and to lighten the mood I told Newton, this is my assistant, Sonakshi. Isn't she beautiful? He said, I only know beautiful when I paint it nude. Sonakshi recovered quickly. She said, in that case you will never know if I am beautiful. I said, this is why I like this girl. Newton said he liked her too. He laughed and I laughed and after some time Sonakshi also laughed. We laughed and smoked and just then there was a call on the landline from Bangalore.

Newton's mother had died. And I thought, yes, this is how it was with Newton. Laughter followed by tears. We spent the rest of the day getting him a seat on the night flight to Bangalore and then we dropped him to the airport. Sonakshi packed his case because he doesn't know how to pack. He does not know how to pack and he does not know how to fly. We stopped at a pharmacy I know, where I picked up a strip of Anxit and a strip of Valium-10. He said he would take one Anxit and one Valium for each hour of the flight, meaning he would take seven pills in all. As I watched him walk to the departure gate I noticed he had the shuffle of an old man, and I worried for him, and for myself, and for all those who offer themselves to the most insatiable of the gods. I mean goddess, the insatiable goddess of art and sacrifice, Saraswati become Kali. Sonakshi too watched Xavier as he shuffled into the terminal and searched his pockets for cigarettes or identification documents or anxiety medication. Poor old man, she said. Poor, poor man. Save your pity, I told her. Pity is wasted on the pitiless. Then I parked at the first shop on the Ring Road and picked up a packet of Gold Flakes and a Clipper lighter. This time I didn't want a shower, I enjoyed it.

Zusi Krass, writer and translator, interviewed by Dismas Bambai at the Shamiana Coffee Shop, Taj Mahal Hotel, Bombay, March 2005

I went to California on family business but I was nervous, so nervous. They have the death penalty there, you know. The Swiss abolished capital punishment in the forties. We evolved before the rest of the world. Do you know Switzerland has separated and recycled trash since the mid-seventies? Long before you people knew, we knew. The future depends on garbage. Imagine a Swiss woman in California where the death penalty is still in effect. Imagine her state of mind and the crisis she must negotiate. To put it plainly, it made me crazy and I walked around a lot. This is how I deal with anxiety, I am centred by the rote physicality of one step following the other, the meditative quality of it, you know? I walk around aimlessly but purposefully, as if I'm going somewhere. I don't want it to look like I'm drifting or they'll be on me in a second.

And so I was out one evening walking around. It had been a couple of hours and I didn't know where I was, some quiet part of town, and I don't know how it happened but I tripped over my own feet. I looked down at my toes encased in sensible Swiss sandals and I was thinking to myself that I liked the look of my sandalled feet navigating the sidewalks of America – and I fell over and hurt my elbow. I was bleeding but I got up right away. I didn't want to take a risk. What if someone saw? They'd be on me. It was a long American street, endless in both directions, an endless stream of cars and I was the only pedestrian. All the people driving saw me fall. They were so surprised to see me get up bleeding but nobody stopped to help. I'm the only pedestrian, bleeding on a road in California, and nobody stopped because of the death penalty.

The linearity of it was clear to me. It was something I thought about a lot when I was there, that they put a person to death as if it is a normal facet of civilised life when actually it is the exact opposite, it is a remnant of the barbaric life. The government brings the entire force of its administrative, bureaucratic, and legalistic might to kill a man, which, as we know, is not an easy thing to do, the spark is not easy to extinguish.

I thought about it as I was walking or limping along and I thought how badly I needed a coffee, but the pedestrian walkway was narrow and then it disappeared into the freeway or highway or whatever they call it. Finally I scrambled down a small hillside to an even quieter street where I tried to hail a taxi. There were no taxis. I could not believe it! I was in a city, and not just any city, I was in Hollywood, and there were no taxis, no pedestrians, no shops, nothing, just cars zipping by all day and all night. Is that any way to live?

I walked and walked. It felt like I'd been walking for miles and by then it was dark and I could hear the animals in the brush. I heard a wolfhound or vampire, a long howl on a moonless night, and that scramble of paws, enough to set anybody's heart a-thumping. By now I really needed a coffee. I was bleeding and shook up and I needed to calm down. Plus, I was so thirsty I could have cried. Just as I was reaching the end of my patience, my superhuman patience, I saw a pop-up-storefront-on-the-street type of gin joint, just without the gin. I tried to compose myself. I tidied my hair as best I could, after those hours in the carbon monoxide I must have looked a fright. I patted down my hair and smoothed my dress and went to the counter and asked the man for an espresso. I thought I'd have an espresso to start, followed by a flat white and then I'd feel human again. The guy behind the counter gave me coffee ice cream because he thought that was what I had ordered. Turned out, they served only ice cream. The only place open on that entire stretch of California freeway or highway or sidestreet, the only sign of life for miles, and all they served was ice cream. You know what I did? I ate it. You know why I ate it? Because they have the death penalty in California. What else was I going to do? I ate the whole bowl of American ice cream and with every bite I wished I was sipping hot coffee and it occurred to me that I had not had a decent espresso since I had landed in the damned sunshine state.

All of a sudden I realised I truly disliked everything about California. I couldn't stand it. The pruned palm trees, the million cars, the lack of pedestrians, the permanent sunshine, the shorts and slippers, the perky cheery upbeat fucking bonhomie. California. I knew in my heart it was a travesty of the true essence, the opposite of joy. Not only because of the cars and carbon and diner coffee and capital punishment. The thing I most could not stomach was their regressive policy regarding zoophiliacs. I want to ask them, is it not backward to legislate love? How primitive must a mind be to tell another mind what is allowed and what is not in the realm of the tender emotions? In California if your boyfriend is a dolphin or a seal you are breaking the law. They prosecute you if you love a non-human species. They prosecute zoophiliacs everywhere in America except Colorado, which may be a reason to live in that godforsaken place. But I was born in Zurich, first in order of precedence of the cantons of Switzerland. I cannot live in Colorado. I was thinking about these layers of complexity and I gave myself a fever. I'm eating the terrible coffee ice cream with a false fever from nerves and I'm thinking, I need to get out of here.

Excuse me? Can we get some service? What's happened to this place? Time was, they'd hover around your table until you wished they'd go away.

When I finished the ice cream I knew that the only way I was going to be able to deal with this was to find something solid I could focus on, something real. So I rummaged in my mirrorwork jhola bag and found the poems and got back to work. I used to carry the jhola everywhere, it was my true home. I had a couple of manuscripts I was working on, my Marathi–English dictionary, some letters and photos and my passport. I remember I was translating Narayan Doss's *My Name is Kamathipura* series and I picked up where I'd left off, a poem about Shantibai, a woman whose unique selling point on the street were the acid burns on her face and breasts. I started work on the poems or I resumed work on the poems and it calmed me. I was able to forget the ice cream, the coffee, the persecution of zoophiliacs, the immense fact of capital punishment, the inescapable presence of California. I was able to forget everything and focus on Kamathipura 11th Lane and Shantibai. I stayed in California for a fortnight and I finished the translation and then I flew to Bombay, from Hollywood to Bollywood with the complete translation in my jhola. It was my Diwali gift for Narayan.

This was in the days before email. Now it's hard to imagine such a time. I mean, what did we do before? We wrote letters and postcards. Except I hadn't written to him, I had turned up in Bombay expecting my friends to be waiting for me and I met everyone except for Narayan. They told me he was on one of his trips, somewhere up north or visiting family in the interior or just lying low on some kind of bender. I waited for two weeks, for three. I met a publisher, met friends, studied the stray dogs of the city, but all the while I was waiting to hear from Narayan and I never did. It upset me. I was living in a hotel on Marine Drive and one night I heard voices in the stairwell behind my room. What should we do with her, they were saying. And in a voice that was pitched higher, in a voice that strived to differentiate itself, a woman spoke. She knows everything, this woman said. It was as if she wanted me to hear and then she said it again in a curiously flat way. She knows everything. It started to rain and I stepped out on the balcony of the hotel and when I looked down I noticed that everything was wet except for a rectangular dry spot directly in front and a woman stood there looking straight at me. I couldn't see her face but I knew it was the woman I had heard talking in the stairwell. First I went back to my room and checked the locks and then I packed my things and sat on a chair and waited for dawn. I left the lights on. The next morning I left that hotel and checked into another. Later I changed my ticket and flew out of the city. I didn't meet Narayan on the trip. When we met again it was in America. He'd flown there on some government freebie junket type thing.

Hello, we're waiting to order. Can we get some service? At least one person on this table is white?

Philip Nikolayev, poet and editor, interviewed by Dismas Bambai at Ramanna Ashram, Rajouri Garden, New Delhi, October 2006

I started a business to make money and I worked from home but I was working all the time. That's the thing when you work for yourself. You end up working harder than ever in your life. I did not stop writing. I continued work on a collection of immured sonnets and a series of linked essays and I continued publishing my magazine once a year. But now I also had a daytime job. It couldn't be helped, I had a family to support.

One day in 2000 or 2001, I'm not sure when, in any case it was one of those apocalyptic years of the early two thousands, and the phone rang and a voice said, hello, is that Philip? I said it was. And the voice said, oh good, I'm glad to hear it because I'd love to talk with you about the mystic beard of Tagore-da. Then he laughed and I knew. I said, one minute. I put the phone down and went to the landing of my apartment where I've placed an armchair and a blanket and an ashtray. I took a look at my view, which is an inch of Harvard Square, a tree, a few buildings, some sky. Not much of a view but it's mine. I looked at it for a long time and I took a deep breath. I inhaled the calm air of Boston, the ordered streets and evenly spaced trees, the groomed Charles, the mild manicured sunlight, the absence of car horns and shouts, the absence of a hundred layers of noise. What I was doing, I was inhaling the opposite of disorder, the opposite of the river and the ghats of Benares. When I was ready I went back inside and picked up the phone. I said, hello Narayan. He didn't bother saying hello, instead he went into a kind of promotional lecture about himself. He mentioned a long poem, a small epic about the geographical features of Kamathipura, in which each street was numbered and dated in the manner of a gazette or authorised legal document or public journal published by the municipal government. Then he informed me that a Romanian magazine had interviewed him and the interview had been published in its latest issue and ran to more than three thousand words, possibly because the Romanian was more long-winded than the English. In the interview he said that Indian poetry had reached a stage of exhaustion caused by eight decades of battle over which languages were allowed and which, meaning English, was disallowed. After some more of this kind of boasting and chitchat, all of which had to do with his own life, because he asked nothing about my work, about my wife's books, about what I had been doing in the years since we had last met in Benares, he got to the real reason for his call.

Isn't B____ a friend of yours? he said. Yes, I replied, though the alarm bells were already ringing in my head. When Doss asked for B____'s phone number I gave it to him. What else could I have done? All he had to do was call the magazine where B____ worked, which was only the most prominent literary magazine in the country, and ask to be connected. So I gave him the number and forgot all about it.

A week later I got a call from B____. Did you give my number to this Indian guy called Doss, he asked. Yes, I said, I hope you don't mind? I mind, said B____, and you should too. The guy calls me out of the blue and asks to meet for coffee. He said he was around the corner from the office and he was a poet from India and an old friend of yours. I told him to meet me at the diner across the street from the building because I was on deadline. And it was the truth, I was copy-editing the magazine's lead review. I put on my parka and walked over to the diner and found him easily enough. He was the only Indian. Furthermore, he was wearing a suit jacket and dress shoes on a snowy New York day. I sat down and the waiter appeared with a pastrami sandwich for him and a beer. I ordered coffee. He didn't waste much time. He said he was visiting the United States for the first time in his life, which was already evident to me considering it was winter and he was wearing a thin jacket. It was something he had always wanted to do, he said. Then he told me he was sick. He was dying of a rare blood disease. He told me the name but I'd never heard of it. I said that I was sorry he was sick and I hoped he would get better and so on. Then he asked if I would publish him in the magazine and he handed me a poem. I told him I was a copy editor not the poetry editor. I said the magazine already had a poetry editor and she was doing a damn fine job as a matter of fact. I said even if I had been the poetry editor his publication strategy lacked finesse. Then I let the strong coffee get the better of me and told him he had a nerve. I asked if this approach had ever worked for him, to say he was dying and ask someone to publish him? I had never met him before and I didn't know whether he was insane or some kind of conman but either way I was furious. I handed back his poem, folded my arms and leaned against the red leather of the booth. I waited for him to defend himself and tell me I was wrong and produce a medical certificate that proved he'd been telling the truth all along, or simply to apologise for his foolishness. By now he'd polished off the sandwich. He took a last sip of the beer, a dark possibly imported stout as I recall, and then he excused himself and left me with the bill.

Zusi Krass, writer and translator, interviewed by Dismas Bambai at Shamiana Coffee Shop, Taj Mahal Hotel, Bombay, March 2005

He was sent to the United States by an Indian government body that managed to survive the end of socialism. I forget the name but it was one of those crazed acronyms that Indians love. This one had a lot of Cs, it might have been CCCP or ICCU or PCPC, I don't know. Let's call it the Indian Cultural Commissars Regime. It sent deserving writers and artists to conferences and festivals in various parts of the world, although the government's definition of deserving differed from almost everybody else's. Mostly it benefited the poetasters, apparatchiks, and freeloaders, who used it as a way to promote their cronies. Narayan was selected on the basis of some untouchable quota, an unofficial system where one or two writers are chosen to represent the unrepresentable classes.

My mother was living in California. She'd moved to the United States because she met a man who made swimming pools and she wanted to learn how to swim, which sounds crazy but it's the truth. After a year of correspondence and vacations in various obscure parts of the world they decided to move in together. I went to visit her in California in the fall of 2001, not my favourite spot on earth in case you didn't know by now. They did have a hot tub, which I learned to like. I would sit in the tub and read.

Earlier that year I'd been at the University of Chicago and I'd looked at the papers of A. K. Ramanujan. Only one other scholar had ever studied them, a writer with a Spanish name. What interested me most was Ramanujan's account of a two-day hallucinogenic experiment that he titled *Mescaline Notes*. For me, as a reader, the weird thrill was to connect the demure demeanour of the scholar poet Ramanujan with that of a man tripping wildly on mescaline. It was similar to the feeling I got when I read Aldous Huxley for the first time and came across those passages about hallucinogens written in dry, detached, boring prose. I made a note to ask some friends of mine why Ramanujan's mescaline account had never been published as a book. I mean, wouldn't it be a bestseller, wouldn't it be the publishing event of the decade? But as with many thoughts that occur to me when I am up, I forgot all about it when I came down. I forgot Huxley. I forgot the unforgettable Ramanujan because I was in California in September and everything else went out of my head. I was in California and it felt wintry and uninhabitable because of the pictures I saw when I closed my eyes. I felt paralysed. All I could do was sit in front of the television and watch those repeating images, the building, the plane, the crash, the people falling like leaves. I didn't want to go anywhere or do anything.

Some weeks later I saw a message in my inbox from Narayan Doss. He was in New York on an Indian government poetry junket and he wanted to know if I knew someone in the poetry world he could meet. I told him I would do one better. I'd don my Florence Nightingale getup and come to see him. If he needed rescuing I would do the needful. I asked my mother to buy me a ticket because by then I was eager to leave sunny happy California. At least on the island of Manhattan people were murderous to your face.

My mother booked me into the Chelsea and they gave me a nice room because Stanley knows my mom from the old days. We used to stay there when we visited New York and I always called him Uncle Bard. I loved that name when I was a kid. I thought of him as my bardic uncle with the long hair and funny face. When I say it was a nice room, yes, well, there's nice and there's nice by the standards of the Chelsea and what I mean by that is, I got a room with no KY stains on the wall and no used condoms in the shower. For small mercies we must be grateful. I checked in and sent Narayan a message and then I went into the lobby and looked at the paintings, the hundreds of paintings, good, bad and ugly, that Stanley had acquired over the years as payment or tribute or the spoils of war. But I didn't see any of it. All I saw was Narayan's face, the face of a boy, a wicked boy perhaps, the face of a corrupt cherub out of Caravaggio, the kind of face you don't want to wake up with or give your heart to, not if you're at all sensible.

Amrik Singh Dhillon, founder, Amrik Singh Dhillon Associates, interviewed by Dismas Bambai at the opening of *66*, Gallery K. Hardesh, Chelsea, New York City, September 2003

I want to say something about poets and longevity, but I fear it might be a tale about the opposite, poets and the will to oblivion. Because here we are at a retrospective of a life in art and the artist is nowhere to be found. Has he disappeared into his own work? Is he taking a powder? Does he need assistance? I have no idea and I'm guessing you don't either. I suppose what I really want to talk about is how I met Newton and how we became friends and how strange it is to say that we're friends at all.

I don't know where he got my number. He called and introduced himself as a Goan-American artist based in New York. I'd never heard it put that way, 'Goan-American'. I didn't know it was even a category. I thought, if Goan-American is a category maybe Sikh-American is one too. Why doesn't he describe himself as Indian-American, like everyone else? I knew who he was because he'd been in the news in the days immediately following Nine Eleven. A newspaper called him for a comment and he'd said something about America's pigeons coming home to roost, which didn't make him the most popular person in New York City, I think it's safe to say. I have my own Nine Eleven story and he must have sympathised on some level. I think that's why he contacted me. He called at about seven in the morning on one of those milky New York dawns, cold and quiet. I'm an early riser. I was on the treadmill getting started on my morning and he said, do you think we could meet? I have a professional question for you. He said a friend needed some help. What, do you mean right now? I said. He paused as if that wasn't what he'd meant at all. Then he said now was fine. So we met at a Starbucks on Curry Hill and the first thing he wanted to know was whether I had gotten over what had happened to me. At that point I wasn't over anything, I was still in the middle of it. I suppose I was in denial. I told him my experience had changed my idea of my self in relation to my surroundings. I was beginning to understand that my skin colour and beard and turban marked me as a foreigner in a city I'd always thought of as home. It was like waking up from a dream or waking into a dream. Otherwise I was like any other New Yorker trying to process the fact that a distant war had landed in my backyard. Newton was quiet for a while, we both were. We sipped our coffee and thought our own thoughts and then he told me about his friend, a poet who was in town on a trip sponsored by the Indian government. His friend wanted to defect to the United States. Was this at all a possibility? Of course it was not. To defect to the United States you had to be a chess prodigy or violinist from the Soviet Union or Cuba. India was not considered a repressive nation, I said, on what basis would he request asylum? India is both repressive and regressive when it comes to caste, Newton said. My friend wants political asylum based on his status as an untouchable in a society where caste determines one's destiny, political, economic, and social. I said I didn't think such a category of asylum existed because if it did it would open the floodgates. As I thought, said Newton. When we got up to leave he invited me over to his place the next day, a Saturday.

That night I went to my parents' house. My mother had just had a cataract treatment done, a new procedure without surgery. It entailed a huge amount of pills that had to be taken several times a day. My father had an alarm on his watch and all evening he was at her side telling her when to take the pills. My brother Sukh and I drove to a place off Maria Hernandez Park in Bushwick and got fish and steak tacos to go and that's what we had for dinner. My parents had no say in the matter. According to my father Mexican food is Indian food gone wrong. But when the tacos were on his plate he had no complaint. On the way back home I picked up the *Post* and found a story about the guys who'd tried to attack me on Nine Eleven. There was a photo and their names were in the caption. There was also a story about a Sikh man who'd been shot to death in Phoenix, Arizona. The killer had mistaken him for a Muslim because of his turban. The story got to me. The murdered man's name was Balbir Singh and he looked a little like my father, or my uncles, and it made me wonder about the country I was living in, a place I had always taken for granted, where freedom of worship and expression was enshrined in the constitution and difference was celebrated and immigrants made welcome. I didn't bring it up at dinner. My mother is anxious enough after what happened to me.

On Saturday morning Sukh and I took the six into town and I showed him the story in the *Post*. He had a gig that night and he got off downtown with his gear. At around eleven or ten thirty the doorman took me up to Newton's apartment. I rang the bell and nobody answered. I rang a few times and I was thinking I'd call him on my cell phone when his partner Goody opened and said Newton was asleep. He'd had a bad night. I waited in the living room while she put on coffee. I was sitting in a kind of plantation chair with extendable leg rests and I noticed there was a prone figure on the couch. I saw the back of a youngish man in shorts and a T-shirt and just then he pushed himself up on his elbows and stared at the couch as if he was trying to remember something. He felt under it and found a short bottle of vodka that he uncapped and lifted to his mouth and drank without once stopping for breath. I could smell the vodka from across the room. He didn't know I was watching him. I saw him down the vodka and I felt the bile rise up in my throat in a wave of acid reflux. I knew I was looking at someone who wanted to die, whose only ambition was to die, someone who would soon be granted his ambition while the world watched in horror or glee. He drank most of the bottle in one swallow and then he replaced it under the couch and passed out again.

After some time Newton and Goody appeared and we had a financial conversation without the participation of the intended beneficiary of our scheme. It was a strange feeling to discuss the finances of a man who was passed out drunk in a corner of the room. I told Newton it wouldn't be too difficult to invest an amount of money in his friend's name, a nest egg that he'd be able to access from anywhere in the world. Newton's questions were to the point and they painted a picture for me. Could I structure it so that his friend would not be able to access the capital but would receive a monthly income? Yes, I said. Could I structure it so the capital would grow for a certain period, say ten years, after which his friend would be able to withdraw the money if he wanted? Yes, I said, but how much money were we talking about? Newton glanced at Goody, who shrugged. I agreed to draw up a reasonable plan.

Before I left I used the bathroom in the hallway. Later I'd become familiar with the apartment but on that first day it seemed to me like something out of a movie, an old black-and-white movie about a pair of bohemians in New York City, artists who do not know how to separate work from life. I saw unfinished canvases and photographic equipment everywhere, in the bedroom, the corridors, even the bathroom. It was the opposite of my bathroom, which is uncluttered and full of natural light. I thought to myself that perhaps it was true what they said about artists, but it was still a surprise. I mean, this is the United States of America, you are part of the system whether you like it or not. You are scrutinised and boxed in a hundred ways. You're taxed, insured, policed, controlled. I didn't think it was possible to live a messy life in this country.

Zusi Krass, writer and translator, interviewed by Dismas Bambai at Shamiana Coffee Shop, Taj Mahal Hotel, Bombay, March 2005

We'd met only once, six years earlier.

I took a course called 'The Internationalisation of English Literature', taught by an American, a jazz drummer and professor who'd lived all over the world and written books on the drift-turned writers of the Caribbean and the Indies, the sundered writers of South East Asia and the United Kingdom, the water-locked writers of Africa, and the shipwrecked writers of New Zealand and the South Pacific, an American, in short, who had written about all the writers of the world except those from his own North American terrain. India was a subject he revisited periodically, particularly the unmapped world of Indian poetry, a world known only unto itself. In the late eighties he published a book that became a cult object, a kind of detective story or a piece of sustained investigative journalism about the Bombay poets. It was the first time anyone had compiled charts, birth dates, publication details, educational histories, romantic imbroglios and substantiated gossip, marital and family data, work experience, everything relevant to the topic and some things that were not. Late in the semester as an exercise he asked us to translate some of the Marathi poets into English. I chose Vilas Sarang, Arun Kolatkar, and Narayan Doss, poets who wrote in both Marathi and English, and once I'd translated a few poems, well, I got the bug. I couldn't stop. I put together about fifty pages of material and sent it to an academic imprint that agreed to publish a book of translations when and if I finished. Bruce King, the professor who had caused the new turn in my life, suggested I visit Bombay and he gave me some names and addresses.

I bought a round-trip ticket and on Bruce's advice I booked a room at the YWCA on Madame Cama Road in Colaba. I decided that of course I would try to meet the three writers I wished to translate but I would also attempt something more and less obvious. I would try to understand India by scrutinising the way it treated its dogs and poets. I like poets and I love dogs and I find it is a useful way to gauge the nature of a society – by marking the way it treats its marginalised figures. When looked at in that way, I'm not exaggerating, it will blow your mind, the number of stray dogs in that city and how precariously they live. I mean, it is astronomical, beyond computation, they're everywhere and at night they take over. The poets are less organised. They are never in charge, not even at night, but they too are plentiful in number.

On Bruce's advice the first person I met was Nissim Ezekiel at the PEN office in New Marine Lines. Ezekiel was the best known among the Indian poets who wrote in English. He knew everyone and everyone knew him. I spent an hour in his office and he gave me so much material, phone numbers and addresses and suggestions for reference books. The next day I got to work and made appointments with Sarang and Kolatkar who struck me as similar in some ways, solitary men not given to much conversation. They preferred their own company and I could tell they wished our business would be concluded as soon as possible. But they were polite to me and forthcoming enough once I mentioned Bruce and the book of translations I intended to publish.

Establishing contact with them was a walk in the park compared to Narayan Doss. He had no fixed address and no phone number. Every morning after breakfast at the YWCA – always the same breakfast, toast, milk tea, a dollop of jam, a dollop of butter, and two eggs scrambled, fried or made into an omelette – I would go to the reception area and use the phone to try to make appointments for the day. There was a woman called Mrs Sonalkar at the switchboard. She appointed herself my guide. She had the best advice, where to go for vegetarian food, where to find a tailor, where to buy silver jewellery and how much it should cost. One morning I was on the phone trying to track Doss as usual and she asked if I meant the poet Narayan Doss. I said I was surprised she had heard of him. Was he so well known? Mrs Sonalkar laughed. She was easily delighted. She said her son knew all the poets and he would be able to help me. Right there she dialled a number and said a few words in Marathi and gave me the phone. Her son sounded like he had just woken up but he gave me the number of a man who was an old friend of Doss's. Mrs Sonalkar connected me to the man, whose name was Rama Raoer. I told him I was trying to get in touch with Narayan Doss and he said he would try to help. I was not hopeful. He seemed uninterested or reluctant and I was sure it was another dead end. Exhaustion was always with me in Bombay. I would eat breakfast, make some calls, take a little walk to the shops on the corner for fruit or toothpaste or bottled water, and I would be done for the morning. I would have to go back to my room to rest. It's something about the air in that city, makes you old before your time. What a surprise when Raoer called me back a day later. He said Doss would meet me that evening at a school in Vile Parle where he was giving part-time language classes. I took a train to the suburbs and an auto from the station. It took two hours but I got there early. Hurry up and wait. There was no Doss, nowhere. The classrooms and grounds were empty. Nobody was around except for a woman sweeping the courtyard with a large broom. December, late evening, and there was that hushed feeling schools acquire after dark. I heard crows and the scratchy sound of the woman's broom. I sat on a bench and watched odd joyous movement in the trees above me, feral shadows that melted like dreams. Bats! Immediately I gathered my hair into my hands because I knew baby bats are easily entangled in a girl's hair. As I sat there with my curls in my fingers I became aware of a tall shape moving toward me in the twilight, a boy with long hair, exceedingly frail, wearing a denim shirt open on his chest. He was beautiful to look at and I couldn't stop myself from staring. When he introduced himself and shook my hand all the possible things I could say in response popped into my head and evaporated in an instant. Finally, just to say something, I asked how he had known it was me. He laughed and lit a cigarette, one of those leaf-rolled skinny cigar-type things. It had a pungent smell that I would ordinarily have found unpleasant. But watching him smoke I wanted a drag too. You weren't difficult to find, he said, you're the only white woman here. Matter of fact you're the only person here other than the security guard.

That was my only meeting with Narayan. Now here I was years later about to meet him in New York. In the intervening years I'd returned to Bombay and tried to find him, without success. I'd thought of him many times, particularly when I was translating his work. Translation is an intimate thing, like entering someone's head and feeling your way around. As I waited in the lobby of the Chelsea all kinds of thoughts came and went. But mostly I kept circling around the same one. This time, I told myself, this time I would seize the initiative. I would make something happen.

I'm ashamed to say I didn't recognise him when he walked up to me. I must have had a big question mark on my face. Zusi, he said, it's me. He had changed so much, even his face was different, darker, with a reddish tint on the skin, and broader, much broader. His cheeks had puffed out and his hair was streaked with white. He was not much older than I but he could have passed for my father. I had made up my mind and I wasn't going to let a change in appearance stop me. I stood up and put my arms around his neck and kissed him on the lips. I smelled the alcohol on him. Alcohol and tobacco, I liked it. He didn't know what to do and it pleased me to be the one in charge and to see he was the flustered one this time. I led him upstairs to my room. He tripped on the stairs and swayed all the way and I took charge again, which I enjoyed so much. In the room he fell into a chair, complaining about pain in his stomach. I thought he didn't like me and he didn't want to kiss me. But he was sweaty and he kept pressing the exact centre of his chest and then he was pacing the room and gasping. I went down to tell Stanley the situation. Of course it wasn't the first time he had been faced with an emergency at the hotel. He arranged a taxi. Then I realised that Narayan was not ready to go, some last-minute reluctance, and I had to pull him to his feet.

At the hospital they kept him waiting on a stretcher because he had no insurance. All night on a stretcher, in pain, hardly able to breathe. I admit I panicked, and so I did what I always do when I'm confused. I called my mother. As soon as I told her where I was she started to give me a lecture and I hung up on her and went back to my spot by Narayan's stretcher. What are we going to do, I said. Narayan pulled out a little notebook and on the last page was a phone number, a friend he wanted me to contact. I made the call and we waited and every now and then he would moan gently, as if moaning made him feel better. A junior doctor would come by and check his vitals and ask a few questions. On a scale of one to ten how bad is your pain? Nine, Narayan would say. The junior doctor would go away and another junior doctor would appear and ask the same question. Nine, Narayan would say, nine going on nine point five. It seemed a long time later that Mr Xavier arrived with a friend. He paid the hospital in cash and finally things started to happen. They took us seriously. The operation took four hours. I went to the Chelsea and had a shower and changed my clothes and when I came back he was still in anaesthesia. They'd removed his gall bladder with some kind of new camera technology. A week later he flew back to Bombay and I never saw him again. Now I never will.

Philip Nikolayev, poet and editor, interviewed by Dismas Bambai at Ramanna Ashram, Rajouri Garden, New Delhi, October 2005

I was twenty-four when I first visited India. A friend worked at a small industrial plant north of Calcutta called Titagarh Steels Limited. I accompanied him to work one day. When he mentioned that I was a poet from Russia a small crowd gathered around me, steelworkers all, rough men who worked with their hands. There was great excitement not only because I was a poet but also because I was newly arrived from the Soviet Union. Bengal has one of the longest-serving communist governments in India and the word 'Russia' is enough to make some Bengalis teary-eyed. They made me recite my poems at great length in Russian, although they didn't understand a word. In return some of the men recited Bengali poems. I was surprised to learn that the plant boss had given permission for this exchange and that the whole factory had come to a halt for the duration. I live in Boston where poetry is an obscure priestly pursuit. I thought to myself, Calcutta's air is thick with a million fumes but here a poet can breathe easy. Perhaps I'd been affected by Bengali sentimentality, after all I'm Russian.

After that first visit I returned several times. I've travelled in Uttar Pradesh and Maharashtra and stayed in ashrams in Delhi, Benares, Haridwar, Rishikesh, Dehra Doon, and rural Bengal. A pilgrim's progress and a poet's progress. I learned Urdu and Hindi to the point of some fluency. When I visit India, which isn't as often as I'd like, I use

Calcutta as my base and branch out from there to Delhi, Bombay, Madras.

I met Xavier and Doss toward the end of my first visit when I attended the poetry conference. I had done some translation, Pushkin, Mandelshtam, Brodsky. When Xavier asked if I could contribute to the anthology I thought he wanted my translations from the Russian. But why would he want Russians in an anthology of Indian poetry? When I realised what he was getting at I didn't agree right away. I didn't know if my Urdu was good enough to translate poetry into English. Of course that was the point. Doss and Xavier came up with the idea of anthologising the kind of poets who had never before been anthologised, outliers, rebels, hermits, dangerous faces unwelcome in polite society. They found poets no one had ever heard of, or had heard of once and quickly forgotten, or had heard of many times over a period and then never heard of again.

I think there were some clear guiding principles that shaped the anthology. Mainly they went out of their way to eschew sentimentality. Too far out in my opinion, Newton particularly. I think he'd read too much hardboiled noir set on the mean streets of Los Angeles or Saratoga or Louisiana. It was no guilty pleasure either. He used those books like fuel. Once I asked him to send me a reading list. This would have been in 2002, the year I compiled such lists from some of my friends. Newton was in New York and he sent me his list by email. It numbered in the hundreds.

I made a partial list from his original. As you will see he survived on a diet of poetry and pulp with a preference for vanished poets. I am speaking of course of the modernist trinity of Srinivas Rayaprol, Lawrence Bantleman, and Gopal Honnalgere, poets who had been forgotten by everyone except the odd scholar or barkeep to whom they owed money. If for nothing else, the Hung Realist anthology should be acknowledged for reinstating these three lost souls to the stage or street corner or gang to which they belonged. But also I found it pleasurable to see the way obscure American and Indian poets rubbed shoulders with vanished thriller, pulp, and sci-fi authors. My friend Ben Mazer with the pseudonymous Richard Stark and the Marathi poet Manohar

Oak, self-proclaimed charsi who once asked to borrow five rupees from me, five, not fifty, which I thought was kind of him because I would have given him fifty if he'd asked. He was homeless at the time, or almost homeless. Toru Dutt, Nitoo Das, Monika Varma, Gauri Deshpande, Reetika Vazirani, Arundhathi Subramaniam, and Anindita Sengupta were grouped together, which seemed correct. But so were Ed Wood, Anis Shivani, Ajithan Kurup, Temsula Ao, H. Rider Haggard, Raul de Gama Rose, Tishani Doshi, Seicho Matsumuto, Revathy Gopal, Karthika Nair, Sridala Swami, and Zulfikar Ghosh, a grouping that seemed incorrect though I am still unable to say why. The baroque racism of the reclusive H. P. Lovecraft had been set against the sweet rhymes of the reclusive Vijay Nambisan. Lovecraft and Nambisan, now there are two names you would never normally see in the same sentence! Saleel Wagh, Indira Sant, Vilas Sarang, Arun Kale, Mamta Kalia, Bal Sitaram Mardhekar, Vinda Karandikar, Damodar Prabhu, and Dilip Chitre may have belonged together as Marathi poets of a certain age, but why distance them from Narayan Surve, an orphan poet who grew up on the streets of the city, or the future publisher Hemant Divate, or the future trouble-maker Bhalchandra Nimade, or Bandu Waze (what a name and what a story, the poet and painter who gave up writing and painting and moved into a temple near Poona), not to mention Sadanand Rege, Vasant Dahake, and Namdeo Dhasal, all of whom had equally dramatic, if not melodramatic life stories? He was also reading a selection of the English modernists of course, A. K. Ramanujan, Nissim Ezekiel, Adil Jussawalla, Dom Moraes, and Arvind Krishna Mehrotra, but they had been lumped with the detective novelists Georgette Heyer, Dorothy L. Sayers, and James Crumley, and the formalist Vikram Seth. Then there were the combinations that seemed so oddly fitting I thought there must be something more to it. Kynpham Sing Nongkynrih, Cornell Woolrich, Anna Kavan, Leela Gandhi, Chester Hines, C. P. Surendran, Bhujang Meshram, Vivek Rajapure, Subhashini Kaligotla, Alexander Trochi, Keki Daruwalla, James Hadley Chase, Anjum Hasan, Margaret St Clair, Max Brand, Bruce King, Catherine Moore, Gurunath Dhuri, Patricia Highsmith, Rukmini Bhaya Nair, Anand Thakore, Bhanu Kapil, William McIlvanney, Imtiaz Dharker, L. Ron Hubbard, Dashiel

Hammett, Kamala Das, Herbert Huncke, Philip José Farmer, Easterine Kire, Menka Shivdasani, Ranjit Hoskote, Ken Bruen, Alexander Baron, Curtis Bauer, E. V. Ramakrishna, and Richard Bartholomew. And the combinations that seemed purely bizarre. Sudesh Mishra, Robert Bloch, Stephen Dobyns, Mickey Spillane, Mani Rao, Ravi Shankar (the poet, not the sitar player), Mamang Dai, Gary Phillips, Elizabeth Hand, Desmond Kharmawphlang, Jim Thompson, Suniti Namjoshi, G. S. Sharat Chandra, K. Srilata, Kazim Ali, Mary Erulkar, Hubert Selby Jr., Edgar Rice Burroughs, Bibhu Padhi, Manohar Shetty, Jim Carroll, Helen Zahavi, Robin Ngangom, Santan Rodrigues, Anupama Raju, Natsuo Kirino, Ruth Vanita, Priya Sarukkai Chabra, Samuel Loveman, Vivek Narayanan, Monica Ferrell, Gerard Malanga, Leigh Brackett, Elaine Sexton, Saleem Peeradina, Melanie Silgardo, K. Satchidanandan, H. Masud Taj, John Rechy, S. Santhi, Malay Roychoudhury, Tulsi Parab, and of course the father of them all, not Michael Madhusudan Dutt, who stopped writing in English at the advice of an English poet, but Henry Louis Vivian Derozio, who had no tongue but English, who died at the age of twenty-two, in 1831, when Madhusudan Dutt was all of seven years old.

Anyway, as I was saying, to hear those guys talk you would think sentimentality was the enemy of poetry. But there was more to it than that. I want to go back to an evening in 1984 at the World Poetry Conference, perhaps the same evening the Parsi kid was talking about, or it could have been another night. We were walking on the ghats and we passed a flower shop and I stopped for a few minutes to take a closer look. I was interested in the way the flowers were handled by the vendor. Floristry has a distinct and complex interpretation in India, which responds to climate of course but also the cultic and ceremonial uses of flowers, as well as tradition, taste, and who knows what else. I am no proponent of the binary but sometimes it can be useful. I was watching the vendor work and it came to me that the west thinks in bouquets and the east in garlands. A flower shop expresses India as much as a temple. How they stack the flowers, how they wash them, how they bunch them, how they decapitate them, how they weigh batches of flower heads on scales, pile them high, spread them on water trays, package them, break them up into loose petals, festoon them, wreathe them, colour-coordinate them, scrutinise them to remove faults. It's a craft of a million things I can't pretend to know enough about. Also, let's not forget, flowers heads are offered to the gods as prasad. I always thought this beheading of plants was a vegetarian version of the goat sacrifices at Kalighat. That evening I bought a packet of marigold petals, cheaply and for no reason. It was completely fresh. As we walked I held up the petals and said, this marigold was a poet not long ago. Doss and the Parsi boy did not hear or they pretended not to hear. But Xavier! I'll always remember the expression on his face, as if a cold hand had closed around his heart. He looked at the flower like it was the face of a friend who had disappeared a long time ago. It lasted for a few seconds no more and then he was back to his usual self, the world-weariness he wore like a cloak or a mask. But in those few moments I had seen him and I knew. His aversion to sentimentality was a pose. I think that was when we became friends.

Amrik Singh Dhillon, founder, Amrik Singh Dhillon Associates, interviewed by Dismas Bambai at the opening of *66*, Gallery K. Hardesh, Chelsea, New York City, September 2003

Newton called to say his friend had disappeared the night before and he'd gotten a call from Lenox Hill where the guy had been admitted with severe stomach pains. Could I meet him there? Doss was on a gurney near the emergency room, lying unattended in a corridor for twelve hours. He was relieved to see Newton, believe me. There was a woman with him, a Swiss woman who was taking care of him. She was the one who'd called. Doss had an inflamed gall bladder and he needed an operation, but he had no insurance. Newton motioned to me and we went to an ATM that was conveniently located in the lobby for just such an occasion, I'll bet. He made a large withdrawal and we went to the cashier where he paid in advance and only then did they attend to Doss. He had not even been given a painkiller. American health care sucks, what else can you say about it?

It was months afterwards that I saw a photo of Doss in an online review of the Hung Realist anthology. It turned out he was a well-known poet in Bombay and my premonition about him was correct, the premonition I had when I watched him drink vodka that morning. I heard he died on a railway station platform with an empty bottle near his feet.

Doss's story reminded me of another friend of Newton's, a poet who had immigrated to Canada, Anglo-Indian guy by the name of Larry. According to Newton his career was similar in some ways to the French poet Arthur Rimbaud. Like the Frenchman he'd produced a body of work in extreme youth and then given up poetry and moved to a foreign land where he'd taken up a new career and died young. What a name for a poet. It always reminded me of a lawyer or Republican. Lawrence Bantleman.

The year after all this happened there was an anniversary celebration for the Hung Realist anthology. I was working for Newton by then as agent and general consultant, I suppose you could call it. To tell you the truth business is the least of it. We hang out. The event was held at a bar in the East Village with a Russian name and a faded red velvet vibe. Mainly it was a conversation between four poets in the anthology, all of whom were currently living in the United States: obviously we couldn't afford to fly anybody down. Afterwards Newton was signing copies and at the end of the line was a guy who had brought something for him, a manila envelope full of photos and photocopies of newspaper articles. He was a friend of Larry's, though I got the feeling they were more than friends. Maybe lovers, maybe family, I don't know. The guy was in tears. He'd come all the way to the East Village from god knows where to deliver the envelope. And the photos! Colour pictures of homeless guys, junkies, friendly down-and-outers in puffy jackets, craggy loners clustered around an apartment building in Vancouver in the winter. And there was a photo of a plaque on the building, the Bantleman Court Housing Society, "named in honour of Mr Lawrence Bantleman who devoted many years of his life to improve the quality of life of all who lived in our community". According to the friend or lover, none of Larry's colleagues knew that he had once been a poet.

It struck me as an Indian story. A young poet publishes a few books before the age of twenty-five. The books disappear without a trace. There are no reviews and hardly any sales and the disappointed poet decides to change his vocation. He gives up writing and takes up drinking. He moves to another country where he works for the poor and dies too soon. Many years later a couple of poets publish an anthology that resurrects his memory. Sorry, my mistake, the last sentence should not be part of this story if it's about an Indian poet. When those poets die there is no resurrection. They simply vanish, like Narayan Doss and Larry Bantleman. Having worked for Newton I guess I have a handle on those guys. Their poetic struggle was to survive the circumstances of the poetry.

Rama Raoer, former professor of English Literature, Bombay University, interviewed by Dismas Bambai at Dolly Mansions, near Dadar Station, May 2005

Didn't you interview me more than twenty years ago about the same subject, Xavier and Doss? And didn't you write a book about the poets of Bombay, a gossipy thriller type thing? Oh, I read it, of course I did. I couldn't help myself. And now here you are again, planning an oral history of Xavier. I'm going to tell you something I should have told you the last time. I think you're obsessed with Newton Francis Xavier, which makes you a footnote to a footnote and that is a sad thing. Do you understand? I think you suffer from a sick obsession. As for your questions, I will reply in the form of an anecdote. Last year I was travelling in the United States at the invitation of a publishing house that specialises in poetry in translation from around the world. It is now in its eighteenth year, so it isn't doing too badly. I asked the publisher if he had heard of the Bombay poets, Nissim Ezekiel, say, or Dom Moraes, or Newton Xavier, or Narayan Doss, or Eunice de Souza, or Adil Jussawalla, or Dilip Chitre, or Namdeo Dhasal, or Arundhathi Subramaniam, or Ranjit Hoskote, or, well, I won't bore you and myself with the entire list. Do you know what he told me? He said the only

Indian poet he had heard of was Arun Kolatkar. I said something about how strange that was, considering the poets I mentioned wrote in English and had each produced a substantial body of work. He said it was possible that he had not heard of them precisely because they wrote in English, after all his area of expertise was poetry translated *into* English. But did he not specialise in poetry from all over the world, I asked, and was he saying that if someone were to translate the work of these poets into Marathi or Bulgarian or Roma and then translate it back into English there would be more of a chance that he would be interested? He said I had made an interesting proposition but only in a theoretical sense, as it did not carry much traction – this was the word he used, as if he was a marketing professional or orthopaedic doctor – it had no traction, he said, in the practical world. He said he did not wish to be combative but wasn't it true that if these poets were as significant as I thought they were he would have heard of them? This was New York, he said, the centre of the wide world of publishing. Do you know what I did? I thanked the man who had dismissed my history and my milieu with a single sentence. I did not say what was on my mind, that he and his colleagues were fighting cancer with a Band-Aid, that they were arranging deck chairs on the *Titanic* and they were not even aware that the ship was sinking. I simply thanked him and shook his hand. And now I'll thank you and if you don't mind I'll skip the handshake and ask you not to contact me again.

Zusi Krass, writer and translator, interviewed by Dismas Bambai at Shamiana Coffee Shop, Taj Mahal Hotel, Bombay, March 2005

I decided I would never go back to Bombay because I didn't want to return to the scene of my early turmoil and by that I mean Narayan Doss, who I think of always as my black angel. Even today if sometimes I pray, I pray to him. I say, my black angel of Kamathipura, spread your sharp wings over me. Also, there were one or two small episodes of mental flux that struck me in the city that never weeps, the heartless city of Bombay, some voices I heard, a woman's voice and the terrible thing she said, unpleasant experiences, bitter memories, and so I thought Bombay was over for me. My black angel had gone and my Indian journey was over and after all there are other places in the world, St Petersburg and Mexico City and Saigon. Why Bombay? I decided I would never go there again. And then a guiding voice boomed in my ear. Zusi, never say never! And of course I returned a year and a half ago because my book of translations appeared at last.

The publisher sent review copies to Indian journals and newspapers but no distributor accepted it because of the price, a prohibitive price for poetry readers, most of whom have no spare change, as you know. There was some interest in the book and some favourable reviews, though one young fool said the poetry in Narayan's work had been found in translation. I wrote to Nissim Ezekiel and asked if he would host a reading at the PEN Centre. He agreed even if I got the feeling that he didn't remember me. Why would he? It had been a long time since my last visit to India. I convinced my publisher to give me some copies on author's discount and I took them with me. When I met Nissim I knew immediately that he was a shadow of his old self, not even a shadow, a shadow of a shadow, a white shade that passed at times over the wire-rimmed glasses and the shamed accusing eyes. I knew it was the wing of madness. It resembled the confusion some call Alzheimer's but I knew it was the same wing and the same shadow I have suffered under.

Naturally I had no great expectations for the event. A handful of people at the most, I thought, considering Nissim's advanced state of disinterest and my lack of experience in organising a literary event. And then, a surprise! Forty or forty-five people came, many carrying copies of the Hung Realist anthology. The hall filled up and some had to stand at the back near the glass cabinets where the rare books were displayed. Nissim made a small and unexpectedly lucid speech. The Marathi script, he said, was denser than the English because the overhangs and underhangs took up more space. Then, without explanation, he said, "Ladies and gentlemen, please join me in welcoming Miss Susie Strauss." I didn't bother correcting him and I didn't really mind the mistake. What difference did it make, Zusi or Susie, Krass or Strauss? And I remembered a story Narayan told me. When William Golding came to Bombay to deliver a lecture Nissim had introduced him as William Goldman. If it didn't bother Golding why should it bother Krass? I read some poems and a protégé of Nissim's read the originals in Marathi. Then I said a few words about Narayan Doss. I said that he had had two simultaneous and overlapping careers, one in English and one in Marathi, and that he had never combined the two even though he had been quite capable of translating his own poems from one language to the other. I said my book was an opening salvo in that project and I hoped there would be more. There were questions from the audience and really they weren't questions but expositions in the French sense. The first person to speak said Dalit poetry was superior to Dalit fiction and the assertion dropped into the room and sank without so much as a ripple. A man in a frayed kurta with the wild look of a homeless person or homeless poet explained (in English) why modernism came to Marathi before it came to the other languages of India, particularly English. Someone stood up and disputed this notion. It turned out the man with the wild look in his eyes was a reputed publisher and his interlocutor was a young poet and the dispute was longstanding. Afterwards a line of people appeared in front of me. They wanted me to sign copies of the anthology, which of course I said I would not do. How could I sign a book I had not translated or written? No, no. A student asked where she could find a copy of the Narayan Doss translations. Could she send away for it? I told her the price in dollars and she asked if she could borrow my copy for a day. She said she wanted to photocopy it. I remembered something Narayan had told me, that in the early days the Bombay poets used to cyclostyle copies of their books to distribute to friends. It was the only way they were able to read each other's work. Of course I lent the girl a copy, and after thinking about it for a minute, or a second, I told her she could keep it.

Afterwards I gathered my book bag and prepared to walk back to the YWCA where I'd managed to reserve my old room. I noticed that Nissim was still sitting in his chair on the podium. He hadn't left the seat all evening, nodding to himself as if he was in the midst of a great debate. By then the audience had left and we were alone in the dusty room full of old books and smeared photographs of dead writers. He looked at me as if his thoughts were far away, on a frozen field in the north of Germany or in the farthest icy reaches of hell. I asked if he would like to have a cup of coffee and I expected him to make excuses. He agreed immediately and when he got up he was his old self, confident and thoughtful, his pale intellectual face alert to everything. We went to a South Indian place across the street from PEN, a place Nissim had been to a thousand times. I signalled for coffee and asked if he would like something to eat. He ordered a dosa and so did I. While we waited for the food I noticed that the cuffs of his shirt were caked with black dirt and his collar too was dirty, more than dirty, filthy, and his trousers were frayed and shiny, as if he owned no other clothes. He looked like someone who slept on the streets of the city, this man who was admired as the father of English poetry in India, who for many years had been its face, and a handsome face at that! Where was his family, his long-suffering wife? It was all too heartbreaking to consider. We talked about the new politics in the country, about how much the city had changed and how the Anglophone Bombay of the seventies had turned into its evil twin. We discussed the meaning of his name. He said the Lord called Ezekiel as a watchman and prophet to the rebellious House of Israel, and Ezekiel predicted for Israel a future of war, and the Lord gave him a scroll and commanded him to be not rebellious and to eat and fill his belly, and when he ate it was in his mouth *as of honey for sweetness*. We talked about poetry. He had just finished proofreading a new edition of his collected poems and there was a new edition of Dom Moraes expected and two books by Arun Kolatkar – all this in the same year. Then he started to talk about Bombay and water, the catastrophic effect of the ocean on peoples and coastlines, and the future of cities by the sea. He had never feared the sea around Bombay, he said. Salt water was a part of the landscape. It gave the city meaning and it destroyed the city too. You could see its effects all around you. No sooner was a building painted than the sea would begin its corrosion. We had more coffee. I asked for the bill and paid and it struck me then that he had no money. It was plain to see in the skeletal cast of his face and in the expressions of the waiters. As we left the restaurant, I to the YWCA and Nissim to where I don't know, I asked if he was in need of money. He shook his head. He had more than enough for his needs, he told me. I insisted. I gave him whatever notes I had on my person. Then I said goodbye and left him on a sidestreet near Churchgate Station. At the end of the street as I turned left toward the telegraph office, I looked around. He was on the corner where I left him, surrounded by beggar children who grabbed at the currency notes he was handing out, the very notes I had just given him. What struck me was the smile on his face. He looked so happy.

BOOK SIX

Alien of Extraordinary Ability

Saint Goody

or Gudiya, or the Goods, or Ms Lol,
whose forgiveness I do not deserve;
first passion, and then its passing, all
was decreed by the Summoner of love,
all that we are, all whom we fail,
all that we in the end must leave.

from *The Book of Chocolate Saints: Poems* (Unpublished)

1.

They took a train from Bangalore to Delhi because (Goody complained) he'd rather spend days traversing the dust plains of Central India than sit in an air-controlled aeroplane for two and one half hours. He was sixty-six, he replied, a senior citizen entitled to his sweet maladies. Goody made a production of stocking up on drawing paper and magazines and postcards she'd been meaning to write. She charged her camera and cell phone. She packed moisturiser and hand sanitiser into Ziploc bags. The trip to Delhi was forty hours if the train was on time. If delayed they were up for a two-day stretch. But Xavier was happy not to fly. He said boredom was akin to happiness because it described the absence of crisis. After the calamitous events of the recent past – the booze; the hospital and his escape from it; his return to the Infantry Road apartment to find Goody with her suitcases packed, waiting by the front door for a taxi, which sight had heralded his unravelling because he could not imagine being without her; the wild promises he made, he would relearn the sober life, he would take his medication and take better care of her and they would move to Delhi; his promises, her tearful declaration that she had said she would leave and she had to keep to her word, his shaky avowals, their raised voices, a drama that had played until dawn – after all that here they were, with nothing expected of them but to stay on the train like packages waiting to be delivered.

"Admit it, this isn't too bad," he said, aiming for lightness because that was the important thing, a certain lightness of spirit even if the spirit was saying, je suis un vieux fou. And here was a voice in reply, non, tu es fou à lier.

Goody said, "Jet lag is preferable to other kinds of lag."

"Jet lag is the time it takes the body to catch up with the mind."

"Or the body to catch up with the body."

And train lag is the opposite of jet lag, he thought. The mind slows down to meet the body. You sit in your seat and look out the window. There is nothing else to do and it is a kind of bliss.

They had facing upper berths close to the train's metal roof and were subject at all times to raw draughts that tasted of cinders and coal dust. But they were in close proximity and heading north into the new unknown. He hoped it would teach them how to be with each other again.

"I'm already bored," said Goody.

"Boredom is an upper-class privilege," he said. "Count yourself among the fortunate."

They shared the compartment with other travellers, including a family of three. The woman nodded as the train left the Cantonment station.

"On-time departure."

"Yes," said Goody.

"A good beginning is important."

"Always."

"I'm Purnima, Saraswat Brahmin from Mangalore," she said. "We are Saraswats but rationalists. You're maybe too young to understand how important was rationalism. I am talking about Partition time but today even more important! See, I am Purnima and this is Anand. We are rational and pious, scientific and pious. Now do you understand? We have no time for Sai Baba and the Shankaracharya and that Sri Sri Sri Sri fellow."

"Purnima," Anand said. "Please."

"Saraswats are dying out," said Purnima. "We are facing a full-blown crisis. We are borrowing from our children but we will not pay the debt. It will be paid in full by my daughter's generation."

"I'm sorry," said Goody. "I don't understand."

"Too many Saraswats are marrying outside the community."

"What about your daughter?" Goody asked. "Will she marry outside or in?"

The daughter's thumbs froze on the message she was punching into her cell phone.

"She is free to make up her own mind but she'll find it difficult to adjust outside."

"So," said Goody. "You're a rationalist but not when it comes to your daughter."

Purnima nodded happily. Puzzlingly, the daughter too was smiling.

Xavier watched as the city's last outposts flickered past. Night had fallen. Karnataka was receding but not swiftly enough.

"Are you going out for a smoke?"

"Yes, Goody, a little stretch, a wee amble or pre-amble, a teeny shot of nicotine to get the blood moving and disperse the stress if you please."

"What I want to know, what I cannot seem to get my head around, how did I end up living with a smoke factory?"

Purnima said, "This is the problem with us Indians, no sense of physical culture. Like they say on TV, we are like this only."

Goody said, "Only we are like this."

Xavier said, "Like, are we only this?"

Purnima clapped her hands and told Goody, "For seven lifetimes you must have watered the holy basil to get a husband like this one."

"Seventy lifetimes," Goody said, "I want my money back."

Purnima said, "Tomorrow is my daughter's happy birthday."

"How old?"

"Twenty-one."

"Keep her away from this one," Goody said, nodding at Xavier. "He likes them young."

Purnima said, "No!"

"Oh come now, please, I've not been right in the head."

"Superfine excuse. I'm crazy, excuse me while I act the pig."

Xavier backed out of the compartment. He lit a cigarette and smoked it down and lit another. He missed Dharini, if truth be told, missed her kindness and the uncomplicated way she met the world. Spending time with her was like sitting in a garden innocent of sin. The word 'love' never reared its treacherous head, few words did. This made for ease and comfort, communication brought down to its non-verbal essence, all possibility of misunderstanding sidestepped. She had given him nothing but sweetness. In return he had left her in a hospital where in all likelihood she still was waiting. And here was he, trapped in a battle unto death with Goody the Mahamaya whose purpose was to show man that Time, like Art and Life and Love, was little more than an illusion, perhaps the last illusion that remained before his consciousness surfaced from its pool of stagnant water. He pulled at the cigarette and remembered Dharini with a sense of regret.

Yellow lights swam up out of the dark as the train passed a small town or village. At a crossing he saw a dog with red eyes and a terrible wound on its back. It was a common sight, unremarkable in every way: maimed animals and humans in every small town and city. A subcontinent of the maimed and the soon-to-be-maimed, where if you got to the age of sixty or fifty without encountering horror you were unaccountably lucky. Even the air was against you, even the water.

To cope he lit another cigarette.

When he returned to the compartment, Daddy, Mummy, and Baby Saraswat had fallen into a deep family sleep. Goody was awake in her bunk, staring at the rusted grille of the ceiling fan just inches from her face. When he climbed into the facing bunk she turned on her side away from him.

Husband and wife were up at six to wish the girl happy birthday. They were boisterous morning people; they wanted Goody and Xavier to get up and join in; they wished to have a little party. Goody's only question on waking was whether her bags were still under the bottom berth or if they had been stolen in the night. Xavier, badly slept and too tired to care, took his morning pill and went into the hallway for a cigarette. He opened the heavy outer door and stood smoking in the slipstream. The train was moving slowly but they were well into the middle of the country, Andhra Pradesh or Madhya Pradesh or some other desolate Pradesh beyond the ken of God and man. He smoked the cigarette down to the butt and shut the door and went back to the compartment where he took a seat by the window. One of the other passengers was also up, a man with an Army crewcut who was lounging in his bunk and staring at the women.

Purnima took a seat beside Xavier. His morning surliness didn't appear to bother her. Anand worked in a bank in Bombay, she said. She too worked in a bank, but in Bangalore. They lived apart for the sake of their daughter. Xavier understood. Everything was for the sake of the daughter, who was awake now and blinking at him and tidying her hair into a coil. She seemed shy and awkward but there was something in the eyes. Was it intelligence? Or interest? And was she staring? He looked away before it became apparent to Purnima that his proximity to her daughter was every bit as dangerous as Goody had predicted. There was nothing he could do about it. Women his own age filled him with the opposite of desire, for a good reason. They were not desirous themselves. They were mothers and grandmothers and they had given up on the sexual life. They had given men a pause. He'd liked young women when he was a young man and why wouldn't he like them now that he was a certified old goat? He'd aged but his tastes had not. There was no call to fight it. And besides, it wasn't an either slash or choice. It was a multiple choice. He also liked mothers and grandmothers.

In his late teens he had been drawn mainly to older women, particularly those who might lead him astray. He had married the most unseemly of them all, Miss Henry of the throaty laugh and bi-lingual leanings, Soho habitué and lauded bohemian whose nude portraits were painted by the noted artists of the day, including Xavier. She had seduced him when he was eighteen and she twenty-nine and one of the first things she said to him was, darling, I'm not sexually attracted to the penis as a rule but in your case I will make an exception. They met at a bookshop run, after a fashion, by the man who would soon publish Xavier's first book of poems, who had also published the first books of Dylan Thomas, George Barker, and David Gascoyne, a man so spectacularly unfit to operate a business that he would run his father's inheritance into the ground and wind up in a room at a hostel for homeless men where he would inevitably kill himself. Miss Henry had just begun work at the bookshop when Xavier walked in one morning on the verge of his great success. The marriage had been a drunken revel that spanned Greece, Israel, India, and the British Isles, and had lasted all of four years; and then Xavier left her for a woman who was her opposite in every way.

Edna was only five years older than he, soft-spoken and self-denying, with the complexion of a milky rose. Their lovemaking was almost entirely missionary and always at his instigation. She would shut her eyes and wait for it to be over. She never removed all her clothes and it occurred to him some time after the marriage had disintegrated that he had never once seen her naked. In the span of four or so years they had a daughter, they stopped sleeping in the same bed, and his drinking escalated to a bottle a day. She was the only one of his wives who had walked out on him. When she died he happened to be in London, on a week-long binge in a squat near London Bridge. He heard about her death from a reporter who had tracked him down for a quote. He hit the man in the face and walked to the off-licence for another bottle of Teacher's and stayed drunk for three weeks, moving from the squat to a couch in Holborn, too full of shame to call his daughter. He dreamt of Edna still, vivid dreams in which he would try without hope to kiss her pale unforgiving lips; and he would wake in tears, unable to speak or get out of bed.

His third marriage had lasted longest. They had travelled the world as journalists and drunk their way through a river of whisky and an ocean of vodka. Lula's classic celluloid features had survived the alcohol, the miscarriages, and the incessant travel. But she had had to give up her movie career because of Xavier's unhinged jealousy of her leading men and directors. His behaviour had been self-destructive and humiliating. And then he left her for an unimpeachable reason: her screaming fits aimed at the neighbours in the voice of his mother during her final dementia. In his paranoia he had begun to wonder if she were doing it on purpose. Did she hope to drive him into the madness that had engulfed his mother? Toward the end she began endless renovations of the Bombay apartment they shared. The floor was misaligned, she said, and the workers would arrive for months-long corrections that had no discernible results. He began to sleep with his wallet in his hip pocket. He accepted whatever engagements came his way and he spent as much time as he could in New York, where his father had left him an apartment. One smoggy winter he checked into a hotel in Delhi. Word spread that he was in town and then began the clamour of the journals. He agreed to an interview request from a magazine with the unfortunate name of *Closed* by a woman with the happy name of Goody Lol.

He heard the ringing of a phone. The ringtone was a woman's voice singing slow morning vowels that climbed unhurriedly into the scale, the notes full of wisdom and a kind of calm joy telling of a lifetime of riyaz at dawn. It was a birthday call for the daughter. Father, mother, and slyly smiling twenty-one-year-old took turns to speak into the instrument.

Goody descended from her berth and opened the packed food they'd brought along, homemade rotis and vegetables.

We are pure vegetarians, said Purnima, perhaps suspecting that Xavier, with his Christian name, was an impure one; but she consented to try some of the potato.

From the middle berth the daughter handed Purnima her phone. On the screen was an old photo of Xavier and an interview from the days when he still gave interviews.

"You're famous," said the daughter.

"Famous, famous," said Purnima, scrolling. "You never told."

"Depends what you mean by fame," said Xavier. "I'm famous at Koshy's and at Dewar's. I suppose you could call me the pet laureate of MG Road."

The daughter laughed silently, watching him all the while.

"Don't deny your fame," she said, her eyes shining.

She took the phone back from her mother and her thumbs moved furiously for a minute and this time she handed the phone directly to him. On the screen was a review of the New York show. Without reading it through he passed it to Goody.

"'The poet of Hung Realism, at the age of 66, rings wily changes on his past,'" Goody read aloud. "'Saintly figures collapse into their containing shapes, never to rise again. Unnamable colours threaten and brood. Although filled with retrospective grandiosity, the show is nowhere nostalgic. It suggests instead the flash and sizzle of a new career.'"

Goody stopped reading and counted.

"Fifty-one," she said. "They call themselves an online journal of the arts and they've reduced your career to fifty-one words. How do you like that?"

"Criticism is a reduced tradition. One must expect truncated thought and half-formed expression."

"The key to happiness is low expectations," said Purnima's daughter, winking mysteriously.

"Lowest," said Purnima, "lowest expectations, best!"

The Army man ordered breakfast from the pantry and so did another passenger, a young Sikh. In berths in the corridor were two medical students on their way home for the holidays. As far as Xavier could tell they were talking about women possessed by ghosts and taken advantage of by temple priests and exorcists. Some people are more vulnerable than others to possession by a violent spirit, said one of the students. I'm using the word 'spirit' because spirits are different from ghosts. What's different about them? asked the other student. Spirits are eternal and ghosts are not, the first student replied. Ghosts are helpless bundles of memory and rage stuck between one world and the next, yearning for release and for the sensations they enjoyed in their old lives. This was why so many ghosts were found in the trees of their village begging passers-by for a mouthful of rice, or a smoke, or a drink of toddy. The other student told him to be more specific. He couldn't say some people were more vulnerable to spirits and leave it at that. Okay, said the first student, small children, particularly girl children, are more vulnerable than adults; and those who are grief-stricken or permanently disaffected for whatever inscrutable personal reason; and those who had recently suffered immense reversals of fortune; and those who wished to die and had wished to die for as long as they could remember. One minute, said the other student, maybe I should write this down since you seem to be an expert and all. Then she laughed.

The Sikh got up and introduced himself to the students. He was a salesman of dental equipment – "the latest, from Germany" – and he had brochures. He offered a brief capsulated version of his sales talk, with pain-inducing references to spoon excavators, retractors, cone burnishers, and probes (sickle and straight), and he ended with the promise of a soon-to-be-available high-speed air drill with a patented friction hand piece and a Christmas tree blur, though Xavier wasn't sure he'd heard the last phrase correctly. Very difficult to pass the time, said the Sikh apologetically on his return. He wore a blue button-down shirt and blue turban day and night through the entire trip and he complained with pleasure about the inadequacy of the dining car and the inconvenience of train travel. Most of the time he followed the lead of his crewcut neighbour and stared at the women.

It was the one constant of travel in India, Xavier thought, the only thing that never changed. The sexual desperation that Indian men took no trouble to hide. Once on a holiday in a beach town in the south they had stopped for dinner at a restaurant facing the ocean. Immediately three men had squatted on the sand and stared at Goody's knees, which were barely visible under the table. It was dark and there wasn't much light on the terrace. What did they hope to see at that distance? She'd been wearing a dress and her legs were bare; this was enough. The men sat and smoked and looked in her direction. They would not go away. It happened everywhere. Men stared; they brushed against her; they scratched their privates and fondled themselves; they urinated in full view. Goody got into fights. On a bus she slapped a man and nobody said a thing. They were used to it. She was on a bench at Wanker's Park, sipping water and digging in her handbag for sunglasses when she noticed an old man in a white kurta standing a few feet away and masturbating in his pyjamas. He was seventy-five at least. He had white hair and a kindly face and he swayed on his feet as his hand pumped his pocket. There were people everywhere, couples on benches and joggers and park employees, but nobody objected. They were used to it. In England they had a name for it, Goody said, lewd behaviour, and it landed you in jail with the other freaks.

Xavier imagined the men dying horribly in cramped spaces. He imagined them tortured with spoon excavators and a pair of pliers in the back of a windowless van, garroted at a urinal, buried alive in a basement closet, electrocuted in elevators or on staircases. He fantasised crimes in which he would cut their femoral arteries and watch entranced as they were lifted up in great waves of blood. He invented murder scenarios in which knives played a larger part than guns. The only firearms he allowed were shotguns that took away half his victims' faces and left sucking wounds in the chest and unpluggable excavations in gut and groin. He preferred hunting knives because he wanted to be intimate with his murders. And now he was imagining the castration and killing of the sullen Army man who did nothing but stare at the women in the compartment. Openly he stared with his hand in his lap.

That night the train stopped in the middle of nowhere for no apparent reason. He hauled open the metal door and stood in the doorway. On all sides the fields flowed outward into the dark. Pale grey trees and timeless village sounds. He heard a dog bark and the chirp of crickets and a well rope creaked and a metal bucket scraped against stone. He thought he heard an animal somewhere close, laughing or coughing.

Someone came out of the bathroom and stood beside him, Purnima's daughter. They stared without speaking at the night. More shapes became discernible in the brush, small dogs perhaps, or children whose eyes shone with a sick yellow light. The air was close and humid. He brushed past her to go into the toilet she'd just vacated and she watched him and her face was expressionless. He nodded at her. Come here. Obediently she came and shut the door and held him close. He felt her heart beating through both their chests and he was surprised at the hunger in her kiss. There was a smell of metal in her hair. When he pushed his hand into her jeans her mouth opened in a sharp hiss but her eyes stayed the same, expressionless. Your beard is scratchy, she said in a stoned voice. Rub it here, she said, pulling up her shirt and indicating a spot on her belly. The train lurched. He got on his knees and she pushed her jeans down and held him tenderly by the ears. She watched him lap at her as if she had no idea who he was or how they'd come to be so intimately positioned. But she shook her head when he stopped to catch his breath. Keep going, she said. Don't stop. He heard a whistle blow and the train changed its rhythm, speeding up or slowing down. Then she was pulling him to his feet. I want you to do it, she said. Do it now. As if she could not call what they were doing by its name. She bent over to hold the metal washbasin in her two hands and offered her behind. He unzipped obediently. He smelled urine and looked at the hole in the floor that was the toilet. The tracks blurred below. Another whistle blew. As he began to hoist himself into her he caught sight of his face in the mirror by the sink, his old man's face with its white beard and broken nose, and he saw the girl in her disarray taking great gulps of the fetid air, her face rapt in yellow light. It was the face of an anxious child. He felt his erection dwindle. When he straightened up she hissed at him. Why? Why aren't you doing it? Not like this, he said. And he kissed her chastely on the forehead and went back into the compartment.

Early on the morning of the second day the train passed a field of sunflowers and yellow mustard plants tall in the sun. He felt the colours seep into his brain like ink. Purnima saw his eyes fixed on the flowers and offered a penny for his thoughts. They were the only ones awake.

"A penny," he said. "No more, no less?"

"A pound, a pound for your thoughts."

"Rothko," he said. "Saint Markus. I wonder how he would have responded to the immovable object that is India if by some chance he'd visited here in the last years of his life. It might have been a good thing or it might have been the death of him. And why am I saying this as if I have some definite prior knowledge? Because I do, I do have prior knowledge. I stopped over to see him before he died. He was under house arrest by his doctors but he took care not to mention it. He seemed happy to see me and this struck me as strange because he was not a happy man. He had no aptitude for happiness, which is a gift like any other, a skill that can be developed or neglected according to one's temperament. Mr Rothko set no stock by happiness. It was not a quality to which he accorded any kind of value, negative or positive. He saw no artistic potential in it, I suppose. Moreover, he was the lifelong exile, the permanent immigrant. In his head he was still the ten-year-old Russian boy newly arrived in a hostile land. So when I saw him smiling I should have known something was wrong. I'd never before seen him smile or heard him laugh, not once in all those years. But here he was in his slippers, shuffling like an old man or a much older man than he was at the time. He kept trying to light a cigarette but his hands wouldn't work. Finally he said, could you do me a little favour, please, Newton? I haven't been to the bank, not feeling up to going out at the moment, nothing serious, just old man's woes. Could you nip down to Garnet's and pick up a bottle of vodka for me, and some cigarettes?

Actually make it two bottles and save me a trip. This is Mark Rothko, my old friend and mentor. The man who introduced me to the art world of Manhattan, whose homes were a haven to me when I had no home, who taught me that it was possible to drink and be disciplined at one and the same time. What was I going to say? No? I didn't know that his doctor had said that a binge at this point in his life was just the same as stepping in front of a train or jumping off a building – a little like my own condition at the moment, if you see what I mean. After he died there was a joke going around town, a New York art world joke, which is to say the kind of joke resorted to by soldiers, doctors, undertakers, and thieves. They nicknamed me The Man Who Killed Rothko. They said it was the vodka I gave him that did him in. Not true. What did him in was old age, according to his own insightful analysis, what did him in was the suspicion that his best was behind him and all that was left was a kind of creeping obsolescence that gets worse by the hour."

Purnima said, "I knew something like this is what you would say."

They stopped at a station named Daund. It was still early and the platform was deserted but for a pair of sadhus. The older man had a cottonwool beard that corkscrewed to his collarbone. He was winding a turban around his head. One foot was drawn up under him on the bench and slowly he shaped the white cloth to his skull. His companion's kurta and mirrored vest and lungi were shades of saffron that varied subtly in texture and hue. Producing a hand mirror from a saffron shoulder bag he combed his beard with his free hand and used the mirror to check the underside of his beard, the back of his turban, and the malas looped around his neck. Critically and thoroughly he examined himself. As a last touch he pulled loose a lock of black hair from under the turban and adjusted it over his ear. Now he was ready. He put the mirror into a quilted cloth case and returned it to the bag. When he smiled to himself Xavier experienced a moment of transference. To step out of his life and into the sadhu's, to sit on a bench in the sun and groom oneself like a cat, consciousness without self-consciousness, wholly free of everything but the body and the pleasure of the moment. How much better than his own tight life!

Agra Cant went past. The train slowed but didn't stop and Xavier said, why can't Agra? If Delhi can, surely Agra can too? Purnima covered her mouth with her hand when she laughed. He imagined setting up house with her in a middle-class dwelling of one or two rooms. She would wake at four to bathe. She would put on a fresh sari and go into the kitchen where she'd contentedly stay for hours making idlis, coconut chutney, filter coffee, and Saraswat sambar. He would not be expected to make an appearance until brunch. He would never enter the kitchen. It would be understood that he was incapable of making a cup of tea. Lunch would be early, rice and curd a staple, after lunch, a nap. Their sex would be furtive and silent, the quick coupling of married Indians accomplished with a minimum of fuss. She would not expect foreplay, much less an orgasm. On festival days he would buy her a sari or a gold bangle and she would shed tears of joy. The happiness would keep her going for weeks. When would he work? All day and all night, the household would revolve around his work and he would be energised by the newness of it all. What would it not do to his output? He was visioning a pile of manuscript pages and vast arrays of fresh canvases when Purnima's daughter descended from her bunk and went to the toilet without a glance in his direction. He waited five slow minutes before he excused himself. The girl was waiting in the corridor. She put a piece of folded notepaper in his hand and squeezed his crotch so knowingly it made his heart race. Then she hurried off. She'd written her phone number, no name, just the number and the words 'call me'. He put the note away; his hands were shaking.

They had stopped at a small station called Bhooteshwar – Place of Ghosts, Xavier said automatically to himself – and there were no people, no dogs, no sign of life until the train started to move and he caught sight of a man painting a railroad buggy. The wheels were chilli red and the buggy bright blue, violent bits of colour against the blank grey day. The train passed shanties built on the side of the tracks, toxic slum clusters and caved-in dwellings constructed from detritus. Children played kith kith in the dust. Even the fields were covered with plastic rubbish and sewage. A woman sat with her sari around her hips and her back to the train for modesty. A tin of water stood beside her and she chatted to another woman who sifted through the rubble. What was the second woman looking for? Blasted brown fields stretched on every side. Small bodies of water thick with green slime or black, liquid matter turned solid.

Poverty, filth, distress: they were in the north, arrived at last in the Republic of Rape. Purnima, Anand, and the daughter had lapsed into silence. Goody was still asleep. He felt strangely protective of this impromptu family.

They were nearing Delhi, he knew, because the train had slowed and the debris and disarray had increased. They passed shrines to nothing in the middle of nothing, Muslim shrines with no indication they were living places of worship. A single stunted tree was the only thing upright on a long stretch of rocky scrub. Two men were seated against the trunk. They had positioned themselves carefully to make use of the slender shade. Others, without the strength to look for shade, lay splayed as if felled by sniper fire. Soon the flat-roofed one-room structures gave way to corrugated tin shacks and tarpaulin weighed down with broken bricks; mounds of garbage spread evenly over vast open areas; excrement and children and starved maimed dogs.

The train pulled in to New Delhi railway station and on the platform they said goodbye to the Saraswats. Goody gave Purnima an invitation to Xavier's party, a card with a time, an address, and *66* in embossed numerals. Outside they settled their suitcases into the back of a taxi. In a pocket Xavier found the notepaper given to him by Purnima's daughter and he let it fall to the floor of the car. It was late in the afternoon and the air was dry with a hint of smoke; anything seemed possible in the mild sunshine, even hope.

The taxi took them to the house of a journalist Goody knew from her time in the city. Paro took immediate charge. They were to rest from their travels and familiarise themselves with the city while she found them an apartment to rent. For now they had a guest room facing a stand of frangipani trees and Paro threw a small party that she called a get-together.

It was the time of tsunamis and bombs.

The day before three explosions had occurred in the city's most populous shopping district and in the news photos Goody noted, as always, the women's shoes and slippers strewn over the bombsite.

"So there are monuments in Delhi, so what?" a transplanted Bombayite told Goody.

The woman had moved to Delhi when she married. She'd been a professional party-thrower in Bombay, a job she called event management. She was still throwing parties but for a classier crowd.

"If every second fool made a monument to himself in Bombay we'd also have thousands of them. I moved here because, what, capital city, has to be more secure, right? Wrong! You're out buying jeans, which, just remember, you're buying cheap jeans, and dishoom you wake up legless in a hospital."

"How long have you been here?"

"Let's see, eight, no, nine years. My god, has it already been that long? I think I need another gin-tonic."

"Nine years and you still sound like a Bombayite."

"Darling, I hope I never sound like a Dilliwalli."

Goody heard this a lot, how awful the city was, how inhospitable, how unsafe for women. But Delhi was her town. It was where she had grown up and where she returned after she left London and she wanted to show it off to Xavier.

People filled their plates with samosas, kebabs, and paneer on skewers. They sipped punch from shot glasses and gossiped about the Gandhis.

It was the time of tsunamis and bombs.

"Paharganj, Govindpuri, Sarojini Nagar," said Sonia Grover, a lawyer who knew more secrets about politicians and industrialists than most journalists. She was a friend of Goody's mother. "See what places they target. Markets where the middle class and the working class do their Diwali shopping. Why not pick on the rich?"

"I'm sure they will," said Goody.

"Not that I'm complaining but pick on someone your own size, you get me?"

"I get you, but it's penis size that's the real problem. The bombs, the rage, the religious screeching, all that is compensation."

"You're a woman now. I remember you as a schoolgirl. How temperamental you were, endearingly anti-social. Your mother didn't know what to do with you."

"That may be the perfect epitaph for me. Her mother didn't know what to do with her and neither did she. And you know what, I think I might be a little anti-social still."

"You artistic types," said Sonia. "What can I say?"

She patted her hair and downed a shot of punch. Immediately Paro brought around a tray of glasses filled to the brim and Sonia took another. She shook Goody's hand in a businesslike way and went to a group of men smoking on the balcony.

Goody found Xavier in the bedroom, alone, staring at the only decoration on the walls, a poster of Gauguin's Jacob wrestling with a yellow-winged angel on a flat ground of vivid red. It wasn't the wrestlers he was looking at, but the peasant women in the foreground. He seemed entranced.

"No," he said, his eyes on the poster. "I think, I don't think I can go out there. I have nothing to say. I'm dry as a bone. I want a shared spiritual experience not a wrestling match."

She made excuses to the guests. He was train-weary and crotchety, she said. Coming down with something, Delhi belly, maybe, or chikungunya or dengue. Who knows? He'll be out at some point, I'm sure. Best to just let him be.

But he did not come out. He stayed in the room until long after the last of them had left. He was doing nothing, as far as she could see, other than staring at the Gauguin, the peasant women in their white bonnets sharing some kind of religious experience, yes, their eyes shut and hands folded in prayer, their great pale heads lovingly detailed in comparison to the indistinct figures of Jacob and the angel.

Their arrival in the city coincided with a downturn or upturn in Xavier's condition. With the medication taking hold he was no longer excitable. Sometimes she missed his manic phase. Was it better for him to be energised and falling for a procession of young women, or depressed and not producing? Undoubtedly the former but it made him unmanageable.

To get him out of the house she rented a car and they went to the Q'utb Minar. They kept the driver waiting and walked toward the structure, which was roofed and pillared but open on all sides. At the centre was a narrow tomb of faded marble. The Q'utb's lack of doors and oversight had extracted a price. Names had been scratched into the tomb. There was graffiti on the walls and grillework. There were lists of all kinds.

Ronita I love you.

Kuldeep I love you.

Neha loves herself.

I love you Kavita but you don't love me Bhola.

Deepak, Neetu, Dhiraj I love you.

Dial 36219837 and enjoy.

And at the end of these oddly promissory slogans was one in the past tense. *Mansoor loved Afsana.*

"Love," Goody said.

"This was once the tallest tower in ancient India," said Xavier, who had perked up in the presence of ancient buildings. "The strict lines and clean shape? It's the Muslim architectural line, human separated from divine and only the divine worthy of consecration."

"Do you think we'll learn to love each other again?"

Without waiting for a reply, she walked ahead to a television monitor. For twenty rupees it gave you the view from a video camera attached to the top of the Q'utb. They were close enough to the tower to see the fine work on its upper storeys, the marble and red sandstone, but the monitor showed live action footage of the unexceptional buildings nearby. Goody saw a sign: Remote Presence Facilitation System. Such a grand name for a camera pointed the wrong way. When they reached the Quwwatul adjacent to the Q'utb she felt a little faint, like a woman in a nineteenth-century novel. The words 'smelling salts' came into her head, though it was water she wanted. The question she had asked came back to her like a cave echo.

"The oldest extant mosque in India," Xavier said in his special voice, "and one of the oldest indications of Hindu–Muslim collaboration and competition, which is what makes for the charged architecture."

He seemed to have revived, or he was making an effort. He had revived and she had wilted. They edged around massive stone screens inscribed with geometric designs. She caught sight of the inner masjid, the perimeter supported by dozens of stone pillars, like no Muslim building she had seen. There was a proliferation of deities and the abundant female figures found on temple walls.

"But it looks so Hindu," she said.

A plaque said the mosque's cloisters had been built using pillars, carved columns 'and other architectural members' of twenty-seven Hindu and Jain temples taken in their entirety to the site of the Q'utb.

"In other words, the temples were destroyed to make this. Do you see?" Xavier said, running a hand along a pillar. "More to it than the linear Islamic ache that sublimates desire into calligraphy."

"That's what I like about you, New, you're better than a guidebook. Right now? I think I like you more than I have for a long time."

"Touch it and feel how the pillar curves. Now look up there, see those supports? What's surprising about them? You're not looking. Yes, exactly, four men, facing in four directions. The human figure in a mosque, how did they get away with it?"

The figures were male, Aryan, kingly. They lay against the ceiling, knees bent and dangling upward, looking down at the viewer, the entire figure a refutation of gravity. Each had been given some individualised characterisation, the Brahmin thread or armlets or royal headgear, and there wasn't a flat belly among them. Goody thought: Indian stomachs.

"Take a look at the faces. See how they've been hacked with such force that some part of the chest is missing as well?"

"Look," she said, excited. "There are female figures too."

"But fewer, as if they were slipped in when no one was looking."

The women too had come under the hacker's sword and not a face or breast had been left unharmed. But the destroyers had been in a hurry; some loveliness was still visible in the parts that remained.

Later they drove through the streets of the old city to the Lal Qila. Goody asked the driver to put the windows up. She felt the pollution in her chest and throat. She would carry a handkerchief to spit in, she thought, like a consumptive. She would be one of those women who walked around with a perfumed hankie pressed to the nose, asking for smelling salts. The taxi had to make a U-turn and then it stopped in a crush of autorickshaws, trucks, and Blue Line buses. Ahead of them was a black Ambassador with a sign painted on its back in rural red and yellow. 'HORAN PLEEJ'. They were trapped in a corridor of cars and buses and the driver pressed pointlessly on the horn.

A woman came to the window with her pallu over her head. She had big lips, like Goody's, and her lipstick was a similar shade of brown. She stared and Goody stared back. In one expert glance the woman took in their clothes, the car, their potential generosity. There was a blond boy of two or three on her hip, a thin child playing with a rubber band. Her blouse was wet from two spreading stains where she'd suckled him and Goody had a sudden desire to taste the woman's breast milk. The extended family was camped on the pavement. The men lounged at their ease and smoked, healthier and cleaner than their wives who sold trinkets and begged and raised the children. A girl of three or four left the group and went to a Maruti with a couple in the front. The woman with the blond baby shook her head and the girl moved to a bigger car. The woman came to Xavier's window but she didn't ask for money. She held her baby to him as if in offering and Xavier gave her a note. Her smile was sweet and shy.

Then the traffic cleared and they neared the walls of the great fort, its ramparts converted into a traffic underpass. At the entrance they squeezed past a crush of loiterers and guides and in a corridor of shops she found a framed painting of Ganesh in the pose of a Mughal emperor. He had his arm around a seated woman whose veil had come undone and his trunk was in a state of semi-arousal. Goody considered buying it but the thought of haggling with the salesman was beyond her.

She wanted a fixed price. She wanted a cold drink and air-conditioning. She wanted silence and a nap in a dark room.

They went to the pavilion where the emperor met with his public. A guard with a rifle and fixed bayonet stood in front of the only object in the fort that was still intact, the throne with its inlay of birds and green leaves. Some inlay remained at the Khas Mahal but most of the silver and gold had been vandalised. Near the octagonal tower where the emperor made an appearance every morning there was a latticework door that had rotted at the hinges. Goody noticed that its great feature had survived, two tiny brass elephants whose heads served as handles, the elephants and their mahouts superbly energised and bursting with detail. The trunks formed a loop into which she placed her index finger and she traced the head with her thumb and felt something of the power the artist must have felt as he worked.

The centrepiece of the building was a screen with the image of a pair of scales. Not a panel remained, only a set of discolourations on the wall. The mirror and marble inlay, the gold and silver ceiling work – all had been stolen. Goody asked a soldier if they could take a look at a roped-off section. Area is closed, he said. Then, addressing her breasts, he pointed out which parts of the palace were open for viewing. When she backed away he scratched his genitals with great care, as if the gesture would seduce her on the spot.

2.

The air was thick with emperors, warriors in the wainscoting and dead footsoldiers in the red cotton trees. The dirty sky brimmed with rain light. Everywhere she looked tired gods guarded a pile of ruined stone or a desecrated tomb or a collapsed place of worship visited only by cattle and bandits. She learned to love riding around the city. She ignored the modern and registered only the weather-beaten and ancient, the falling-down mud dwellings and dirt roads unchanged for three hundred years, the camel trains of myth, the veiled herders and yellow-haired babies encamped on the pavement, the blackened pots of cook fires, the nomadic labourers stained with the dust of desert quarries and construction.

They had moved from the winter wastes of Manhattan to the temperate clime of Bangalore to the extremes of a Delhi barsati, or two Delhi barsatis. The first belonged to an alleged officer in the Indian Air Force. He asked to meet at a bus stop near Air Force Headquarters where he waited in full uniform. They met him again to sign the lease – at the same bus stop. It struck her later that they had not seen his office or home and he had not produced identification of any kind. He may have been impersonating an Air Force officer for all she knew; anything was possible in the newly incredible India. They installed air-conditioning, a bed and some of the art, and then they discovered why the apartment had been a bargain. There was no water in any of the taps. Xavier had asked all the right questions about air and light, he had asked if there was a park nearby, but he had not asked after water. He hadn't known that in Delhi the presence of a tap did not indicate the presence of water and that the scarcity of water was the Indian future. When they confronted Yadav, the Air Force officer, he dropped in one morning with his wife and the phrases came so easily off her tongue that they knew they'd been had. *Water harvesting. Tube well. Tankers.*

The Yadavs were con artists, slippery and brilliant. Goody visited the downstairs neighbours and the woman of the house said there was no water in the entire building sometimes for days at a stretch. She had two young children and they needed water for bathing and also for drinking. She said it apologetically, as if it was an unreasonable expectation. Later in the afternoon Goody found her climbing the stairs with a full bucket in each hand. The woman had gone across the street to borrow water. Xavier gave up the month's rent and the deposit as money lost or swindled. They moved.

With Paro's help they found a new apartment in a moderately noisy block in Defence Colony. In days Xavier had made it new. The way she thought of it, he made it New. He converted the bedroom into a studio and office. He put a double bed and a desk in the big living room and potted dwarf palms in the bathrooms. He had the terrace painted yellow, blue and green, so when you sat out under the curved bamboo rigging it was like being on a ship. The bamboo was a premium essential and before its cane sails were installed on the terrace they were woken each morning by extreme heat and light.

She didn't know it then but the burst of homemaking would be the end of Xavier's active phase. Soon he was inert, uninterested in sex, work, or conversation. His explanation for inactivity was simple. He was settling into the city and the city was settling into him. He was sifting and storing the architectural residue of adjacent centuries, tombs from the sixteenth, Victorian memorials from the nineteenth, stone and glass skyscrapers from the twenty-first. One afternoon he saw two women transporting a tree trunk to market, the heavy wood balanced casually on their heads. Their flared red and yellow skirts were tucked into their waistbands and their muscles were stringy and alive. It was an image from an ancient desert past and for someone from the coast, from the forgotten town of Forgottem, for example, here was an image to be stored for future use. Except, thought Goody, all he seemed to be doing was storing up the images. He wasn't working; he was on medication; he was sane and sober and depressed.

Late one night she found him cross-legged on the terrace in the dark, puffing on a cigarillo and scribbling in the blue notebook he carried at all times. He was making a growing list of saints and soon he would need a new notebook. Cigarillo smoke issued in a complex system of rings and tubes. What was he doing exactly out there in the dark? And why was he smoking so much?

He said, "Smoke is a way to communicate with the dead, a more effective method than relying on a medium, whose presence, as in quantum theory, changes the nature of the communication. The medium brings his or her own vibration into the interaction to such an extent that the petitioner will never know how much of the subsequent communication has been influenced by said medium. This is not to say that all mediums are suspect but that a medium (as the word suggests) is a separation, a barrier between oneself and the vast sorrowful community of those who are unable to speak for themselves. Smoke is a better method of communication than words because there is no question of miscommunication, misunderstanding, and inaccurate articulation. For instance, if you examine this plume you will see that it sails upward in the shape of a dismasted galleon. There is a figure in the prow and she is waving but is she waving in farewell or in greeting?"

"I'll always take hello over goodbye. You should too."

"How much time do we have?"

"I don't know, Newton."

"This is not my life and I do rather wish I could get out of it."

"But where will you go?"

"Back to New York, I don't know."

"You hated it there. You said you felt like a third-class third world citizen. You called it an exhausted culture on the verge of its inevitable decline and fall."

"Well. That was before I got here. Have you seen a more exhausted culture than this one? It's more racist than America. The fairness creams. Buri Nazar Wale Tera Muh Kala on the trucks. The jokes about Hubshees and Southies and Chinkies and Dalits."

She heard a ping from her cell phone and reached for him as if she'd been doing it all her life, waking from a night of vivid dreams with the same man in her bed. He remembered nothing of his dreams, not a word or a picture unless he was woken violently. He lived only in the moment or in future moments and what he remembered he kept to himself; he had a private life. She did not, everything in her head she shared.

She had dreamed of Dracula and Mina, which made her remember a film they had seen once in Paris. The director was a woman Xavier had known when she'd been an assistant to a friend of his, a filmmaker with a reputation for drugs and violence. The woman had left his friend to make her own movie and its name was in the air a lot that summer and Xavier had taken Goody to see it. The first half was a fairly standard French art film. Careful frames of cities at night, lamplight on a bridge at dusk, a boat moving on black water, improvised street scenes in the style of documentary footage shot from a moving car with a handheld camera, parked cars on a boulevard and people in overcoats waiting on a pavement, and long sequences where a slender woman with a severe haircut smoked unfiltered cigarettes and a man with a square jaw and a three-day stubble committed petty crimes, and there was unhurried sex without dialogue in hotel rooms with standing ashtrays, in hotel rooms with faded carpets, in hotel rooms with indistinct lighting, and in an aeroplane toilet, all, as I say, fairly standard for Xavier though not for Goody, who had only recently begun to watch European art-house cinema. So when the movie, which seemed like a series of prepared stills that followed one after the other with no apparent purpose, turned without warning into a horror film it caught them by surprise. The scene where the film switched genres was one in which the lead actor performed cunnilingus on a woman whose cries of pleasure turned into screams when he began to eat her in earnest, eat her like a succubus, eat right through her panicked attempts to get away until she died on sheets that had turned black with her blood. The scene went on and on, pitilessly, until it seemed the director must take some special pleasure in the depiction, that it was her own excitement she was pursuing. There was more to follow, scenes of mass slaughter in which manacled women were eaten alive by men and women with dead eyes and sharp teeth, and as the movie progressed it became bloodier and bloodier, until, unable to watch, Xavier turned away. Later he said the film displayed the kind of split personality to be expected from a first-time director and he would have thought more of the exercise if it had been one thing or the other, art or horror, not six of one and half a dozen of the other. She understood that his critical comments were a way to mask his feelings because that night he couldn't sleep. His head was too full of blood images, he said, and he finally dropped off only after he put on a nightlight. She remembered all this and felt a protective surge for him that was maternal and sexual at the same time.

There was another ping. The bamboo sails yawed slightly and in the air-conditioned bedroom the shaded light made a minute adjustment. It had always been this way with her; she had no boundaries. She remembered their first meeting at the Hauz Khas Village café with a view of a tomb in the middle of a lake. I'll teach you how to sin, he'd said. Though he'd never followed up on this promise. She remembered a dream she had had of Newton, blind and exiled to a rock for his crimes. She remembered their first trip together. By then the English boy she'd been seeing had given up on India and on her and returned to London, and she and Newton were an item. Together they went to New York, her first trip out of the country since returning from the UK. In the apartment on Central Park West she learned to let go, she learned to fall. She rode the subway and took taxis. Mostly she walked, whatever the weather. The first time she slept with someone she was abashed and guilt-ridden. She told Xavier about it and he laughed. He said, I think at heart you're a good Indian girl with a solid middle-class upbringing. She applied for a job and started to work and took another apartment and things were coasting along. She too developed a full-blown private life, with assignations, break-ups, crushes, heartbreaks. She was experiencing what she called her bicoastal phase, an uneasy period she would remember mainly for the stress of it. She had girlfriends because she'd always had girlfriends. Sex with a man was useful for the context it provided. You were able to compare penetration to being penetrated, awkward hanging appendage to sleek inward mechanism – there was no comparison really. But then came New with his renewed claim on her and she laid her own claim and now she was as hetero as a soccer mom.

She got up when she heard the third ping. She went to the study and unplugged her cell phone and found a message to herself. Tughlaqabad! They were to collect twenty-eight boxes shipped from New York and sitting in a warehouse on the outskirts of the city.

Xavier didn't like to think of the move to Delhi as permanent, or even temporarily permanent. But it was a city she knew. She liked that it was mired in sex, a stunted society in which women were an endangered and sexualised species. She liked that it clarified and simplified social interaction. There was no room for murky ambiguity.

"I'm on a bus and I smile at a woman," she said. "Anywhere else she'd think I was just being friendly. Here she knows I'm interested. In Delhi everything is sex. To clarify, I look, that's all I do."

"Everybody looks."

"Everybody is so polite. We should be able to do more than look."

"In Delhi?"

"Oh, rape. Men like to think rape is the worst thing that can happen to a woman because they want to believe their puny dicks are weapons of mass destruction. Do you know that sometimes, not always but sometimes, I like it when you use me and you don't care about my pleasure? I like it when you're rough with me and you're not trying to be a good lover, did you know?"

"No," Xavier said.

And he changed his style, fucking her quickly, a half-dozen rabbit strokes and off he'd go. And she asked herself what she'd started.

"New, get up."

"What."

"Get up, we have to go."

"Had a bad night, I was up for hours."

"We're going to Tughlaqabad."

They left the house and drove for an hour past tombs and mosques in varying stages of disrepair. There was laundry slung across fifteenth-century stone and goats tethered to arched doorways and Mughal gardens dotted with dog shit and covered in graffiti. Even in a landscape of ruin Tughlaqabad stood apart, an expression of the element it stood upon, sand-coloured and sand-made, like a giant architectural drawing of a medieval fort rising from the scrub. Rising from or sinking into, she wasn't sure.

They drove into a maze of triple-decker containers stacked like boxes, a city constructed by the insane where the streets led to no conclusion and the windows illuminated nothing, a place without activity of any kind.

And that was when Xavier turned to her and said, "The past is never past, it's present and accounted for. It is with me always, like your love. You keep me steady. Find a way to forgive me, Goody, I'm sorry."

"Don't be sorry," she said, "we'll work it out."

She spoke automatically but the words made her feel better.

The driver took them into an alley lined with the L-shaped skeletons of container-trailers. A graveyard of broken-necked vehicles lay before them, the engines and chassis at impossible angles. The alley was long and perfectly straight and at the end of it, at a right angle, another alley with more broken trailers. The driver parked outside a building that was only façade, the rooms shells, the toilets non-existent. There were flies and mosquitoes everywhere. The sign didn't say England as she had thought at first, but Inland. She followed Xavier up a staircase and past several floors of abandoned rooms filled with gutted or burned furniture. Dental instruments lay in heaps on the floor, the metal tools rusted beyond repair. He asked for directions from a woman sitting cross-legged on a bench. She squeezed coconut oil out of a dented plastic bottle and rubbed it on her toes. This is room 123, she said, gesturing to a doorway. Then she went back to work on her feet. A man sat at a desk in the front of the room and another in the back. In between the two were deskless others collapsed into chairs placed haphazardly throughout.

Dev? Xavier said to the first man. It was the name he'd been given. The man said his name was Faisal and he pointed to the man at the other desk who was now talking into two cell phones. Faisal said they were to wait until Dev was free. Goody thought, what else would you do but wait in interiors such as these, where time had stopped? You wait and prepare yourself for more waiting. You come one step closer to understanding the earth-forged nature of the bardo, the waiting room the soul passed through on its interrupted journey to the realm of the eternal. Room 123 was full of people who had been there for an eternity, exhausted messengers, defrocked managers, couriers who had run out of hope, long-distance drivers holding checked towels to their heads. The drivers would be the former tenants of the stalled machines that lined the roads to the building. They waited with their eyes unfocused and limbs slack and Goody noticed a peculiarity that became more apparent as the day lengthened and they moved from one bombed-out landscape to the next: she was the only woman. Wherever they went she was the object of immediate attention and she resorted to the strategy perfected by the women of the city: she spread her dupatta to veil her hair and cover her breasts.

Accompanied by an assistant to Dev they showed their papers at a security gate and walked past a tower of locked wooden chests and entered a tin-roofed warehouse. Skylights ran along the centre of the ceiling in twin wings, upside-down landing lights that illuminated a world of lost objects, and in a corner they found the things they had shipped to India from New York. Then Dev's assistant raised the first objection.

"One, because DOA is September, TR will not apply. You will have to pay."

The Indian obsession with acronyms – what was he talking about? There was a long discussion and they understood that without a transfer of residence they would have to pay an additional holding charge.

"Two, the size of your TV is larger than specification. Three, CD and DVD are different machines or the same?"

A separate duty would have to be paid on each item. They followed the assistant to a room jammed with tables and the kind of petty bureaucrats Paro had warned them about.

"The customs department is full corruption," she told them when she heard their boxes had been at the clearance hangar for two months. "They will make you pay extra for every day."

Unexpectedly the customs men were amenable. Write a letter to the

Deputy Commissioner of Imports, they said. Explain that you were travelling and that's why you were unable to pick up your shipment. Dev's assistant, their agent in the transaction, seemed disappointed with the new turn of events and he watched suspiciously as Xavier wrote in longhand in English. The official read the letter with some care and told them to wait until the deputy commissioner arrived. He was at the Central Secretariat in North Block – Goody knew the words were tribal power mantras, Central Secretariat, North Block – and he would be back, though the official could not say when. He did not know the DC's schedule; nobody did; all they knew was that he would return, like the Saviour.

After waiting an hour Goody gave her cell phone number to the clerk and asked him to call when the deputy commissioner arrived. They walked back to the car and asked the driver to take them to a restaurant. When he stopped at an establishment that had 'PURE VEG' on its frontage in lieu of a name they were both too exhausted to argue.

Upstairs it was cool and gloomy. The waiter was a boy of about seventeen, who rushed to fetch water and refill the napkin holder. In his haste, rushing, the boy dropped the menu. Immediately he picked it up and dusted it and kissed it. Goody understood. The day had just begun and the menu was an object of veneration, the good book that gave the boy his livelihood.

The Bombay sandwiches they ordered were soggy with butter and chutney. Xavier was lifting up a slice of bread to examine the cucumber and tomato when Goody said, "Last night on the terrace, what did you mean when you said nobody knows how much time we have?"

"It's a useful thing to brood on, I find, it puts life into perspective."

He lit a cigarette. He was cutting down, he said.

"Did somebody die? Is that what this is about?"

"Everybody died if you fast forward into the future. What can I say? What can I say? Let the day perish wherein I was born. I'm sorry, Goody."

"Everybody says that to me. I'm sorry, Goody."

They got into the car and went back to the reception area where Xavier dozed for a few minutes. He was woken up at four by the ringing of Goody's phone. The deputy commissioner had arrived. They went through security and out into the sun-made landscape and they tried to keep to the shade but there were too many things in the way, too many objects that had lain unclaimed for years, piled office chairs and desks, Fords and Toyotas and SUVs, combine harvesters and Chinese armoured trucks. Parked outside the warehouse gates was a customised car with curtains in the back and a blue beacon on its roof. The vanity licence plate said DC SS1. The deputy commissioner's chariot, no doubt, said Newton, as they squeezed around it. Inside, Dev escorted them to the deputy commissioner's office and they presented their papers to a guard who went into the cabin and immediately returned. The DC was waiting for them, he said. They felt sudden new attention directed their way. After a day of waiting they had received the call from the corner cabin; now they were persons of interest to every guard, clerk, and agent in the hangar.

In the cabin three air-conditioning units ran at full blast. A couch and armchairs were grouped in a seating area to the side and behind a large desk sat a man in his thirties. Instead of the bureaucrat's bush shirt and matching trousers he wore a slim-fit Polo, a Stalin moustache, and jeans. On his forehead was a flame of red from his visit to the temple. He waved them to seats and Goody noticed that there were a lot of men in the room.

"Yes," said the deputy commissioner to Goody. "Your company?"

"We work out of a studio office," said Goody. "We are self-employed."

"Studio office," the deputy commissioner said to a man seated on the couch. "Kumar, you know this studio office?"

Kumar was a bearded man in a white kurta and churidars. He took off his dark glasses and said, studio. An assistant brought a bundle of files and attempted to place them on top of other files on the desk. Over there, the deputy commissioner said, pointing to a far corner. He positioned his pen over the files that were nearest. He scanned the first two pages and made a small pout with his lips and signed quickly and fastidiously and moved to the next folder. The files were identical to the file that their agent and his assistant had been carrying all day, in which the letter Xavier had composed had been attached to a checklist of contents, a photocopy of the dollar cheque they had paid, and the shipping form and receipt.

The deputy commissioner looked at Xavier. "Where are you employed?"

Xavier checked his wristwatch and froze.

Goody said, "He is a painter and writer. His retrospective is coming to the National Gallery and his writing has appeared in *Harper's* and *Outlook.*"

"*Harper's* and *Outlook*," said the DC. "Kumar," talking across the room, "who is *Harper's* and *Outlook*?"

"*Harper's*," said Kumar, repeating the word slowly, making it sound like a threat. "*Outlook*."

In Hindi he said, "I don't remember."

Goody started to explain why it had taken them so long to come and collect their things. They had been travelling and work-related decisions had to be made – but the deputy commissioner was not interested.

"Have you done your post-graduation?"

"Yes."

"What subject? From where?"

"International relations and an MA in gender, media, and culture."

"What aspect international relations?"

"Conflict resolution. My subject was Kashmir. I travelled around the state for two months."

"What is resolution to the conflict in Kashmir?"

"Free and fair elections? Something drastic, I'd say."

"Easier said than done. What will solve the conflict?"

Goody said something about the people of Kashmir and the deputy commissioner seemed to like the phrase.

"All these people write books. People with long beards give long lectures but what happens to the conflict? What difference it makes to the people of Kashmir? What can your international relations and conflict resolution do? Painters" – he gestured at Xavier – "paint pictures and journalists make their careers, like that fellow" – and he looked at Kumar, who knew the name his boss was looking for and supplied it – "he made his career with one stupid article on the people of Kashmir.

I used to be a journalist also. I'll tell you, ninety per cent of them are middlemen and money collectors. Some tea?"

There was no question of refusing. He was magnanimous now that he'd put Goody, a graduate of international relations, in her place, and Xavier, a writer and painter, in his. Goody asked for his card and the man slid it over. His name was Sunil Srivastava.

He took her card and said, "Do you work on Saturday?"

"No."

"Did I say something wrong?" he said to the men, who were laughing.

"No, sir," Kumar said.

"Bring tea for ten," Srivastava said to a canteen boy. The tea arrived in small paper cups, each consumed in a single sip.

"It is a problem," he said. "The transfer of residence is a problem but don't worry."

He made a show of signing the file.

He said, "It is waived."

Xavier lit a cigarette. There was no ashtray in the room.

Srivastava understood the man who had made his career with the article on Kashmir. His main job at the newspaper had been to inform on his colleagues and friends, including Srivastava. In this way he managed to stay employed and win promotions. His colleagues' careers depended on the information he passed to the proprietors or kept to himself. That kind of power was intoxicating and addictive. Srivastava loathed the man but he understood him.

He did not understand the painter who kept examining his shoes, old-fashioned shoes that were red in colour. What kind of man wore red shoes? Srivastava knew there was something wrong with the painter, but what? Kumar was intelligent. He had the gift of the gab. He could stand in front of a crowd of people and talk for an hour but the fellow had no insight into personality because he had no interest in personalities. He looked at the painter but did not really see him. What was it about the painter? Srivastava thought maybe it was the eyes. They were too steady and too cold, as if they were the eyes of a criminal who had donated them on the eve of his execution, not from a feeling of generosity or brotherhood but from a kind of egoism. He wanted his eyes to continue seeing in the world. The painter moved his head from side to side like a blind man. Under his misshapen nose a beard hung to his chest, the ragged beard of a ruffian. Smoke stains surrounded the mouth.

Insolent fellow smoking in my office and tapping ash on my floor.

He turned his attention to the woman. She was speaking but he could not understand her. Conflict resolution. What did she know about conflict resolution? Let her try to work in a government office and she would understand that conflict was eternal and resolution impossible.

Boobs too large for her shirt.

It was difficult to keep his eyes on her face. He was a boob man; it was his weakness. Was she saying something about his job? The painter yawned and tapped ash on his floor and settee.

Srivastava said, "Customs? I've been here for some years now."

Goody had asked if a job with the customs department had been his goal as a young man. The deputy commissioner hadn't heard her or he had misheard her, a consequence of doing too many things at once. The signing of files, the ordering and drinking of tea, the remarks to subordinates, the flirting with a woman in the presence of her partner, the casual display of power.

Then Srivastava said, "I am thirty-nine. I never wanted to get into this line. My interest was philosophy and religion."

Actually philosophy and religion were Kumar's subjects, but Kumar was his subordinate and crony. Kumar was his creation. They were close enough to be family members. What belonged to Kumar belonged to him.

"Everything is written on the head, as per fate. I could have landed up somewhere like New York. I went there last year to see the Times Square," he said. "Such a long flight. For fifteen hours I am sitting next to a Negro. Never again."

Goody tried to fill the silence that followed and made a mistake.

She said, "What kind of books do you read? We have lots of reference titles in our studio. We can send you something."

"I'll take your help. I surely will. I'll take books on religion, philosophy, and my favourite, governance. I will come to your office."

"I'll ask my assistant to send you a list and you can let her know which ones you want."

"No. I will come to your office for your help." And it was Xavier he was looking at, as if it was Xavier's help that he wanted. Goody recognised it as his tactic, to speak to one person and look at someone else. "I'll come to see you. Give me your mobile."

He returned her business card so she could write her number on it.

"He'll bring a turtledove and pinch off its head and the blood shall be drained out on the side," said Xavier.

Srivastava said, "What side?"

"Leviticus," said Xavier.

"Kumar," said Srivastava, "what is this levity curse?"

Kumar took a seat beside Xavier. "He is quoting Bible, sir."

Srivastava said, "Why?"

"He is making a comment on power, sir."

Srivastava was comfortable with power. It was one of his subjects. Also he had a special interest in spiritual matters even when they emanated from suspicious foreign sources such as the Bible. This man had mentioned blood. He had the guts to sit in a government office and talk about blood.

"Explain," he said.

Kumar said, "People have many needs and desires. What do they really need? They need the possessions they have accumulated. The phones and TV. They need their families and friends to give them company. They need money to buy some luxuries and necessities. They need to know that their homes are secure and they have opportunities in life. It is the job of power to provide these small needs. What will power receive in return? It receives the goodwill of the—"

Srivastava said to Xavier, "Do you go to Lodi Gardens?"

Xavier said, softly, "There is no peace there, only unease."

Srivastava said, "What are your qualifications?"

Xavier said he had set aside an unfinished list of suicide saints and begun a new one. He was making a list of dark-skinned saints to correct the western historical record that acknowledged only fair saints with blond hair and blue eyes. Many saints were dark-complexioned, swarthy, or negroid, with unwashed hair and poor nutrition. Like Jesus. He hoped to compile a book of chocolate saints, a directory in which there would be no pale faces, only dark and darker, as a counterbalance against the many books in the world that had no black or brown or yellow faces, not to mention greeny faces such as the one he was addressing. Even so it was a partial list, he said, because it could never be complete. There were too many everyday saints, obscurely situated patron saints of the commonplace overlooked by the church and unseen by the laity.

"They may be described as imaginary saints but only by the unimaginative," he said.

"Yes?"

"As you know, everything is prophecy."

Srivastava looked at Goody and said, "Kumar?"

"He is speaking of sants," Kumar said.

Goody said, "Thank you. If we're done, we—"

"Naked came you out of your mother's womb and naked shall you return," said Xavier. "This is my qualification, perhaps my only one. What, I wonder, is yours?"

And now Goody was in a hurry to be off, to take her ailing lover and leave the hellish premises of the customs shed. She asked if there was anything else that remained to be done. They were free to leave, said Srivastava, and it was clear that there had been no reason to sit and watch the man conduct his business; it had simply been his wish.

Early the next day he called to ask if their goods had arrived. He turned up at the studio office unannounced, the blue beacon flashing from the roof of his car. Goody told Payal at the desk to serve him tea and tell him to wait. She came into the reception area twenty minutes later and told Srivastava she was taking a meeting. She said he could help himself to any of the books on the shelves and made an apology and left. When Srivastava finished examining the shelves he planted himself in front of Payal's desk and asked her how much she earned. She told him a figure slightly higher than her salary. He nodded and smiled and put his card on the desk. You should work for customs, he said, sarkari job security is better. She said, thank you, uncleji, I'll keep your card just in case. He said, uncle? No, no, no. Tell me one thing. When I speak to someone like you where should I look, your face or your chest area?

"I think he was asking a genuine question," Payal told Goody. "He really wanted to know. Thank god the phone rang then and I got busy. When I hung up he was gone. Where do you find these types?"

Goody said, "Where do you not?"

When Payal left work at six that evening she didn't notice the car that was parked across the street with a clear view of the entrance to the studio. It had tinted windows and a blue beacon light and a vanity licence plate that said DC SS1.

3.

The sun disappeared in January and the temperature dropped to four degrees. All day the skies were overcast, the streets ruled by fog or smog, ambiguous matter that hung to the ground in a low white veil. For weeks there had been no sign of sun and if you looked up at night you saw no stars, only the impenetrable sky. Goody imagined fleeing the city and driving south, driving without cease until they reached brightness. But car crashes were common and flights had been grounded or diverted: there was no escape. They kept their coats on and huddled around space heaters. The houses of Delhi were designed for the summer; winter was brief and deniable but only for those who lived in houses. The homeless wandered the streets wrapped in blankets or sheets, rubber slippers on their feet. When the cold entered their bones it did so at night and they died in their sleep.

By the last week of February winter had gone and it was difficult to imagine a time when overcoats and sweaters had been an indoor necessity. The temperature rose ten degrees and more from one week to the next; in a matter of days, the city went from winter to summer, from heating to air-conditioning. Then, in April, a rain bird's high cry announced the coming of a storm. It took days to build. The bird called at all hours of the night and the morning, always with the same note of dementia. The breeze smelled of moisture but when the storm came it came in the form of dust, a yellow powder that coated trees and cars and people, bleached yellow that may have fallen from the moon; and there it stopped, there was no rain.

It's working, Xavier told Goody, the fluoxetine, going so well I'm beginning to bore myself. What he didn't say was that he had been cutting down and taking thirty milligrams a day instead of the prescribed forty. He was feeling so much better that he wanted to cut down again by half.

They went to dinner in an apartment in Jorbagh on a terrace screened by tall plants. The apartment belonged to a friend of Goody's, a former classmate who was editing a men's magazine, a thin woman in knee-length boots, hollow-eyed and jittery, with an ostentatious post-nasal drip that she wore like expensive jewellery. Slowly, with infinite patience, she loaded a needle joint with slivers of Manala hashish. And that was when it arrived, forked lightning in the sky for an hour, then heavy drops that wet the plants on the terrace and the lawn below. They moved the dining table into the shelter of the overhang and stood by the long windows and inhaled the year's first shower, a smell of dust and packed heat and moist North Indian desert air that was nothing like the raw earth smell of the southern monsoon. After the heat, the rain shower was more potent than the hash. Goody felt a tint on the skin like a shading of red.

On the coffee table she saw a fish whose scales were shells of a peculiar pale rose. The fish moved in your hands when you held it. And the best thing about it, Goody thought, was that the mouth was a bottle opener. She saw it as something beautiful, a piece of art her friend had acquired somewhere, and tonight, smoking Manala cream from the Parvati valley, the fish was more than art: its function was its beauty.

She said, "Who was it that said things should either be beautiful or useful?"

"William somebody?" said an older man with a shaved head. "Shatner? Shakespeare? Reich?"

Monica said, "And where would you place yourself, Goody, among the useful or the beautiful?"

"Depends, doesn't it, on which day of the week you get me."

"And then there are the days when you're ugly and useless."

"Goodness, Monica," Goody said, surprised. "I had no idea you knew me so well."

Monica was twenty-five and clumsy in a way that felt dangerous. She moved jerkily in spasmodic bursts followed by fractured laughter. She was full of stories about the married executives and managers she slept with and worked for. It's so easy to get them to do what you want, she said. You just tweak their egos. A little tweak will get you anything.

Some famous old filmmaker will do exactly what you tell him. He'll take orders from a twenty-five-year-old woman that he would never tolerate from a man.

"What else?"

"It's a cliché but that just proves it's true. Everybody has his price. Money or cocaine or sex. If you knew how many coke sluts there are in this town, chicks who hang with drug dealers for the free toot and dudes who do the same. It's a free-for-all."

Goody wondered if Monica had become a bit of a coke slut herself. The talk drifted like smoke. After dinner there were more drinks and then Monica dumped a small mountain of white crystal on the coffee table and made a line that ran from one end of it to the other, like a salt line or the line that landed the pink-scaled fish. She and the man with the shaved head started at opposite ends and then everybody took turns. Later Monica tilted her head and tapped her nose and talked about a recent journey she'd taken.

I needed to wind down, she said. I needed to get out of Delhi. You know how it is when you live here. You have to get out as often as you can just to keep your equilibrium. She went to Brazil and there she met an older man who spoke no English, a musician. He came up to her in a park and took her by the hand. They exchanged no words at all or none that she remembered; after all he must have said something to her during the course of the long night they spent together and she must have said something to him, but she could not recall a single thing. It was all too frenzied. They went to his apartment. He didn't sleep or eat all night, all he wanted was cocaine and sex. His penis was too big for her and she had to push him away. She had to hold him at bay with both hands so he would not plunge too deep inside her, or he would injure her. At around three in the morning, sore and exhausted, she begged him to stop. He took a drink out of a thermos he kept by the bed. It was a drink the colour of blood and he did what looked to her like a sitting shavasana, that is, he inhabited the correct parts of the body in the correct order, the crown of his head, his third eye, his heart, his stomach, his balls, his calves and feet and toes. After the meditation, which only lasted about twenty minutes, he placed her on his penis and fucked her in a sitting position. He told her to move while he sat cross-legged. She did it gladly because it was a way to make sure he didn't penetrate her too deeply. She came more than once, more than twice, more than three times and still he would not come. He took another drink from the thermos and when he licked her nipples and her lips she tasted herbs, kava kava maybe, or bhang, or fresh blood from a snapping turtle. He put cocaine on his cock and fucked her from the back and changed positions so he could look into her eyes while he fucked her, fucked her for an hour, and still he would not come. She thought she was becoming delirious because she heard a high voice singing in a language she didn't know. It might have been German, the singer begging the horses of the night to run slow, oh, slower. How did she know this when the language was foreign to her? Her skin felt hot but when she touched her forehead it was clammy. Every hour he took a drink from the thermos without offering her any. She dozed. Toward dawn he fucked her again with his hands around her throat, Monica said, looking Xavier and the man with the shaved head in the eyes. When he came it was as if he'd spurted into my uterus the purest cocaine. I felt hot and cold at the same time. I growled like a dog, like a bitch in heat, and as it was happening I knew I'd fall pregnant. I knew there was nothing I could do to prevent it and of course I did, I fell pregnant, and when I got back to Delhi I had an abortion. The next day my car was stolen and I was knocked down by an autorickshaw. I lay on the road with blood on my dress. I couldn't find my wallet. I'd forgotten how to use my phone. I couldn't breathe. I thought, yes, I have assumed my true form. I am become transparent.

There was a silence and then Goody said, "You shouldn't have had the abortion. Great fucks make great babies."

Monica looked at her without speaking.

Goody said, "It would have been an exceptional child."

They drove home in silence. She looked at the licence plates and didn't count numbers; she was done with counting. Progress, snail's progress, but progress all the same.

They parked in silence and walked up the stairs, Goody first, conscious of the jounce in her hips as she climbed. Inside she switched on all the lights and pulled him to the carpet in the living room. He groped for a condom but she pinned his hands and lowered herself on him. She imagined she was Monica and Xavier the Brazilian musician. Xavier held himself inside her and imagined she was Monica and he was himself, fucking her in Brazil or being fucked in Brazil; and Goody looked at him as if she knew exactly what he had been thinking and when he closed his eyes again she punched him in the belly. Look at me, she said. Then she pulled him on top of her and rode him from below, staying him, making him stop and go and stop again. He kissed her and blackness took his vision, the weird oracular half-pictures glimpsed for a second and retained without context or memory. In his blindness he saw the station at Bhooteshwar and the damaged sky above, a sky dripping at the edges like melted wax or a bowl heaped with dead coals and he heard cries like the cries of cats or infants among the bombed-out ruins of their former homes, a charred landscape in which the buildings were façades and nothing moved except shadows under a night sky on fire. He heard the voices of Bombay's lost poets raised in unison and one among them spoke in Marathi and English and listed the names of the railway stations on the Western Line from Churchgate to Bandra. When he came he yelled some words in a language he did not recognise though he knew the words were obscenities, words of one or two syllables that entered his gullet like an obstruction and would not let him breathe until he spat them out; and still she would not stop, she would milk him until he was dry.

The next day a truck arrived in the afternoon and six sweating men carried twenty-eight boxes to the top floor of their building. The living room became a miniature version of the container terminal. When the men left Xavier opened a carton and there in the Delhi barsati was a hint of fall in New York and the smell of the apartment on Central Park West. Any number of forgotten talismans fell to the floor, books, shoes, kitchen utensils, wool socks and hats, button-downs and corduroys. In the pocket of a favourite leather jacket Goody found a receipt from a New York taxi and a small plastic baggie with the top half-torn. She checked for residue but there was none. Had she used the heroin on the same day she'd taken the taxi, 3 March 2003, the date in fading blue print on the cabbie's receipt? And why had she kept the bag and the receipt in her jacket if not as archival documentation? She stood in a narrow alley between the piles of boxes and scrutinised the time on the receipt and the amount paid. She held the bag to her nose and inhaled.

When their life unravelled it did so in a matter of hours. At one moment they were co-dependents with a shared life and past; and then it ended as effectively as if someone had thrown a switch. She came home to find Dharini in a towel, freshly showered and smoking a cigarette. Her hair had frizzed in the heat. Xavier was apologetically pacing.

"I know this is a bit sudden and all," he said. "But Dharini is here in Delhi and she doesn't have a place. I wondered if, you know, she could stay with us for a bit?"

Dharini looked at Goody and blew a little smoke and smiled. It was a frank appraising smile and she smoked inexpertly as if it was a habit she had only recently acquired. She had a round face and Chinese eyes that she accentuated with eyeliner. Goody thought it was the kind of face people stole glances at or stared at openly on public transport, on a crowded street, in a theatre, or a mall.

She said, "Dismas said Newton was missing me. So I emailed to Newton and came. He said you'd not mind. I hope it's okay?"

Goody went to the kitchen and put away the items she'd bought, a box of green tea, half a dozen lemons, a small jar of cognac honey, and Xavier came in and launched into an excited speech. He was in love. He was sorry to have to say so but he was in love with both of them; it could not be helped. The girl was from a South Indian business family and though she was yet to be educated in culture – which a crash reading course would remedy in no time, a course he had already begun to administer – she would be good for him, for both of them. He knew this and he wanted Goody to know it too. If Goody cared for him she would see the truth in everything he had said. Goody tried to calm him down. She suggested they go out to dinner, all three of them.

At the restaurant Xavier ordered a bottle of Chilean red and drank most of it. Alcohol didn't mix with his medication and she expected him to fall silent. Instead he talked and smoked and his hands shook freely. Dharini slouched in her seat, her breasts momentarily deflated and her legs pulled up under her, showing the restaurant her panties, which were white or whitish. High on the wall behind Xavier was a television with an image of, could it be Benny Time? Yes, Time being interviewed by a news channel. He was wearing his prime time smile. Goody decided to say nothing about it to Xavier, who was excitable enough. On an adjoining table was a group of young Indian expats. Goody assumed they were expats because they had New York accents and the men wore gas station shirts and trucker hats. They were arguing about bagels and why it was that H&H was no longer up to the mark. Too chewy, said one, or he might have said it wasn't chewy enough. That's what I'm talking about, he said. Goody couldn't decide whether it was the accent or the pitch of voice that was more annoying. Or it was a combination of both and it grated in Hauz Khaz Village more than in Williamsburg, comparably trendy locations at disparate points on the globe. More was to come. A group of men in hats and narrow ties took the stage near the entrance to the restaurant and launched into reggae. The singer rapped about poverty and world hunger in a dollar-store Jamaican accent. Offstage he reverted to Delhi English. Goody realised that none of the Indians in the room sounded Indian except for Dharini. Xavier, possibly inspired by the faux Jamaicanese, talked in his lecturer's voice about the sons of Noah, Shem, Ham, and Japhet. Dharini said little during dinner except to ask a single question. How had Xavier and Goody met? Xavier didn't reply and Goody only remarked that everybody asked the same question.

Back in the apartment Dharini shut the door to the guest room and joined them in the bedroom. Goody put her charged cell phone in her pocket and said she was going out to buy rolling tobacco and condoms.

"Back immediately if not sooner," she said.

"No need for condoms," said Dharini, gesturing at Xavier who strolled energetically on the terrace and consulted a paperback edition of *Preparations for Death* by Saint Somebody.

It struck Goody that he hadn't slept in at least forty hours.

"You never know," she said.

It was a poor joke. Xavier was manic (uninterested) or depressed (incapable) or, for the briefest of moments, in the blissful state between manic and depressed (insatiable). Goody couldn't remember the last time she'd had any. Well, she could. It had been the night of Monica's dinner, so long ago it felt like another life though it had only been a month. And the sex had been brilliant. And her period was late.

Dharini said, "In Bangalore he left me saying he was going out to buy cigarettes. I hope someone does the same to him."

Goody took care not to bang the door.

On the terrace Xavier was walking at a brisk pace and reading in a singsong voice from the saint's book.

"The grave is the school in which we may see the vanity of earthly goods and in which we may learn the wisdom of the saints," he sang. "'Tell me,' says chocolate saint Chrysostom, 'are you able there to discover who has been a prince, a noble, or a man of learning? For my part, I see nothing but rottenness, worms, and bones. All is but a dream, a shadow.'"

Dharini was reminded of her father. Bhuvapathi and Xavier, two crazy old men and their fixed obsessions. On an impulse she grabbed her bag and followed Goody down the stairs. The street was deserted but for a sleeping watchman in a sentry box. She saw Goody at the far end of the lane and hurried to catch up. What would she say? She didn't know. Maybe she would simply ask to tag along. She had nowhere to go, she was lost in the city. As she hurried toward Goody she saw a car with its headlights off, a big car with a blue beacon on its roof and tinted windows and chintz curtains in the back. Slowly it moved in the heavy moonlight.

What kind of moon was it?

Bright, shaped like a sickle.

She wondered where the car had come from and why it had stopped near Goody. She tried to read its licence plate but it was too dark. The front windows came down and Goody shouted something she couldn't hear. Then a man stepped out of the car and caught her by the arm. Dharini screamed and kept screaming as she ran. The watchman came awake. The driver discovered it was not easy to drag a struggling woman into a car when another woman had come to her assistance. Dharini hit the man in the face and the watchman joined in with a short bamboo stick. The man said, no, no. He raised his arms against the blows. And now Goody too was hitting him – with a rock.

In the moonlight the four figures moved in a Butoh dance of slowness and death. Then one shadow detached from the others and jumped into the front seat of the car and accelerated away, the door on the driver's side banging open in his haste.

4.

She needed to go somewhere calm, a place without testosterone where her dreams would be free of cannibals and saints. After the calamitous events of the night she wished for no further entanglements with the moon and the men, but this was a long-term goal. For now she wished only for quiet.

At night the city belonged to the men. You sensed them out there wild-eyed, sniffing the air with their intoxicated nostrils, using their meaty hands to break and gouge and caress, the men who swaggered out of the cradle and into the fields, drunk and defecating, whose default mode was sudden rage. They were all out there, the fathers and husbands and brothers and uncles, the guardians and feeders, the predator-protectors, the men.

She hugged her knees in the black and yellow taxi. She put her feet up on the seat and took slow breaths and hugged her knees to her chest. Dharini lit and offered a cigarette, which she accepted hungrily. The elderly driver opened a window and she caught a whiff of something, not pollution but a kind of intermittent sewer stink: the city opening its pores and airing out its privates. She puffed and passed to Dharini, who passed back. They shared the cigarette like a joint. Bit by bit she felt her limbs loosen and her fists relax.

If Paro was surprised to see them she did not let it show. She brewed tea in an enamel pot and served it in old china. She advised against filing a complaint at the police station. It would take years to get to court and Goody would not be able to travel in the meanwhile. At the end of it Srivastava would be free, untouched by scandal, and being a well-entrenched political man, he would look for revenge.

"You shouldn't worry," said Paro. "The men of North India are well placed for karmic retribution."

"I have no idea what you're saying but I like the sound of the words."

"What I'm saying, the male–female ratio up here is screwy, seven women to ten men. And it's getting worse by the year in case you haven't noticed."

"They kill girl children out of the womb, Paromita. It's true all over the country."

"Yes but here it's happening sooner rather than later."

"And this is karma going round and coming round? They get what they deserve?"

"Imagine a city, a state, a nation without women, the unrelieved ugliness of it. They'll be stuck with each other, men on men on men. It is exactly what they deserve."

"A society of men without women," said Goody, imagining. "A definition of hell. And the punishment? That the men, the gross men will have to fuck each other and fantasise about women while they're doing it."

"Serve them right," said Dharini, cupping her hands to her mouth to laugh.

Paro made up for them the L-shaped couch in the living room.

It was late, the moon a dull red. The sounds of Nizamuddin washed into the house. The neighbourhood's dogs howled in concert and went silent and there was the tap of the night watchman's staff and the rare splash of traffic.

They settled for the night in borrowed T-shirts and Dharini asked again how Goody and Xavier had met.

"Tell like a bedtime story, but."

Goody shut her eyes and listened to the ceiling fan. The cotton sheet was cool against her skin. If she let her senses shrink to the immediate everything would be fine, but the immediate was a small island surrounded by the infinite.

"In a minute," she said. "Why do people always want to know how other people met? You'll have to wait. I'm dead on my feet. It's late."

"What he must be thinking? Two women leaving him at the same time, must be a first."

"Maybe not. He's had a few lives, is what, been around a long time."

"Longer than you and me combined?"

"He may not even have noticed we left."

"He noticed. I think so he noticed. Is it always too hot in this city?"

"Sometimes too cold. How old are you?"

"Why don't people wear hats in Delhi? Aren't they afraid of sunstroke? Twenty-three next month."

"Is that a marriageable age in this country? Do people pressure you about it?"

"My mother used to pressurise but she is no more."

"I'm sorry."

"She's from Kerala and my father's from north. They met in college. Once she made me meet a boy. You know what he said?"

"How much dowry will you bring?"

"He asked what I cook."

"And you said, I prefer eating out."

"I said, aloo, pyaaz, tamater, bhindi. He said, together or separate? I said, separate. I was lying. Then he said, rotis? I said, of course, rotis."

"Match made in heaven."

"He said, round rotis or like the map of America? He laughed and I laughed. Then I said, I cannot marry you because I have a boyfriend."

"More lies?"

"Lies, only. I'll not let some boy rule my life. That's why I'm pestering about you and Newton. Tell."

"It's been a hard day. First thing in the morning, okay?"

But in the morning there were missed calls and messages on both their phones, messages that were pleading, angry, apologetic, and unapologetic. They compared call records, eleven to Dharini and twenty-eight to Goody. They compared texts. To Dharini he wrote: *Don't u wanna cum to my last party?* And: *Cum on!* And: *Ari! Listen!* To Goody: *M SORRY!* And: *Benny Time in Delhi. Wants 2 fix press conf.* And: *I need u. Nat Gallery party next month.* And: *U pick a fine time 2 leave me Lucille!* Some messages to Goody consisted of one word collapsed into three letters: *PLS!*

Paro's driver took them to Defence Colony. They stopped at a traffic light and a child knocked on the glass. It was a girl of three or four who put out her hand and said, Didi. Dharini asked the driver to roll down the window and she gave the girl a note. Immediately more children appeared. Then a woman limped to the car, her clothes grained with dirt and grease and her mirrored skirt so caked with grime that it reflected nothing. She wore heavy anklets that rested on bandaged ankles and her face was creased like soft old leather and swollen with alcohol and heat. It was impossible to tell how old she was. Dharini gave her a hundred rupees and the puffy red features seemed to register a kind of emotion, distant gratitude or pleasure.

"Give me your blessing," she told the woman, whose lips had opened in a small toothless grin.

The driver powered up the window and put the car in gear. The interiors had filled with dry, pleasant heat.

Dharini said, "Tell. Now you can tell."

Goody said she would have to go back ten years and it was a long story and maybe they didn't have enough time.

Dharini laughed and settled into the upholstery.

"Time is my bitch, no?" she said. "I own it, man."

When Goody finished the car had come to a stop in front of the Defence Colony studio. They stayed inside in the airconditioning, reluctant to step out into the day.

"And that's the story in its entirety," Goody told Dharini. "What do you think?"

"Hottest thing I ever heard," Dharini said.

When they got to the studio the French windows were open and a fine layer of dust had gathered on the desktops and bookshelves. The bed had not been slept in. The shower stall was dry.

There was no sign of Xavier.

BOOK SEVEN

The Book of Chocolate Saints

Saint Maurice

or Moritz, or Moorish, or Mauritius,
upper Egyptian third-century legionary;
canonised early, before the Holy See
reserved the right to the Pope's sole hands;

turned white in early representation;
a thousand years later, painted as he was,
black soldier, black saint; patron of weavers,
swordsmiths, dyers, & infantrymen.

from *The Book of Chocolate Saints: Poems* (Unpublished)

1.

Up close the sunbird was enormous. Distance revealed her frailty: she was the size of his thumb. As long as he paced she stayed on the terrace; if he stopped moving she would flick her wings, ready to fly. She turned up at all hours, unmistakable, in colours only a master would mix – matt olive and jonquil yellow, a bluish sheen around her eyes. Her favourite spot was the terrace wall near the champakali. To begin he asked a simple question. If it is true that nothing will remain of us but the bits that live inside a machine, then is it true that we will never die? Because machines will live for ever, which means we too will always be available to friends and strangers as information on a screen. The bird tickled her breast with her lovely, slender, decurved bill. He heard her call, why-be, why-be? Haw, he said, you're right. The Internet won't always be confined to a screen. It will be everywhere, in the air, in water, grafted into our skins, which means after I die bits of me will be everywhere too, for ever everywhere. The sunbird in her excitement lifted off the wall into a hummingbird variation. Her wings moved at microscopic speed as she vibrated in place and sang a long bell-like note; then she flicked her wings once and dropped into the trees.

The encounter lifted his spirits enough to make him want to go back into the house and see what the women were up to, though even in his craziness he wasn't going to mention that he had been talking business with a sunbird, which, after all, was one of the most common species of bird on the Indian subcontinent. If you're going to hallucinate a bird make it a peacock, a flamingo, a sarus crane, anything but a sunbird in the moonlight.

But when he stepped in from the terrace he sensed that the apartment was empty. They were gone, both of them. Where? Had they left together without telling him? Had they left him together?

The phone in his pocket buzzed.

"X," said Benny Time, bass-heavy music in the background. "What's the haps?"

"I'll be with you in just a minute," he said and searched the bedrooms, both bathrooms, and the back balcony. "Yes."

"What's the haps, my man?"

"Benny, Benny, if the sixties are back I'll have to get my groovy threads out of mothballs. Man."

"A figure of speech. I'm here in your town mixing it up with Bunty and Babloo."

"A most alarming scenario, Benny. Do I know them?"

"No."

"Lion tamers, perhaps, with a side in firearms?"

"Liquor barons, X, promoters of last night's Benny Time event in Delhi. The Lord works in mysterious ways. Listen, why don't you join us? We're at the, one second, where are we?"

Indistinct voices went in and out of hearing.

"Escalate, is the name of the club. In Gurgaon. I hope you're all set for tomorrow? We're planning on meeting early."

"Tomorrow."

"The press conference. Two p.m. sharp. Everybody will be there. I've got a suit for you, grey pinstripe double-breasted for that unassailable authority silhouette."

"I should have thought white linen."

"I'm white linen and most of the talking, you're pinstripe and all of the gravitas. You sit there with a wise look on your face, say a few words about freedom to worship as one sees fit. You're good with the press, right?"

"Even the crow is a blackbird among pigeons."

"See, that's why you make the big bucks. You're good, X, real good."

"The bucks are never big enough, if you really want to know."

"This is a truth universally acknowledged. When tomorrow do we pick you up?"

"When tomorrow," Xavier sang, stepping out into the terrace again. The sunbird was nowhere to be seen.

"Yes?"

"Well, someone told me once that there's no ease in death but I wonder if that's necessarily the point. The unexamined death is not, you know, worth dying and the question is, will you and I and everyone else continue to exist after life as we know it comes to an end? If it is true that the mind lives for seven seconds after the body dies when does death occur? When the body dies or when the mind dies? If my brain is kept alive am I dead? If I am only body and I arrange to have it frozen indefinitely can I be said to be dead? We the living have this in common and only this, we are born to die. Everything else is speculation but speculate we must. These are some of the questions I am examining tonight, all alone, I might add."

"Now look, stop with the death and dying for one evening. Hop into a cab and come down to Escalate, I mean, up to Escalate, this party will go on some."

He ended the call and went to the kitchen on the slim chance that Goody or Dharini, or Goody *and* Dharini were whipping up a late night snack or making cocoa or cleaning the oven or executing some other cheerful chore; but the kitchen was empty. There was no sign of recent habitation other than cups and unwashed dishes in the sink and a cigarette butt on the windowsill.

He resisted the urge to pick up the phone and call her, call Goody, not the other one whose name had slipped his mind for the moment. Had he really said he loved her? His brain was on fire and his body drowned in ecumenical piss. Caught between the two was he, prodigal son of Forgottem. But he would not call; he would not text; he would not be a needy old man. He'd depend on the dictum of the disco philosopher: he would survive. He thought of Benny Time and his doomed mission, to make a suspect church palatable to pagans and enemies. He deserved Time and Time deserved him. He would help save that which could not be saved and then he would secure his own work. He had a party and a birthday show coming up, a show to end all shows, the work of a lifetime assembled under one roof. He would focus and buckle down. But just as quickly as it came the fantasy passed, exited the stage pursued by a heavy bear. On impulse he went into the bedroom and put on his lucky boots. He wasn't flying but he was going to Gurgaon; he needed all the luck he could get.

He would hop into a cab and escalate.

The walk to the market was disorienting because all the way on the main road women beckoned to motorists, lone women motionless under the trees or strolling into side lanes. After sunset Defence Colony changed character, or revealed its true character, and the respectable neighbourhood became a seething cauldron of iniquity. He found a taxi stand at the market and a turbanned cabbie on a charpoy who agreed to take him to the Gurgaon mall where Escalate was located. For most of the way the cabbie drove in silence. As they neared the mall he asked if he should wait in case Xavier wished to return to Delhi. Xavier told him he wasn't sure when he would return and it was better that they parted ways. The driver said Gurgaon wasn't safe to wander around in after dark and possibly not in the daytime either. He suggested that Xavier take his phone number just in case. They passed metro construction and complex diversions around dug-up sections of road and the car slowed to a crawl. They passed stalled or overturned trucks and entered a long stretch of scrub punctuated only by the burnt-out neon of liquor shops. Then came sudden islands of electric light, malls like giant spaceships, the fortified walls of tower blocks, construction sites the size of football fields, all of it surrounded by the heaving dark of rural Haryana. It felt like the Indian future had arrived, dropped from the sky in prefab chunks, but there was an end-of-times feel to it all. The taxi dropped him at the entrance to the mall and he made a note of the driver's name and number.

He passed through a metal detector and took a lift to the top floor. The lift was mirrored and everywhere he looked he saw his used-up face, the lines crooked or smeared, each new angle recalling the unseemliness of the whole. At the club a slight woman in a black suit stamped his wrist with the likeness of a tawaif in regalia. She led him up three floors to a VIP booth above the bandstand where a small group ate dinner. Benny waved him to a seat and a waiter served him oysters on crushed ice.

"This is Bunty," said Benny, introducing him to a cigar-smoker in a Grateful Dead T-shirt and sequinned dinner jacket. "On your left is the beauteous Meeyami and you know John."

"I know John and my nose knows John."

"Mr Xavier, great to see you again. Glad to see your nose has healed, and again, my apologies. What are you drinking?"

Meeyami picked up a dripping bottle of champagne and filled his glass. He lifted it to the dim yellow light cast by the chandeliers and examined the flute's extended stem, the endless happy bubbles lifting to the brim. He took a small sip and his throat constricted with an involuntary spasm, future body knowledge, distress telegraphed from brain to gullet. He took a breath and tried again.

"It's spelt M-I-A-M-I but pronounced Mia Me," the girl said. "Do you like to drink?"

"I do like to drink," he replied. "I must confess I do rather like to drink."

She nodded seriously and touched his glass with hers.

"Meet Casa Dungdung," she said, indicating a woman of the same age as she, somewhere in the lissome mid-twenties, with similar hair, straightened and dyed, wearing a similar strappy dress, so short the hem needed constant adjustment.

Bunty clapped him on the back and said the band would be on in a minute and he'd love them, three guys from Oakland, California. The highlight was the singer back-flipping into the audience.

"The singer is a big white guy, yeah?" said Bunty, talking around his cigar. "Is a sight to see, bru."

A waiter came around with a tray of shots, vodka possibly, presented in a swirl of dry ice. Xavier took two, one for each hand. Benny and Johnny Starr were deep in conversation, their heads together across the table. Benny told him they were planning the press meet for the following day and the three of them needed to have a sit-down at some point.

"Not right now," said Bunty. "Here come the boys from Oakland."

They gathered at the balcony as the lights dimmed. Xavier got up and filled his glass with champagne and found a face he knew, a gallerist from the old days, friend and colleague to Warhol, Basquiat, and Rene Ricard, based now in New Delhi.

"Newton," said Tungsten, "tell these whippersnappers. Haven't I always been a dinge queen? Why else would I live in this hellhole? What do I always say? Give me an Iranian oil wrestler or a Tamilian stud muffin any day of any week!"

"He is and always has been," Xavier told the two young men with Tungsten, "a dinge queen."

"I'd rather have sex with pupae and larvae than fuck a Caucasian."

The band was well into a fast rap over rock power chords. It was their hit anthem. Rise up, get over, throw off the chains of the oppressor, not today or tomorrow but someday. In the Spanish gut-string guitar break the singer made his move and somersaulted into the audience. Instantly the crowd parted; there was nobody to break his fall. Even three floors up Xavier heard the impact.

"Oh fuck," said Bunty.

"Fuck, fuck," someone else said, perhaps it was Babloo, and both men left the room.

Roadies carried the shaken frontman from the floor. The band called an end to the show and hurried from the stage.

"I'm a poet," Casa Dungdung was saying. "I've always been a poet. When other people are talking about this and that, in my head a poem is birthing. Right now for example. They're talking hip-hop and I'm thinking, 'nuclear kiss', or I'm thinking, 'sample this'. I'm doing my make-up and I'm thinking, 'apricot death'. I'm thinking, 'foundation is fugue'. Poetry works in mysterious ways but it begins with verbal anarchy. We cannot legislate the unacknowledged legislators. What do I do? I'm an anaesthetist. Six days a week I'm in the operating theatre doing needlework and in my head my lines are writing themselves. Late at night I'll be home having a drink and staring out the window and I'll note the poetic nature of staring out the window with a drink in my hand and I'll think, I'm a poet, inside and outside I'm a poet. What do you do?"

"I drink," Xavier said, picking up a glass of red wine from a passing tray, though to give credit where it was due this was no glass. This was a goldfish bowl of wine.

"Ha ha," said Casa, "you do. I was being naughty. I know who you are. You're the painter and poet, founder of the Hung Realists. You founded the Bombay School of Experimental Autists with Ara and

Husain. Some call it the School of eX. I loved the motto and adapted it into my own life."

"Oh, did you now?"

"Anarchy and anonymity!"

The party moved downstairs to a table by the bandstand. Casa Dungdung and Mia Me danced the twist and mimed the words, "bully for you, chilly for me, got to get a raincheck on . . . pain", with exaggerated hand gestures. More champagne arrived. Bunty returned to say that the Oakland band had cancelled their India tour because the singer had injured his back. The sponsors were not pleased. Bunty wanted whisky.

"What was white boy thinking?" he said. "This is Delhi, nobody gonna catch you when you fall."

He joined the women on the dance floor.

"Madder music, stronger wine!" Xavier said, obscurely.

"We'll have a police presence tomorrow," Benny Time shouted in Xavier's ear. "They're taking the threats seriously."

"Do they know who's making them?"

"They don't. Landline calls to newspapers and television channels. Cleverly effective, don't you think?"

Xavier took a mouthful of wine and felt the bass in his prostate, a juddered vibration slightly slower than his pulse rate. For the first time in days he felt contained in his skin, solid and comfortable.

I have been faithful to thee, Goody, in my fashion.

"Listen, I wanted to say you don't have to do this. I do appreciate it but things are different now that there's a possibility of violence. I'm saying I'll understand if you opt out," said Benny.

Xavier felt for his phone and sent a text: *M SORRY*.

He said, "We're in it together, Benn, old boy. I'm going to help you navigate the merry puddle and you're going to help me throw the party to end all parties for the Delhi opening of *66*."

The DJ played a remix of 'Choli ke Peeche'. Bunty and Mia Me performed a series of chesty Bollywood moves. Casa Dungdung was dancing with herself and Xavier picked up his refilled bowl of wine and joined her. He held the glass carefully but a spray of red appeared on his white shirtfront.

He woke on a bed, possibly a bed in a hotel room, fully dressed except for his boots, which were nowhere to be found, not under the bed, not in the closet, not in the bathroom, not in the hallway outside. He could not find his boots but in his trouser pockets he found a dangly silver earring and a butter cookie. He remembered some things from the night before, dancing, taking a lift with people he didn't know, texting someone, Goody probably, and the clearest memory of all, he was dancing in darkness and when he looked up there was the night sky and all its stars. He was on a rooftop designed to resemble a dance floor and someone passed him a joint. He remembered all this but he could not remember getting to the hotel. He could not remember losing his boots. The room was low-end business, meaning it was bare of everything including the essentials. There was no water in the minibar, much less a cold beer or miniature vodka. There was no phone and of course there was no room service. He went into the bathroom and splashed water on his face and went back to bed. He dreamed of his old friend, Dom Moraes. They were sitting in the Casbah, a beloved Bandra dive. You don't understand, his friend kept saying. I'm not dead at all. I'm like jazz, I smell funny but I'm still here. You're dead, Xavier said, I was at your funeral. I'm here, said Dom, and I'm thirsty. There was a banging on the door. Don't wake up, Dom said, we have a lot to talk about.

It was Benny Time with a pinstriped suit on a hanger, as he'd promised. He waited in the lobby while Xavier showered and dressed and came downstairs barefoot. They stopped at the hotel restaurant for breakfast, or it might have been lunch, and Xavier chased the ache from his eyes with a glass of beer. His head felt porous with light, his vision soft around the edges, cataract squiggles floating out of sight. He had stopped taking his medication, perhaps these were the side effects? If so, he was all for it. More porousness! The waiter brought the bill and he had an idea, a solution to his immediate problem. Let me buy your slippers, he said. The boy hesitated for a minute, then shyly took off his worn rubber slippers and presented them to Xavier. He refused to take money in return.

When they got to the hotel where the press conference was to be held there was an unexpectedly large police contingent and in a matter of minutes Time was surrounded. There was security everywhere and television crews roamed the lobby. It was only when a young man approached Xavier for a statement that he learned what had happened: Johnny Starr abducted by persons unknown. Benny Time returned, distraught, and took him to a corner. The press conference would be rescheduled to give them time to formulate a response, but what response?

"John was taken from the street," said Time. "Full daylight, picked up by three men and shoved into an SUV. The hotel guard says he saw it happen but didn't do anything because this is Gurgaon. Shoot-outs on main street are standard. Three men bundling someone into a car is just guys having fun. Jesus! The tour can't go on without him. How did they know?"

The crowd in the conference room was immense. Xavier had to take off his suit coat and roll up his sleeves. The dancing girl stamp on his inner wrist had smeared in the humidity and the waiter's rubber slippers felt like a blessing. A reporter asked if someone had taken responsibility for Starr's abduction. Another asked whether it was right-wing Hindus or Muslims. A policeman sent to monitor the conference said nothing had been ruled out. Then a print reporter stood up and asked Xavier for a comment.

"I'm here as a friend to the Church of Time and I'll keep my comments brief," he said. The reporters leaned forward as one, the better to hear him. "Johnny Starr is an American citizen. As we know, the Americans do not forgive the taking of their citizens as hostages. I, on the other hand, I am free and unaffiliated except to God and Time. Whoever you are, Hindu Muslim Buddhist Christian, perhaps we should talk."

"You're offering yourself in exchange for Mr Starr?" someone asked.

"Not necessarily."

His phone started to buzz as the conference ended: Goody, calling from the real world. Her voice would be grounded and reassuring, perhaps offering reconciliation. He dismissed the call and the phone rang again, an unknown number, and he fantasised briefly about dropping the device into the bin under the desk. Start with the umbilical cord of the cell phone, then sever other workaday ties to the world, eliminate all urgency and busyness, leave only unvexed thought and the promise of serenity.

But he was hurried into the street by Benny Time, who had acquired a companion, a policeman in a safari suit.

"I can't let you do it," Benny said. "You didn't sign up for this. I appreciate it, I do, but we're in outer space now. All bets are off. According to my friend here it's either a Hindu or Islamic faction."

"And they picked Johnny because he is the singing voice and he was easier to get than you."

"He's closer to me than anyone."

"Welcome to the future, Benny, a world where it's impossible to tell the conservatives from the radicals."

"Anyway you're off the hook. Thank you but I can't expect you to put yourself at risk. If anyone should take responsibility for this it's me."

Xavier's phone buzzed and he touched the accept button.

"Hello."

"Sir, NDTV this side, I am calling to—"

He cut the call and considered the phone as it buzzed again. Goody. His throat and nose felt scratchy and his head was loose on the pivot of his neck, as if he was coming down with something. The timing could not be worse.

"I say, could you drive me to the hotel at all? I think I need a bit of a lie-down."

"X, the conference is done, you can go home now. I don't know what comes next. You should go home."

But he got off near the airport turn-off. It took him some time to locate the restaurant he had had breakfast in, which was the only way he knew to find the hotel. There was a theka next door and he picked up a nip bottle of gin and two beers, which he took to his room. He saw a pad and pencil on the night table and understood that the sensation he had been experiencing all day, as if he was coming down with something, was not a prelude to illness at all. He was on the verge of a poem and he had forgotten the feeling – the fullness in the chest, the headiness. He took the cap off the bottle of gin and drank some and poured himself some beer in a water glass. He took up the pen and pad and began to write. The lines came fast and soon he had a workable first draft. After a while he made a clean copy from several sheets of crossed-out and corrected lines. He titled it 'For Dis', set it aside and began another, and another, working deep into the evening, by which time the alcohol was gone. He stretched out on the unmade bed for a quick nap and when he woke it was morning. There were sixteen missed calls on his phone, most from Goody, some from Dharini, and the remainder, he assumed, from journalists. In the bathroom mirror he saw a startled man in a stained once-white shirt. He washed his face and used the hotel toothbrush and went to the lobby. He had an idea that he might buy a shirt and a pair of shoes. He missed his lucky boots. He was standing in the lobby blinking at the light when the waiter who had given him the slippers appeared by his side. He said, are you okay, sir? One minute, Xavier replied. His pocket was buzzing. Without looking at the caller, he clicked off the phone and handed it to the boy. It's yours, he said in Hindi. Change the sim card and you won't be bothered by calls. Then he shook hands with the frightened waiter and stepped unsteadily into the street.

Warily he examined the day. Next to the airport flyover, the street consisted entirely of vertical signs for hotels, bars, and spas. Some of the neon signage was lit though it was not yet noon. He stopped at Hotel Waves and ate a paratha, chewing it slowly, unaccustomed to the taste of food. The only other diners were a couple at a table near the door. The woman's nails were too long to push the buttons on her handset. Tenderly she patted the phone and held it to the man's ear. He spat a bit of meat or bone into his plate and laughed. Correct, he said, correct! Xavier called for the bill. Outside, the midday sun was a curse on his head. A blue bus went past at speed and a small dog moved out of the way just in time. He passed a bar that had just opened and went in and ordered a brandy and club soda. The waiter lent him a pen and he took out the poems he had been working on the night before and smoothed the pages on the table. He started to make corrections to the second poem, 'Saint Augustine', and the third, 'Saint Nicholas', and made notes for two others and wrote a list of words and phrases in the right-hand margin – meek, mean, meat, nitid, itch, madden, midden, peace, pearl, buzz, froth, egg, scream, spin out knee-deep in death & egesta, rat chat, snake hissance, lizard fizz, bug thrum, beast din, fetid, feed, grot hilde, grimm the reaper, sore, soar, petal, laughter, water, word, world – for future rhymes, half-rhymes, and supra-rhymes. He watched his hand move into a steady independent system and when he finished the brandy he clapped his hands for the waiter who was watching cricket. This was what Indians did in a room with a television: they found a cricket match because somebody somewhere was always throwing a bat against a ball. He held up the empty glass and waited for the man to bring him another. He drank brandy and soda and found the correct arrangement of words on the page, a heroic activity at any time but especially in the middle of the afternoon in the last bar on the last street in the last city of the world. He finished the poem and began another. He drank and wrote and in time the sun's bald glare receded and he put down the pen and looked at his hands.

What do I do now?

He was wearing the same shirt from the day before, from days before. He would try to call Benny Time. He walked against the traffic on the narrow street of bars and spas but could not find his hotel. The sun beat its old curse on his head. He stepped off the broken pavement to look up at the building signs and see if he could recognise the hotel's name. He stepped off the pavement and heard a man shout and turned in time to see a cycle rickshaw swerve. Its back wheel rode over his foot. The pain was not unbearable; it didn't feel like any bones had been broken. The rickshaw-wallah gave him a look and didn't stop, as if it was his fault, which it was. His foot throbbed. A bruise was already forming and he wished for his boots. Where had he left them, he wondered, and who was wearing them now? He limped a few paces and looked for somewhere to sit. He couldn't find the hotel; he had misplaced it and he would never find it again. He felt a pain in his side and stepped into the first establishment he saw, a workingman's bar where the customers bought nip bottles and plastic sachets of water and drank standing up, the floor covered in litter of all kinds. He took a bottle of extra strong beer and drank it leaning against the wall and a man spoke to him in words he could not understand. Inanity, he thought, thy name is human speech.

I am for the birds.

To be run over by a cycle rickshaw, the most antiquated mode of transport in this antiquated land, not even an autorickshaw or a halfway-decent car. A cycle rickshaw, inanity and insanity, onward and onward. His foot throbbed and the pain in his side was no longer localised.

He was falling into himself, through madness and folly into himself. He was becoming light at last, sheer as a sheet of glass, each inflamed nerve visible from afar. He was invisible and his mind was invincible. The vulnerability of the body did not matter because he had fallen finally into happiness; and still holding the bottle of beer he walked out of the bar, grunting with effort like an old man. It reminded him of his father. He grunted like Frank but he was mad as Beryl. For no reason at all he remembered Dimple the pipe-maker, the model for a painting he had not offered for sale. He numbered in his head the pictures of Goody he would not sell. Goody nude, dressed, supine, floating. And what was it all worth in the end? More than money, less than time.

Behold, he putteth no trust in his Saints and his Angels he chargeth with folly.

The pain or ache in his side had spread to his arm and there was a circle of pain tightening around his chest. He wondered if he was having a stroke. He limped into a storefront with frilly window curtains. Such an odd word, stroke, such a tender word for so brutal an event. There was a woman at a counter and three chairs against the wall and the mentholated scent of eucalyptus oil. Hello Kitty waved from a table. He heard Chinese flute music and sat heavily on a chair and the woman asked him what kind of massage he wanted. He said something in reply but she didn't hear him.

"Excuse me?"

"Boredom is best."

He settled his shoulders against the wall to ease the tightness and the woman spoke again. When he did not reply she came around and examined his eyes, which were open. She slapped him lightly on the cheek, once, then again, and then she rang a bell. She pried loose the bottle gripped in his hand and locked the door of the shop. When the boy appeared, she told him to help her carry the man to the alley in the back. They dragged and carried the body out of the room and then the madam returned to the parlour and quickly unlocked the front door and went behind the counter to wait for custom. In the alley lined with air-conditioning units, the boy checked the man's pockets. He took what cash there was and he took the driver's licence and credit card. There was no phone; instead he found some pages of hotel stationery covered in cramped English writing. He let the pages fall into the alley's shallow puddles where they lay undisturbed, the words still legible in the fading light.

2.

You become a repository for voices you don't recognise. A jingle or aphorism that does not give up its meaning, a country-western whippoorwill too blue to fly, lucid gossip heard at a party, your father commanding No, something someone said about refinement and cruelty and the Taj Mahal; you become shortwave messages bounced back from the ionosphere.

Dismas was promoting *The Loathed*. He travelled, gave readings, signed books. And he read from the opening, a long paragraph about Xavier:

> America, which has no history or too brief a one, and India, which swallows history and spits it out whole, are the two poles of this tale, and if you're asking me to tell you my side of it, I'm going to have to go back a bit, to NYC, because that's where I first met him, when he tried to send me on a murder quest, tried to make a detective out of me, and he gave me a nickname, the Bombayman, because he said only Bombaymen felt obliged to put the city down. I'd brought along some poems as an introduction. He said he liked them, because at least I was conscious of the sullen craft, which was more than could be said for most Indian poets, who seem to think all you need are feelings, who seem to forget that everybody in the world has feelings and the purpose of poetry is, and I quote, to get away from your fucking feelings. He said my poems were hindered by my conception of myself, which is a hell of a thing to tell a twenty-five-year-old. But I wasn't the only one, all of us were, we Bombay poets, hindered by the self-destructive incendiary poet's mythology we carried like badges of honour, like armour against the workaday world. I added a personal ingredient to the mix, my inescapable place as outcaste, outside caste, the

affiliation that annihilated everything, my foreign education, my ambitions for myself as a writer and journalist, my hopes of raising a family untainted by a caste name – the reason I had changed mine to Bambai. I knew he was right. I was hindered by my own image and so I found it in myself to betray him, and here I must take a deep breath and say, Goody, as in the proper noun, Goody Laugh out Loud, Goody Lollipop, and I must say that in my guilt I attempted to reconstruct his history for the kind of biography I would never write, such false remorse directed at my friend, the poet and painter Newton Xavier, the consonant X, my doppelganger and hypocrite twin, X and I, another set of poles around which this story revolves, all this happening in the west of course, and that loaded phrase 'in the west', which, when I hear it, isn't a locational indicator for me, I don't hear it in terms of geography, it's not a place name but placement, anthropology, an attempt at classification, a social science reference, all the categories of inside and outside you think of when you hear the word the way Xavier said it, Amurka, the stunned vowel first and last, a interrupted by murk, not abecedarian but aeolian, as said by the harshest consonant, X, who, once upon a time in the west, said, "Bombayman, your tragedy is you are the king of the jungle and you don't know it. The beast of the east eats the best of the west. Welcome to Amurka slash Amurkaka." He said it in an Indian accent: "The best of the vest." He made an aphorism out of it, a jingle. We were in Chelsea somewhere, and he was drinking black coffee and vodka out of a red and green Christmas cup, it being the holiday season. He mocked the idea of a coffee chain named after a whaling saint but he drank the coffee, his glasses cloudy, and he kept nodding although I hadn't said a thing. He asked about my visa and I told him I'd have to leave the country soon because it was about to expire. He said that was no reason to leave a place. He said I wasn't a book borrowed from a library, though that was our fate in the end, to be books, borrowed or forgotten, and if we were lucky we would find ourselves on a shelf leaning against a friend. He said I should get myself an O-1, the extraordinary alien's green-to-go card, speaking in the whisky-and-cigars voice he had earned, and when I think of him now, if I think of him at all, I remember him as a ghost, a once-friendly ghost I'm trying to raise.

The day after the Agra launch he was in one of the city's few coffee shops when a picture of Xavier flashed on the television above the cash register. The sound was turned off and his first instinct was to turn away, as if by looking elsewhere he could change or delay the news. He brushed bagel crumbs off his shirt. He asked the waiter for iced water. Then he turned back to the screen and read the words scrolled across the bottom, X'IAN PAINTER NEWTON XAVIER DISAPPEARED, FEARED DEAD. They had summed up his life in three bullets.

- Don Newton Pinter Xavier, painter and poet, disappears.
- Co-founder of Hung Realists. Co-founder of Autists Group that included Husain, Souza, Padamsee, Mehta, and Ara.
- Posthumous retrospective opens in New Delhi next month. National Gallery calls it 'most important museum show of the century'.

Disappeared, feared dead. It had the ring of an epitaph. Delhi wasn't far from Agra. This was the time to go to Goody and pay his respects. He would make his case and hint gently at X's fecklessness. But the man's disappearance had robbed him of something, some closing push and necessary drama. Even in absence Xavier was the better thief, thought Dismas, as he finished his breakfast.

To skip his own party, what an instinct for showmanship!

He asked the counterman to turn up the volume. The news about Xavier had been usurped by an interview with a French music producer who had first arrived in India as a hippie in 1973. He had lost or given away his passport and had stayed on in the country for years. Dismas listened with some suspicion. The man spoke in English and there were Hindi subtitles, but the subtitles did not match the words. Soon after he arrived in India, the producer said, his guru introduced him to a woman from Kerala. Go with her to the mountains, the guru said, she will be your guide. But the subtitles said it was the Frenchman and the guru who walked to the Himalayas. There was no mention of the woman. The producer said that he and the woman walked from Kerala, through Karnataka, Maharashtra, Madhya Pradesh, Uttar Pradesh, and Nepal, thinking it would take a month or two, maybe three months at the most, but they walked for a year and more. They made a strange couple, a white man in a dhoti, his long hair twisted into a bun, and a matronly South Indian woman with a nose ring and sari. People teased them. They sang Hindi film songs, 'Mera Naam Joker' and 'Awaara'. It didn't bother me because I didn't understand Hindi in those days, said the Frenchman, in English. It bothered her. The subtitles said: *We had many wonderful adventures! Indians are very hospitable! They invited us into their homes and fed us with their own two hands!* A year and three months after they began the journey they came to a forest in the foothills. At first the woman was frightened because there was no village nearby, no electricity, no humans for miles. She would cry when I went to fetch water from the river, said the Frenchman. Don't go, she'd say, don't leave me alone. Now there were no subtitles at all: the translation had stopped altogether. After a few months in the forest the Frenchman left the woman and returned to the city. He found a job and got married. He forgot his life of wandering. He bought a house and became a father to two daughters, a man of the world, a businessman and householder, but he never forgot the journey to the north with the woman from the south. Some years later he returned to the spot in the forest where he had left her. She was now in her fifties and she welcomed him as if he had left only a moment ago, as if he had set off that morning to fetch firewood. She made milk tea for him. She put out a bowl and cried, mongoo, mongoo, and a mongoose family gathered and sipped the tea. Birds ate from her hand, a deer visited, and a snake. People came too and some of them said she was the first female hermit of India. But I think of her as a saint, said the Frenchman. Now the subtitles reappeared. *Indians are saints!* Dismas changed the channel hoping for a music station that with any luck would be screening the new Rihanna video. There was an update about Xavier on Channel Zee and another on Doordarshan. An unnamed friend to the artist had suggested that his disappearance was in fact a suicide.

Later that day among the sand-coloured rooms of Fatehpur Sikri, Dismas heard the echoing voice of a pair of drunks. They glared at a group of Muslim travellers from the hinterland who threw coins on the empty crypt where the bodies of the prince and his lover had been buried. Sab Mussalman hai, the drunks told each other. Sab, Mussalman. They were guides, resting up between spiels aimed at the foreign tourists. They didn't care about the locals and they cared nothing for Mussalmans. They treated the crypt like an echo chamber into which they flung their voices. The louder of the two shouted Om at two-second intervals. In the mausoleum the sound fell like a projectile.

Dismas walked around and fell into melancholy. He bought a thumb-sized replica of the Taj Mahal and an illustrated history of Fatehpur Sikri and he listened to the fictions of the tour guides.

"This flower was made hundreds of years ago, please touch it, you see? It is alive!"

"This is the dovecote from where pigeons carried messages to the generals and brought back news of the battle for Akbar. This one was the dovecote of the most prized pigeon of them all, Akbar's favourite, the Hindu pigeon Birbal."

"Here is the entrance to a secret tunnel built by Akbar to connect Fatehpur Sikri to Delhi, Lahore, Kabul, and Peking. If you stand here you can see exactly where it was blocked up by the British."

From Agra Fort facing east he caught a view of the Taj through the fort's jaliwork. He saw a slice of silvered river and blue sky, and the dome and its minarets rising into filigree. He took a picture through the jaliwork and zoomed in to the top of the main dome and that was when he saw it. The culmination of the dome was a bronze spire and at the very tip was a sickle moon, its horns pointing upward to God. But the Muslim moon had been placed so that a lotus shape bisected its centre, Shiva's trident. You needed a telephoto lens to see the Hindu trident at the pinnacle of the Taj Mahal.

At the entrance to the mausoleum he paid a fee and took off his new red leather wingtips and left them, reluctantly, on a pile of discarded footwear. He climbed the marble stairs in his socks. From a parapet he saw a vista of river and scrub dust and he examined the great dome. The marble had recently been whitened and to see it up close was to see that time had worked very little damage on the stone. The colours of the jasper inlay jumped out at you as if they'd just been set. No two inlays were alike. The dome itself was so white it was without feature but the eye took it in small sacramental sips, the frozen teardrop that marked the deaths of so many. Nearby, a mason squatted on scaffolding and repaired slabs of black stone that had fallen from the siding around the marble. He cut each stone, working the rough edges straight. His name was Abdul Wahid, he said, and before taking up the job of repair at the Taj he'd been working for three months in Delhi on the Q'utb Minar. Was Dismas from Delhi too? What was his country? His name?

Then, suddenly intimate, he asked, "Are you Muslim?"

Dismas made his standard reply. He was from Bombay.

"Ah," said the mason, as if this explained his foreignness, his friendliness, and his interest. Dismas might have said he was from Pluto.

"The spire on top of the main dome, isn't it Hindu?"

"What?"

"Doesn't it look like a trident?"

"Many men made this thing."

"Many men over many years."

"They were brought from everywhere," said Abdul Wahid. "They worked hard."

"Many did not survive."

"It depends from which direction you are looking, depending on your position it is Hindu or it is Muslim."

The Taj Mahal is refinement and cruelty, X had said. Only the Mughals could have built it.

Pinter. Not Francis but Pinter. Had the TV station unearthed his birth certificate? How had they discovered the name?

On his way out Dismas was relieved to find his new shoes unstolen under a pile of second-rate footwear. He let the crowd carry him out of the Taj. Now he was in a hurry to leave for Delhi. At the hotel he packed and made quick arrangements at the reception desk. Dusk was falling as the taxi left the hotel and followed the course of the Beas from Manali down to the plains. The river was to his left, a silver thread banked by high crags where palm trees sprouted at impossible angles. What tide had brought the trees? How had they survived in this climate? Late at night as the taxi neared the city the river's silver faded to a dull trickle and disappeared into the filth of the Yamuna. They entered a wall of sound and particulate matter. And soon, the early part of the journey, the river, the displaced palms, his anxiety, all seemed false, like memories of a city he had never visited.

3.

The maid called him to the phone. It was Dhruv, the teenage son of his Delhi hosts.

"Listen, Uncle Dismas," he said. "You better get down here right away."

"I don't think so, Delhi in June, it's brutal out there."

"I'm in a gallery at the mall in Saket. Art gallery. There's a exhibition here and you're in it. You knew Xavier, huh, the artist? That's awesome."

The gallery was full of media, women in saris and men in suits, and outside it was forty-five degrees. Dhruv was in the front room where the show's title was projected on a wall:

Ties & Binds
Photographs, Sketches, Fragments, 1992–2006
GOODY LOL

Dhruv motioned to a picture captioned, 'Dismas, 2002, New York City'.

"Goody Lol," he said. "Sick."

"Is she here?"

"Not in person. There's a video interview on permanent loop. Can I talk to you sometime about Xavier? I write about art for the *Noida Tribune*."

"Impressive," said Dismas, in a tone that implied the opposite.

"How come you missed the funeral?"

"Funeral? He disappeared."

"They found him. Someone recognised him from the news."

"What was the cause of death?"

"Heart attack. There were six people in total at the funeral. I hear he had more enemies than friends."

"Goody?"

"She was there, couldn't miss her. So, how did you meet him?"

"Called him up."

"You can do that? And then?"

"And then I went to meet him and met Goody."

"You did, you surely did."

Dismas looked at the image, his tied hands behind his back, shirtlessly leaning against the reflected lights of the city; and he felt no connection to the man in the picture.

"I want to hear all about it, how you met him, what he said."

"Buy *The Book of Chocolate Saints*, my next book, an oral biography of Xavier. It's all in there."

"I hear he staged his death like performance art."

"I wouldn't know. Why don't you talk to Goody?"

"She doesn't, yo. Talk, I mean. No photographs, no autographs. Check the video and you'll see what I'm saying."

The photographs were studies of solitude and sexual frustration, frail bodies stretched against walls and curled on the floor, dwarfed by the tiny spaces in which they were placed. The photographer's gift was to make even a small area seem large and forbidding. A young Sikh on his knees in a doorway, white light streaming into the room, hair loose and body twisted, his hands bound by a length of crisp black cotton. The light in the photograph was concentrated on the man's oxblood kurta and the black fabric on his wrists. The caption: 'Amrik, Albany, 2003'. A woman sitting on a rock, her head bent in such a way that you saw only back and hips. The grainy black and white gave her skin the same texture as the rock, as if the entire assemblage had been carved out of one element, even the elaborate ties and knots that ran from her throat to her groin. It was captioned, 'June, Central Park, 2002', and he recognised the woman as the waitress in the Fourteenth Street diner where he and Goody had once had coffee. There was a picture of the same woman on an unmade bed, her knees drawn up to her chin. She had stuck her tongue out at the camera and thick kajal smeared her face like fright make-up. A double strand of hemp was looped twice around her eyes. The camera's focus was so acute that you saw the exact status of the peeling paint on the walls, the aged light fixtures, a wire snaking its way across faded bed sheets. The room was standard American motel, dull furnishings and generic fixtures: 'June, New Jersey, 2002'. He had met Amrik and June in life but in Goody's hands they were rendered unrecognisable. They had been snatched from time and flash-frozen, made anguished and monumental.

The bulk of the exhibition, titled 'Equality', was a group of portraits of bound men; men in elaborate silk sherwanis and churidars suspended from ceiling rigs like human chandeliers; working-class men in uniform, in overalls, in underwear, tied to bathroom fixtures and doorknobs and heavy furniture; men in business suits divested of trousers and hogtied; men in suits, tied up and supine on the broken pavements of an old city; men roughly tied up and hanging by one leg from the ceiling, the rope-work coarse and rushed; and in one enormous portrait, two dozen paunchy men in white Y-fronts, tied to each other by the elbows and made to stand against a concrete wall, glaring suspiciously at the camera.

How had she managed to convince so many to submit to her lens? He knew the answer because he too had been her subject. She had put them in poses calculated to humiliate but all they had seen was a woman photographer and a camera. Their egos had filled in the rest.

The work from 2004 and 2005 was on two walls, one for each year, portraits of Xavier taken indoors and out in all kinds of light. And a curious thing, as the eye followed the portraits to a wall left entirely blank, a story took shape: X leaving his life one frame at a time. There were two portraits of Goody in costume and playing dead. The titles were in Xavier's hand but he had signed her name. And there were line drawings, damning self-portraits in which she made herself appear misshapen. You could see the speed with which she'd done them and there was something of Xavier in the confidence and off-handedness of the line.

He went to the video screen. A rotund young man waited on a narrow pavement in a residential Delhi neighbourhood. She stepped into the frame and pulled a dupatta around her head like a veil. When she saw the interviewer she stopped short and shook her head.

"I don't want to talk to you," said Goody.

The man said, "Please, madam, just two questions."

"Don't beg, it's not worth it."

"Madam, how has life changed after the tragic sudden death of one of India's greatest artistes?"

"Artist, not artiste," Goody said automatically, walking away.

The interviewer followed.

"Alleged suicide or alleged murder? A great mystery surrounds."

There was no reply. The interviewer hurried behind her and the camera followed.

"What about the controversy regarding authorship of his last works? Some are made by you?"

"That's a laughable allegation."

"Is the photography project ongoing? Critics have said it is controversial but original."

"There's nothing original about it. It's not originality I'm aiming for but documentation and anonymity."

Cut to the interviewer on a narrow pavement in a residential neighbourhood. Goody steps into the frame and the conversation repeats itself.

The monkeys roamed in marauding packs, their ponderous heat-scarred bodies bleached in the desert sun. How did people manage? The city wasn't fit for habitation. He was living with family friends in Safdarjung and most of the time he stayed indoors under a fan, sweating, looking out over the rooftops of the city. He saw bedraggled crows, dust storms, fever visions of parched langurs. He reduced movement to a consolidated minimum: no action unless absolutely required and only when combined with other action.

He put it off for a day, for two days, but then he gave in and took a taxi to the Defence Colony address he had noted in the video.

A familiar face answered the door.

"I know you," said Amrik.

"I know you too. Aren't you a long way from home?"

"Home? Maybe, maybe not," he laughed. "My first time in India. I have family here I've never met."

"In Delhi?"

"Delhi and points north."

"And how's it going so far?"

"Nice to be in a place where skin colour isn't the first thing people notice about you. I'm looking forward to growing my hair and relearning how to tie a turban."

"Look, I didn't mean to turn up out of the blue."

"No apology required. I'll tell her you're here."

But she was already there, holding the door wide and motioning him inside. He followed her into a room that had the unmistakable feel of the Central Park West apartment. Stacked in deep rows against the walls and corridors and every available surface were numbered packages, canvases and photographs and indeterminate objects. She had put on some weight, which had changed the shape of her face, and her hair had turned white. She looked very frail.

"You," said Dharini, who was on the couch.

"It's me, it's me. Hello, hello," said Dismas, unable to stop repeating himself.

Goody said, "The retrospective opens on schedule. Amrik brought down most of the New York work. He'll be sourcing New's Indian work and liaising with the National Gallery. Benny Time is in charge of the opening party. I hear he has big plans. Come if you can."

Her accent was newly Indian, all trace of London obliterated. She lit a cigarette and this was another bit of newness. As far as Dismas knew she'd never been a smoker.

He said, "How are you holding up?"

"I don't know. I don't know."

They went to the terrace where cane chairs had been arranged under a bamboo awning. The sun was starting to set and a sliver of moon was already visible. Then Goody told her story, slowly in the new accent.

"He was like Superman on kryptonite, hated what the pills did but without them he was out of control. Mania or monotony, nothing in between. Made jokes about doing himself in, throwing a week-long bash at the best hotel in the city and no worry about expenses because he wouldn't be paying the bill. He'd send everybody home and take himself home too. I asked who would clean up the mess and he said, you, who else? In that way he's completely conventional, expects a woman to take care of everything. Well, I did, I took care of everything. I've done my job and now I'm through. I'm not insane enough to be an artist above all else. I'm not cruel enough. I'm not New."

"What happened to the man who was abducted?"

"A conservative Pentecostal group called God's Blood. They released him on a street in Fort Kochi but only after carving a swastika on his forehead."

"Conservative Pentecostals?"

"Holy war is contagious and everybody wants in. The future is holiness. We'll all be saints, to quote New."

She lit another cigarette, cupping a red and white lighter that he recognised before he saw the word 'Kuwait'. She took a deep drag and exhaled and considered the smoke. Then she stubbed it out.

She said, "I shouldn't be smoking, I'm pregnant."

Silence for a beat and then: "He left something for you."

Her bare feet made no sound at all as she went into the apartment.

Dharini caught his eye.

"Answer your question? She's not okay. She says she's sick of art. I think she's not handling it so well, the pregnancy."

Dismas shook his head. Pregnancy was an insurmountable word, moated and garrisoned. What could you say in response?

He looked at the crowded walls and the books and furniture that had filled the last of the many rooms of Xavier's life. He made a note in his head of the pencil drawings on the walls, self-portraits, X as satyr, as Aztec priest bathed in blood, as half-dog half-angel with mournful eyes.

Goody returned with an office envelope on which she had written Dismas's name in a neat cramped hand.

Goody said, "It's not the fact of not having him around to talk to that bothers me. I'm perfectly capable of carrying on a one-sided conversation, indefinitely if need be. What bothers is that nothing you say makes a difference."

"What do you say when you talk to him?"

"We could have found a way, changed medication, changed towns, changed our names. We could have started over."

It was then that Dismas said what he had come to say and even as he offered himself as a replacement, or a substitute, he knew the futility of his suit. Goody went to Dharini's side. The women looked at each other in silence. Amrik had stepped quietly out of the room.

Goody said, "I understand something about you that I hadn't understood before." She turned to face him. "You're a critic. There's no worse thing that can be said about a man. When your book appeared a journalist called him for a response. That's how he heard the things you said about him, self-promoter, self-plagiarist, and so on. And the made-up controversy about Moraes and Kolatkar and Ezekiel: not a shred of evidence, hearsay held up as truth, but so many people took it seriously. He knew why you did it. Murder sells books. He said you were your own enemy and he forgave you. Who knows, in time I might too."

The cabbie had his radio tuned to Punjabi rap. He drove with one hand. With the other he tore open a shiny packet with his teeth and emptied the contents into his mouth. The sick-sweet smell of chewing tobacco, paraffin, paan, and lime filled the car. He was about to ask the cabbie to turn down the volume when he saw in the rearview that the man's eyes were half shut. Maybe he needed the music to stay awake. The colony's main gates were closed and they had to turn around and go back the way they came. Dismas looked out at the leafy streets cramped with parked cars.

What was there to forgive? He had embellished a little and created a controversy out of coincidence. Compared to Xavier's crimes his own were insignificant. She would forgive X but not him.

When you've been driving for eighteen hours you'll take whatever you can get to keep yourself going, the driver said, including this gutka that will give me mouth cancer.

Why opt for eighteen-hour shifts, then, work eight-hour days like normal people, Dismas said.

Saheb, said the driver, I am a poor man with a rich man's bills.

Pregnancy, a word that existed on its own, that could not be argued or negotiated with, a word that would not settle for less than everything.

What can I possibly say in reply?

The driver turned up the volume on the radio but it didn't drown out the sound of traffic because now they were on a flyover on the ring road and hedged in by vehicles.

What was there to forgive? How unforgiveable a crime was embellishment? Was it more of a crime than forgery or cruelty?

I too am a poor man with a rich man's bills.

As the cabbie turned into Safdarjung, he opened the envelope and shook out a water-stained page. The words were smeared but legible.

To Dis; or, Assertion of Provenance

Dawg, just so you know, I didn't need the money.
I lied, but bad X was running the show, stab-
Stabbing for revenge. Well, good X forgives you,

Betrayer, though even he does not do it easily.
O, Bambai, you are better than you know.
May your base instinct expel itself like bad
Blood and may you rise to shame, as I am un-
Able to do; I sink daily, deeper into bad mud,
Yea, verily I sink. Even so, I certify the Two
Marys, signed *Xavier 96*, are comparatively
Authentic, painted by the writer of this poeme,
Newton, for Dis, retrospective acrostic dedicatee.

If the posthumous jump in the price of Xavier's work was any indication, one day the handwritten poem might be worth a lot of money. There was no doubt that the National Gallery show would be a success, critically and commercially, and there was no doubt that the value of the Two Marys would rise tenfold.

He could feel it coming, a groundswell and detonation point in the Xavier bazaar. Not that he had any intention of selling the pictures just yet; he would hold on to the Marys and get started on his next book. He knew already the shape it would take. He'd borrow a leaf out of Q Ball Li's opus and write a memoir of his time in America composed entirely of the things he had bought. A life in consumer items. He would call it *Shopping: An American Life*. But first he would publish *The Book of Chocolate Saints*, his oral history of Xavier, using a representative sample of X's poems. For that he would need Goody's permission. She had the rights to his estate. It was a reason for them to meet again.

He told the cabbie where to stop and reached in his pocket to pay.

Epilogue

And now as I prepare the final pages let me leave you with a picture of Goody Lol in the future where all of us will eventually reside. Not the far future, not afloat in the great river of forgetfulness and oblivion. I will draw her for you in the apartment in Delhi where, not long ago, the rooms had been full of commotion, so full it seemed an army of ghosts must camp there.

Now it is just she, just the one ghost at a window facing a small park.

In the room that used to be her study Ari is waking up. Soon Goody will go back to bed and stretch out for a moment beside her. She has been up since dawn, cataloguing the art Amrik brought from the Central Park West apartment. There is a lot of it, from video, 16 mm film and documentary photos, to installations, paintings, line drawings, and multimedia. There is the art they had stopped thinking of as art: wall drawings, a painted door, symbols carved into the windowsills and doorjambs, shelves that had been painted or written on, kitsch, psychedelia, a collection of door stoppers made into humanoid shapes, newspaper and magazine pages painted over with grids and figures, the converted advertisements, the unpublished poems and unclassifiable prose, enough to fill a good-size book, enough to load with ore the massive Newtonian retrospective that will now open in the winter.

It is her job because there is nobody else who can do it and for now she is happy to be curator and archivist not artist.

How little the surface has changed. Life has changed beyond measure, beyond repair, but here is the house and the street and the neighbourhood, untouched, unscathed, unmoved. Even the shoe rack near the door drives her to distraction. Running shoes and boots and dress heels that will survive those who wear them. It drives her to distraction but who is she to expect change? Hasn't she come back to live among the wreckage of the past?

The room's dimensions are comfortably odd. The side that faces the street narrows like the prow of a ship. The flooring is different. The tiles are of wood not stone, as if the entire park-facing side was a late addition. Perhaps it was, perhaps when the building was first built this had been open ground. According to Mrs Rathod, the downstairs neighbour who can no longer meet her eye, the building began modestly and grew in stature. The theory is as likely to be true as anything and it explains why the room opens into a corridor that runs the length of it and no two rooms are the same.

At a narrow window is a writing desk and chair that came with the apartment. She likes to imagine a woman fanning herself as she dreams of ships, a thin nervous woman with a ferocious way of scratching pen across paper who pauses in her writing to gaze at the dusty trees outside; Goody knows what it is to be her.

The day after her return Mrs Rathod rang the doorbell. She was dressed in a pink tracksuit and high heels and a CD was on offer.

"Some music for you," she said, her eyes on the floor. "Something to distract you. Some of my favourites and three versions of 'Ave Maria'."

She had declined coffee as if Goody's condition was contagious. And she hadn't let her heels tap too loudly against the tiles as she went down the stairs. She was considerate, Mrs R. She was a paragon of consideration, a rock to which the newly bereaved could cleave. Except old Mrs Ratface knew nothing about bereavement. She had no idea, for example, that grief could not be distracted. It *was* distraction. It was distraction multiplied exponentially until the bereaved felt she too had died. How could music correct such a condition? It could not. But late at night she listened to all three versions of 'Ave Maria' and put the one she liked most on repeat, the one by the soprano whose name was the song's title. She took to playing it at all hours, so loud that Mrs R would surely feel the vibrations. For some reason it worked, the exalted keening and the slowness of the lament.

It is only now that grieving begins.

She had to put the perils of the past behind her; she had to give in. The giving in is the easiest thing in the world. And in the years to come she will feel she is finally past the grief, she has *moved on* as they say.

Then all of a sudden grief will return, as fresh and red as ever.

This morning she plays 'Ave Maria' at a low volume because she doesn't want to wake the house. As always she comes out of the music heavier and more substantial if only to herself. As always she lights a cigarette and exhales slowly to watch the pictures in the smoke, to communicate with the dead.

She is one by two; she has two brains, two pairs of lungs, and two sets of genitals.

She has two hearts.